THE
SUNCATCHERS

THE
SUNCATCHERS

JAMIE
LANGSTON
TURNER

THOMAS NELSON PUBLISHERS
Nashville • Atlanta • London • Vancouver

Published in Nashville, Tennessee, by Thomas Nelson, Inc., Publishers, and distributed in Canada by Word Communications, Ltd., Richmond, British Columbia, and in the United Kingdom by Word (UK), Ltd., Milton Keynes, England.

Scripture quotations are from The Holy Bible, KING JAMES VERSION.

Library of Congress Cataloging-in-Publication Data

Turner, Jamie L.
  The suncatchers : a novel / Jamie Langston Turner.
    p.   cm.
  ISBN 0-7852-7911-3 (pbk.)
  I. Title.
PS3570.U717S86 1995
813'.54—dc20
                                   95-14275
                                      CIP

Printed in the United States of America

1 2 3 4 5 6 7 - 01 00 99 98 97 96 95

Dedication

to Daniel

*As the apple tree among
the trees of the wood, so
is my beloved among the sons.*
Song of Solomon 2:3

Part 1
CANDLELIGHT

When his candle shined upon my head, and when by his light I walked through darkness.

Job 29:3

Chapter 1

Perry had opened a dozen boxes hoping they'd be this one. He didn't know why he should feel so relieved but he did. He knew he should have labeled all the boxes on the outside: Office Supplies, Glassware, Linens, etc. That's what Dinah would have recommended if she'd been supervising the packing. But she hadn't been. She had sorted through everything in the other house, though, and stacked his allotment against a wall. She'd even gotten empty boxes from somewhere and set them along the same wall. Dinah could be very efficient when she had something she wanted badly enough. Then she had taken Troy and gone to her mother's while Perry cleared out.

He reached down inside the box and carefully lifted an object wrapped in a blue-flowered pillowcase. He could feel the heavy, hard roundness of the glass globe and sense the gentle sloshing of water inside. He unwrapped it and spread his palm over the smooth dome. He had always called it a music box, and Dinah had always said no, a box was square or rectangular and so this was a musical snowglobe. Anyway, it played a tune when the knob was wound and created a snowstorm when turned upside down. It hadn't been in the pile of things Dinah had set aside for him, but he had taken it anyway. It wasn't hard to imagine how furious she had been when she noticed it missing.

He was still holding the music box when he heard the soft, regular swish of sweeping next door. He walked to the kitchen window and looked out. That must be the woman his sister Beth had talked so much about—Jewel Blanchard. Taller than he had imagined and a little younger. Or younger-looking. But it was hard to tell from this distance.

He knew for a fact she was forty-five, that's what Beth had told him. He realized now that he had already given her a face and a size and even a personality over the past month or so, and it startled him somewhat that he had been so far off in her looks. He wondered what she'd do if he opened the window and yelled, "Hey, you're not supposed to look like that!" Perry couldn't remember when he had started doing this—wondering how people would respond to startling statements. It had become so much a habit with him that sometimes he had to stop and think very hard to remember if he had only imagined saying something or if perhaps he really had. One of his worst fears was that someday he was actually going to carry through and humiliate himself.

Sometimes in a concert or a crowded store, he would get a panicky feeling imagining the shocked expressions, the sharp intakes of breath, if he suddenly stood on a chair and shouted something crazy. He found himself more and more wanting to know if the responses would be as dramatic as he imagined. Maybe everybody would simply look straight past him as if nothing had happened. Or maybe his outburst would trigger a whole series of similar responses from those around him. Maybe everybody was just waiting for someone else to start it all. Maybe now if he yanked open the window and told Jewel she wasn't supposed to look like that, she'd just holler back, "Yeah, well, this broom's made out of cat whiskers!" and calmly go on sweeping.

He wished she would lift her head so he could see her better. She had her hood up, but the hair he could see looked dark, almost black. He had pictured it as lighter, a sandy brown going to gray.

He watched her make her way slowly down the driveway. The broom was a sorry excuse, with only a short stubble of straw left on it. She needed a new one. Maybe he should get her one after his year here was up, as a parting gift when he was ready to move on. But by then she would know what he had been up to and she might not want a broom or anything else from him.

But he had nothing to worry about, he told himself again. He had kept reminding himself of that as he drove all day yesterday. What he was doing wasn't *wrong*. Not at all. He was going to study these people and then write about them, simple as that. He'd done it before and had never suffered any pangs of conscience. That's what research was all about, and that's what writers all over the world did; they studied people just as investors studied the stock market. Anyway, he would tell these people sooner or later what he was doing, but not right off. He wanted them to act natural as long as possible.

He used to envy writers like Charles Kuralt, who were always aboveboard with the people they interviewed. Whenever somebody like Kuralt sat and chatted with, say, a country fiddler in Galax, Virginia, or ate hot tamales with the cook at Bigger's in Imogene, Mississippi, or toured Winston-Salem, North Carolina, with a man who used to make bricks for factories and schools by hand, six at a time, he always told them up front about the book he was writing. He didn't go around on false pretenses, encouraging people to talk freely, casually, innocently, then spring the news on them later, after he had his story.

But, of course, that was a different kind of book altogether—a collection of journalistic human-interest stories, not at all on the same level with true sociological research. Whereas Kuralt was *selecting* his data and rearranging it to tell a story, almost picaresque-style, a sociologist had to collect and organize all the facts, regardless of whether the subjects or the readers *liked* the picture that resulted. What would it be like, Perry had wondered more than once during his early days of research, to be able to relax and just write whatever struck his fancy?

The woman outside stooped to pick up something in the driveway, turned it over in her hand, then slipped it inside her coat pocket and resumed her sweeping. Watching her from behind the curtain, Perry couldn't help wondering how she would fit into the book he was going to write. For the first time he felt the faintest stirring of interest in the project—the moment he used to call "the spark," a moment that had always happened much earlier during the research for his other books.

But he was rusty at all this. It had been eight years since he had last done this kind of writing, although at one time he had intended to make it his life's work. "A brilliant ethnographer, all the more phenomenal for his youth," he'd been praised on the dust jacket of his third book, the one entitled *New Verena,* in which he had revealed the inner workings of a tiny community of Lithuanians in central Illinois. "Scholarly yet delightfully readable," another critic had written of the book. He clearly remembered Dinah holding the first copy of the book reverently in her hands when they received it from the publisher. "Book number *three,*" she had said, leafing through its pages. "What does it feel like," she had asked him, "to be successful?" The question had embarrassed him, but she had kept pressing it. "No, come on, now, tell me. How does it feel to be a big hit?"

A big hit? His books maybe, not him. It was funny—he never associated his writing with himself, which he realized in the split second before he opened his mouth to answer Dinah would be impossible to explain. When he wrote, he wasn't Perry Warren. Perry Warren was a quiet, tongue-tied, nondescript sort of person you wouldn't even notice if you passed on the street. Perry Warren was *not* a big hit. But there stood Dinah, sincerely believing she was married to someone famous, someone from whom she expected a breezy, pithy answer to her question.

So he had taken refuge in comedy, the kind of impromptu bluster he could pull off only with Dinah. "It feels, my dear, as if you're dangling helplessly at the end of a fraying rope above raging waters teeming with starving crocodiles. If it's real, you face the burden of being expected to do something heroic, and if you discover it's all a dream, you drive yourself insane wondering what you would do if it really were true." And Dinah had laughed as always, then set about cutting the celebration cake, which she had made and decorated to look like a large open book, topped with small white candles arranged to form the numeral 3.

But a few days after the last piece of cake had been eaten, he woke up one day and realized he had lost the thrill of it all. How it had happened he had no idea. He could well remember his first book—waking early every morning, skipping meals, walking through rain and snow, worrying Dinah sick with his single-mindedness, all for the joy of recording every observable detail at Lifegate, a private preschool for orthopedically handicapped children. Then the second book published three years later—a study of an artists' colony outside Beloit called The Lemon Grove—had absorbed his interest just as much. Then *New Verena* two years later. Then it was over. If it had been a telegram, his research career would have read *Lifegate, The Lemon Grove, New Verena* STOP.

In less time than it takes to blow out a candle, the desire was gone. His work began to seem inconsequential. Not that the lives of the children, the artists, or the Lithuanians seemed trivial, but his writing about them had lost its purpose. What *difference* was he making going about observing these subcultures and reporting on everything from toilet schedules to spices used in cooking to experimental sculptures made out of things like the pulltabs of soda cans and raw, abstract splatter paintings with titles like *Routing the Octuple Niches*? He saw himself as sneaky and nosy—a busybody peering over people's shoulders, slinking around corners, eavesdropping, yet unable to answer the most elemental of questions: Why?

Shortly after his third book, he had been approached about coauthoring a textbook for college sociology, and had in fact sat in on a preliminary meeting before he bowed out, unable to tolerate the thought of systematizing all that information. As the other sociologist—a small, intense, bespectacled woman in her late fifties named Natalie Reinhardt—had sat across the table from him excitedly laying out a chapter outline for the textbook, Perry had been overcome with boredom. Why would he want to spend two years of his life working on a book to introduce students to a field of study with which he himself was so thoroughly disenchanted?

He had let Natalie get all the way to chapter nine before he said anything. She was just saying, "And then that chapter will lead very naturally into the next one on ethnic relations, and I *do* feel it needs to be a separate chapter, not just an addendum to the one on social strata" when Perry had politely interrupted. "Excuse me," he had said, "I don't believe I can do this," and he had simply gotten up and left the room. Natalie had gone on to write the book alone, and he had heard that it was very good. He had even looked through it once—had felt almost ill scanning the glossary of terms: *anticipatory socialization, ethnocentrism, gemeinschaft, primary deviance, rate of natural increase, utilitarian authority*. On and on they went, all the way to *zero population growth*. He could have rattled off definitions for them all, would have even suggested rewording several of Natalie's had he stuck with the project, but all he felt as he closed the book was extreme relief that he had escaped.

His agent had tried to interest him in a new book about a highly respected adoption agency near Chicago, but Perry had declined, and eventually he had done what any weary researcher would do—simply quit. Trying his hand at fiction writing, he found he could do it, and for the past eight years he had been writing stories. At least he saw a purpose in what he was doing, even if it was the dubious one of entertainment. Most of his novels so far, dozens of short mysteries and adventures targeted mainly at adolescents, had been set in Indiana and Illinois—a region as familiar to him as the letters of the alphabet.

Then there were his more recent science-fiction fantasies set in outer space, which Dinah had begun saying was a place he knew well. It was sometime during this last series of books that Dinah had changed. One day she was leaning over him from behind with her arms clasped over his heart, her own heartbeat steady in his ear, reading and proclaiming what he had just written to be witty and imaginative, and the next day she was on the telephone in the next room, telling her newest friend in his hearing that "my husband, yes, Perry Warren—Ph.D., sociologist, and novelist—is as out of touch with life on the planet earth as he is with how to make a woman happy."

A few months ago—had it really been so recently?—Dinah had calmly announced to him one morning at breakfast that their marriage was choking the breath out of her and she wanted out, or rather she wanted him out. Dinah never was one to work up to something gradually. He had been so stunned he hadn't even replied, and she had left for work taking Troy with her to drop off at school.

He had hoped she'd forget about it, but when she returned that afternoon, she came into his study and said briefly, "I meant it, Perry, every word of it." He had stayed in the house another two months, avoiding her by holing up in his study and trying to pretend nothing had happened. He continued to look over Troy's homework papers and start the dishwasher when it was full and bring in the newspaper, but it didn't work. He couldn't ignore the chill in the house. Troy sensed it, too, and started waking them up with nightmares.

Dinah had known Perry wouldn't fight back in the end, and she was right. He would rather die than go through what he had often heard referred to as a "messy divorce." She had filed the papers, and he had signed them. And he had finally packed up his boxes and left. So now he was here, bag and baggage as they said, in the South. The divorce would be final after the required separation period, so all he had to do was wait for it to "go through," as if it were a loan for some major purchase.

Things had happened fast once they got underway. His sister Beth had offered him her house for a year, and his agent and good friend, Cal, had contracted him for a new book, though one Perry still wasn't sure he wanted to do. In the wake of several widely publicized scandals among so-called "fundamentalist" Christian leaders, the publisher Cal had bargained with wanted a writer who would go to one of these churches for an extended period of time, become involved, observe the members, and then write a full-length book about his experience. The publisher particularly wanted an established professional writer but one who could tell a good story, not just a researcher in academia. "So, see, you're perfect," Cal had told him on the phone. "This guy's getting them both, a researcher and a storyteller. He's read your stuff. He knows what a deal he's got."

It would be a good challenge, Cal kept telling Perry, something to take his mind off things. "You could look at it as lucky timing," Cal had said. "I mean, I know the divorce is rotten and all that, but think about it. There's your sister's house sitting empty for a whole year, and where is it? Right in the heart of Bible Land. And what kind of job do I line up for you? A book about fire-and-brimstone fanatics—and you even said yourself that your sister lives right next door to a family of Bible thumpers. Think about it, Perry. You're a lucky man. This is the perfect thing to get you back on track. Your novels—well, they've done fine, don't get me wrong, but the research will be good for you."

Perry looked down at the music box he was still holding and shook it a little. He was dismayed to see that during the move one of the little figures had somehow broken loose and was drifting around with the fake snow inside the globe. He curved his hand back over the glass dome and thought suddenly of the big glass doorknobs in old houses. You turned those knobs and walked into strange dark rooms with high ceilings. And you got the same kind of feeling he had now, of being alone in a cold, dark place and wishing you were back home.

The woman outside was still sweeping steadily. He moved into the living room to see her better. It didn't seem to be the quickest way to sweep, going in only one direction, right to left. A lot of wasted motion.

But then he realized he had never really swept a driveway; maybe you did it that way to direct the dirt so it didn't swirl up and around and sneak in behind you again. He'd always used a leaf blower. Well, maybe Dinah had used it more than he had, but he was the one who had gone down to Sears to buy it. He didn't even know if they'd owned a broom, now that he thought about it. He couldn't remember having seen one around the house anywhere. Maybe there had been one, though, and Dinah had kept it for herself, which wasn't very fair considering she had kept the leaf blower.

He heard somebody call—a full, resonating voice—and Jewel turned around and squinted toward the house. Maybe it was the old lady. The one Beth had called "a real case." Or maybe the boy. He saw Jewel shake her head and smile a little at whoever it was. "In a minute," she said. "When I'm done here," and she turned back to her sweeping. She was working along the side of the driveway now, closer to him. Some of the dust and leaves flew over into his driveway, but she didn't seem to notice it. Thanks a lot, lady, he thought.

Why not go out and meet her now? He could pretend to be getting something from the car, and then he'd catch sight of her and say, "Oh, hi there, I was just getting something from my car," and then she'd say something and they would introduce themselves and then that first awkward step would be over. Dinah had always fussed about that— what she called his overplanning everything and using little ploys to avoid being straightforward. He supposed he could just go out and say he'd seen her from the window and wanted to meet her and his name was Perry Warren and he was Beth's brother. Or maybe he should just wait till later. "You're like a little old woman," Dinah had told him not too long ago. "You fret over the stupidest details. Just quit worrying and stalling and *do* something." Grown men weren't supposed to worry, she had told him. "And sociologists are supposed to have all their hang-ups worked out." Dinah was always getting sociology mixed up with psychology.

It was uncanny the way Dinah could read his mind. He'd be sitting in his recliner—just sitting there not doing a thing—and she'd walk by and say, "Oh, stop it! Stop thinking about that proposal! Writers get their ideas rejected all the time! Get on to something else!" Or "Who cares what my mother said about Troy? Get over it!" And the remarkable thing was that she was nearly always right; she always knew exactly what he was thinking. Only once could he recall her being wrong. He had been watching her dust the bookshelves in the den, stretching up to reach the top ones. He was noticing how slim her waist still was, how nicely curved her calves were when she turned around suddenly. He glanced away immediately but didn't have time to readjust his expression. Passing him on her way to the living room, she had said, "Thinking up a new heroine for your next book, huh? Hope she's as beautiful as the last one—Asdrilla, wasn't that her name?" He hadn't answered. What could he have said? "No, I was just admiring your figure"? You didn't say things like that to your wife. At least *he* didn't.

Well, anyway, the driveways in this neighborhood weren't very long; the woman next door was going to be done with the sweeping soon so he'd better get on with it if he was going to do it. What could be simpler than meeting a new neighbor? He hoped he could look her in the eye.

He opened the front door and stepped out into the yard. She was down near the curb now but stopped and looked back when she heard the door open. It was then that he realized he was still carrying the snowglobe. Well, too late now with her standing there looking at him.

He began talking as he walked across the patchy grass in the front yard. Might as well get it over with. "Hi. You must be—Jewel, isn't it? I'm Perry Warren, and I'll be living here for . . . but I guess you already know that . . . or do you?" He should have thought this out better. He wasn't really looking right at her, more at the telephone pole across the street.

He could tell she was smiling at him, though. "So you're Beth's brother. She told us you'd be moving in sometime this month." She put the broom behind her, holding it with both hands like a tap dancer's cane. He was glad she didn't offer to shake hands. There was something too personal about that—an expectancy of trust.

He saw her looking at the music box. "I've been unpacking," he said.

"That's always a chore," she said, and he nodded. She lifted her head a little, and he looked at her eyes. A pale but startling blue, the color of those clear, ice blue candies wrapped in cellophane that looked so cool and fresh but turned out to make your mouth burn. Aquamarine, that was the color. It was the birthstone for some month, he thought, but he couldn't remember now which one. He focused again on the telephone pole.

"Beth told us you're a writer," she said.

"I guess so. But not for a day or two right now. I haven't found my computer yet in all the boxes . . . it's a mess in there." He motioned back toward the house.

She laughed. He couldn't remember seeing a woman her age with such pronounced dimples. Didn't dimples untuck as a person's skin aged?

He didn't look right into her eyes but rather in the corner where the skin bunched up into a little fan of pleats. Forty-five had sounded older than it looked. Or maybe he had gotten the age wrong.

"We saw your car and the U-Haul late last night when we got home," she said. "Sorry we weren't here. Joe Leonard would've helped you carry things in."

"That's okay, it didn't take all that long really. There wasn't anything too big. Beth left most of her stuff here for the year . . . and all." He shifted the snowglobe to the other hand and looked down at her feet. Navy blue Keds with white socks.

"I was going to see if you could come eat supper with us tonight," she said. "But I wasn't sure you'd be awake yet on a Saturday."

He hadn't expected this. He guessed Southern women still did this sort of thing, some of them anyway, but he hadn't thought about being invited over so soon.

"Well, sure . . . I guess so. I don't usually eat much supper, though . . . but thanks."

She smiled. "I can tell you're not a big eater from looking at you," she said. "But you just might be hungry after a day of unpacking." Perry found himself wondering why her eyes didn't shine more as she talked. They really should, being that color. Maybe she bore some personal burden that snuffed the sparkle out of her life. He could identify with that. "We eat around six," she added, "so come on over anytime before then. It won't be fancy." She took the broom from behind her and swung it with one hand at a few curled brown leaves along the curb.

"Sure. Okay, thanks," he said and turned to go.

"I told Beth I'd watch out for you," she called after him. "Let us know if you need anything."

Back inside, he set the music box down on a small end table and looked around the living room. Beth's sofa, Beth's old hi-fi, Beth's bookshelves, Beth's rugs, Beth's knickknacks . . . and his boxes. But it could be a lot worse, he reminded himself. At least he didn't have to go to a motel to live the way he'd heard of some ousted husbands having to do. He had a whole house to live in for a whole year. Even if it was in a blue-collar neighborhood like this and in a state like South Carolina—that regularly scored forty-ninth in quality of education. He wasn't sending anybody to school here anyway, so what did he care?

The broom was still swishing outside, and he was surprised to see Jewel slowly heading back up, sweeping his driveway now. He remembered the sinking feeling last night when he had arrived and found that Beth's driveway was adjacent to the neighbors'. There was something about adjacent driveways that forced a closer relationship than he felt he wanted to think about.

Jewel was a careful sweeper, going all the way to the edges. Had she been planning to sweep his side all along? Maybe so; or maybe she was afraid he had noticed her sweeping stuff from her driveway to his. He ought to go out and tell her not to bother, that he'd take care of it later, but that might seem ungrateful. Maybe he should stick his head out the door and yell a friendly thank you. But he didn't do either.

He picked the snowglobe back up and slowly wound the silver knob underneath. Immediately he wished he hadn't, but there was no way to stop it now. As the music started, he turned the glass ball upside down and watched the flurry of snow cover the tiny plastic people and the tiny plastic snowman. The loose figure floated lazily in the snowstorm. It was a little boy, he noticed now—a little boy somersaulting dizzily and finally landing face down beside a little evergreen. Small white granules settled on the roof of the miniature house near the snowman and slid off onto the ground.

He and Troy used to build snowmen. They tried to see how many different things they could use for eyes. He still remembered the time several years ago when Dinah had come home to find a pair of her enormous glittery red earrings dangling from the snowman's eye sockets. They had all three laughed about it; the earrings were only cheap

Kmart ones, and that was back when Dinah still thought everything he did was clever. Perry distinctly remembered wondering as they stood in the yard that day whether he would always be as happy as he was then. Well, he knew the answer to that now.

It had been snowing steadily when he had driven out of Rockford early yesterday. They could get some pretty heavy snowfalls in February. He wondered if there had been enough to build a snowman. Would Troy try building one by himself now? He couldn't imagine Dinah helping with something like that. Would she think to check over Troy's arithmetic problems?

As he watched all the snow inside the glass ball settle and listened to "Winter Wonderland" seven times through, he thought about how stupid he must look standing there. Somebody ought to take a picture of him and label it "Regrets Only."

Chapter 2

All the houses in this neighborhood were more or less alike—small brick rectangles with little porches just big enough for a couple of chairs or maybe a swing if a person swung in moderation. The area, known as Montroyal, had all been planned and constructed in the early fifties by the big textile conglomerate that had once fed the economy in this part of South Carolina. Montroyal had financed the houses for their employees at reasonable interest rates and even landscaped and equipped a couple of corner lots as parks for the kids. By the time they had closed down operation in the late seventies and moved their main plant nearer to Columbia, Montroyal had made a nice little profit from their real estate venture and three or four hundred families had their own modest little homes—but no jobs now, at least not here in the town of Derby, South Carolina.

A few of the people had stayed on after Montroyal relocated, but mainly it was the older ones ready for retirement. Most of the younger ones had sold their houses and moved to Columbia with the company or taken jobs at a new Summerweave plant up in Greenville. A big Gerber baby-food plant had moved to Derby a year or so after Montroyal closed down, so that took up the slack a good deal.

All the streets in Montroyal were named after flowers. Daffodil and Violet and Daisy and Rose and Iris. Those were all Streets. Then there were the Avenues—Hyacinth and Petunia and Tulip and others. And a few Lanes—Pansy and Lily and Geranium. Then there was the one Circle, where Beth's house was, tucked away in the far northwest corner of the subdivision—Blossom Circle it was called. Perry wondered if whoever had named the streets had run out of specific flowers by that time. He knew for sure there wasn't a Chrysanthemum or Rhododendron Street, but maybe they figured those would be too hard for the mill people to spell. Blossom Circle was actually a cul-de-sac and should have been a Court in Perry's opinion, but evidently the community planners hadn't known the rules about naming streets.

Perry remembered how proud Beth had been to become the owner of one of these little brick boxes two years ago. The family she bought it from had bought it from one of the original Montroyal families. At the time, Perry had questioned her using their mother's money on something so inelegant. He had put his down on a $200,000 place Dinah had fallen in love with. Not a very smart move now that he looked back on it since it seemed that her falling in love with the house had coincided with her falling out of love with him.

In her lucid moments, Perry's mother used to call Beth the practical one and Perry the experimenter. Perry had always wondered whether her labeling them that way had shaped their destinies; maybe she had seen Beth one day at the age of, say, three or four stacking up her pennies in neat little piles while Perry pushed his through the slots in a heating vent, and from that day on she had decided their futures. Forget what they might have done the next day or the next; her mind was made up now. Beth was neat and logical; Perry was inquisitive and creative.

And so Beth had grown up to be a math teacher and pay cash for a $50,000 house and remain unmarried. And Perry had become a writer and gone into debt and married a woman who now hated the sight of him. "Two roads diverged in a yellow wood" and all that. But the two roads in that poem by Frost were equally attractive to the narrator, Perry recalled, which certainly wasn't true in this case. Perry had never wanted to be a math teacher, and Beth often said she'd go mad sitting around fiddling with words at a computer all day. "To each his own." There, that was a more appropriate quotation.

Perry waited until the digital clock said 5:59 before he left to walk across the two driveways to the Blanchards' house. He hoped they would eat right away so he wouldn't be expected to sit around before the meal and make polite talk. It was bad enough when you had something to do with your hands, like hold the silverware. "For somebody supposedly so interested in people—I mean a *sociologist* no less—you sure are a dud in a crowd," Dinah had told him once after a party. But for Perry, observing people and interacting with them were two totally different things, and the one usually got in the way of the other, he had discovered long ago. Participant observation wasn't his style.

The Blanchards' porch light was on—one of those unshielded bright yellow bulbs. Perry walked up the steps to the front door and stood beside a large white wooden goose listing to one side. The words

"Welcome, Friends" were stenciled on its stomach, and an enormous green bow hung limply around its neck.

He heard the doorbell ring inside—or rather buzz. Another sign of a cheap house, he thought. There were three little square windows in the front door at eye level, but he was careful to keep his eyes down. He was standing on what appeared to be a piece of leftover carpet, and he suspected he'd see the same olive shag in a room somewhere inside.

The door began to swing open slowly as if it hadn't been firmly latched in the first place. But then he saw a face peering around the edge at him—an old woman with short, straight metal-gray hair and eyebrows as thick as caterpillars. His first impression was that she was scowling at him, but when he looked more closely, he understood that she meant it for a smile. She must be tall, he thought, unless she was standing on a stool behind the door.

They stood there looking at each other for a moment, and then he heard Jewel's voice from behind her. "Well, for pity's sake, Mama, let him in." Jewel opened the door wide and motioned him in.

"He was standing right in front of the screen," said the old woman. "It wouldn't be very cordial to smack him in the face, now would it?" She had one of those sticky voices that made Perry want to clear his throat to help her out. "Besides," she said, "I wanted to look him over good." She stretched her mouth wide, her eyes narrowing to dark incisions, and laughed a deep, honking laugh.

Jewel looked at Perry over the old woman's shoulder and smiled.

Perry stepped inside and wiped his feet on a mat with a border of red teddy bears holding hands and "We LOVE company" stamped in the center. The room was a splash of different colors, and it was so hot Perry wondered if he was getting sick. Why was he doing this, he asked himself. Not just the supper invitation but the whole business. What he was planning to do suddenly seemed so ludicrous to him that he wanted to laugh. What made him think he could move into town and crank out a book about these people when he had turned his back on sociological research more than eight years ago? He had probably lost the knack for it by now anyway. He ought to just excuse himself and go to the Hardee's a few blocks away.

He realized that the old woman had just said something and was looking at him for a response. Dinah had always been after him to keep his mind on what was happening right then. "Half the time you don't make any sense whatsoever when you open your mouth because while the conversation has been going one way, your mind has been going the exact opposite," she told him once after an evening out.

It had been an awful night, the kind Dinah was always dragging him to, the kind Perry hated, with people clustered together pretending to be interested in what the others were saying and then wandering off to reassemble in another huddle in another room and go through the whole charade all over again. That was the time the interior decorator had asked him if writers ever thought of their pieces as undiscovered constellations in the solar system, and he had snapped out of wherever he withdrew to at such times and replied with a quotation from *King Lear*: "A man may see how this world goes with no eyes." He could still picture the woman cocking her head as if the relevance of what he had said could be grasped if she only pondered it a while.

This was terrible. The old woman had said something else now, and both she and Jewel were staring at him, waiting.

So he did what he often did—smiled and bobbed his head. He'd have to do better than this—a lot better. Paying attention was pretty fundamental to observation. He was going to be earning money for observing and writing about these people—that is, *maybe,* if he went through with it—so he'd better start tonight.

Jewel was talking now, so he looked directly at her mouth. Her two front teeth overlapped each other just a little but were white and strong. Not the sort of thing you'd ever want to put braces on to correct. It was a nice smile, really. Combined with the blue eyes and dimples, it looked like a girl's.

". . . with Mama if it's okay—oh, and I'll get Joe Leonard to come in here and meet you too." Jewel turned and left the room. Perry's stomach felt unsettled. It was so hot in here—and so bright.

Maybe he should have offered to help Jewel in the kitchen. But that was laughable since he couldn't even keep straight which direction the blade of the knife faced whenever he tried to set the table. At one time early in their marriage Dinah had thought it was comical, his confusion over such details when he could remember others with vivid clarity, like the intricate paisley design of a scarf she had often worn when they were dating. He had drawn the design for her several years after they were married and even colored it in with Troy's crayons. And she had dug the scarf out of a drawer somewhere and compared it with the picture. "You aren't a normal human being," she had told him after studying the two for a few moments.

The old woman turned and motioned for him to follow. She was one of the largest old women Perry had ever seen. She had to be close to his own height of six feet, with broad shoulders and wide hips, and she walked with the waddle of a pregnant woman, which was a ridiculous comparison, he realized. It wasn't that she was fat necessarily, she was just big all over. She wore a shapeless lavender knit dress with a long-sleeved black cardigan over it and a long string of lavender beads with matching earrings. She walked over to the sofa and sat down heavily at the end closest to a gas heater. Perry could sense the waves of hot air emanating from it, and he pushed up the sleeves of his sweater.

He chose a straight-back chair across from her on the other side of the small living room. The seat was cane and sounded like a creaky hinge when he sat down. It was then that he noticed the old woman's feet. She was wearing black rubber boots, the kind with the little metal clasps down the front, like children wear, except many sizes larger. Above the boots he could see what looked like the tops of plastic bags cinched to her calves with garters.

He realized he must have been staring because she lifted her legs and held them straight out in front of her. "Poor circulation," she said. "My feet get so cold! This here's something I read about in a magazine. You coat your feet all over with Vaseline, and then you put them in plastic bags to trap the heat. Then you put socks on over that. I got on three pairs. And then you wear rubber boots on top of those." Her thick eyebrows drew together as she smiled broadly.

Perry couldn't think of a reply at first. He watched her silently for a moment on the outside chance that she was teasing. "Does it work?" he finally asked.

"Pretty much," she answered. Perry wondered how she cleaned the Vaseline off her feet afterward. Maybe she just left it on and layered over it every day. What would that look like by springtime? He looked away quickly.

A thin, gangling boy walked partway into the room and stood at the other end of the sofa looking embarrassed. His whole face was spattered with reddish-brown freckles, as if he had leaned over a hot skillet of grease. His jeans were neatly rolled up several turns, and his flannel plaid shirt was tucked tightly inside and buttoned up snug to the neck.

"This here's Joe Leonard," said the old woman, smiling at the boy proudly. "He's fourteen and is learning to play the tuba." No wonder he looks embarrassed, thought Perry. Joe Leonard came forward awkwardly and extended his hand. Perry was surprised at the firmness of his grasp. But he supposed that hauling a tuba around would have to develop finger strength. As they shook hands, Joe Leonard gave a lopsided grin and studied the carpet—olive shag, Perry had already noted.

Perry relaxed somewhat as he always did when he saw someone

who looked even more uncomfortable than himself. "What grade are you in, Joe Leonard?" he asked.

"Ninth," said the old woman.

"You like sports?" asked Perry.

"He's too spindly for football," said the old woman. "For which I'm grateful since he doesn't have any business playing that anyway. Nobody does unless they're bent on killing theirself."

"I like basketball," said Joe Leonard. His eyes met Perry's briefly.

"And tennis too," the old woman added. "He and his mother play together some. She can usually win, but he's improving, she says. I used to play myself when I was younger." An image filled Perry's mind of the old woman serving an ace in her black rubber boots. He narrowed his eyes and stared hard at his knees.

No one spoke for a few moments. Perry glanced quickly around the living room, which had the look of an overcrowded souvenir shop. Everything was in its place, but there was so much of it that the first impression was one of clutter. There was a long shelf mounted on the wall above the gas heater, holding a collection of ceramic owls. Perry tried to imagine how hot they must be.

He wondered what made it so bright in the room. Did they use special lightbulbs? Or maybe it was just the contrast from Beth's plain, dull little house next door. He wished he could have borrowed some of this brightness last night when he had arrived to find the electricity off. Beth must have anticipated it, for there were assorted candle stubs laid out on the kitchen table, along with a book of matches and a note in Beth's bold script: "Electricity comes on Sat., the 18th. Use candles in a pinch. Extra blankets in hall closet." Leave it to Beth to cut it that close. But then how was she to know he would decide to leave Rockford a day earlier than he had said? He had lit all the candles and set them in the living room on saucers, then carried in all his boxes and piled them in front of the bookcase. Then he had blown out the candles and slept in his clothes on the sofa. Welcome, welcome to your luxurious quarters, distinguished guest, he had thought before drifting off to sleep, wrapped in borrowed blankets. Sometime early in the morning the electricity had come on; he heard a sudden low hum throughout the house and was dimly aware of a digital clock somewhere in the room insistently flashing its red numbers.

Perry looked around Jewel's living room and counted five colorful afghans—two folded over the back of the sofa, two draped over chairs apparently as replacement upholstery, and a small one laid across the piano bench. He was going to ask the old woman if she had made them when it occurred to him that he didn't know her name. It wouldn't be Blanchard since she was Jewel's mother. And he couldn't very well call her "Mama."

"I'm bad with names," he said, trying not to look at her boots. "Jewel probably told me yours at the door, but I can't remember."

"No, she didn't," she said. "It's Rafferty, Eldeen Rafferty. You can call me Eldeen."

"Eldeen?"

"E-L-D-E-E-N, Eldeen," she said. "Not a name you hear very much, is it? We had us some real original names in our family." She began laughing silently, shaking all over.

"Is it a family name?" Perry asked. Joe Leonard had disappeared, he noticed.

She picked up a photograph from the dozen or more on the table beside her and motioned him over, wiping her eyes. "This is me, here, and my sister Nori, N-O-R-I, and my brother Klim, K-L-I-M, and my other brother Arko, A-R-K-O. Get it? Eldeen, Nori, Klim, Arko?" Perry didn't.

She set the picture down and sighed. "Nobody ever does," she said. "I don't know what got into my mother naming us that way. She was a character, she was."

He still didn't understand.

"She couldn't ever do things the way everybody else did," Eldeen said. "Not that I would of wanted her to. No sir, she made life real interesting. See, about the names—my mama wanted to name her children after everyday things around the house, to remind us of our humble beginnings, which we never would have forgot anyhow. But instead of just naming us the thing itself, she turned it around and spelled it backwards."

"Oh, I see," said Perry slowly, studying her eyes. No twinkle of mischief and she wasn't smiling. Standing over her this way, he caught a strong whiff of Mentholatum. He noticed also for the first time that the soft down of a mustache feathered her upper lip.

"Eldeen, needle . . ." he said.

"Yes sir." She laughed a throaty laugh, showing teeth too perfect to be her own. "Well, like I always say, I guess I'd a heap rather be named Eldeen than Needle." And she laughed again as she set the picture back in its place.

Perry's mind wheeled. He thought of other words Eldeen's mother could have chosen to spell backwards for names. Words like *tar* and *mud*. Could this be possible? Was this woman leading him on? *Straw* and *rail*. Hello, my name is Warts. Glad to meet you, mine is Liar. *Tub* and *knits*. He grew feverishly hot. He felt dazed trying to imagine the mother of this old woman sitting inside a little house somewhere, looking out the window, maybe writing down lists of what she saw, sounding out all the words backwards and trying them out as names for her children.

"She already had Dees and Eram picked out for the next names," said Eldeen, "but then she had female problems and never could have any more babies. She was satisfied with four, though, since she never expected to have even one. She used to say she was such a ugly little girl, looks-wise that is, that people thought she'd been in some kind of a accident. But then my daddy saw her one day when he was helping his uncle build a barn in Fiona, Arkansas, when she brought out some pie and iced tea for the men in the middle of the afternoon, and he just fell in love with her laugh, he said, and she always said she was sure glad that rooster had flapped its wings and scared that fat man or else Daddy never would have heard her laugh. She always dreamed of marrying and having babies but never thought it would come her way. I don't know how many times I heard her recite that verse when we was kids, 'He maketh the barren woman to keep house, and to be a joyful mother of children. Praise ye the LORD.' She was sure a fine, fine mama, she was. And I never once looked at her and thought she was ugly." She shook her head briskly. "No sir, not a bit of it. To me she was the prettiest mama in the world!"

Perry looked down again at the photo of Eldeen's family. If he wrote something like this in a work of fiction, he could never get away with it. A mother who would name her kids Needle, Iron, Milk, and Okra spelled backwards would be just too weird.

Chapter 3

As Jewel had promised, the meal wasn't fancy. The four of them ate at a dinette table in the kitchen, and Perry was glad to find out that it wasn't as hot in the kitchen as it was in the living room. Afterward he felt slightly stunned from the whole experience. It wasn't the food exactly or his three dinner companions or the conversation or the kitchen itself; it was just everything together. He had never spent an evening that so overloaded his senses.

The food was better than any he had eaten for a long time, but the combination was unusual. Jewel had made a ground beef and macaroni dish that she called Burger in a Skillet, though it was in a Pyrex dish, and with it she served baked squash, hash browns, black-eyed peas, applesauce, corn bread, and iced tea. No one else seemed to think it funny that all the food was a shade of brown or gold. Even the dishes were tan with a sprig of golden flowers painted in the middle.

Jewel asked the blessing, concluding with "And we pray your loving watchcare, Lord, on this, our new neighbor, and your hand of success on all his daily endeavors, in the dear Savior's name, amen." No one spoke at first, and Perry busied himself arranging his napkin in his lap.

"What exactly do you write, Warren?" asked Eldeen as she handed him the Burger in a Skillet to start around.

"Warren's his last name, Mama," said Jewel. "Remember, it was Beth's last name too. His first name's Perry."

Eldeen emitted a noise that was part laugh and part snort. "Now aren't men's names funny that way?" she said. "My first husband had a name like that. Norton Malcolm. And people used to get it mixed up so much that half the time I forgot whether I was Eldeen Malcolm or Eldeen Norton. I had a uncle the same way. His name was Palmer Westwood, but it could just as easy been Westwood Palmer. And I had a second cousin once named McLeary McSpadden of all things. They used to call him Big Double Mack, but that was way back before them hamburgers came along. He was the *tallest* man you ever seen! And there's that poor old man at church named Mayfield Spalding, you know, Jewel, the one who sits in the back that I think looks a little like Barney Fife. Anyway, it sure was a relief when I married Jewel's daddy and got somebody with a name you could keep straight—Hiram Rafferty. Least I never *heard* of anybody with the last name Hiram, though I reckon somewhere on God's green earth there's probably a Mr. So-and-so Hiram. Maybe over in one of them Arab countries."

Perry glanced at Jewel and noted her bland expression as she passed the hash browns to Joe Leonard, as if all she heard was some background music on the radio. Eldeen's speech rolled on.

"But when I work on remembering a name, I can usually do it. Perry Warren, not Warren Perry. Perry Warren, Perry Warren, I'll put it in my file box up here." She pretended to open a lid at the top of her head. "Here, take a helping of Jewel's applesauce. We thought those little old wormy trees out back never would bear, but then all of a sudden they must of healed theirselves because we started getting the prettiest little green apples."

"We sprayed them, Mama, remember?" said Jewel. "We talked to that man at the nursery and he told us what to do."

"Well, whatever happened, it worked. Anyway, a name's a funny thing. Joe Leonard here, you'd think his real name'd be Joseph Leonard, but it's not, it's just plain Joe Leonard. That was Hiram's middle name—Leonard. And the Joe came from his daddy, of course. Joe Bailey Blanchard, but for some reason the Joe didn't stick with him, and he was just Bailey. Bailey Blanchard, that's another one of those names you could say either way. Bailey died three years ago this June. I didn't know if you knew that or not."

Jewel reached over and set the glass lid on top of the casserole dish with a loud clap. Beth had told him Jewel was a widow but never talked about her husband.

"But a name's just something you get stuck with and can't do anything about," said Eldeen. "'Course even with the prettiest name, you can make people think it's ugly by the way you act. And vice versa. A good name's better than precious ointment, the Bible says."

Perry was beginning to breathe more easily now that he realized he probably wouldn't be called on to do much talking. He wondered if Eldeen had ever had some kind of throat operation that made her voice sound that way. One of those Sesame Street characters had talked like that, Perry recalled. Was it the one named Grover?

The corn bread was wonderful—crisp on the outside and soft and warm and mealy on the inside. Perry wasn't fond of squash but took some to be polite. It was surprisingly good, though, with a slight tang of what must be some kind of spice or herb. Perry wondered if the family ate food this good all the time. Jewel refilled his tea glass.

Eldeen stopped talking for a moment while she chewed a spoonful of black-eyed peas. Joe Leonard was sopping up his bean juice with a piece of corn bread, and then he dipped what was left of it into his applesauce. Could the boy have already eaten his helping of Burger in a Skillet? Perry wondered.

"Now what was I asking you?" said Eldeen. "Oh, yes, what exactly is it you're writing?" Her bushy eyebrows were drawn down as she looked at him, but she was smiling. It was that same peculiar grimace with which she had met him at the front door. She looked back at her plate and stabbed a forkful of hash browns.

"It's something new," said Perry. "I haven't really gotten a good start on it yet." He didn't want to come out and say he hadn't written even the first word.

"Is it going to be a book or what?"

"Well, yes, it's a book."

Joe Leonard scooted his chair back suddenly and got up. Eldeen jumped.

"That makes the awfulest sound, Joe Leonard! It sounds like a hurt dog." Joe Leonard got an ice tray from the freezer and brought it back to the table. Jewel took it from him and gave it a quick twist. Then she lifted out ice cubes one at a time with just the tips of her fingernails and began dropping two or three into each glass.

Eldeen was still looking at Perry as she chewed a large mouthful of something. "Is it going to be a romance or a mystery or something like that?"

Perry hesitated. "Well, no, it's not exactly a . . ."

Jewel stood up. "Mama, Perry might not want to talk about it. I heard that writers don't like to tell their stories till they're all finished. Here, somebody take this last piece of corn bread. I'm keeping some more warm in the oven." Joe Leonard started to reach for it, then darted a look at Perry.

"No, you go ahead and take it," said Perry. "I've still got some." He watched as Jewel fit a quilted mitt on her hand and slid the muffin pan from the oven. Then she grabbed the top of a muffin and set it quickly on Perry's plate. He wondered how women could touch hot food without flinching. Dinah had been like that. She'd take baked potatoes right out of the oven with her bare hands.

"Joe Leonard's read one of your books, haven't you, Joe Leonard?"

The boy nodded and said, "Beth gave it to me." He started to say something else but must have swallowed wrong, for he began coughing.

"Drink some tea! Drink some tea!" Eldeen said, and he did.

Finally the boy cleared his throat and said, "It was *Ice Planet Countdown*. It was a real good mystery."

"Oh, a mystery!" cried Eldeen. "I just love a good mystery book. I've read every single one of Agatha Christie's. I think it's the most fun to try to figure out who's the guilty one before that man Hercule whatever-his-funny-last-name-is or Miss Marple sets everybody down and explains it all. Sometimes I guess right too! Have you ever read *The Murder of Roger Ackroyd*, Perry? You haven't? Well, I tell you, *that* one's a real stumper. I *never ever* would of guessed who it was, not even if I'd of read it a million times."

Thankful that Eldeen had left the subject of his writing, Perry gave her his full attention as she explained the entire plot of the book.

"Mama, you're spoiling it for him if he ever wants to read it," Jewel said at one point.

"No, it's fine," said Perry. "Really, it's all very interesting."

"You're welcome to have more," Jewel said after Perry had emptied his plate and sat back. Joe Leonard had finally quit eating, having cleaned his plate to a slick shine, and was busy folding his napkin into different shapes, first a triangle and then a diamond. Now he was working on a hexagon.

"Oh, I can't," said Perry. "I've had a lot more than I usually eat."

"It was the funniest thing," said Eldeen, "when Jewel was just a little girl and I married her daddy and fixed our first meal together as a family. I can still remember what we ate that night. It was pork chops that I fried way too long, and they ended up hard as Hiram's work boots. When I asked Jewel if she wanted another one, she looked up at me with them big blue eyes so solemn and said, 'I've had a sufficiency, thank you, and any more would be a loathsome burden.' I like to died laughing. Hiram told me her first mama had taught her to say that. I've never forgot it. You can imagine *that* coming out of the mouth of a little six-year-old. She was the shyest little thing."

Jewel smiled and shook her head. "Mama loves to tell that story." She started picking up plates to carry to the sink. Joe Leonard took all the glasses over and then folded up the place mats and shook them out one at a time over the garbage can. Eldeen dipped her spoon into the applesauce bowl.

"I didn't use it before this," she said to Perry. "I don't want you thinking we're not sanitary-minded around here." She opened her mouth wide and turned the spoon upside down on her tongue. "Mmmm, nobody's applesauce is as good as Jewel's." Perry noticed a tiny crumb of corn bread clinging to the hair above her lip.

Eldeen got up slowly and took her spoon and the applesauce dish to the counter. Then she walked over to a small pantry, her rubber boots squeaking on the linoleum. Inside the pantry Perry saw rows of glass jars filled with what looked like more applesauce. From a top shelf Eldeen got down a box and brought it back to the table.

"Do you like Chinese Checkers?" she said. "We usually play it every night after supper."

Jewel turned around from scraping off dishes and shot Perry an apologetic look. "Mama, Perry might rather just talk." Joe Leonard was filling one side of the sink with soapy water but turned to watch Perry's response.

Perry shook his head. "No, no, this is fine. Chinese Checkers is fine. Really."

Eldeen brushed her hand across the plastic tablecloth. "Joe Leonard, bring the rag over here and wipe up this sticky place. I hate a gummy tablecloth."

Perry helped her set up the game board and fit all the pieces in the holes. He tried to remember how many years it had been since he had played Chinese Checkers. It must have been at least twenty-five. He and Beth had played it a lot during summer vacations at their aunt and uncle's cabin in Wisconsin when they were kids, but Beth usually won since working out a tidy, systematic plan and fitting things into place suited her temperament perfectly. Perry had always grown restless after a game or two and started experimenting with creative, roundabout jumping patterns or had played defensively by trying to figure out and block Beth's next move, which always rankled her.

Eldeen must have asked him something because he looked up to find her staring at him.

"I'm sorry," he said. "My mind wanders a lot. Did you say something?"

"No," she said shortly. "I was just noticing your mouth. It reminds me a lot of Beth's, the way your lips are kind of thin." So what were you supposed to say, Perry thought, when an old woman started discussing your lips? "And your eyes too—" she went on, "they're exactly like hers, dark and set in deep. Why, you two could be twins! I never thought of that—*are* you?"

"Oh, no," said Perry. "Not at all."

She laughed and reached over to pat his hand. "Well, your hands sure aren't like hers, not one bit. I like a man's hands that are big and sinewy like yours," she continued. "So many men you see have these little pale, milky-white hands without any hair on them at all. You half expect to see their nails painted pink. I don't like to see a man with fingernails. You've got you a pair of real man's hands. Hiram had hands like that. Big and rough. And Bailey did too."

Dinah used to say the same things about his hands, only not in so complimentary a tone. She had fumed over his nail-biting and complained when he stroked her knee, saying he'd ruin her stockings with his rough skin. So he had started picking at his nails instead of biting them, peeling off the thinnest little strips and dropping them onto the carpet when she wasn't looking. And he had begun keeping his hands off her knees.

"I bet you got thick, dark hair all over your arms too," Eldeen continued. He must have looked surprised because she patted his hand again. "Oh, don't worry. I'm probably old enough to be your grandmother, so I can say things like that. How old are you?"

"Thirty-eight," he answered.

"Let's see, I was seventy-nine my last birthday, so when you were born, I was . . . yes, that would of worked. I *could* be your grandmother!"

Perry couldn't help wondering how different his life would have been had this woman actually been his grandmother.

"I like a man with dark hair," Eldeen went on. "'Course, the hair doesn't make the man, not by any stretch. My first husband was nearly bald by the time we married—his daddy lost his hair real early too, so it had to of run in the family although I read one time in Joe Leonard's science book that it's really the mama and not the daddy who's to blame for the boys in the family going bald. My second husband sure wasn't bald, though. Hiram had hisself a head *full* of dark, wavy hair just as dark and thick as yours, though of course like I said *his* was wavy. He was tall like you, too, but a little more plumped out. I think Joe Leonard's going to be a string bean just like you. I bet neither one of you's ever going to have to worry a minute about getting fat." She drew a long, straight line in the air with her index finger. "Like a rail—both of you!" She laughed and repeated the process, this time using both index fingers. "Just like a pair of rails!"

"We're going to miss Beth," Jewel said from the sink. Perry was grateful for the change of subject. He felt like he had undergone a physical exam. "I hope she's going to enjoy her time up in Washington,

D.C." Joe Leonard was washing the dishes and Jewel was drying. Perry hadn't seen anybody wash dishes the old way in almost as many years as the last time he had played Chinese Checkers.

"You couldn't pay me to go live in Washington, D.C.," said Eldeen. "I never could figure out why Beth would leave here for a whole year and go off to someplace like that where all them corrupt politicians live and they have blizzards and protest marches on a regular basis. A lot of nasty things go on up there. That's where that man killed all them teenage girls last year and chopped 'em into little pieces and threw 'em into the Potomac River in plastic bags. Them big Hefty Cinch-bags I read in the paper. Fourteen or fifteen girls in all. What a horrible way to meet your death. I'm still wondering what got into her. Beth, I mean. Looks like she could of found a place to do her studying closer to home."

Perry couldn't understand it either. Although his mother had branded him as inquisitive when he was barely old enough to hold a spoon, his inquiring mind evidently hadn't extended to geography, for all his life he had hated leaving home. It was odd, really, considering the inadequacies of his home; a normal person would have longed to escape. Beth certainly had. She had shaken the dust of Rockford off her feet the day after high school graduation, had left the Midwest to attend college in Virginia, then had moved to Colorado for a master's degree, then to South Carolina for a teaching job in a junior college, though why she'd chosen one of the poorest-paying states in the nation Perry had never figured out. She didn't want to live in a big city like Columbia, where she taught, so she had scouted out the surrounding area for a fifty-mile radius and had moved to Derby. Beth had always been like that, studying everything out and going where the so-called "best opportunities" opened up, although her definition of opportunities often stymied Perry. Now it was a doctoral degree she had set her mind to. And she'd get it, too, he knew, probably finishing with the highest math scores in the history of the university. "I can't live my whole life knowing my big brother's got more education than me," she had told Perry when she decided to go to Washington. He had almost corrected her grammar—"than I, Beth," he had wanted to say, but had let it go.

"Well, Mama, bad things happen everywhere," said Jewel. "And anyway, Beth sure is plucky to be going after a doctor's degree." She looked back at Perry. "She sure was glad it worked out for her to start on it in January instead of having to wait till fall."

"Yes sir, she was one happy gal when she found out there was that opening back before Christmas," Eldeen said. "And it just all fell together like a puzzle! That man who used to have her teaching job over in Columbia wrote the college a day or two later and asked if they could hire him back again 'cause his other job wasn't working out so good. Then she came over another day a few weeks later and told us *you* might be moving down here to look after things at her house while she was away. My, my, it sure did happen fast."

Jewel nodded. "I told her she'd be so smart when she was done that she wouldn't be able to carry on a regular conversation with normal folks like us." Jewel stopped suddenly as she was reaching to set a plate in the cupboard. "Oh, I'm sorry, Perry. I didn't mean anything by that. I just now remembered Beth said you had a doctor's degree too."

"Don't worry about it," said Perry, shaking his head. "Those degrees are . . . well, they don't mean a whole lot really."

When Jewel and Joe Leonard finished the dishes, they both sat back down at the table, and they started the game, which turned out to be highly competitive. With four players, the middle of the board was a thick jumble of different colors for a good while. No one spoke much as they played, and Perry was surprised at how serious they all seemed to be about it. Even Eldeen kept quiet most of the time, with her thick eyebrows drawn down like an awning.

When Joe Leonard won, Jewel had the courtesy to suggest stopping the game there. It was obvious that Perry would come in last. Joe Leonard returned the game pieces to the box and then marked a tally beside his name on a sheet of notebook paper taped to the inside of the pantry door.

"We can have our dessert now," Jewel said. Perry wondered what it would be. Maybe pecan pie or chocolate cake. It would have to be brown to match the rest of the meal.

It was brownies with a mound of chocolate ice cream in each bowl beside the brownie.

"Would you like to come to church with us tomorrow morning?" asked Jewel when he walked into the living room to leave several minutes later.

"Joe Leonard's playing a solo on his tuba," said Eldeen, and Joe Leonard frowned down at his black canvas hightops.

"Thank you. I'd like to go very much. I . . . yes, I would," said Perry. This would work out fine. After all, the church was probably going to be the focus of his attention for a good while—if it met the requirements, that is. He might as well check it out right away.

Jewel was just opening the front door for him when Eldeen clapped her hands. "Wait, hold on a minute, I want to show Perry what we got," she said. She walked to the large front window, grabbed the drapery cord, and gave a sharp tug. The draperies, made of a cheap, nubby mustard-colored fabric, parted violently. "Looka there at our suncatchers," Eldeen said, pointing proudly to the window. Perry studied them silently—a cluster of decorative trinkets fastened to the glass by small suction cups. "You'll have to come back when it's light out and the sun's shining on them," Eldeen continued. "Ooooh, the colors they do throw out!" She pointed to a red apple. "That one there's about my favorite—that deep red color and the pretty little green leaf. It's real glass too. Some of them's just plastic, but on a sunny day they'll all just about dazzle your eyes out, plastic or not! That little yellow cat's a pretty thing, and so's the bluebird. They're all just so cheerful and every one of 'em's different! They're a lot prettier in the daytime."

Perry nodded and smiled. "I'm . . . sure they are," he said. "They're nice—all of them. Well, thanks again for the meal." He moved toward the door.

"We'll see you in the morning," Jewel said, and as she closed the door behind him, Perry heard Eldeen say, "He sure is a quiet boy."

As he passed by on the sidewalk in front of the window, he saw the draperies close with a jerk. The suncatchers clung to the glass like dark moths.

Chapter 4

Beth had told him that Jewel and her family were religious. "They make Mother Teresa look like a slouch" was actually what she had said. Perry had been instantly interested. And he was even more interested when she told him it wasn't a particular denomination they belonged to but some kind of small, independent church. She had done some checking, at Perry's request, and found out that, yes, the people at their church did call themselves fundamentalists. Perry supposed Cal had been right in a sense about all these circumstances being lucky. When he had first learned of the book contract, he hadn't known he'd end up living next door to some of the very people he'd be studying.

Cal had already told Perry that this part of the South was full of colorful, eccentric little churches. "You'll find the place crawling with religious fanatics," Cal had said. "Leftover Puritans. They don't believe in having fun and don't want anybody else to either. It'll be the perfect place to write the book." Cal ought to know. He'd grown up in Georgia.

It had been decided that they would all go to church together in Jewel's station wagon because of the tuba. They left at 9:45 for Sunday school, Jewel had told him, so at 9:44 Perry pulled his front door closed and walked over to the Blanchards' driveway. Eldeen was already in the front seat of the car waiting, with a swatch of her bright red dress caught in the door and hanging out the bottom. Perry wondered if she was wearing her black boots to church today.

Jewel was holding the kitchen door open for Joe Leonard, who was lugging a huge instrument case.

"Need some help?" Perry asked, but Joe Leonard shook his head.

"He's used to it," said Jewel, "but thanks anyway. Here, you can open up the back of the car for us, though." She tossed him a set of keys.

On the way to the church, Jewel told him that Sunday school classes were by age group and he'd be in the Fishers of Men class.

"Unless you'd feel more comfortable coming to my class," she said, glancing at him in the rearview mirror. "We're called the Willing Workers."

"I think I'd rather do that . . . if it doesn't matter," he said.

"You'll like the teacher of Jewel's class," said Eldeen. "I wish I was in the Willing Workers so I could hear Harvey Gill every Sunday. He's a saint, that man is. Smart as all get-out too."

Eldeen went on to tell about her own class, the Autumn Gleaners, and her teacher, Marvella Gowdy, who obviously waited till Sunday morning to prepare her lesson every week.

The church, which was on the other side of town from Montroyal, was set sideways on a corner lot. It was a small white frame building with one of those encased marquees standing out front. "THE CHURCH OF THE OPEN DOOR," the letters inside the case proclaimed, although Perry noticed that the front door of the church was securely closed. An elderly man in a long, dark overcoat stood outside greeting everyone, though, and handing out a paper of some sort as they walked in. Jewel parked the car in the gravel lot and gave Joe Leonard the keys to get his tuba out. Then she went around to help Eldeen.

"Oh, Mama, you had your dress caught in the door," Jewel said, bending down to inspect it. "I hope it didn't make a mark," and she brushed at it briskly. Then she took Eldeen's arm and together they stepped gingerly across the gravel, with Perry and Joe Leonard following. Perry noticed that Eldeen was wearing opaque brown stockings and large, black, rubber-soled, lace-up shoes this morning. It looked as if her feet had been stuffed into them and then inflated. She wore a gray tentlike cape over her red dress, and a large black pocketbook the size of a duffel bag swung from her arm.

"This old gravel irks me all over again every Sunday," Eldeen said. "I wish they'd pave it. Somebody's going to stumble someday and hurt theirself bad."

As they approached the front steps, the elderly man smiled and opened the door for them. "Glad you've come, glad you've come. It's a little warmer today, yes, just a mite warmer all right," he said, handing each of them one of the papers. On the front of the paper Perry read, "Wash me and I shall be whiter than snow." Under that was a picture of a dense forest smothered with snow, no doubt many miles from South Carolina.

"Shirley Grimes types up the bulletins every week," said Eldeen, smiling down at the snow scene. "That's a real pretty picture, real pretty." Under the picture Perry read the words "THE CHURCH OF THE OPEN DOOR OF DERBY WELCOMES ALL OF YOU ONE AND ALL." Evidently Shirley didn't proofread for redundancy.

"We meet in here first for opening exercises," said Jewel as they passed through the lobby into the auditorium, and Perry had a brief vision of all of them standing in the aisles doing calisthenics the way he'd heard Japanese workers did in their office buildings every morning.

They sat down in a pew near the front, and Eldeen smiled and nodded to everyone around them, calling out their names softly. "Myrt, Mr. Simpson, hello, Grady. There's the Pucketts, Jewel, look, they must be back from Spartanburg already. Nina, hello there. Beverly, I see your mother's gone and curled your hair up pretty as always. Good morning, Bernie. Hoyt, how's your back doing today?" Joe Leonard carried his tuba case through the door by the organ and came back out without it.

It had been years since Perry had been inside a church. His mother had taken Beth and him to an Episcopal church several times as children, but mostly just on Easter and at Christmastime. All he remembered was staring in awe at the high vaulted ceilings and richly tinted pictures on the windows.

And the summer he was thirteen, when his mother had been taken to a hospital for something mysterious that was never explained to Perry, he had been sent to stay with his uncle Louis in Wisconsin. Uncle Louis and Aunt Marsha had taken him with them to their church—a large Baptist church where everyone looked wealthy—and had even sent him to the denominational Youth Camp for one week. Perry still remembered his intense discomfort that whole week, watching all those people smile so much and sing what they called "youth choruses" and hearing his counselor pray every night for "the teens here in this very cabin who still haven't yielded to God's call." Perry had remained at his seat during the closing service of the week—a candlelight ceremony during which the campers had been invited to light their own small candles from a large one up front, to signify a "commitment to God"—and had shaken his head when a man had asked him if he wanted to go to the prayer room. He would never forget the wonderful relief of boarding the bus at the end of that week and heading back to Uncle Louis's.

He hardly knew what to expect today at the Church of the Open Door, though. He'd known a girl once who told him that the people in her church—a place called The Bread of Life—moved around a lot during the services and even swayed to the music and shouted with joyful abandon during the preacher's sermon and hugged each other. He'd seen things like that on TV too—on the religious channel where men wearing bola ties and middle-aged women with bouffant hairdos sometimes conducted healing services. He certainly hoped no one would try to hug him this morning.

As a portly man in a rust-colored sportcoat walked to the platform, Jewel slipped out and went to the piano. Perry was surprised as she started playing; he hadn't known she was the pianist. It was a bright and happy song she was playing, and when she hit the final bass chord, the large man stood up behind the pulpit and smiled jubilantly.

"That's Willard Scoggins," whispered Eldeen. "He's our Sunday school superintendent and the song leader both." The man had a round, congenial face, and all his features seemed to have drifted toward the center of it.

"Let's all sing the song Jewel just played," said Willard, and off he went, starting on a slightly lower note than Jewel but adjusting his pitch quickly. He waved his arms vigorously, his full baritone voice filling the auditorium. It was a song Perry had never heard before, one about counting your blessings and naming them one by one. Eldeen sang quite loudly and an octave lower than the other women, Perry noticed. Joe Leonard's voice was high and reedy but not at all timid as Perry would have expected. The boy sang out with confidence in a section where all the voices seemed to be repeating snatches of the refrain at different times.

After the song, Willard asked if there were any visitors. Eldeen immediately raised her hand and spoke out. "We've brought our new neighbor with us. This here's Perry Warren. He's Beth's sister, I mean she's his brother." Everyone laughed. "Oh, well, the two of them's brother and sister," said Eldeen. "Some of you've met Beth before on visitation."

Willard nodded. "Yes, we remember Beth. She's the one we all prayed for several times." Perry wondered if Beth knew this. She had never mentioned coming to this church. What was "visitation" anyway? It sounded somewhat sinister to Perry, like people sitting around participating in eerie ceremonies involving visions and levitation. Were these people praying for Beth behind her back? And what for?

Willard went on to announce a churchwide Sunday school social coming up in March and requested prayer for a couple of people he called "shut-ins," a term Perry had never heard before. After another lively song, one in which the repeated phrase was "Send the light!" everyone got up and headed through the two doors at the front of the auditorium, talking cheerfully. Perry heard Eldeen call to a small, black-haired woman, asking if her daffodils were up yet. The woman gasped and reached back to grab Eldeen's hand. "Oh, honey, you should see the ones on the creek bank!" she said. "They look like a picture!"

Harvey Gill, teacher of the Willing Workers, appeared to be around sixty. He was almost totally bald but had a firm, lean face and the posture of a military officer. He held his Bible spread open in his left hand the entire time he spoke, and Perry marveled at the freedom of his gestures; never once did he catch the edge with his other hand and flip it over or let it tilt and slip off, not even when he read some verses near the back of the Bible. He often made large, sweeping motions with both hands to emphasize some point, all the while keeping his Bible balanced perfectly. He never seemed to tire of holding his arm out in the same position, and when he turned pages to read different verses, Perry wondered how he could find them so quickly since there didn't seem to be any markers in his Bible.

The lesson was titled "The Hidden Manna" and centered on God's provision for his people. Jewel shared her Bible with Perry since he hadn't brought one. He didn't even own a Bible, he realized, and he made a mental note to get one as soon as possible. Perry noticed that the margins of most of the pages in Jewel's Bible were filled with handwritten notes and many verses were underlined. The cover was limp and beginning to split at the binding. It appeared to Perry that she needed a new Bible almost as much as a new broom.

Harvey Gill shook Perry's hand heartily afterward and invited him back to the Willing Workers class. "It's always an honor to have visitors," he said. "Next week we'll start a series on the Fruits of the Spirit." As Perry looked into Harvey's steady, gray eyes, he felt certain that the man had already gotten a good start on next week's lesson.

"I've got to go warm up with the choir," Jewel told him. Perry imagined them all running laps around the church. "You can go on to the sanctuary and sit with Mama if that's okay," she said. "Joe Leonard and I'll join you later."

Perry was glad to see Eldeen already seated in the same pew they had sat in earlier. She patted the place next to her. "Sit on down here and tell me how you liked Harvey and the Willing Workers," she said.

"Well, it was all quite interesting," he said. "We learned about manna."

"Uh-huh, we did too," Eldeen said. "All the adult classes have the same lessons. But I'm sure Marvella's lesson couldn't hold a candle to Harvey Gill's. She hummed and hawed the whole time." Perry thought of Marvella humming through the lesson. He wished he'd quit picking apart everything these people said. It was a distracting habit of his, always had been, but now was an especially risky time to be doing it. He was afraid he'd laugh out loud right here in church if he didn't stop it.

The choir filed in a few minutes later as Jewel played the piano, a slower and more sedate song this time. Joe Leonard stood in the second row with the men, who were greatly outnumbered by the women, Perry noted. Willard was on the platform again, towering over another man in a well-tailored gray suit. Standing together, the two of them looked like a comedy duo. Compared to Willard, the other man was small and compact, built like a gymnast. He had a slightly receding hairline, but the hair he did have was riotously curly, whereas Willard's hair was thin and straight with the beginnings of a pronounced bald spot on top.

Eldeen leaned over and pointed. "That's the preacher up there with Willard," she said. "Brother Hawthorne."

Perry had already noticed that the paper he had been handed earlier had a list on the back called "Order of Worship," a kind of agenda he supposed they would follow—which they did, starting with the "Welcome," a cordial greeting from Willard. As if he hadn't just seen all of them in these same seats an hour earlier. Then there was a song, listed as "Congregational Singing—'At the Cross.'" Perry turned to the right page number and read the words as everybody sang. He glanced around after the phrase "For such a worm as I," but no one else seemed to think it odd. Another song followed, one called "Only a Sinner." During this one he saw that Eldeen had her eyes closed and was slowly wagging her head from side to side as she sang the words.

"Announcements" followed, during which Willard asked for more nursery volunteers and someone to sign up to iron the communion cloths for next month. He reminded everybody of the Wednesday service, visitation on Thursday night—there was that word again—and repeated the list of shut-ins. The theme of the Sunday school social in March was going to be "Springtime," he announced. Perry expected someone to snicker at the lack of originality, but no one did. They needed people to decorate Fellowship Hall, Willard said, and there was a sign-up sheet in the lobby.

Then Brother Hawthorne took over for the next part, "Offering." There was a sudden stirring over the entire auditorium and a great rustling of purses unzipping and unsnapping and wallets being wrestled from hip pockets. Several men holding shallow baskets walked down the aisle and stood in front of the pulpit. Someone behind Perry ripped out a check, and several coins rolled onto the floor and stopped at his feet.

"Oh, looka there, some little person's gone and dropped her offering," Eldeen said in a loud whisper. She craned her neck to look behind them. Perry bent down and picked up three nickels and a dime. A small child started crying several rows behind them and someone whispered, "Shhh!"

"We got your money, Missy honey," Eldeen called softly. "Pass it back," she said to Perry. A large hand was thrust forward beside Perry's shoulder, and he dropped the coins into it. He heard a ripple of fond chuckles as the coins exchanged hands.

He noticed Joe Leonard slipping out of the choir and disappearing through the side door. When Brother Hawthorne prayed for "these sacrificial gifts," Perry saw Joe Leonard come back into the auditorium and mount the platform carrying his tuba, this time out of its case. He felt a flash of admiration for Joe Leonard. That instrument had to be heavy. Perry couldn't imagine having to hold it up and blow into it at the same time.

As the men started the baskets up and down the rows, Joe Leonard nodded to Jewel and began playing what was listed on the schedule as "Offertory—Special Youth Music." It was a song Perry recognized from a number of years ago, when some popular singer on the radio had sung it in a swingy, blues style. "Amazing Grace, how sweet the sound! That saved a wretch like me!" He still remembered most of the words.

Everyone was listening with serious, attentive expressions, even the children. Perry didn't know much about brass instruments, but he suspected, listening to Joe Leonard play, that the boy was pretty good. The notes rose full and deep. Perry thought of Joe Leonard's high singing voice and smiled at the contrast. He wondered what had been behind the boy's decision to play an instrument like the tuba. Joe Leonard finished the song the first time through and then played it all over once more after Jewel had filled in the break with a few notes. No one clapped after it was over, but several people, including Eldeen, said, "Amen."

"Wasn't that a blessing?" she whispered to Perry, and he nodded.

Joe Leonard quickly rejoined the choir, which Willard then led in a song that started out with "I stand amazed in the presence of Jesus the Nazarene, And wonder how He could love me, A sinner, condemned, unclean." It occurred to Perry that these people didn't seem to have a very high opinion of themselves.

He glanced over at Eldeen, who had her hands clasped together under her chin and her eyes closed again. He saw that she was mouthing the words to the song the choir was singing. He studied her hands—almost as large as his own, with big purple veins running like twisted tubes beneath the wrinkled, discolored skin. Her nails were grayish, thick, and square.

He looked up at Jewel playing the piano. She was beautiful really, with her soft, dark hair, the long neck, those eyes the color of a blue mist. Perry wondered if she knew she was pretty, or if all she saw when she looked in the mirror was a worm, a wretch, a sinner condemned and unclean. He looked at Joe Leonard, whose chin was lifted high, whose Adam's apple throbbed above his brown bow tie as he sang, "Oh, how marvelous! Oh, how wonderful!" How would this boy ever survive in the cruel world?

He glanced at others around him and wondered who they all were. Did they act this pure and pious all the time? The couple in front of him with the three children. Did they ever fight? Did the husband ever throw things? Did the wife ever make harsh, sarcastic remarks to the children? The preacher, Brother Hawthorne, gazing meditatively at his open Bible as the choir sang. Did Brother Hawthorne enjoy a good joke? Had he ever gotten drunk and given anybody a black eye? Cursed? Did he ever watch R-rated videos? The plain little woman playing the organ. Maybe she was a chain-smoker in real life. Did she ever have the urge to jump into a swimming pool fully clothed? Or naked? He watched Willard Scoggins waving his arms expansively in front of the choir. Did Willard ever break the speed limit? Had he ever held a knife to someone's throat or gambled away his family's grocery money? Harvey Gill sat across the aisle from Perry with a tall, matronly woman who must be his wife. Had Harvey ever had a lustful thought? Did he like beer and pretzels? Or did he survive on manna?

Chapter 5

When the phone rang on Monday morning, Perry knew it was Cal.

"So what's up?" Cal asked. "Did you scout out the church yesterday?"

"Yep, morning and night both," said Perry.

"Is it going to work you think?" Cal asked.

"It's just what we wanted—small, about a hundred and fifty people or so, no denominational affiliation, fundamentalist."

"Great," said Cal. "And did they try to get you saved, born again, converted, regenerated, baptized, and sanctified?"

"Not really," said Perry. "They just did their thing and I just watched."

"Well, I don't believe that for a minute. Don't kid yourself, Perry. They were watching *you* is more like it. And they'll be coming after you before long, count on it."

"Well, maybe so," said Perry. He knew what was coming next. He'd heard it a dozen times already. Though Cal claimed to despise his religious upbringing, Perry couldn't help noticing how much he enjoyed talking about it.

"I grew up in Sand Hill, Georgia, remember, right in the middle of it all," said Cal. "I got my exercise by walking the aisle—or I guess my mother got hers from dragging me down it. Public profession of faith, Sunday school, Training Union, Daily Vacation Bible School, Camp Victory every summer, baptism by immersion, the whole works. They had their claws in me before I was out of diapers. Thank God I got away from that place. Trust me, Perry, they won't let you rest until they think they've rescued you from the wolves of the world and brought you to the fold."

Perry suspected Cal was right. He wouldn't be surprised if Harvey Gill had already called a special prayer meeting to pray for him.

"What are the neighbors like?" Cal asked.

"Nice. They're real nice people. But different—it's just a whole different culture."

"Didn't I tell you? Part of it's the South and part of it's the religion. Every one of those little towns down there is spooky. You step inside one, and it's like you're in some kind of time warp. It could be anywhere from the nineteen forties on. Unless you get around some teenagers and hear the music, you'd never know what year it was. At least teenagers are good for something, I guess." Perry recognized the sigh that followed as an invitation to ask Cal how his daughter was, but he didn't feel up to listening to the answer.

After a pause Cal continued. "Watch the kids at this church, Perry. That's where the rottenness shows up. I remember hating Sundays with a passion. My brother and I had to think up all sorts of things to make it through without dying of boredom. Did I ever tell you about what we did during the communion service that time?"

"Yes," said Perry quickly.

Cal laughed. "Well, anyway, keep an eye on the kids. Especially when they get to be twelve, thirteen. That's when they start getting fed up with all that crap they've been told all their lives. That's when I checked out. And *that's* where you can prove the failure of the system."

"I'm not trying to prove anything, remember," said Perry. "That's not what I do in a book like this. I'm just writing what I see." He had sensed from the beginning that Cal had a lot more interest in the success of his book than just that of an agent for his client. He had wondered, in fact, how the whole project had originated, though he had never asked. It wouldn't surprise him a bit to learn that Cal had been the one to cook up the whole idea and had then presented it to one of his editor friends, suggesting Perry as the author so he could keep a finger in the project. Cal had a lot of friends in high places in the publishing field and had proved himself to them over and over with his unerring instinct for what would work.

"Well, I'm just trying to give you some tips, that's all," said Cal.

Perry thought of Joe Leonard and wondered if he ever considered telling Jewel to shove it when she said it was time to leave for church. He thought of the tuba solo and wondered if the boy had been forced against his will to play it. What kind of music did Joe Leonard listen to when he wasn't at church? Was he fed up with the Church of the Open Door and ready to ditch it all? Had he ever thought of emptying the grape juice bottle before communion, as Cal had done, and replacing it with real wine laced with Budweiser?

"Have you talked with the preacher yet?" Cal asked. "What's he like?"

"They call him Brother Hawthorne," said Perry, "and he clears his throat a lot when he preaches. Probably close to my age, went to some Bible college in Florida, and uses a lot better grammar than you said he would. Has a red-haired wife who sings solos and probably outweighs him by ten or twenty pounds. Has some little kids too. I told him last night after church I'd like to come see him sometime this week."

"Bet he's excited. He probably thinks his excellent preaching put you under conviction, as they like to say. Or maybe he's expecting you to apply for membership. That really wouldn't be a bad idea, you know, Perry."

"We talked about that already, remember? I'm not going to join or sign anything or recite an oath or go through any kind of initiation. I'm here to observe and write. I'm not going to pretend to be one of them."

"But you'll be attending all the time. Eventually people will start to assume you're a member anyway."

"All the more reason not to go through the hassle now," Perry said.

"You'd get a better view of things from the beginning if you were a member. They'd let their guard down more."

"No. We went through all that already. I never did it in my other books, and I'm not starting now. I don't want to try to participate and research at the same time. That's not me, it never has been. Besides, it's not even honest."

"Well, if it's *honesty* we're talking about, how honest is it to go to a church all the time and pretend to be interested when all you're really doing is writing a book about it?"

"I'll tell them sooner or later," Perry said. "I'll have to."

"Yeah, but in the meantime, they're thinking you're somebody you're not. Don't throw that honesty bit at me, Perry."

"It's not dishonest to attend a church regularly," Perry said testily. "I'm not making any kind of commitment by sitting in a pew. Anyway, they'd ask me all sorts of questions if I applied for membership, and I have no desire to be quizzed about religion."

"Okay, okay. But you're going to have to put up with people bugging you *all* the time instead of just a one-shot thing. Get your answers ready. 'If you died today, do you know where you'd spend eternity?' 'Are you on your way to heaven?' You wouldn't have to go through all that if you went ahead and . . ."

"No."

There was a pause. Perry pictured Cal holding the receiver out in front of him and staring at it, bewildered. Perry seldom questioned anything Cal suggested and never so emphatically.

"Well, carry on," Cal said at last. "I'll talk to you later."

After he hung up from talking with Cal, Perry refilled his cup of coffee and took it back to the guest bedroom, where he had set up his computer on the dressing table. It was one of those low-sitting old mahogany dressers, with a little round stool that fit into the curved center. The large oval mirror could be tilted to any angle; Perry had moved the dresser away from the wall and aimed the mirror downward so he wouldn't have to look at his face every time he glanced up. He had moved a kitchen chair in to replace the stool and had laid a towel across the dresser top with a piece of shelf board set on top. On this rested his computer. Not exactly the setup of a professional writer, he thought, but it would do. In fact, it might be good for his writing to have to adjust to a new room, even lower his standards of comfort.

He stood in the doorway and looked at the mahogany dresser. He knew it had been foolish not to bring his sturdy oak desk from Rockford. His sister had scolded him over the phone for leaving almost everything behind with Dinah. "You're stupid, Perry," Beth had said. "You're going to have to start all over and buy everything from scratch." But the thought of that was better than the thought of leaving gaping holes behind him in a house where he had once been happy. It was really for Troy anyway, though he hadn't told Beth that. Maybe one actor was offstage, but at least Troy would have the security of the same set and props.

Perry glanced at the clock. Troy was probably just getting to school about now. Mondays had always been hard for him. After being home for two days, he never wanted to go back to school. Dinah had always blamed Perry for this. "What do you expect?" she had said once. "You make him think the weekend is some kind of uninterrupted partytime where nobody ever has to work. Friday afternoon till Sunday night, solid, you're letting him drag you around wherever his heart desires. A movie? Oh, sure, Troy Boy, which one? Sledding? Okay, but first let's buy you a new sled. That other old thing must be at least two months old. Pizza? Fine. Call all your buddies and invite them to come too. On and on, every weekend. Then Monday morning, bang. Reality. School. Weeping and wailing. It wears me out, Perry, and it's not healthy for Troy."

Perry wondered what Dinah and Troy had done this past weekend without him. She was probably exhausted.

He had heard the car start in Jewel's driveway next door about an hour ago. He had been up for a good while already and by then was on his third cup of coffee. He had watched through the kitchen window as Jewel opened the back of the station wagon and Joe Leonard hoisted in his tuba. He heard Jewel say something and they both laughed. Then while Jewel started up the station wagon, Joe Leonard had run back into the house and come out with a zippered satchel and a couple of books. The car sputtered and died once, but Jewel started it again, gunned it backwards, and they were gone. He remembered Beth saying Jewel was a teacher, but he realized now that he didn't have any idea what she taught.

Looking out the side window now, Perry imagined Eldeen sitting by the gas heater inside the house smearing her feet with Vaseline, with a box of Baggies nearby.

He sat down at the computer. The screen was blank except for a heading he had typed in before the phone rang. GOSPEL LIGHT BIBLE CHAPEL. That would be his new name for the Church of the Open Door. For a project like this he had to use fictitious names in accordance with the standard ethics for sociological science research, and he had discovered years ago that it helped to choose the names for everything and everyone right at the very beginning. It was an easy way to get something down on paper, and even if he went back later and changed the names—which he often did—he still had the feeling of having begun his research in a substantial way. He had already decided that Jewel would be Opal, Harvey Gill would be Gilbert Hadley, and Brother Hawthorne would be Brother Frazier. There were others he hated to give up, though. Eldeen, for one. He thought he might go with something like Lorena or Ila. Or maybe he could do something with Vaseline. Valina? Evaline? Salveena? Lavinia? Now there was a possibility.

He typed a list of names as he thought of them, then closed the file and named it "Name Bank." He knew he had to get his first impression of yesterday's services down before the day passed, so he opened another file. He had taken notes inside his Daytimer, and he got those out now. He could still see Eldeen's nod of approval as she had watched him writing in church yesterday. "I filled up a whole heap of notebooks in my day," she had whispered, "but it's harder to keep up now with my arthritis, so I just listen real close."

Perry started typing and the screen quickly filled. After Joe

Leonard's tuba solo in the morning service, the congregation had sung another song entitled "Must I Go and Empty-Handed?" and then a plump redhead had stepped out of the choir and stood behind the pulpit. She had a pretty face, one of those fresh, guileless faces you'd see in ads for milk or Ivory soap. "That's Brother Hawthorne's wife, Edna," whispered Eldeen. "She has a voice like a angel." And it *had* turned out to be a nice voice—a cross between Dolly Parton and Julie Andrews, Perry thought, and she sang so earnestly, leaning forward to scan the faces of the audience: "Have you any room for Jesus, He who bore your load of sin? As He knocks and asks admission, Sinner, will you let Him in?" Brother Hawthorne stared up at his wife pensively while she sang. Perry wondered what he was thinking.

Many people indicated their approval with hearty "amens" after Edna Hawthorne finished. The choir then got up and filed down to sit in the congregation while Jewel played another verse of Edna's song. Edna Hawthorne sat on the front row with three children who had caught Perry's eye earlier. The little boy, probably four or five, had received numerous pokes from his sisters seated on either side. Now he moved over to sit on his mother's lap. Perry tried to imagine how soft that must feel.

Jewel returned from the piano and sat beside Perry, with Joe Leonard next to her. Brother Hawthorne moved to the pulpit and bowed his head for a moment of silence that stretched out so long Perry wondered if someone had forgotten a cue. But then Brother Hawthorne began praying aloud, quoting phrases from all the songs they had sung and heard that morning, weaving them together into an eloquent supplication for mercy—almost poetic. Perry tried to see if he was reading his prayer from a script but saw only a closed Bible on top of the pulpit.

The sermon that followed wasn't at all what he was prepared for. Cal had led him to expect a ranting stream of rhetoric ludicrously illogical in content and clumsy in style. Brother Hawthorne did not rant, however, although he did speak with intensity and briskness and gestured frequently. He sucked in his breath audibly before making a major point, cleared his throat after making the point, was fond of the phrase "by the way," and maintained close eye contact with his listeners. At one point he stopped talking and gazed sternly at his son on the front row, who, having crawled out of Edna's lap, had slapped a hymnbook shut with such a loud smack that Eldeen had said, "Mercy me!" right out loud.

In a way, Perry thought, the sermon *was* ludicrously illogical. The title of it had been "Ten to Two" and had dealt with what Brother Hawthorne called "the distillation of the Law of Moses."

"If you obey these two commandments," Brother Hawthorne had said, "you will have no trouble keeping the ten that were engraved by the hand of God onto the stone tablets at Mount Sinai." He had first read three verses from the book of Matthew in which Jesus answered a question posed to him by a Pharisee: "Which of the commandments is the greatest?" He had then gone on to read each of the Ten Commandments in order, from Exodus 20, and had explained briefly how each would be obeyed by simply, first, loving God with all your heart, soul, spirit and, second, loving your neighbor as yourself. And in obeying these laws, a man could find what Brother Hawthorne called "a purpose and joy in living." It sounded so neatly formulaic.

Perry stopped typing and looked into the mirror in front of him. He saw the reflection of his fingers resting lightly on the keyboard. He stared at them a moment, wondering what thoughts would flow into them and onto the computer screen in the form of words and sentences over the course of the next several months. He often saw his life as something projected back at him from a mirror—not the real thing but an image, light rays bouncing off the flesh-and-blood reality and producing a painted still life.

His life as husband and later father had always troubled him for this reason; it had never seemed real. He had seen himself in a role, his name in fading letters on a script, his lines recited with amateurish inflections. He had often stopped in the middle of something where the three of them had been together—once during Dinah's birthday dinner at a restaurant, he recalled—and pictured what they must look like from a bystander's perspective. He imagined his words being recorded by a foreign movie director and then played back for analysis: "This is a typical American male speaking to his wife and son. Notice the phrasing of the dialogue." Even his work as a writer seemed a step removed from reality; he was always a spectator of life, never a participant.

He read over what he had just written. The sermon had been so simple, and Perry couldn't help marveling that he had been seated in the midst of over a hundred people who by all appearances truly believed life was this easy. Do this and this will happen. Push that domino and all the others will respond in swift, orderly succession. Be good and you'll be happy. Love God—how did you do that anyway, was it just an oath you took?—and he will enfold you in his embrace. Love others as yourself—now there was a hefty assignment, or was it?

Perry had never in his life felt anything approaching fondness for himself, at least not on a rational, conscious level. Of course, he had no doubt that he would struggle to survive as fiercely and instinctively as the next person if his life were endangered, but somewhere deep in the core of his soul he seriously questioned whether his life would be worth saving. Anyway, where was he? Oh, yes, love others as yourself, and God would smile upon you. He would rock you in the lap of his approval, a lap of privilege as warm and soft as Edna Hawthorne's.

There was no doubt about it; these people really believed happiness was permanently attainable, like some kind of medal you earned and then pinned on your chest to show you had accomplished a basic skill. They seemed to put so much stock in every moment, every action, every thought. What a simple way of looking at life, yet complicated too. How could you ever get through a day if you stopped to weigh the consequences of everything you did?

He was still staring at the keyboard in the mirror when he heard a knock at the door, followed immediately by the door buzzer.

"I'm not staying but a minute," Eldeen said when he opened the front door. "Don't worry, I know authors need their private time, but it dawned on me while I was having my devotions a minute ago that you might not of gotten anything at the store to eat yet and might like some of Jewel's muffins she made this morning." She held out a tin pie plate covered with foil. "I was reading in Romans 12 about feeding your enemy if he's hungry and giving him a drink when he's dying of thirst, and I know you're not my enemy, of course, but all of a sudden it hit me: 'Now I wonder if Perry's fixed hisself any breakfast.' Did you?" She looked at him longingly, with the transparent plea written all over her face: Please say you didn't, that you're about to starve to death and were just this minute wishing for some homemade muffins.

"Well, I did have a little something," said Perry. "But not enough to satisfy my appetite," he hurried to add when her eyes clouded. Her face wrinkled with delight, and she held the plate out farther. "Oh, here," Perry said, "come on in. Here . . . I'll take those . . . thanks," and he stepped back, motioning her in.

"They're still warmish," Eldeen said, walking inside. "They've been setting on top of the stove."

"Thanks," said Perry. "I'm sure they'll be good . . . thanks. Come on in." He knew he was repeating himself.

"They're best with a smidge of butter—do you have any?" Eldeen's gaze darted to the kitchen. She had on the same gray cape she had worn yesterday, and under it a long pink chenille bathrobe hung down to the toes of the black boots. Her stiff gray hair stuck out from behind one ear as if pulled by a magnet.

"I'm going out this afternoon," said Perry. "I'll get some then. But I'm sure the muffins will be . . . fine without it . . . the way they are. Thanks."

"Here, look at them," said Eldeen, reaching forward and yanking back the foil covering. "Aren't they the nicest little muffins? Jewel's the only one I know of that makes them kind of muffins. And there's a surprise in the middle." She clamped her hand over her mouth. "Now there I go ruining it."

Perry didn't know what to say. What did she mean, a surprise? They looked good—small golden brown domes rising above the crinkled pastel papers.

"Go on, taste one," said Eldeen, and as he bit into one, her eyebrows lowered and her face tightened into its painful-looking grin.

"See? See there? I *told* you it was a surprise, now didn't I? That's what they're called—Surprise Muffins." And she clapped her large hands together as she laughed.

It was jelly. There was a dollop of blackberry jelly right in the center of the muffin. The muffin itself was sweet like cake, and the jelly spread inside Perry's mouth like warm, thick syrup. He nodded his head and smiled.

"It's good," he said. "Very good. I like the surprise . . . it's good."

Eldeen was still laughing. "I get the biggest kick out of seeing people bite into them jelly centers." Perry could picture her, walking around the neighborhood handing out Surprise Muffins, then watching for a response with the eagerness of a child.

"Well, I need to get back home," said Eldeen. "I don't want to miss Brother Hawthorne's radio talk at nine-thirty. And you need to get back to whatever it was you were doing." She looked around for signs of his work, then slowly turned toward the door. Seeing the musical globe on the small table beside the door, she pointed. "I always liked them little things," she said. "Someday I mean to get me one." She picked it up carefully and shook it around a little. "Oh, now that's a shame," she said. "That little feller's done gone and broke off inside of there. He's just floating around with the snowflakes." She studied the little figure gravely, then shook her head. "Wouldn't that feel funny? I always wished I could go up in a space rocket just once to see how it'd feel to drift around like a feather." She set the snowglobe on the table and walked to the door. "It's still a pretty thing—mighty, *mighty* pretty—even with the little person broke off that way and all."

"Thank you for the muffins," said Perry. "I'll have another one with some coffee . . . thanks . . . they're good." He opened the door again, wider this time, and Eldeen stepped heavily across the threshold onto the porch.

She turned back toward him. "Did you say you were going out this afternoon? Well, I know you did say that; I heard you with my own two ears. But what I mean is if you need somebody to show you the best place for groceries, I could. Fact is, I need to use up a couple of coupons before they expire, and Jewel's not going to the store again until payday a week from Friday." She drew her eyebrows together and studied him hopefully.

He didn't know what to say. How could he tell her that he'd rather look around Derby by himself? That he didn't want to be slowed down by someone the age of his grandmother? That he didn't even know if she could stoop down and fold up enough to get into his compact car? That he might have some other errands to run besides grocery shopping? What if she had some kind of stroke or seizure while they were wheeling a cart down the aisle? He didn't know anything about old people really. He was a little wary of them in general. He remembered as a child going with his mother to a nursing home in Chicago only once, to visit an elderly aunt who had thrown her lunch tray at one of the aides; he remembered his mother's blanched face when the aunt had let loose with a string of profanity. What would he do if Eldeen lost control of herself and started throwing things or shouting? What if she needed to use the bathroom all of a sudden?

"Well, all right," he said.

"Oh, you are the nicest thing," said Eldeen. "You just come over and knock when it's time to leave, or better yet—just toot the horn a little bit. I'll be sitting on ready." And she put one large hand up close to her face and gave a tiny, slow wave like a shy child.

Chapter 6

At five o'clock that afternoon Perry stood at the kitchen counter unloading two bags of groceries. Removing a jar of spaghetti sauce from the sack, he noted how heavy it felt. He had never known grocery shopping could be so physically draining. For almost two hours he and Eldeen had walked up and down every aisle of Thrifty Mart—very slowly, with Perry pushing the cart and Eldeen fingering through a shoebox labeled "Dr. Nebergall's Ortho-treads" that served as a file box for her coupons. They had had to backtrack to several different aisles: once to hunt for muffin papers which they had overlooked the first time on Aisle 8; another time to get a second box of strawberry Jell-O on Aisle 6 after Eldeen grew worried that the recipe for Berry Berry Swirl, which she wanted Jewel to make for the upcoming spring social at church, might call for a large box of jello instead of a small box; and then all the way back to Aisle 3 to exchange vanilla wafers for graham crackers after Eldeen had examined her coupon for any Nabisco cookie product more carefully.

"See, there's a picture of graham crackers right smack in the middle of all them cookies," she said, pointing to her coupon triumphantly. "I'm glad I noticed it. I like graham crackers a whole lot better than vanilla wafers. Vanilla wafers are bad to go soft, and I can't stand a soft cookie. I like them crisp. If I want something soft, I'll eat cake, thank you, not a cookie. Cookies oughta *crunch* when you bite down."

She stopped suddenly beside a large display of peanut butter at the end of an aisle. "Now here's something I plum' forgot to put on my list, for crying out loud. You can't eat graham crackers without peanut butter, and Joe Leonard nearly cleaned out the jar last night after church. Have you ever tried graham crackers and peanut butter together, Perry?" But before he could answer, she gave her throaty laugh and swatted his hand. "Oh, what in the world am I thinking of? 'Course you've tried it. Everybody has. I bet all you little Northern children had graham crackers and peanut butter for snacks after school, same as we did."

Perry nodded. A whole compartment of his childhood suddenly unlocked. He hadn't thought of it for years. In fifth and sixth grades he used to come home after school and sit down at the white enameled table in the kitchen with a box of graham crackers, a jar of peanut butter, and a knife. His mother would be at the sink or washer or sewing machine or ironing board, usually listening to an old Cole Porter or Mills Brothers album. Perry would eat slowly and quietly, taking in all the sounds: the splash of the water at the sink, the steady thunk of the washing machine, the rhythmic ticking of his mother's Singer sewing machine, the hiss of the steam iron, but most of all the words to all the songs. "You're the Top," "I've Got You Under My Skin," "Opus One," "Paper Doll," "Glow Worm"—he had learned them all and used to sing snatches of them for humorous effect: "I get a kick out of you" the time he tried to teach Beth to punt a football, "Don't get around much anymore" when he sprained his ankle, "You always hurt the one you love" after Beth stepped on the cat's tail, "I know a little bit about a lot of things" when he guessed the right answer on "Final Jeopardy." The only problem was that no one at home ever laughed at his little musical jokes, and he had finally quit trying.

There was one the Mills Brothers sang entitled "Dinah." He remembered singing it to Dinah: "Dinah—is there anyone finer in the state of Carolina?" The song went on to describe the charms of gazing into Dinah's sparkling eyes. Perry had put in all the same inflections when he sang it, just as he'd heard it on the album—scooping up to notes, holding certain ones out longer, and punching at others to add a syncopated effect. Dinah would laugh and shake her head when he got to the part of the song in which the speaker worried that his beautiful Dinah might grow tired of him someday and change her mind about loving him. Not a chance, she'd say. Not a chance in the world.

He tried to remember the last time he'd sung the song to her. It must have been at least five or six years. Why had he stopped, he wondered. Funny how he'd wound up in the state of Carolina and Dinah had indeed changed her mind about him.

At some time or other his mother had stopped listening to her record albums. He never knew why. She had also stopped buying graham crackers and had started buying boxes of graham cracker crumbs for her cheesecakes and pies. Gradually Perry had begun going directly to his bedroom after school and had stopped sitting at the kitchen table for snacks anyway.

". . . and would eat a jar every day if his mama would let him." Eldeen was still talking as she sifted through her coupons. "Here we go. Skippy—fifty-five cents off. Now let's see here." She bent close to the shelves to examine the prices. "That's what I thought! Now that's just exactly what I thought!" She straightened and pointed to the jars of Skippy. "Even with this coupon, that kind is going to run me almost forty cents more than the Lucky Lady brand. And it's not a bit better. Not a bit!"

She picked up a jar of the Lucky Lady and set it firmly in the cart, then placed her unused coupon on top of a Skippy jar on the shelf. "There, I'll leave that right there in case somebody's just dead set on getting Skippy and doesn't care about sticking to a budget. It irks me when a coupon is for fifty-five cents anyway. They won't double anything over fifty cents, so the way I see it, a coupon for fifty-five is gypping me out of forty-five cents if you know what I mean." She looked at Perry as if expecting an answer; he frowned and nodded. What in the world was she talking about? "It's for the chunky kind anyway," she continued, "and I'd much rather have the creamy."

On the graham cracker aisle Eldeen's face suddenly creased with pleasure as she pointed to a woman headed toward them. "Why, there's Martha Joy Darrow! Martha Joy, it's been so long since I've seen you, honey."

Martha Joy, a tall, pale woman with limp, shoulder-length hair and thick glasses, looked up and squinted toward them, craning her neck forward. Suddenly she smiled widely and said, "Well, if it's not Eldeen Rafferty, you sweet thing you. I couldn't figure out who you were at first."

Eldeen immediately introduced Perry as "my tall, handsome young neighbor who offered to bring me grocery shopping with him." Martha Joy stuck out her hand, and as Perry took it, he noticed that her orange lipstick overlapped her lips by an eighth of an inch all the way around. Maybe it was a beauty tip for making thin lips appear fuller. And it would probably work fine if you didn't get up too close to anyone. Or maybe she was extremely farsighted and couldn't see what she was doing in the mirror. Martha Joy smiled at him and said, "I saw you at church yesterday morning, but I slipped out early, so I didn't get to visit. You don't meet many gentlemen nowadays, that's for certain. It's mighty nice of you to offer Eldeen a ride to the store. It's a pleasure to meet you."

"How's Burton getting along?" Eldeen asked her, and then she and Martha Joy talked for several minutes. Burton, who was evidently

Martha Joy's husband, was suffering from diverticulitis, which Martha Joy said was "tying his insides in knots."

Perry walked on down the aisle and exchanged the vanilla wafers while Eldeen talked. As he returned to the cart, another woman with a baby and two toddlers in her cart turned down Aisle 3. He heard Eldeen gasp. "Well, I'll be. If it's not *another* one of my favorite people in the whole wide world. Imagine it, meeting two of my nicest friends here on the same day." The three women laughed and hugged one another.

The new woman, named Crystal, told Eldeen and Martha Joy that she'd had to miss the last two Sundays because of the children. "They can't all of them get well and stay that way for more than a day or two," she said. The little girl in the cart lifted her dress to cover her face, exposing a pair of blue panties. The other toddler, a little boy oozing thickly from his nose, was clapping two cans of peas together. The baby started waving his arms and crying like a weak lamb.

Eldeen asked Crystal about her houseplants. "Did the fertilizer I gave you help any?" Crystal said she'd never gotten around to trying it, and Eldeen patted her arm. "I know, honey, you've got lots more important things on your mind than puny violets." They talked a few more minutes before one of Crystal's toddlers ripped open a bag of rice and she quickly wheeled away. "That poor woman, I feel so sorry for her," Eldeen said to Martha Joy, and they stood side by side, sadly watching Crystal round the corner.

A stock boy in a green Thrifty Mart apron passed at the end of the aisle. "Gordon!" Eldeen called, waving the top of the coupon shoebox. "Gordon! There's been a spill here on this aisle! It's a safety hazard! Bring a broom!"

Martha Joy said good-bye and left, but Eldeen stayed to watch the cleanup. "Over there's some more," she told Gordon, pointing with the shoebox lid. "Crystal's had a hard time of it," she said to Perry. "She's got four more children besides them three with her. The oldest one is ten or thereabouts, and it's all up to Crystal to put clothes on their back. Her husband is just a no-account. He sure needs Jesus, that man does. I need to pray harder for him." She closed her eyes right then, and Perry saw her lips moving. He looked down at Gordon in embarrassment and then back at Eldeen, who still had her eyes closed. Perry ran his foot under the edge of a round revolving rack displaying cakes of toilet sanitizer and sponges of various sizes. Several grains of rice scooted across the floor, and Gordon swept them into his pile.

Eldeen opened her eyes. "Every time I see Crystal, my heart just breaks in two for her. Some folks have such a hard time in life it doesn't seem fair, does it? But Jesus knows, Jesus knows. The steps of a good man are ordered by the Lord, the Bible says, and I reckon that includes a good woman too." Gordon finished sweeping and held out his dustpan, which was full of rice. Eldeen nodded approvingly. "There, that's got it," she said.

By the time they had covered the whole store, the cart was full. Perry had stacked his things in one half of the lower section at Eldeen's suggestion, using a jumbo box of Corn Flakes as a divider. Eldeen's purse and box of coupons took up most of the smaller top section. A large bag of potatoes and two economy packs of paper towels filled the flat shelf on the bottom.

"Jewel will be so glad I got all this," Eldeen said as they finally headed toward a checkout lane. There was only one cashier working, so they got in line behind two other people. A small, elderly man stood directly in front of them, shoulders hunched forward and chin resting somewhere near his sternum. His scalp shone like a bright pink balloon through his thin, oily, yellowish hair, which straggled untidily around his ears.

"My, but a buggy can sure fill up fast, can't it, Mr. Hammond?" Eldeen said loudly, tapping the man's arm lightly with the shoebox lid she was still holding. He slowly pivoted and scowled up at Eldeen from deeply sunken eyes. "Seems like you no sooner get started than you run out of room," she continued cheerfully, motioning toward her cart. Perry wondered if she really did think it had happened fast. The man's cart held only four small tubs of cottage cheese and a big jar of apple juice, he noticed. The old man stared at Eldeen for a moment without answering, then solemnly studied their loaded cart. "I used to like sausage," he said in a hoarse whisper, "but it doesn't set with me anymore."

"Well now, that's a shame," Eldeen said. "I guess if it's not one thing it's another, isn't it? Now me, I used to pour a gallon of Italian dressing on my salad, and then all of a sudden it started upsetting my digestion something awful. I can't take even the slightest little taste of it anymore. But sausage—now *that* would be a hard, hard thing to have to give up." Without responding, the old man turned back around and inched his cart forward as the woman in front of him finished unloading her groceries onto the moving belt.

Eldeen began digging in her purse, unzipping several interior pockets and extracting folded bills. "That poor old man, he's just shy of being totally and completely deaf," she announced to Perry without lowering her voice. The old man gave no sign of having heard her. "His name's Otis Hammond, and he lives all by hisself, he told me one day," Eldeen continued, "and he said he comes to the store every day. I see him in here all the time. It just gives him something to do I reckon. I keep inviting him to come to church, but he says he doesn't see any sense in religion, that his brother-in-law was a preacher and the worst bag of hot air in the country. I'm praying hard for him, though, and I keep having this dream that I'm setting in church one Sunday and I look up and there he is, coming in through the back door. He's got a heart problem—I mean besides his *spiritual* one—and then some days he can hardly talk on top of that. It's some kind of nodules on his thyroid that just keeps growing bigger and bigger. And he won't have a operation. Thinks doctors are a bunch of butchers and thieves, he says."

The old man stooped to pick up his purchases and place them on the belt. The small bones running down the back of his hands protruded like taut cords as he grasped each carton one at a time. He coughed weakly and appeared to be lost in dark thoughts.

Eldeen poked Mr. Hammond again and pointed to a tabloid beside the candy rack. "Now if that's not just the biggest bunch of flimflam!" she shouted. "Looka there at that: '*Ninety-year-old Woman Marries Teenage Siamese Twins.*' They must think we're a nation of idiots to believe that. '*Alien Dog Emits Beta Rays.*' And to think there's people that *buys* them papers and reads that stuff!" She laughed and pointed. "There's a good one: '*Farmer Teaches Pigs Spanish.*' Ha! Wouldn't you like to hear 'em? Wonder how a pig oinks in Spanish!"

Mr. Hammond frowned up at Eldeen, then over at the tabloids. He leaned forward and studied one, squinting fiercely, his lower jaw jutting forward angrily.

"There, Mr. Hammond, she's ready to ring you up now," Eldeen called loudly. Turning to Perry, she smiled with anticipation. "You'll like this little checkout girl," she told him. "Her name's Helena, and she's the sweetest little thing. She finished up with high school last year and is taking some night classes at the vocational school in Hodges, trying to make something of herself. I always admire a young person for pushing ahead that way. So many teenagers today don't have any get-up it seems. They'd just as soon take a job at a filling station—which is all right if it's the best a body can do. Helena's going places, though."

Helena looked to be around eighteen, short and plump with smooth, dark skin. She worked incredibly fast, Perry noticed, flashing each item across the scanner with lightning speed and shoving it behind her with her left hand while she reached forward for the next item with her right. She smiled the whole time, revealing two rows of straight white teeth as she kept up a steady stream of talk.

"Hello there, Mr. Hammond," he heard her say. "You loading up on cottage cheese today, huh? Gonna have you some cottage cheese sandwiches I bet. It's a good buy this week, but you shoulda got you some more. This here won't hardly last you no time. The apple juice is two for a dollar ninety-nine. You're wasting a whole penny just buying one." She obviously didn't expect an answer, and the old man never even looked up at her. "That'll be three eighty-six, Mr. Hammond," Helena said, flapping open a brown paper bag. The man twisted his head to read the digital numerals on the cash register, then slowly reached deep into the pocket of his limp brown overcoat. Helena had already finished filling his sack. She whipped off the register receipt, dropped it into the bag, and stood grinning at him with her hand outstretched. She raised her voice. "Come on, Mr. Hammond, fork it over."

Eldeen poked Perry. "She's a real cutup. I get so tickled at her."

Mr. Hammond was unbuttoning his overcoat now and fumbling inside the pocket of his trousers. His frown had deepened, and he was mouthing words.

"You trying to pull my leg, Mr. Hammond?" Helena was still smiling, but she put her hand down. "You forget your money or something today?" she asked. Mr. Hammond's mouth dropped open, and he looked up at her helplessly.

Eldeen pulled the old man's cart backward out of the way and stepped forward to stand beside him. She leaned down close to his ear. "Can't you find your wallet?" she shouted. He didn't look at her but shook his head.

"Well, here, Mr. Hammond," she said loudly. "Don't you worry the least little bit. I got me a little secret place in my pocketbook here where I keep some emergency money just for rainy days like this. Even though it's not actually raining outside of course." Eldeen laughed loudly and stretched open her enormous purse, reaching deep inside. Helena looked back at Perry, raised her eyebrows, and shrugged good-naturedly. Perry heard a solid click from inside Eldeen's purse, and she pulled out a five-dollar bill. "This here is yours, Mr. Hammond," she announced, placing it in his small, wrinkled hand and folding his knobby fingers over it. "It used to be mine, but now it's yours." And she gave his hand a firm pat as if he were a child being handed his lunch money. "There now, pay your bill."

The old man looked up at Eldeen sternly for a long moment before

Helena finally reached forward and took the five-dollar bill from his hand. "Well, looks like somebody's watching out for you, Mr. Hammond," the girl said. "That's what I call a good neighbor. But you better look out there. I think Eldeen might be making a pass at you. You know what a flirt she is." She laughed heartily as she slapped the change into his palm. The old man turned again to gaze up at Eldeen, then slowly dropped the change into his sack of groceries, picked it up, and shuffled toward the door.

"Well, if that don't beat all," said Helena. "Eldeen, he didn't even give you back the leftover."

Chapter 7

Walking across the church parking lot on Tuesday morning, Perry clearly heard a line of poetry spoken aloud. This sort of thing happened to him so often that it had ceased to startle him, but he still marveled over the curiosity of it all and wondered if others had such experiences. It was as if the audio track of his life kept replaying itself. He would do something—the simplest thing, like open a drawer or tie a shoelace or see a mail truck—and suddenly remember exactly what he had been saying or hearing or thinking the last time he did the same thing.

Today it was looking down at his feet as he walked across the gravel parking lot at the Church of the Open Door that triggered the memory. The last time he had been here was Sunday night, with Eldeen, Jewel, and Joe Leonard. As they had pulled into the lot that night, Eldeen had been talking about a woman named Flo, who made crocheted place mats and sold them at the "G.O.O.D. Store," which, she explained to Perry, stood for the "Golden Oldies of Derby." Eldeen herself contributed sets of pillowcases to the G.O.O.D. Store to sell. "I sew little lamb designs on them to fancy them up," she told Perry.

"I sure hate it that Flo doesn't see how much she needs the Lord," Eldeen had said as she slowly swung her legs out the car door and searched with her rubber-soled shoes for a firm footing on the gravel. Hefting herself up and out of the car, she had looked up at the church's small steeple, dark against the February dusk, and uttered solemnly, "Because I could not stop for Death/ He kindly stopped for me."

"What did you say, Mama?" asked Jewel.

"It's a poem I read in Joe Leonard's English book," Eldeen had said, taking Jewel's arm. "It was about this lady who went out for a buggy ride with this man, who turned out to be Old Mr. Death hisself. He took her past all the places she was familiar with, like the schoolhouse and the farms and so forth, and he just kept driving so slow and easy, not in any hurry at all, and the lady started getting cold because she wasn't wearing proper clothing, only a thin little gown. He'd come a' callin' when she wasn't expecting him, see, and she didn't have time to change into something sensible. And when they finally stopped at the end of their ride, guess where it was? It was a graveyard."

No one had spoken for a moment as the four of them crunched their way across the gravel.

"So, see," Eldeen said, "if Flo doesn't go on and get saved, she's going to find herself in a buggy with Mr. Death before she's ready. She's always saying she's too busy for church, that Sunday's one of her main crocheting days. But I keep telling her you've got to stop and get yourself set to die before it sneaks up on you." Eldeen clucked her tongue and shook her head. "Jesus might come back, I tell her, and you sure as sure can't wear a crocheted place mat to heaven. No, sir, you got to be dressed in a robe of pure righteousness, I tell her."

"Because I could not stop for Death/ He kindly stopped for me"— Perry heard the words again now, as clearly as if Eldeen were walking right beside him. He never would have expected her to read Emily Dickinson, much less quote her. It was funny how Eldeen's voice, deep and muffled, sounded almost normal to him now after having heard it so much. It had seemed so odd only a few days ago.

The poem was one Perry had studied. And liked too. Dickinson had always been a favorite of his. He liked her elegant phrasing, her tight metaphors, her breezy dashes, her slant way of looking at things. In fact, it was largely because of Dickinson that he had started out as a literature major in college before switching to sociology.

Other lines from the poem came back to him: "The carriage held but just ourselves/ And Immortality." The word "civility" was in there somewhere and something about "fields of gazing grain." And later on, "For only gossamer, my gown/ My tippet—only tulle." Interesting. He didn't know that he had ever connected that line with being unprepared for death, the way Eldeen had. True, he had always had a clear visual picture of the lady in the carriage wearing a delicate, gauzy gown and a filmy shawl, but he had never seen it as a lack of foresight on her part and he'd never really felt the chill of being on such a journey so ill-clothed. Probably a teacher somewhere along the line had pointed it out, but it had not taken hold; he had always been better at forming mental images than at feeling.

But that wasn't right either. He *did* feel, he knew he did despite Dinah's arguments to the contrary; but what he felt was so confusing and required so much work to figure out, and then even more to get it to the surface and express it, that it was easier to keep quiet and concentrate on pictures, something he could see. He used to wonder if he could have become a painter or sculptor instead of a writer. Cal always told him that his descriptive passages knocked editors dead; if he could describe things with words, couldn't he probably do the same with paints and clay? It came to him now that all of the scenes he pictured in his idle moments were like silent movies; he imagined people doing things but rarely were there any sound effects and never any talking. In his novels, though, he had been shocked to discover that he could invent dialogue—lots of it—quite easily. The repartee between two characters in his most recent book had been so brisk and witty, in fact, that Cal had asked him if he was sure it wasn't from an old Cary Grant movie.

The church door was unlocked as Brother Hawthorne had said it would be, and a door labeled "Pastor's Study" stood slightly ajar off to the left of the foyer. Perry heard the metallic squeak of a swivel chair from inside the study, and before he could knock, the pastor had opened the door and was extending his hand. He wore a white shirt and a bold red tie, and Perry caught the gleam of his polished wingtips without looking down at them. Perry wondered fleetingly what a man like Brother Hawthorne did all day in an office like this. He glanced at the big metal desk against the wall. A sheet of yellow legal paper had been inserted into a manual typewriter, and a few lines had been typed. Several open volumes were spread out on both sides of the typewriter. Next to the desk lamp sat a large framed picture of Edna Hawthorne, her hands clasped dramatically beside her smooth, round face, her head tilted, her lips slightly parted, and her eyes turned upward as if admiring something very delightful just out of her reach.

Brother Hawthorne was shorter than Perry by several inches but gripped his hand firmly and spoke with hearty confidence as he led him to a pair of small wingback chairs slightly turned to face each other beside the window. Perry was reminded of a job interview, and in a sense he supposed that was what this was all about.

"Have a seat, please," said Brother Hawthorne, and he waited until Perry had sat down before he took the chair facing him. The pastor crossed one leg over the other and set his Bible on top of his thigh, both hands resting on it. His nails were clipped short, Perry noticed, and his wide gold wedding band caught the sun from the window and glinted. Perry thought again of plump Edna Hawthorne and wondered if this man made her happy. He glanced down at his own wedding band, which he still wore, and wondered how a man went about making a woman happy anyway. He had thought it was so easy at one time, had even been secretly scornful of husbands whose wives left them, sure that the men had been guilty of some heinous misconduct they weren't admitting.

"Let's pray before we begin," said Brother Hawthorne. Again he paused for a long moment before praying aloud, and Perry wondered what went on during those seconds of silence. Was he thinking of how to start? His prayer was short this time, and when he finished he smiled at Perry and asked, "Now how can I help you, Perry?"

Perry took a deep breath and started. As he explained the book he was going to write, the pastor's eyes never left his face.

When he stopped, Brother Hawthorne cleared his throat before speaking. "And so you will be attending our services and activities regularly for the sole purpose of writing about them?"

"Yes."

"And you will change all the names—to protect the innocent, isn't that the expression?" The pastor smiled faintly.

"That's right."

"What about our church members? What about your neighbors? Jewel and Eldeen? Don't you think they should know what you're doing?"

"Maybe they should, but I'm not sure I want them to . . . for the time being at least," said Perry. "I've found in the past that . . . well, if I could just go about my writing quietly, it will move along better I think. I wanted you to know, and of course eventually the others will have to know. But for now I was hoping we could . . ."

Perry trailed off. He had been afraid of this, that it would all sound too underhanded to the pastor. Maybe he should just get up one Sunday in church and tell the whole congregation what he was doing. Maybe he could have it printed in the bulletin as part of the agenda, maybe after "Offertory—Organ Solo." They could list it as "Special Brief Admission of Purpose by Frequent Visiting Non-Member."

The pastor cleared his throat again and tapped his fingers lightly against the cover of the Bible in his lap. He inhaled sharply. "This book you're writing—will it be . . . well, is it your purpose to write an *objective* report? I don't mean to offend you, but it seems peculiar to me that anyone would want to spend a year here just to watch us—unless there were some . . . ulterior motive. I know you said you've written other books similar to this, and I really do hate to sound so suspicious, but I have my people's interests at heart here, you know."

"I know," said Perry. "But it really is exactly what I've said. The book is supposed to be about a church that practices fundamental Christianity, and that's what I've been told you are here. I'm not trying to dig up dirt or anything. I'm just supposed to find a relatively small church that meets the requirements and conduct a well-documented study about . . . what it's like . . . and all." He shrugged his shoulders.

"*Any* fundamental church? Why ours?" Brother Hawthorne leaned forward a little.

"That part is just luck I guess," said Perry. Maybe he shouldn't have said *luck*. He doubted that these people believed in luck. "What I mean," he went on, "is that my sister's house just happened to be sitting empty for a year, and she knew about your church, and so it worked out for me to come live here while she's away, and . . ." He couldn't think of what else to say. This was what he hated so much about conversations in which he was forced to participate. He could never end his part right, was always trailing off lamely and leaving thoughts unfinished. People would never guess he was a writer from the way he talked. Maybe he should suggest using pencil and paper for a conversation sometime; he was sure he could come across better if he could write his responses.

Pastor Hawthorne pinched the crease in his pants and ran his fingers down it slowly. He looked back at Perry, frowning slightly. "Just out of curiosity, what is your religious background, Perry? Are you from a Christian family?"

Perry shook his head. "I don't think I'd call it that, no," he said.

"Do your parents belong to a church?" Brother Hawthorne asked.

Again Perry shook his head. "My father died when I was only five . . . he drank himself to death. And my mother never saw much fairness in that, I guess, because she never talked to us about religion." He paused, but when the pastor said nothing, he continued. "I mean, she did take us to church a few times, but it wasn't a big part of our lives . . . or anything like that."

He remembered the trouble he and Beth had gone through trying to decide on a minister to conduct their mother's funeral. They didn't know any. The funeral director had finally gotten somebody to do it, but Perry couldn't even remember now what kind of church the minister was from.

"So you have no quarrel with fundamental Christianity, am I right?" said Brother Hawthorne. "You simply have very little experience with it—maybe we could even say no interest in it until you started this book? Is that right?"

"I guess you could put it that way," said Perry. "I just want to see what . . . you do here, and . . ."

Brother Hawthorne nodded and patted his Bible. "I believe you, Perry. Normally I'd be wary of something like this, but I think you're truthful. We certainly don't have anything to hide here, so I'm going to approve the arrangement for now. It interests me a great deal, to be honest with you. I never thought anybody out there"—he made a wide gesture toward the window—"cared what we Christians did in our churches. I don't want to worry you, but I'm wondering who's going to buy your book." He smiled and held out his hand again. "I won't tell anyone about this, but it's only fair to warn you that I'll be praying for you. This is a unique opportunity for me, and one that I'll take every advantage of."

"Well . . . thank you," said Perry. He guessed he was thankful, although he felt a little uneasy about this "opportunity" Brother Hawthorne had mentioned. He stood up, immensely relieved that the session seemed to be over. "Oh, I can show you a portfolio if you'd like to check my credentials," he said as they walked toward the door. "In fact, I have it in the car, along with a copy of one of my books. I can go get it all if you want to see it. I wasn't sure . . ."

"That would be interesting," said Brother Hawthorne. "Not that I distrust you at all, but I'd like to see what kinds of things you've written. Here, let me get my coat and I'll walk out with you."

Neither man spoke again until they neared Perry's car. Brother Hawthorne cleared his throat, then breathed in slowly and deeply. "End of February. I always like this time of year because you know warm days aren't far ahead." Opening the car door and reaching inside, Perry wondered if the people here really thought this qualified as cold weather. "Hope you're not overly fond of snow, Perry." The pastor chuckled. "We had a blizzard a couple of years ago I guess it was. Four whole inches."

"I can live without it," said Perry, handing Brother Hawthorne the binder and the book he had left on the front seat of the car.

Brother Hawthorne flipped through the notebook, then looked up and smiled. "I'll get these back to you."

"No hurry," said Perry.

"Oh, say," said the pastor, frowning slightly. "I just thought of something I should have mentioned in the office." He squinted and gazed upward as if planning how he should word it. "It might cause problems for the church if, say, you were seen around town doing things our people have strong convictions about—for instance, drinking or . . . well, even smoking. I mean if the people of Derby assume by your regular attendance that you're one of us, then the testimony of the church might suffer if . . ."

"Don't worry," said Perry. "I've always been what people call a 'stick-in-the-mud.'" He could still hear Dinah complaining about his lack of social vices. "You could at least take a cocktail and *hold* it," she used to say. "It would give you something to do with your hands, for pity's sake! You always walk around fidgeting like a little kid about to play a piano recital."

Brother Hawthorne was nodding his head. "Well, good," he said. His face brightened. "You've got some very nice neighbors, by the way. I know they'll take good care of you. I've never met nicer people in all my years of pastoring."

Perry nodded, then had a sudden thought. "Jewel's husband—did he die . . . or . . . ?"

"Yes, close to three years ago now, I guess it's been."

"Was it an accident or did he . . . get sick or something?"

"He drowned," said Brother Hawthorne, looking out toward the vacant lot next to the church.

"Oh." What else was there to say? Perry felt like a block of ice had fallen to the pit of his stomach. He had always imagined drowning to be the worst of deaths. He used to dream about being caught in an undertow and would wake himself up screaming and thrashing around. "Well, I wondered," he said. He dug a small hole in the gravel with his heel, then smoothed it out with the toe of his sneaker.

"Jewel took it hard," said Brother Hawthorne. "She's never quite been the same since."

Perry wondered what Jewel's husband had been like. His name was Bailey; he remembered Eldeen mentioning it at supper that night. Marriage was certainly unpredictable. One minute you were happy, and the next minute you felt like you'd been to hell and back. Or just to hell. He'd often chastised himself in recent months for having grown so dependent on Dinah that he could hardly function for days at a time once he'd lost her. Why should a person lose his footing in life just because of one other person? But marriage was like that. You didn't even realize it was happening until one of you shifted and the whole thing fell down and buried you underneath. Brother Hawthorne cleared his throat. "I think Jewel or maybe Eldeen told me you were married. Is that right?" He had tucked the folder and book under his arm, Perry noticed, and had shoved both hands inside his overcoat pockets.

"Yes, I was. I'm . . . not anymore. My wife . . . well, we're divorced, or at least will be . . . when it's finalized and all."

Brother Hawthorne shook his head. "I didn't realize that. I'm sorry."

Perry opened the car door wider. Brother Hawthorne leaned down as Perry slid into the seat. "I used to have one of these," he said, patting the roof of the Toyota. "Mine was a '75 Corolla. Dark green. Edna never liked it, though. She called it a 'toy auto.' I accused her of wanting to start a family just so we'd have to get a car with more room." Brother Hawthorne stopped talking suddenly and closed the car door. Perry rolled the window down so as not to appear rude.

Brother Hawthorne stood upright and reached inside his overcoat to his shirt pocket. "Here, take one of our church welcome cards. It has my phone number on it—here at the church and at home too. Call me if I can do anything."

Perry took the card. "Thanks." He turned the ignition key.

"I mean it," said Brother Hawthorne.

Perry nodded and rolled up the window. As he drove slowly out of the parking lot, he glanced down at the card. "Church of the Open Door" was printed in the center in plain boldface, and underneath that "Theodore Hawthorne, Pastor." Theodore? Was that what Edna called him? Or did he go by Ted? Or Teddy? Or Theo? Or maybe she called him Brother Hawthorne too.

Pulling out onto the main road, he saw the sign again: "Derby City Limits, Population 23,000." And it happened again; he plainly heard Eldeen's voice from Sunday night: "Every time I see that sign I wonder just how far off it is. It's been up for five years now, and anyway, that number couldn't of been right for more'n a day or two when it first went up! Why just think of all the changes just since Christmas. Crystal had her baby and so did Bernice's daughter-in-law. And the Tiptons over on Daffodil adopted that little boy from Korea. And then, my goodness, all the people who've died—Buford Gray and that poor dentist's wife who had cancer and Denny Pyle's mother and Coretta's boy and Harvey Gill's brother we prayed so long for . . ."

Joe Leonard had spoken up. "He lived in Raleigh, though."

"Well, still," said Eldeen. "And there's people moving in and out, in and out, in and out all the time. Why, that one house on the corner of Lily and Daisy's had three different families in it in just one year."

"Maybe it all evens out every year," said Joe Leonard. "All the moving and all the births and deaths."

Eldeen had swung her head slowly from side to side. "No, sir, I don't believe it for a minute. I hear of new babies here and there, but not near as much as people dying. They just die right and left, right and left."

Jewel had driven on in silence, leaning forward and gripping the wheel tightly.

Chapter 8

Wednesday night was what Eldeen called Prayer Meeting. "You don't need to keep giving me rides," Perry had told her that afternoon when she had called on the telephone to invite him to go with them. "I know the way to church now." He immediately worried that he sounded ungrateful. "I mean, I do want to go, and it's not that I don't like riding with you, but . . . well, you don't need to feel obligated to keep asking me . . . that's all I'm saying."

She had made a raspy sound as if she'd swallowed something wrong. "Now it would be purely wasteful if you was to drive your car to the very same place we're headed. Where's the sense in that?"

Perry hadn't answered right away. He could hear chewing sounds on the other end of the phone.

"Well, sure, I'll go . . . if it's no bother," he had said after a moment.

"*Bother!* Why, I'd like to see the day when giving somebody a ride to church is a bother!" Eldeen had said.

They sat in the same pew as on Sunday—third from the front on the left—and Perry noticed that others sat clustered closer to the front tonight in the first several rows. Harvey Gill stepped across the aisle to shake Perry's hand. "Glad to see you out again," he said, and his wife leaned forward, smiling, and said, "Is that Eldeen treating you nice?" Perry nodded and smiled back, and Eldeen said, "Oh, Trudy, you know me—I'm as ornery as always!" Then she sat back and, without lowering her voice, said to Perry, "Harvey and Trudy Gill has got to be one of the nicest couples in the world. He's a perfect gentleman—and so *smart* in the Word—and Trudy's just a queen, a absolute queen!"

Edna Hawthorne glanced back from the front row and waved to Jewel. Her little boy was peering over the back of the pew, only his large eyes showing. His sisters, both of them wearing enormous bright pink bows in their tightly braided pigtails, had their small heads together. Two children sitting directly in front of Eldeen turned around and grinned. "Hey, Chief Lightning Bug," the older one said, and they both giggled. Eldeen raised her right palm and dropped her voice. "How, little Twinkling Star and Pecan Tree."

Then suddenly she slapped both hands on her knees and leaned over to Perry. "Now *that's* what I kept meaning to tell you about in the car on the way here—our Peewee Powwow we have every Wednesday night with the little folks," she said. "I knew there was something I was wanting to tell you about, but I reckon we got busy talking about some other subject."

Eldeen had been the only one talking on the way to church, Perry recalled, and it hadn't been only one subject either. In fact, the swiftness with which her mind ran, and the ability of her tongue to keep pace, amazed Perry more every time he was with her. He would have to try his game with her sometime—really it was more of a mental exercise— in which he tried to retrace a train of thought. He often realized in the course of a day that his mind had been wandering; while he had started out thinking about, say, getting the oil in his Toyota changed, he had ended up recalling a spoiled cantaloupe his mother had found thirty years ago in the back of the refrigerator. Then he would start back- tracking to see if he could fill in all the steps that had led him so far from his original thought. He'd have to try it after one of Eldeen's monologues sometime, see if he could trace it back to its start. That would be a challenge.

"While the grown-ups have prayer time here in the sanctuary," Eldeen was saying, "we take the children back to a Sunday school room and have Peewee Powwow."

"Peewee Powwow?" said Perry.

"Isn't that the cutest name?" said Eldeen. "Joe Leonard thought it up." She raised her voice a little. "He's got the cleverest mind, that boy does."

Joe Leonard was absorbed in reading over some handwritten sheets of notebook paper and didn't look up.

Jewel walked to the piano and began playing. Willard Scoggins came forward and whispered to her as she played. She looked up at him and said something, then listened to his reply and said something else. How can she do that, Perry wondered—carry on a conversation and keep the music going at the same time?

Eldeen was still talking. ". . . and to make it more fun and keep up with our Indian theme, we said we'd let them make up names for theirselves. This was a good while ago, way back in the summertime I guess, and we took them all outdoors one night while the adults were here inside, and we told them to look around at all God's mighty, wondrous creation and pick theirself out a name. And Jewel wrote them all down on a pad. It had to be something God made, we told them, and you shoulda heard some of the things they came up with. One little boy—well, it was Levi Hawthorne is who it was, he's the preacher's son—named hisself Mud Puddle." Eldeen broke off to laugh, so loudly that people all over the small auditorium looked over curiously and smiled.

As Willard Scoggins rose to announce the first song, Eldeen lowered her voice to a gravelly whisper. "We let them give *us* names too. Jewel's is Chief Broken Branch and Joe Leonard's is Chief Hopping Cricket and I'm Chief Lightning Bug." As the congregation began singing the first verse of "Sweet Hour of Prayer," Eldeen leaned over and spoke directly into Perry's ear, very slowly, pronouncing each word with exaggerated clarity. "When it's time to split up, you can either come to Peewee Powwow with us or you can stay in here with the regular folks."

Brother Hawthorne came striding briskly down the center aisle during the chorus of the song and stood beside Edna on the front row. From the back, Edna's soft roundness contrasted sharply with the wiry compactness of her husband. As Levi moved from the other side of his mother to wedge in next to his father, Perry saw Brother Hawthorne glance at Edna with a fond smile, then place his hand on top of his son's white-blond curls.

The service was different from the ones on Sunday. For one thing, Willard Scoggins asked the people to call out four requests to sing, and like eager bidders at an auction several numbers were shouted out. They sang only one stanza of each, and it was easy to tell these were favorites. One of the songs, "Victory in Jesus," had a line that struck Perry as odd: "He loved me ere I knew Him, and all my love was due Him." Many people sang the poetic archaism "ere" as if it were "air," Perry noticed.

After the songs, Brother Hawthorne stood up and faced the congregation. He set his Bible on a small lectern beside the piano and then picked the lectern up and moved it closer to the center aisle. He paused before speaking, studying the faces of everyone in the audience.

"Continuing our family emphasis," he said, "please turn to Ephesians chapter five." There was a light rippling of pages, and Eldeen held out her large-print Bible for Perry to share.

For the next fifteen minutes Brother Hawthorne expounded on only one verse in the chapter, the twenty-first: "Submitting yourselves one to another in the fear of God." The man had a natural gift for public speaking, there was no doubt about it. Perry wondered if he had taken classes in oratory at the Bible college he attended or if he had just been born with the talent. He could easily imagine Theodore Hawthorne as a young child standing among his toys and stuffed animals, pretending to preach to them, or out in his backyard with small woodland creatures in an attentive circle around him.

After listening to Brother Hawthorne's opening remarks, Perry slipped his Daytimer out of his pocket to take notes. The first sentence he wrote down was a simple statement the pastor repeated three times in a row, each time emphasizing a different word: "In marriage, *submitting* means always thinking of your partner first. In marriage, submitting means *always* thinking of your partner first. In marriage, submitting means always thinking of your *partner* first." That one sentence was as far as Perry got in his note-taking.

Later, looking down at the single line of small, neat manuscript he had written, he failed at his old game of retracing his thoughts. He knew where they had started: with a sudden vision of Dinah brushing her hair. Amber was the color he had always called it, and he used to lie in bed watching her in the bathroom, his eyes half closed so that if she suddenly looked at him she would think he was asleep. She would stand in front of the mirror over the sink, swinging the shiny curtain of her hair first over one shoulder, then the other, brushing slowly from the crown of her head all the way down to the lightly curled ends.

He had loved the long pastel nightgowns she had worn, the delicate arch of her small wrist, the hypnotic motion of her brush. She would hum as she brushed, never a recognizable melody but just a rise and fall of mellow notes, and then when the ritual was ended, she would stop humming abruptly and gather the loose hairs from the sink with her fingertips, turn and drop them into the wastebasket, then dust her palms together.

She certainly hadn't thought of Perry's wishes first, though, when she had come home one day two years ago with her hair cut as short as Troy's. He still remembered hearing her come into the kitchen through the back door that afternoon. He had been writing a particularly slow-moving chapter in a new adventure novel entitled *Galactic Battlements*. He had just typed the phrase "charging with murderous fury, blind and bloody, toward the golden light" and then quickly deleted it. He had used all those words before, maybe in different arrangements, but still, they sounded too tritely overstated, like something he had read a million times. Besides, Cal had cautioned him to downplay the gore in this book since it was aimed at younger readers.

He had rubbed his eyes and gotten up from his desk. These days Dinah still smiled sometimes when he came up behind her and kissed her ear, though he hadn't tried it in many weeks. She had been running water into a saucepan when he quietly eased into the kitchen, hoping to judge her mood before he approached her.

But he stopped just inside the doorway. He knew it was Dinah from the set of her shoulders, the royal blue blouse she wore, her narrow waist. He knew no other woman would be in their kitchen running water at the sink. Dinah turned off the water and placed the pan on the stove, then twisted the burner knob. She bent down, opened the cupboard under the sink, and got out several small potatoes. She rummaged through the silverware basket in the dish drainer and found the peeler. Then she must have sensed him in the room because she had suddenly whirled around and clutched at her throat.

"Oh, Perry, don't do that!" she had said. "Don't sneak up on me like that! You know I hate it!"

He had stared at her without speaking. The short haircut made her look taller for some reason. It accented her cheekbones, it lengthened her neck, it widened her eyes—it changed her in so many ways that he could very well have believed her to be someone else if she hadn't been standing here in their house preparing to peel a potato.

He had turned and left the kitchen, bewildered. She had never once mentioned wanting to cut her hair. What had come over her? He had gone back to his desk and squeezed his eyes shut. All he could see was Dinah sitting in a chair with a plastic cape around her shoulders, some maniacal beautician poised above her with gigantic silver-bladed scissors, while thick cascades of amber hair slid in shining pools to the floor.

He wondered what they had done with her hair. Had someone swept it up with all the rest and thrown it in a trash bin? He took quick, shallow breaths. Then he looked up at his computer screen, lifted his fingers, and typed, "charging with murderous fury, choking convulsively as crimson bubbles frothed from his charred lips, tearing savagely with vulturelike claws at his own empty oozing eyesockets, shrieking with terror as he groped madly for the golden shards of warm light that had vanished." Later, of course, he had deleted that one too.

"Always thinking of your partner first." That was how Brother Hawthorne had started. But what was the magic formula? It sounded good, but who really did it? Dinah certainly hadn't. A few minutes after he had disappeared to his study that day, Perry had looked up to see her leaning against the doorway. "Do I take it from your hasty exit that you're not exactly overwhelmed by my new look?" she had said, and he had kept typing, not trusting himself to speak. He was overwhelmed all right.

From Dinah's hair, Perry's thoughts during Brother Hawthorne's message had scattered in so many different directions that he couldn't begin to get them in order. He did know that he emerged from his private world in time to hear the pastor's closing illustration in which he told about the early years of his marriage to Edna. He had enjoyed coming home after a long day of graduate classes at the college where he was attending, he said, and propping his feet up while he took a short nap. Then he would pour himself a glass of orange juice and open the paper. Edna would usually arrive home about this time, after having spent the entire day since 8:00 A.M. typing and filing medical reports for a group of doctors. "There she was, working to put me through Bible school," Brother Hawthorne said, "and then she would come home a little past five o'clock and go straight to the kitchen to start supper, not even taking time to change into something more comfortable."

"It never once hit me," he continued, "that I had a pretty easy time of it compared to Edna. I would hear her night after night opening and closing cupboard doors, setting dishes on the table, walking back and forth across the tile. Every night I heard the clink of silverware, the whir of the mixer, all the normal kitchen sounds—and it never sank in that here was this wonderful gem of a wife I had married, in there still working—and for no pay—while I was taking it easy.

"One evening after we had eaten another good meal, Edna cleared away the dishes and then came to the little desk where I had my books and papers spread about. She said she wanted to talk with me, so I put my studying aside and sat with her on the couch."

Brother Hawthorne paused here and looked at Edna. Her face was lifted toward him as he spoke, but Perry couldn't see her expression. "She didn't know I was going to share this with you tonight," Brother Hawthorne said, "but I don't think she'll mind." Edna shook her head.

"She put her hands in mine," Brother Hawthorne continued, "and said she was struggling with resentment and wanted my help. I assured her that she would have any help I could give. She then told me plainly yet gently that she didn't mean just a few words of encouragement and a prayer; she meant my *literal* help—the kind where your hands get involved. She pointed out that if I would help her in the kitchen each night, we could eat earlier and get things cleaned up earlier and move on to our evening's work earlier."

Brother Hawthorne looked down at his Bible for a long moment.

At last he looked up again and continued. "Of course, the selfish part of me immediately rose to my own defense and started listing all the long, hard hours of classes I faced each day, the studying I did in the evenings, the papers I had to write, the sermon outlines I had to prepare. That hour of relaxation before supper was richly earned, I told myself.

"But then I paused long enough to look at it from Edna's perspective. Where was her hour of relaxation? I asked myself. After supper she often sewed; several ladies in the church we were attending paid her to make clothes for them, and this money was part of our budget. She also typed all my papers and sometimes did typing for other students. Many evenings she did housework since she didn't have time for any of that during the day."

The auditorium was quiet. Even the children were still. Brother Hawthorne narrowed his eyes as if he were straining to see something far in the distance. "I felt ashamed," he said. "I had never even thought about helping her in the kitchen—not once had it entered my mind. Here I was studying for the ministry so I could meet the spiritual needs of others, yet I had failed to meet a very simple physical need in my own home." He cleared his throat and looked into the faces of his small congregation. "Sorry, men, I know this won't be one of my more popular Wednesday evening talks." There was a shifting of bodies and a low murmur of laughter.

"By the way," he said, "I did change. Edna can tell you that." Edna's head bobbed gently. Brother Hawthorne closed his Bible and walked around to stand in front of the lectern. "It's no excuse for a Christian husband to say, 'But that wasn't the way I was brought up' or 'Kitchen work is for women.' Did you notice that the pronoun in Ephesians 5:21 is plural—*yourselves*? The principle of submission runs in two directions, men. Let's not demand something of our wives that we ourselves don't demonstrate."

Perry hardly knew what to think about this story. First of all, he hadn't expected anything like this. Cal had told him once that all fundamentalists rejected the motto "Times change" in favor of "*Times* change, but don't expect *us* to." It was a little thing, he supposed, but he wouldn't have thought these people would be so modern in their views of men's and women's roles. This was important enough to include in his book; he'd have to try to get it down on paper tonight after he got home.

He tried briefly to imagine what Dinah would have done if he had shown up in the kitchen to help her. Like Brother Hawthorne, the idea of pitching in to cook supper and clean up had never crossed Perry's mind. He had grown up in a home where his mother had spent most of her waking hours in the kitchen. She had never expected his help; she had probably never even wanted it. Looking back now, Perry could see that kitchen work had been his mother's escape from all the disappointments she had borne in other rooms of the house. The only times he remembered seeing her smile were when she slid something from the oven or hung up a freshly ironed dress.

When Perry had gotten married, he had come into the kitchen only to eat. Of course, in the early years of their marriage before Dinah had taken a job—the job being another example of her failure to consider his wishes first—she was home all day. Preparing meals was part of her daily routine; it was all part of the homemaker package.

In those days he had worked a part-time job writing copy for an advertising agency, and then spent the rest of his workday writing his dissertation, shut away in what he called his study—at the time a storage nook under the stairway in their apartment, outfitted with a card table, a cheap word processor, and a small lamp. It wasn't like he was loafing all day while Dinah slaved at home. He had had his work and she had had hers.

Then later, after he had earned his doctoral degree and researched and sold his first book, he had dropped his part-time job to become a full-time, self-employed writer. He was busy then writing or researching all the time—well, most of the time. And Dinah was still a homemaker and everything was fine. They had moved before Troy was born to a house with three bedrooms, one of which became his study, and everything was still fine. Dinah had seemed happy—hadn't she? He hated to admit that his memory of trivia, like the abbreviations of all the elements on the periodic chart and the middle names of all the U.S. presidents, was keener than his memory of the first ten years of his marriage.

But when Troy started to school, Dinah suddenly wanted a job and promptly went out and got one. It had shocked him senseless, though he never let on. She started as a part-time receptionist and typist for a realtor, then after a few months took a couple of night courses in real estate, and before he knew what had hit him, she was having her own business cards printed.

Not that she had totally neglected her role as homemaker. Frankly, Perry couldn't recall that things were that much different after she had begun her job—at least not in the everyday details like having supper on the table and clean sheets and towels. But she had started to drift from him in small, subtle ways. In her real estate scurrying, she had found her dream house, and Perry had agreed to use his mother's inheritance money as a down payment, and then—well, then he had ended up here in Derby, South Carolina, living in his sister's house.

Would Brother Hawthorne have him believe that helping Dinah clean the house and cook meals would have saved their marriage? She had never even asked him to help her. If she had wanted his help, she should have come to him as Edna had gone to her husband, taking his hands off the computer keyboard and gently placing them inside hers and telling him she had a problem and wanted his help. But no, not Dinah; she had filed for divorce instead.

Anyway, it wasn't as if he didn't do *anything* around the house, Perry argued silently. He had regularly started the dishwasher when it was full and taken out the trash whenever Dinah set it beside the back door. He even remembered once when he had helped Dinah fold sheets warm from the dryer. Well, he had *tried* to help. She had become so exasperated with him that she finally yanked them away and said, "Oh, I can do it faster by myself."

Perry was suddenly aware of movement around him. Jewel and Joe Leonard were sidestepping their way from the pew out to the center aisle. Twenty or so little boys and girls had come to life and were eagerly surging out of the auditorium through a side door. "You coming with us to Peewee Powwow?" Eldeen whispered as she rose.

"Oh, sure," said Perry, and as he followed Eldeen out, he heard Brother Hawthorne say, "Now who would like to be the first to share your prayer burden with us?"

The children were lined up, giggling and squirming, at the door of a small classroom in the back hallway. Inside, Joe Leonard had put on a feathered headdress made out of construction paper and was spreading rug squares on the floor while Jewel, wearing a less elaborate headgear, admitted the children one by one and assigned them a rug. After they were all seated, Eldeen looked down inside her big purse and extracted a red Tootsie Roll pop. This must have been part of the regular procedure, for Perry noticed all eyes upon her. Eldeen lifted the Tootsie Roll pop high and waved it around. "Looka here what I got. This'll be for whoever's the best little brave or squaw tonight. Is everybody going to try their *very* hardest to win the Peewee Prize tonight?"

All the children sat cross-legged with their hands folded in their laps, nodding eagerly as their eyes followed the Tootsie Roll pop closely. They reminded Perry of little frogs ready to nab a fly. Perry sat in a chair against the wall as Jewel stepped around quickly, setting on each child's head a paper headband sporting two paper feathers.

Joe Leonard unsnapped a black case and lifted out an autoharp. Perry hadn't seen one of those since elementary school. It brought back a memory of Mrs. Stubblefield, the jolly music teacher, strumming her way violently through "Wabash Cannonball" and "Skip to My Lou" while the boys all snickered at the jiggle of her fleshy upper arm with each brisk stroke.

Joe Leonard set the autoharp on a small table and sat in front of it, holding the pick poised above the metal strings. He leaned over the instrument, pressing several of the key selections with his left hand as if practicing silently. Jewel nodded to him, and he began strumming softly. As Jewel began singing, the children's voices joined in. "This little light of mine, I'm gonna let it shine!" they sang joyously. Eldeen came over and sat beside Perry, her thick voice an octave below the others as she sang: "This little light of mine, I'm gonna let it shine, let it shine, let it shine, let it shine." The second verse admonished against letting Satan blow out the little light, and all the children blew a puff of air on their pretend candles to illustrate what they weren't supposed to do.

Next Jewel led the children in a rousing verse of "Onward, Christian Soldiers." Levi Hawthorne, seated on the carpet square closest to Perry, belted out "Onward, Christian Shoulders" but no one, not even Levi himself, seemed to notice the error. After another song with one line that said, "The gate to the fort of my heart is the Bible"—a fairly complicated metaphorical idea for children, Perry thought—Joe Leonard moved three metal folding chairs in front of the children, then quickly set up a pair of poles on flat wooden bases on each side of the row of three chairs. Jewel unfolded what looked like a tablecloth and tied the two top corners around notches in the poles so that the cloth was stretched between the poles like a tight curtain.

During all of this Perry studied the children in disbelief. They were watching the procedure with expressions of anticipation, a few of them moving their hands in silent clapping motions. How can they sit so still? Perry wondered. These kids were abnormal; everyone knew children were supposed to wiggle and squeal. He remembered Troy's last birthday party—ten eight-year-olds inside their house on a rainy Saturday afternoon. He had vowed after that to have all subsequent parties at large rented facilities far away from their house.

But these children were all younger than Troy and his friends by three or four years. Maybe that was why they were so good. Maybe if you got to them early enough, you could train them to be mutes. But what had Jewel, Joe Leonard, and Eldeen *done* to make these children so tame? Perry counted—there were twenty-two of them, more than twice the number of guests at Troy's party. Was the secret in the Tootsie Roll pop? Eldeen had set it on top of a storage cabinet, and Perry noticed the children's eyes straying to it frequently.

Jewel removed a large grocery sack from the cabinet and carried it behind the makeshift curtain; then she, Joe Leonard, and Eldeen sat in the three chairs behind the curtain, which shielded them from the children's view. Joe Leonard gave both Eldeen and Jewel one of the handwritten sheets he had been reading earlier. The children stared intently at the top of the curtain with rapt expressions. Seated to the side, Perry didn't know what to expect. What was going on here? Everyone seemed to know except him.

Then he saw. It was supposed to represent a stage. Above the top of the curtain appeared two puppets—a large mouse dressed in overalls and a straw hat and a raccoon wearing a little sailor cap. The children laughed with delight, then grew quiet. Perry recognized Jewel's voice as Philip the Field Mouse and Joe Leonard's as Bandit, Philip's sailor cousin who had come to the farm to visit. No one seemed to question the logic of a mouse and raccoon being cousins.

The gist of the story was that Bandit was a troublemaker, never wanting to follow the rules, always looking for shortcuts and reveling in mischief. Philip tried to influence him not to play near the thresher, and Mrs. Field Mouse, played by Eldeen, even made a brief appearance to lay down the law about what was off-limits.

In the end, of course, Bandit disobeyed, and Joe Leonard gave a very convincing performance of the naughty raccoon in convulsive agony after getting his striped tail caught in the thresher, which Eldeen represented by holding up a toy tractor and emitting a series of deep, husky rumbles. In the final scene Bandit slowly turned around and showed the children his backside, now missing its tail. Levi Hawthorne put both hands over his mouth and stared wide-eyed. Perry wondered where the tail had gone. Had Joe Leonard yanked it off behind the curtain, mutilating the raccoon just for the sake of this one lesson? Maybe it had only been pinned on in the first place.

After "prayer request time," during which a snaggletoothed kindergartner asked for prayer for her grandfather, who had a disease called diarrhea, and a swarthy little black-haired boy requested prayer for his cat which had "gone to sleep" at the vet's, Jewel led the children in another song called "God Answers Prayer." Then Eldeen prayed, mentioning every child's request individually. When she paused at one point, Perry saw her wiping her eyes. Was she crying, he wondered, or chuckling over something one of the children had said?

The Peewee Prize was awarded to a little girl named Sandra Sue, who smiled shyly and refused to come forward for the sucker when her name was called. Joe Leonard stepped between rug squares to hand it to her, and Sandra Sue lowered her eyes away from all the longing looks of the other children. Again Perry marveled at the self-control exhibited here. Any one of the children would have every right to kick up a fuss about not being the honored recipient; as far as he could tell, they had all behaved faultlessly.

Before they dismissed the Peewee Powwow, Eldeen stood up and announced, "We have a visitor with us tonight, I'm sure you little Indians noticed." As Perry felt the eyes of the children upon him, he wondered if Eldeen had ever heard of the term "Native Americans." He doubted it; she probably still used the word "Negro" too.

Eldeen smiled broadly and swept her arm toward Perry as if introducing a dignitary. "This here is Perry Warren," she said, "and he just might come back again sometime. Now if he does, we need to give him a name so all you braves and squaws'll know what to call him. Can anybody think up a good name? Remember, it's got to be something our Almighty Creator God made." Immediately Levi Hawthorne's hand shot up. "What's your idea, Levi honey?" Eldeen asked.

Levi pointed at Perry solemnly and said, "Chief Field Mouse." How fitting, thought Perry. Even this child could tell that Perry's counterpart in the animal kingdom was nothing strong and heroic, like a lion or a stallion; nothing noble and beautiful like a deer, swift and free like an eagle, soft and useful like a sheep. No, people took one look at him and pegged him right off: the common field mouse.

Chapter 9

On the following Monday morning, a little before nine o'clock, Perry was in the kitchen refilling his coffee cup when he heard the Blanchards' side door open and close, then the sound of heavy shuffling across the driveway. He watched Eldeen from the kitchen window. Could it have been only a little more than a week since he had first met her? It seemed that he had known her for years. She had her black boots on again, and a dark green scarf was tied tightly around her head. She hefted herself up the steps to Perry's side door and rapped loudly on the pane. When he went to open the door, he saw her face against the glass, circled by her large gloved hands. Her breath had already made a dense foggy patch on the pane.

"Oh, good, I was hoping you were up," she said as soon as he opened the door. She stepped inside. "I really wasn't sure how late you like to sleep, so I was a little afraid to ring the bell, although I guess writers as a rule don't lollygag in bed too long since the stories must just be *itching* to get out of their heads. Isn't this just the awfulest cold snap?" she said, drawing her thick eyebrows together in a gnomelike grimace. "It's down to twenty-eight this morning and supposed to get even colder tomorrow."

"It's cold all right," Perry said, recalling that the weather map had shown the temperature to be between zero and five degrees in Rockford over the weekend. These people in Derby didn't know what cold really was. He wondered if Dinah had been using the fireplace. To his knowledge, she didn't even know how to start a fire; he had never thought of that before. Troy didn't either, as far as he knew. He pictured the two of them huddled next to the heating ducts.

"If it's going to be so cold as all this, I wish it'd just go ahead and snow," Eldeen said. "But I don't expect any. We didn't get diddly-squat last winter and only some little old flurries the year before that. It always misses us. We did get us a few inches about three years back, though." She smiled proudly, apparently unaware that she had just contradicted herself.

"Well, you never know," Perry said. "The weather forecast shows a chance." He saw Eldeen glance at the kitchen table. "You want to sit down?" he said.

"Well, only for a minute," she said, moving toward a chair. "I see Beth left you all her things to use. That was nice of her. Beth's a real sweet girl, but I don't need to tell you that. It just must run in your family, sweetness must." Eldeen's boots squeaked against the tile floor as she settled herself in the chair and smiled up at him. Perry turned quickly and reached for the coffeepot, then realized his cup was already full. He opened the cupboard and got out another cup.

It was funny, but Perry had never thought of Beth as sweet. She'd always been picky about small matters like keeping a neat room and wiping off the bathroom mirror and making all A's. It used to get on his nerves the way she took off her shoes at the door, even as a child, and pestered everybody else to do the same. She cleaned her glasses at least a dozen times a day, and in high school she'd started keeping a Daytimer. In Perry's opinion that said it all; a person who was zealous about Daytimers had stepped over the line into the Extreme Zone. Never content to organize just her own time, Beth had begun sending Perry a Daytimer for Christmas the past several years. He kept it in his pocket and always enjoyed leafing through its mostly blank pages. Sometimes next to, say, 3:00 P.M. on a Tuesday he might find a note jotted to himself about something he was writing: "make boy's brother older" or "mention color of stone in pendant—symbol?"

It was nice of Beth, though, to offer him her house for a year. He knew how anxious she must be up in D.C. wondering if she would find her furniture scratched and her dishes chipped when she came back home.

Eldeen was still talking. ". . . a favor to ask you, but I don't want you to think a thing about it if you can't do it. Now, here's my question. But first, let me tell you that I'm not aiming to bother you like this on a regular basis. You took me to Thrifty Mart last week, and I appreciated it a lot, but like Jewel told me—and I agree with her two hundred percent—I can't be asking you to carry me all over town just because you got you a car and are home all day. I know you got to keep regular working hours just like if you had you a desk job in a office somewhere. 'Course, I guess you *do* have you a desk job, being a writer and all, don't you?"

She broke off to laugh at her joke and then began untying her scarf.

"Whew, that wool gets awful scratchy after a while," she said, laying the scarf across her lap.

Unless she addressed him point-blank with a question, Perry was always fearful of responding to Eldeen's remarks. She was so easily diverted that he was afraid she'd never get back to the original point if he interjected remarks of his own. Of course, he could rarely think of anything appropriate to say anyway, at least not fast enough to slip into a pause, so his silence was easier all the way around.

"Do you like wool?" she said.

"Well, sure, I guess so," Perry answered. "It keeps you warm. Here, I poured you a cup of coffee," and he set the cup on the table in front of her.

"Oh, no thank you, honey, I didn't come over here meaning for you to offer me refreshments. Besides, I don't drink coffee like I used to." As she unbuttoned her coat and loosened it around her neck, Perry sat down across the table from her. This didn't have the makings of a short visit.

"After I married Hiram, I took up drinking coffee and pretty near got addicted to it," Eldeen said, soberly gazing down inside the cup before her. "Isn't it a wonder how something so innocent-looking can grab ahold of you? That's why I never am one to say, 'Why, I don't see how *anybody* can let theirself get drunk' or 'What a stupid thing to go around smoking them little tubes of nicotine.' I don't mean I think drinking and smoking's all right. No, sir, not on your life I don't. But I do know how I used to think coffee was the nastiest stuff in the world, and then all of a sudden there I was, drinking twelve cups a day. Addiction is addiction, no matter what it is you're addicted to. It's all part of the devil's steel trap I always say, and I know how easy it is to get your foot caught in it. Yes sir, just like that—snap! And it's rusted shut!" And she clapped her hands together loudly.

Perry jumped slightly and spilled a little of his coffee onto the table. He hadn't even seen her remove her gloves. Eldeen leaned down and sniffed the coffee. "My, that does smell good, though." She pushed it away a few inches.

It amazed Perry how much space Eldeen took up. Not just physical space, though she was a big woman, but she had such a strong presence that whenever he was around her, his senses began to tingle, like a circuit breaker was about to flip. He couldn't have blocked her out if he'd wanted to. There was so much to see and hear and think about that he wanted to yell, "Wait, reduce the wattage! Cut the power!"

Saturday Night Live. That was it. Eldeen should be on *Saturday*

Night Live. She could just talk. She wouldn't have to have a script; she could just say whatever came to her mind. People would love it. They would say she was a brilliant new comedienne, so talented, so fluent, so *funny.* And they'd never ever know that she wasn't even trying. She wouldn't have to go to the trouble of creating a character, like Gilda Radner's Emily Litella or Lily Tomlin's telephone operator; she could just be herself and knock people over. Everybody would be saying, "You've *got* to see this old lady they've got on *Saturday Night Live* now, she's a stitch." Eldeen could make a fortune.

"I just hope and pray every day that Joe Leonard's not going to get addicted to anything," Eldeen said, raising her voice vehemently. "There's so much wickedness to tempt youngsters nowadays that it's a scary thing. The devil's out to get them all, all our little children. He wants to snatch them away from their mamas and daddies and lead them to everlasting destruction. He's got such a tender heart—Joe Leonard, I mean. He's always had a soft heart, just like his daddy did."

Perry wished he had someone he could exchange glances with. It surprised him to realize that that was one thing he missed about Dinah. Whenever they used to meet someone eccentric or see something amusing, they rarely talked aloud about it; they just looked at each other. Just deadpan, no rolling of the eyes or raising of the eyebrows, not even the hint of a smile. Dinah used to say they didn't need to talk; they communicated through thoughts. But that was a long time ago. More recently that was the grievance she aired most often: "You never *talk* to me." She must have said it a hundred times at least.

The turning point had been a series of seminars she'd attended entitled "The Inner Door"—all about things like "verbal bonding" and "breaking the marital sound barrier" and "mining the psyche's ore." She had come home each night ready to lay bare her soul. Worse, she wanted Perry to do the same. He had read some of her notes and handouts and had even tried taking a quiz and participating in what she called an "exploratory exchange."

Dinah hadn't liked his answers, though. In a section of the exchange called "Sharing Your Spouse's Future," she had asked the question, "What do you most dread in the future?" and he had answered, "The next question on this quiz." She had pressed her lips together and gone on to the next one: "What do you most look forward to in the future?" He had answered without a pause: "The end of this quiz." At which point she had exploded. "Oh, well, okay, just forget it! Just stay inside your hard little shell and spin your make-believe stories!" His first thought after her blowup was to deplore the mixed metaphor. She could have worded it so much better: "Just stay inside your hard little shell and hide from me the pearl of your soul!" or "Just shut yourself away in the storeroom of your imagination and spin your fanciful straw into golden tales!"

Eldeen was chuckling as she fingered the stiff fringe along one edge of her scarf. ". . . bought it for me for Christmas, bless his heart, so I just *have* to wear it so he'll know how much I like it. I'm hoping it'll soften up some. You ever have something give to you like that, that you just *had* to use so the other person wouldn't feel bad?"

Perry nodded and took another drink of his coffee. As a matter of fact, he had. He thought of the tweed beret Dinah had bought him one year. He had always felt like an idiot wearing it, but he could never get out the door without Dinah reminding him to put it on. "It gives you such a jaunty air," she said. Now he wore it out of habit. He should tell Eldeen that she'd soon get used to the feel of the scratchy wool scarf and would even miss it when she didn't wear it.

But there wasn't time. She had started in again. "Now, where was I? Oh, I remember. I was telling you about needing to go somewhere. You see, Jewel normally drives me wherever I need to go after she gets home from teaching at four, but this is a special thing that I don't want her knowing about, and you'll understand why after I tell you what it is." Which might be sometime next week, Perry felt like saying.

"She's such a angel that she'll be embarrassed to death over this, but I'm going to do it anyway. You know, Jewel doesn't ever expect anything for herself, and she doesn't hardly know what it means to just let down and set your work aside and have a good time. She used to, but ever since Bailey died, Jewel's just never come out of it. She used to be real lively and talkative, but then after Bailey's accident, she just changed, that's all. It's like she's still roaming lost in the Valley of the Shadow of Death and can't find the path out or else doesn't want to, I don't know which. And Jewel's not the kind you can just sit down and question and pry things loose from. She keeps it all balled up inside. It's hard to understand, but that's the way she is. Me, now I'd be the kind to find comfort just talking about it."

Perry realized that he didn't know anything about the exact circumstances surrounding Bailey's drowning. Brother Hawthorne had given only a sketchy account, and Beth had never mentioned it—if she even knew. Suddenly he wanted to know, very much. But Eldeen didn't stop for questions.

"And so, anyway, I got me a plan all worked out for her birthday coming up next week. I already talked to Brother Hawthorne about it and Marvella and Birdie and some of the others, and they all think it's a real nice idea. We'll do it after church this next Sunday night back in Fellowship Hall, and it'll be a surprise. She won't be expecting a thing because her birthday's not till a week from tomorrow, on the seventh of March. She's got the same birthday as my brother Arko, isn't that a coincidence? And that's not all—Arko's boy, Tate, was born on *Hiram's* birthday, which was only two days after Joe Leonard's, which is the day before Flag Day on June the fourteenth! Aren't coincidences just the funniest things?"

She started shaking with laughter.

"How did he die?" Perry asked quickly.

"Who, Arko? Oh, he's not dead. He's alive and well. He and Tate both. And Arko's wife, too, Prissy, bless her heart, although she's as weak as a little kitten. They live in a duplex in Rubicon, Arkansas; Tate and his family takes up one side and Arko and Prissy the other half. Rubicon is close to where I was born, in Chester, Arkansas. People are always thinking Arko's named after Arkansas, but he's not. Did I ever tell you how Arko and me got our names?"

Perry nodded. "I mean Jewel's husband. How did he die? It was a drowning, wasn't it?"

"Oh, Bailey? Why, I thought you knew. It was the saddest thing." She broke off, shaking her head slowly and nibbling on her lip a moment. "It was a fishing accident. They still can't figure out what exactly happened. But he went out fishing one day all by hisself and just never came home. He didn't come and he didn't come and he didn't come, and finally Jewel called the police. And she rode with 'em out to the little lake where Bailey liked to go so much, and there was his car pulled up next to the bank, and way out in the middle of the lake was Bailey's little green boat just bobbing up and down—empty as a dry gourd."

"Did they ever find him?" Perry asked.

"Sad to say, they did," Eldeen said. "'Course I guess it was a blessing in a lot of ways 'cause if they'd never of found him, it would of preyed on Jewel's mind even worse, wondering where he was. They got some diving men to go down under and hunt for him, and they finally found his body a good piece away from the boat. It was all real odd. His fishing line was tangled up every whichaway inside the boat, and his tackle box was upside down and all topsy-turvy."

"And they never knew what happened?" said Perry.

"No sir, never for sure, they didn't. They said it could of been this or it could of been that, but what it boiled down to was that nobody knew. There wasn't a soul out there fishing besides him; at least nobody came forward to give any testimony. They examined him good at the autopsy but didn't come up with anything like a heart attack or anything, and they didn't think it was any foul play that happened. No sir, to this day nobody but God in heaven knows what killed Bailey Blanchard and broke Jewel's poor little heart."

Neither of them spoke for a moment. Perry heard a muffled click as the refrigerator turned on. Somewhere outside a dog barked—one of those yippy hysterical kinds. Eldeen sighed and started rebuttoning her coat. She put on her gloves and then tied the thick wool scarf around her head again. With a grunt she stood up and walked to the door. Perry followed her. She turned back to him as she reached for the doorknob.

"But our Lord Jesus can see a little sparrow fall. We know that. Yes sir, he saw his precious saint fall that day, and we know Bailey Blanchard is resting content and happy in his bosom today." She shook her head. "But it's mighty hard to see Jewel still suffering over it. I keep praying and praying that she'll get her spark back. And God can do it, I know he can." She closed her eyes and lifted her face to the ceiling. "'For thou wilt light my candle: the LORD my God will enlighten my darkness.'"

Eldeen turned the knob and opened the door a crack.

"Didn't you want to ask me something before you left?" Perry said.

Eldeen released the doorknob, tilted her head backward, and raised both hands in consternation. "Well, of all things that ever were or will be! If I didn't almost walk right out without even finishing my request. If that doesn't just beat all!" She closed her eyes and laughed with gusto, stopping suddenly with a choking snort. "What I was aiming to ask you," she said, "was if you could just spare maybe a half an hour sometime today and take me by the bank and then real quick by Wal-Mart so's I can get the party things for Sunday night?" She looked at him wistfully.

"Well, I guess so, sure," said Perry. "I could take you this afternoon if you don't mind waiting a few hours."

"Why, not at all, not at all!" cried Eldeen. "As long as it's before Jewel gets home, I'll just be tickled and grateful to go anytime."

They settled on two o'clock, and Eldeen finally made her way out the door and down the four steps to the driveway, turning back several times to add random details about the morning's conversation.

First, "Arko and Tate used to operate a hatchery down in Rubicon. It was the most interesting place to visit—all them little separate pools for the different sizes of fish. Now Tate runs it by hisself with his son-in-law, Buddy, helping him out."

Then, "It's funny how I was the only one of the four children in my family to take after their name. Arko hates okra something awful, and Nori never did iron a thing—always wore the wrinkledest clothes—and poor Klim was allergic to dairy products of all kinds. But me, I took a liking to the needle right off as a little girl and have done stitching all my life. Isn't that odd?"

Then, "I guess it's kind of another coincidence in a way that my whole family's always been involved in raising fish—and catching and eating them, too—and then my poor little Jewel had to go and lose her Bailey in a fishing boat. My husband Hiram just thought so much of Bailey, and the first time Jewel brought him home to meet us—that was when we used to live in Felix, Alabama—Hiram took that boy fishing with him, and they came home just busting their seams 'cause they'd done caught 'em a bucketful of the biggest catfish you ever seen."

She paused at the bottom of the steps and looked up at Perry. "Life's just full of turnarounds, isn't that so, Perry?"

"Yes, it is," he said.

"But it sure is a blessing to know that he"—here she pointed skyward— "knows about every single thing that happens to us and has a divine, almighty reason for it all—the good and the bad too."

He stood with the door open, watching her plod across both driveways. The metal clasps on her boots gave a faint jingle with every step she took. As she started up the steps to her own door, she looked again at Perry and shouted, "We fried up those catfish, too, and had us the best supper that night! After supper Bailey asked Jewel to marry him." She finally made it to the top of the steps, and before opening the door, she laughed and called back merrily, "I guess I don't need to tell you she said yes!"

Sitting down at his computer again a few minutes later, Perry tried to get back into his notes on the service the day before, but he kept seeing an empty green boat drifting in the middle of a lake.

He shut down the machine and thought maybe he could spend some time with pencil and paper, trying to decide on the best way to approach the book he was going to write. He remembered now how much he had always hated the organizational part of a new book, figuring out the order of things. That's why he had grown to like fiction so much more than a book like this one. With fiction you could let the story tell itself, but this book was going to take some premeditated structure. Maybe he ought to call in Beth for consultation. She loved arranging details; she could probably come up with a neat, symmetrical outline in no time flat.

So far, he had simply been taking copious notes on everything he observed about the church and the people. But behind every stroke of the keyboard was the niggling worry that all this would sooner or later have to be wrestled into some kind of format.

And it wasn't just the structure of the book that troubled him, now that he thought about it. It was everything, his whole life. What if these people at this fanatical little church were right? What if every detail *meant* something? What if the joys and sorrows—the "turnarounds of life," as Eldeen called them—had some kind of specific purpose in the huge scheme of a man's existence? What if everything that happened to Perry Warren ultimately fit together tightly into a preplanned chapter in the great Book of Mankind?

Chapter 10

As Perry had suspected, the trip to the bank and Wal-Mart ended up taking a great deal more than half an hour.

It was a windy day. Eldeen wore fuzzy tan earmuffs clamped over her green scarf, and her voluminous gray cape billowed as she slowly made her way toward Perry's car promptly at two o'clock. A brown parcel stuck out the top of her handbag.

"I do believe the wind was fixing to carry me off like Elijah!" Eldeen shouted as Perry leaned over to open the passenger door. She laughed softly as she lowered herself onto the seat and then lifted her feet in one at a time. Under the long dark blue dress she was wearing, Perry could see loose black velour pantlegs that came to the top of her boots. "There, I finally got my hind leg in," she said. "And just look at you, will you? Already got the car all toasty warm. I sure like that cap you're wearing. I told Joe Leonard on Sunday he ought to get hisself one like it. The way young people walk around bare-headed, it's just a wonder they don't all catch pneumonia. You lose most of your body heat through your head, you know."

She began to chuckle as she struggled with the seat belt. "You need you a jumbo setting on this here thing," she said. "'Course, these little foreign cars are made with little Oriental people in mind instead of regular-size Americans like us." Perry wondered if Eldeen really did think of herself as regular-sized. He pretended to adjust the rearview mirror until he heard the seat belt click into place.

"I just *love* a surprise, don't you?" Eldeen said as they backed out of the driveway.

"Well, yes, sometimes," Perry said. But the truth was that he hated most surprises. Even the happy ones. He wanted to know about changes well ahead of time. He detested being confronted with something unexpected and then being asked, "Well, what do you think?" If he were Jewel, he would rather suffer physical torture than endure the surprise birthday party Eldeen was so happily planning for her. All those people watching so excitedly for her spontaneous reaction—he couldn't imagine anything more horrendous. Maybe he should warn Jewel so she could get herself used to the idea—or get sick and stay home that night.

As they turned from Blossom Circle onto Lily Lane, Eldeen pointed to a house with a bright yellow birdbath in the front yard. "Isn't that a tacky color for a birdbath? But that little lady that lives there's just the sweetest little thing you'd ever hope to meet. Got her a heart big as all outdoors and then some. Feeds the birds all winter—has her a whole passel of feeders—and in the spring the birds just *flock* to her backyard. She's got the cutest birdhouses, all sizes—even has one for humming-birds, with the tiniest little hole, and they come too! If only she'd see the need to come to church—here, turn left here and head on toward town. I'll show you where the bank is when we get closer. I told you about her, didn't I?"

"Who?" asked Perry.

"Flo Potter."

"I think so." Actually, Perry couldn't begin to keep straight all the names Eldeen wove into her stories.

"She's probably settin' in her house right this minute crocheting some little baby a pretty little blanket. I declare that woman's fingers move faster than a water bug. She can whip up a set of them crocheted place mats of hers in no time. I reckon every woman in Derby's got a set of them by now. They sell a right smart lot of them in the G.O.O.D. Store too. But Flo, she gives away a heap more'n she sells."

Perry remembered Flo now—the one who had inspired Eldeen's recitation of Emily Dickinson in the church parking lot.

Eldeen hung her head and closed her eyes. Perry glanced over at her uneasily after a few silent seconds had passed. Before long she lifted her head and smiled. "There. No use preaching to a body if you're not praying for them is what I always say. I aim to see Flo Potter get saved before I die. She's the nicest little soul you ever saw, kind of soft and twittery and skittish like a bird herself, but being nice won't get you a ticket to heaven I keep telling her." She launched into a lengthy description of Flo's late husband, Purcell, who used to run a wood-working business out of his garage and made all her birdfeeders and birdhouses by hand.

Eldeen had gone on to praise Purcell's brother, an enterprising retiree who set up sno-cone booths all over town every summer, when suddenly she grabbed Perry's arm. "Oh, here it is right here! Turn in here!" She took hold of the steering wheel and gave it a strong yank to the right. Perry's heart lurched as the Toyota careened into the driveway of the bank, barely missing another car headed out. The other driver honked and shook his head. Eldeen waved. "That was Terrence Barnett, I think," she said. "His daughter teaches school with Jewel. She's the gym teacher and has the biggest muscles I've ever seen on a woman. You should see her!"

Perry applied the brakes, and they jerked to a halt. Eldeen's purse slid off her lap onto the floor. "We've come in backwards," Perry said, looking at the three cars lined up facing them in the separate drive-in lanes.

"Well, if we haven't," said Eldeen. "But it doesn't matter. The first one's empty over here, and I like it best anyway 'cause it's got the little drawer that rolls out and you don't have to keep pushing the button to talk." When Perry hesitated, she nudged his arm. "Go on, pull on up there quick before somebody else comes. It'll be handier this way since I'm the one that's got the business to do anyway."

Perry couldn't believe it. He was actually pulling into a drive-in bank the wrong way. Thankfully no one here in Derby knew him.

"Now wasn't that forgetful of me to get so busy talking that we almost missed the turn-in?" said Eldeen cheerfully as they pulled up beside the drawer. She took her earmuffs off, rolled down her window, and spoke loudly to the woman inside. "I was hoping you'd be here today, Belinda! I got to get this cashed," she announced, waving a check. Perry looked steadfastly at the Toyota logo in the center of the steering wheel as Eldeen and Belinda bantered back and forth.

Just then another car pulled up directly in front of Perry's Toyota. Perry kept his gaze on the steering wheel. This couldn't be happening to him. It didn't matter if these people *were* strangers; he was still mortified. Dinah always used to laugh at him about his fear of sticking out in a crowd. "Yes sir, old Mr. Daring, Mr. Who-Cares, Mr. Nonconformist—that's who I married," she would say. Early in their marriage she had laughed about it fondly, but later she had quit teasing. "Loosen up, for heaven's sake!" she would say. "Why don't you show a little backbone and self-confidence? Step out and take a few risks! You've spent your whole life scared to death of making a fool of yourself." It was one of her pet subjects. She had even quoted a favorite line to him from Ralph Waldo Emerson's essay on self-reliance. He could still hear her: "Conformity is the hobgoblin of little minds and statesmen!" As if she had forgotten that he was the one who had introduced her to Emerson in the first place. He had been tempted each time to correct her, to tell her what Emerson had actually said: "A foolish consistency is the hobgoblin of little minds, adored by little statesmen and philosophers and divines." But he had never bothered.

He tried quoting the line to himself now, over and over. It was strange how funny a word started to sound after you kept repeating it: hobgoblin, hobgoblin, hobgoblin. He made a mental note to look up its etymology sometime. The driver of the car in front of him beeped the horn lightly, but still Perry didn't look up.

"Why, looka there, would you?" said Eldeen, waving enthusiastically. "If it's not Edna Hawthorne, bless her heart! Right there in front of us! And she's got little Levi with her." She turned back to Belinda, who was just sliding the drawer back out with Eldeen's money in it. "That's our preacher's wife in front of us," Eldeen said proudly. "She's got a voice as pretty as a nightingale. You could hear her sing if you'd come to church with me some Sunday like I asked you to."

Belinda laughed. "You don't ever give up, do you, Eldeen?"

"Not on your life I don't," said Eldeen. She took her money out of the drawer and then unbuckled her seat belt and leaned out her window. "Aren't we a sight settin' here all switched around?" she called to Edna. "Perry'll back up so's you can pull on in!" She turned back to Belinda. "Bye, honey! Remember, church starts at eleven on Sunday morning and seven at night!"

"They wouldn't let somebody like me in the door," Belinda said, grinning. "But thanks anyway. Bye, Eldeen."

Perry had shifted to reverse and begun backing up when Eldeen grabbed his arm again. "Oh, I forgot to give her something! I plum' forgot! I wrapped it up special for her and then I forgot it. Pull back up quick, it won't take a minute." And she leaned out the window and hollered to Edna, gesturing her backwards with exaggerated motions, "Just a minute, Edna honey! Whoa, back up! I forgot something!" As Edna began backing up, the car pulling up behind her honked loudly. Perry heard an angry shout from somewhere.

He'd have to remember all this later. This would make a great scene for some new comedy—something like *What's Up, Doc?* where the crazy heroine never did anything the normal, expected way.

"Forget something?" Belinda asked as they appeared in front of the window again.

Eldeen pulled the brown parcel out of her purse. It was a grocery bag rolled up in a clumsy tube shape and cinched tightly with several rubber bands. "I promised you a set of my pillowcases, remember?"

she said. "I finished them up last night after church and then almost forgot to leave them with you." She wedged the package inside the drawer and gave it a pat.

"Well, how nice of you, Eldeen," Belinda said, sliding the drawer back inside and removing the parcel. "I'd forgotten all about them."

"Well, and I bet you thought I had too," said Eldeen. "But I was working on them all along. I put my little lamb design on them. See there? I got so tickled when I thought about it last night. Here I have been stitching that same design all my adult life and never once thought about how funny it was to be putting little lambs on a pillowcase—get it? You lay your head down on these little baby sheep and then *count sheep* to get to sleep!" Eldeen laughed with delight.

Perry heard a car horn from another lane. The car behind Edna Hawthorne suddenly backed up sharply and headed for the exit with a squeal of tires. Belinda held up one of the pillowcases.

"Well, now, that's the prettiest thing I've ever seen," she said. "Thank you, Eldeen." She stared through the glass at Eldeen with a puzzled look. "Thank you," she said again, looking down at the pillowcase and then out again at Eldeen. She shook her head slightly.

"They're all ready to slip on your pillows. I washed 'em up fresh and pressed 'em for you this morning. You got to do that after you finish, see, 'cause the little design sometimes shows through, especially if all your stitches don't line up as neat as they should." She laughed. "I'm afraid my old hands aren't as steady as they used to be."

"Oh, Eldeen, I can't believe you did this for me," Belinda said. "You're just a jewel." She waved as they began backing up again.

"That's my daughter's name—Jewel!" Eldeen called. She turned to Perry, her face puckered with pleasure. "I think she liked 'em real fine, don't you? She's got lots of personal problems, Belinda does. But doesn't the whole world?" She sighed and then waved suddenly toward the parking area to their right. "Would you swing in there and stop a minute?" she said. At this rate they should get home by midnight, Perry thought. But he didn't mind really. The thought of writing this afternoon made him weary.

He backed into a space at the end of the small parking lot but left the motor running. What was Eldeen intending to do? he wondered. Go inside the bank to follow up on her conversation with Belinda? Flag down Edna for a chat? Count her money? That was always a good idea. He'd discovered errors more than once by doing that. He glanced sideways at Eldeen and saw her with her eyes closed once again. Her forehead was deeply furrowed, and her eyebrows formed a thick, shaggy ridge. Her lips moved slightly and she exhaled a soft moan. Perry turned and looked out his window. Edna Hawthorne was driving by slowly; Levi was licking an orange sucker and staring somberly at Perry. Why couldn't Eldeen have her prayer session while they rode along, Perry thought impatiently. Why had she asked him to stop and park? He depressed the accelerator a little and raced the motor.

Eldeen raised her head and set her mouth in a firm line before speaking. "I've been waiting for the right moment for this, and I feel like it's high time," she said at last. She turned to look at Perry, and he was surprised to see her eyes moist with tears. A sudden feeling of dread and panic seized him. What was happening? Was she going to divulge some painful secret? Was he going to be asked to comfort her in some way? He wished intensely that they were at Wal-Mart now amid the bright fluorescent lights and shiny floors, the neat shelves of merchandise and crowds of people, the friendly salesclerks in their blue smocks.

As soon as she started speaking, Perry realized that this was what Cal had meant when he had said, "They'll come after you before long." Too bad he had neglected to get his answers ready, as Cal had urged.

Eldeen didn't slide up to the subject sideways; she looked Perry directly in the eye and asked, "Have you been born again, Perry?"

He looked over at her swiftly, then turned back to look out his window. Why hadn't he planned something to say? He ought to have known his turn was coming. She went after everybody else; what had made him think he'd escape? He felt as ill-prepared as people who were bowled over by some disaster and afterward testified, "I never thought it would happen to me." It set Perry back to think of himself as *involved* in this whole scenario. He'd been with Eldeen a number of times now but had never seen himself as part of the play. He was merely a spectator as always, observing and recording—invisible. He never thought of himself as arousing her concern—being on the same level as, say, Mr. Hammond or Flo or Belinda. He looked back at Eldeen, who was still searching his face. He was trapped; he would have to say something.

She looked dismayed at his silence. "Oh, Perry, I've just prayed and prayed that I'd do this right. It's not like me to hold off this long, but I could tell right off the bat the first time I met you that you had a heavy weight of trouble on your heart, and I just didn't think you were ready yet to be spoken to about the gospel, although you know it's really during the low, low times of life that we need Jesus the most."

"I know," he said. It wasn't at all what he meant to say or what needed to be said.

"Beth told us, naturally, about your wife and the divorce and all, and I know that's got to just hurt so deep, especially having a little boy like Beth said you had—you must be so lonesome. But Jesus can take your burdens and help you carry them, Perry. He can wash away your sins and give you joy in your heart, that's a *fact*."

Perry watched with wonder as she leaned toward him, her head to one side, her bright eyes glistening, her wrinkled face sagging with the weight of his sorrow. He wondered as he looked at her if he had ever been the subject of one of her conversations. Did she really pray for him? Did she really spend time thinking about him?

"You've been so good to go to church with us," Eldeen continued. "And we've all talked about how unusual it is since we never could persuade Beth to come with us, not even once. But it's kinda like Joe Leonard said last night after we got home. He said to Jewel, 'You know, Mama, I get the feeling Perry's just coming to church with us to be nice to us, 'cause he's afraid it'd be rude to say no.' And then Jewel, she said, 'Well, seems like to me he's really and truly *interested*, but only in the way a newspaper man's interested in a train wreck or some criminal's execution. Like we're some kind of a curiosity he's investigating.' That's what Jewel said."

So he *was* a topic of conversation after all. How odd. He had never thought of these people discussing him, wondering about his motives. He was amazed at Joe Leonard's and Jewel's assessment of his church attendance. They were both partly right, of course. He *had* felt it would be impolite to refuse their offer of a ride, even though he really would prefer at times going alone, and his interest was indeed like that of a reporter. He had been so smug, thinking of himself as an unnoticed observer, almost as unobtrusive as a piece of furniture, but he had been seen and judged plainly by the smalltown mentality of a fourteen-year-old boy and his mother.

"Well, it's a different situation, all right," he said lamely. He wasn't even sure exactly what he was talking about. Everything during the past months had been a different situation.

"It's just got to be," Eldeen said sympathetically. "Being all by yourself down here away from your family and all your friends."

All his friends. That was a laugh. He'd never been much of an attractor of friends. Cal was probably the closest thing he had to a real friend, and their relationship was mostly business-related and mostly by telephone. But then men weren't as big on friendship as women. As long as he had known her, Dinah had gathered friends easily, like flowers from a garden. She was drawn to colorful, dominant, well-groomed types, and rarely did she ever discard a friend; she just kept adding them. She had whole bouquets of them. Perry envisioned her now, surrounded by her beautiful, fragrant friends, all laughing and talking at once. No one would ever pity Dinah for being lonesome, that was certain.

Eldeen laid her hand on his arm. Perry looked down at it, marveling again at its largeness. He wondered if she had to buy men's gloves. "I just felt this morning after I came over," Eldeen said, "that maybe it was time I asked you about being saved. It dawned on me all of a sudden-like that if something happened to you—like a tragic car accident or a heart attack or something really serious like that—that you might be *dead* before I'd talked to you about your soul. And then wouldn't I feel just terrible?" Her face took on an expression of extreme horror. "And wouldn't it just be the awfulest thing for *you,* having to face eternity without Jesus?"

Perry opened his mouth to say something but realized he had no idea of how to answer. Cars were still pulling through the bank in a slow procession. The serious looks on the faces of the drivers as they passed reminded Perry of a funeral. And in a sense it was a funeral, he thought. Every single one of these people, from the youngest to the oldest, from Levi Hawthorne to Eldeen, was moving closer and closer to death. They might be clutching a fistful of money now as they drove by, but sooner or later their hands would fall limp. He thought of the famous lines from *Macbeth:* "Out, out, brief candle! Life's but a walking shadow."

Perry inhaled sharply. These people were getting to him. How morbid. He remembered a time when death never used to cross his mind. Now here he was, coming up with thoughts like something Brother Hawthorne would say in a sermon. No doubt the pastor *had* said something like that.

Growing old had only recently, in the past year or two, become a personal threat for Perry. He often thought of how close to forty he was, then would come fifty, then sixty. In less time than it took to strike a match, he would be Eldeen's age. He thought now of Brother Hawthorne's words at church the day before: "Time is fleeting. Our life is but a vapor. Soon you'll be a year older, then five, then ten, then twenty, then thirty."

Eldeen had leaned over to Perry in the pew and said, "Not me! I'll be dead and buried and singing in heaven long before that!"

Brother Hawthorne had gone on to describe for the congregation the picture of a deceased celebrity he had seen on the news recently. "They showed film clips of her in her youth," he had said, "and, I know

Edna will forgive me for saying this, but she was truly lovely—flawless skin, shining hair, slender form, light voice, graceful movements. Then they showed a picture of her that some persistent photographer had taken five days ago as she was helped from her car into the hospital. This vision of loveliness had somehow turned into an obese, haggard, wrinkled old woman with a tangled bird's nest of hair. And I was reminded of the poet's words: 'Whatever is begotten and born, dies.'" Well, Perry had thought, that wasn't exactly the way Yeats had said it, but it was close, and, anyway, the meaning was the same.

Perry looked down again at Eldeen's hand on his arm. He tried to imagine what it must have looked like sixty years ago. They must have been sitting in silence for a full minute before Eldeen spoke again.

"I'm not going to be pushy, I promise, but do you mind if I pray out loud for you before we go on our way to Wal-Mart?"

When Perry nodded, she pressed his arm more firmly and squeezed her eyes tightly shut before beginning.

And there in the parking lot of First Carolina Union Bank in the middle of a windy February afternoon, Perry heard Eldeen pray specifically for him. He counted eighteen times that she said his name.

Chapter 11

U h-oh," said Eldeen as they pulled into the driveway two hours later. "Jewel's home already. I was afraid this was going to happen when we ran into so many snags in Wal-Mart."

Perry wondered if it occurred to her that all the "snags" at Wal-Mart had been of her own doing—things like asking the elderly door-greeter in charge of offering shopping carts how his trip to Mississippi had gone and then quizzing him for ten minutes about every detail of his son's new job in a Schwinn bicycle factory. Later she had debated at length over which paper party cups were prettiest and even stopped several shoppers—total strangers—to ask their opinion. She couldn't decide whether to get neon-colored birthday candles or pastel ones, so she ended up getting a box of each. The same thing happened with the Hi-C, and she finally got two large bottles of each of the three flavors. Then she dug through a sale bin of discontinued kitchen utensils they passed, explaining to Perry the variety of ways in which each one could be used before she settled on a large plastic spatula because "you just never could have enough spatulas."

When they finally made it to the checkout line, she suddenly remembered that she needed some pink embroidery thread, and when they went back to find it, she spied a display of suncatchers and stopped to choose one—a bright yellow tulip—to give Jewel for her birthday. On the way back she saw a "clearance" shelf of Valentine candy, and she stopped to exclaim over the half-price bags of conversation hearts, informing Perry that she had always "been partial to these little things—used to practically make myself *sick* eating so many of them." She put two bags of them in the cart, then added a third and started telling Perry about all the things she stored in the freezer until she was ready to use them.

Back at the checkout line, she let two women get in line ahead of them since both of them were buying only one or two items, and when they finally made it to the cashier, Eldeen asked for somebody to please check the shelf price on the jars of Hi-C that she thought were only $1.49 but that the scanner had priced at $1.79. Outside, she pointed to the cart-return after they had unloaded their bags into the Toyota and said to Perry, "Way over yonder's where you take the buggies so's they can use them for the next crowd of folks." It seemed to Perry that everything Eldeen did turned out to be so complicated.

Jewel opened the kitchen door now and stepped outside, looking curiously toward Perry's car. "Oh, lands, what am I going to tell her?" said Eldeen. "I know for sure and certain she's going to ask where we been."

Perry rolled down his window and called, "I took Eldeen with me to Wal-Mart. I had some things to pick up. She'll be right in." Jewel nodded and went back inside.

Eldeen turned to him with a spectacular grimace. "You sweet boy, you," she said. She reached inside her purse, and Perry heard the crisp crackle of the candy bag she had taken from the Wal-Mart sack. "It's sure a good thing I talked you into getting you some of that Windex and them lightbulbs that was all on sale," Eldeen said, "or you'd of been telling a story just then." She held out a handful of pastel candy hearts, then laughed happily as she poured them into Perry's hand. "Here's you some treats. I get such a kick out of what's on them. Here's one that says 'Dig you.'" She shot him another grin, then opened her door and slowly swung her feet out onto the driveway. "You go on and take all the bags to your house if you don't mind," she said. "I'll get them tomorrow after Jewel's left for school—oh, except give me my thread and the spatula, will you?" Perry turned to the backseat and rummaged through the bags while Eldeen made her way to his side of the car.

"I sure appreciate your neighborliness in taking me on my errands," she said, smiling broadly. She looked over toward Perry's house, her smile fading, then back at Perry. "I hope you don't mind if I pray for you," she said. "I just have a feeling, a real strong feeling right here," and she laid the spatula over her heart.

"Well . . . thank you," said Perry. He looked down into his palm at the little mound of candies. He took a white one that read, "U R #1" and put it into his mouth; he dropped the others inside his coat pocket. Then he sat for a moment watching Eldeen mount the steps, her cape whipping about and lifting with the brisk wind as she struggled to keep it down. Perry thought suddenly of the famous picture of Marilyn

Monroe with her skirt flying up all around her, and he tried to imagine what a conversation between Eldeen and Marilyn Monroe would have been like. Eldeen would no doubt have asked the sex goddess point-blank if she was born again. And what would Marilyn Monroe have said to that? he wondered. How old would Marilyn be anyway if she were still living? Probably in her sixties. Reaching the top step, Eldeen turned before she went inside and waved the spatula like a small flag.

After carrying in the bags and setting them on the kitchen table, Perry glanced at the digital clock in the living room. It was almost four-thirty. He lay down on the sofa in the living room and closed his eyes; he didn't even take his coat off. Maybe he could sleep through these next couple of hours—the worst time of the day for him since he had come to Derby. He wished earnestly for a time-release drug he could take to knock him out for exactly four hours without any harmful effects. He would take it around three o'clock every afternoon and wake up at seven.

Troy would be home from school now; they were an hour earlier in Rockford. Dinah would be home too—or at least that had been the plan. Perry wondered if she ever stayed late at work these days, if Troy ever had to come home to an empty house. It would be the kind of thing Dinah would have no qualms about. "He knows where the key is hidden," she would say, "and he knows exactly what he's supposed to do after school. Mother can even run over to make sure he keeps on schedule."

Starting about two-thirty, Perry had always begun watching the clock back home in Rockford. Troy's arrival from school was his favorite part of the day. For a whole hour the boy was his, not shared with Dinah or other children. They had a routine, beginning with Oreos and chocolate milk and ending with what they called "art from scratch," when Troy would scribble on a piece of paper and Perry would form a picture of something—a ship or a mythical animal or a clown's face—out of the random lines. In between was the odious task of homework, usually only a couple of papers Troy hadn't completed at school. Perry was often appalled at the boring nature of these papers. Hadn't teachers learned anything new since his own days in elementary school? Didn't any of them have any imagination?

Dinah used to scold Perry frequently for what she called his "pampering" of Troy. "Let him learn some independence!" she'd chide. "Maybe he could get used to the idea that life isn't all fun and games if you'd quit mother-henning him to death!" She had come in on them a few times when Perry had been trying to add some sparkle to the homework procedure—by timing with a stopwatch each arithmetic problem Troy did or doling out pretzels for each correct answer.

Perry sat up suddenly. So many things could happen to a kid by himself in a big house. What if some pervert had been stalking their neighborhood watching for a child who was home alone? What if Troy slipped on the kitchen floor while carrying his chocolate milk to the table and cut his head on a shard of glass? What if he tried to light a match for some reason and caught the whole house on fire? What if a friend came over with his father's gun and tried to show Troy how to load it?

He reached for the telephone and began dialing, wishing desperately that Beth had a Touch-Tone phone instead of one of these old stupid, slow rotary ones. But at least his fingers were finding the right holes—not like the dreams he often had where he was in extreme danger and kept misdialing in his panicky attempts to call the police. There, the phone was ringing now. On the sixth ring it suddenly stopped; there was a bump and a scraping sound, as if the receiver had been dropped. Then Dinah's voice: "Hello?" She was irritated about something. Funny how he could tell that from only one word spoken eight hundred miles away. She was definitely irritated. "Hello?" She spoke again, louder this time, more impatient.

Perry's fingers tightened around the receiver. He ought to hang up now that he knew Troy wasn't home by himself, but he couldn't. He heard Dinah sigh. "Who is this? What do you want?" she asked. In the background he could hear a rhythmic pounding. Was that Troy? What was he doing? He wasn't supposed to bounce balls inside the house. Maybe it was the washing machine out of balance. It was bad to do that.

"Hello?" she repeated, then paused. Then "Oh, for . . ." and she hung up. Perry sat still, clutching the receiver. It felt warm. But he knew that was only because he had been breathing into it. He realized suddenly that he was hot. He started to take his coat off, then stopped when he thought about the effort it would take. "Who is this? What do you want?" she had asked. Simple questions that he supposed deserved answers. What should he have said? "This is your ex-husband, Perry Raymond Warren, and I want things to be like they used to be when we were first married." He couldn't begin to imagine how Dinah would have responded to such a statement.

Slowly he hung up the phone. It was only four-forty, and still there stretched before him the long hours when he should be hearing the sounds of supper in the kitchen, then voices around the table and the clink of ice in glasses and silverware against plates, then the dishes being stacked and rinsed and set inside the dishwasher. There was another answer for Dinah's question: "This is Perry and I want to hear the kitchen sounds again."

His eye caught the television on the coffee table. He had brought along the old one from home—the small set he had kept in a corner of his study, usually stacked with old magazines and mail left unattended. He realized now that he hadn't turned it on once since he had moved in. Where had the past week and a half gone? A couple of errands with Eldeen, he thought, and a few pages of notes about the Church of the Open Door—those were the grand sum of his accomplishments.

He stood to take off his coat, feeling the slight bulge of the candy hearts in the pocket. He fished them out and set them in a little pile on the coffee table, then ate one that said "Hot Mama" on it. He turned on the television and lay back down on the sofa.

Mister Rogers' Neighborhood was on. Mister Rogers had on an apron. He was stirring a bowl of batter as he smiled into the camera. "And I call these cookies Super Special Cookies because I make each one special—just like each one of you boys and girls. But before I show you what I mean, I have some other nice things to share with all my special friends out there." He walked over to a refrigerator and set the bowl inside. Then he took off his apron and put his blue zippered sweater back on, all the while smiling into the camera and singing a song that started off with "No one else is just like you and no one's just like me, But though we're all so different, we're as happy as can be."

Troy had watched Mister Rogers several times when he was four or five, Perry recalled. Then one day he had looked at Perry and said, "Mister Rogers acts dumb," and he had refused to watch him again. Perry had taken it as a sign of superior intelligence then, but thinking back over it now, he wondered if it didn't have more to do with the precocious cynicism of kids today than with intellect. And, too, he and Dinah sometimes passed each other looks when Mister Rogers said something particularly saccharine. Troy could easily have picked up on those.

Perry ate several more candy hearts. One said "Be Mine," another said "No Way," and another said, "Melt My Heart." What a coincidence. That last one was the same phrase Eldeen had used in her prayer in the bank parking lot. Something like "And dear Lord in heaven, melt my heart and make me soft to the needs that Perry has so that maybe, just maybe, I can help show him the way to the cross of Jesus."

Maybe that was how Eldeen and Brother Hawthorne and the others composed their prayers—out of the messages on conversation hearts. He ate two others—one said "One and Only" and the other "Stay True." That was it. They strung these little cliches together, and presto—they had a prayer. "Teach us, Lord, how to serve you as our One and Only God. Show me that your promises can all Be Mine. We know there is No Way to heaven but through salvation and help us to Stay True to the Bible." They might have to skip a few—like "Hot Mama" and "Cute Dish"—but a really creative person could probably come up with something for even those.

Perry closed his eyes again and listened to Mister Rogers talking with a woman named Miss Gardenkeeper, who was explaining about different seeds as she dug little holes in the soil. Of course, Mister Rogers took everything she said and forced his theme upon it: "These little seeds are all special and different, aren't they, Miss Gardenkeeper? And each one will grow into a beautiful plant with blooms of different colors." What must it be like to live with a man like that, Perry wondered. Did his wife ever tell him to shut up? Did he have children of his own? Grandchildren? Was his blue sweater a gift from one of them? Did Mister Rogers always speak so gently to the neighbor children who ran across his flower beds?

Of course, he knew enough about men to know that all of them—including the soft-spoken Mister Rogers—were capable of living private lives that were totally unlike their public ones. Fundamentalists should have learned this lesson by now too. All these TV evangelists who spoke so self-righteously to their adoring audiences and then proceeded to spend the money mailed in by widows on swimming pools for their dogs and sleazy videotaping sessions with prostitutes. He'd read all about them. It was one of Cal's greatest sources of delight. He knew Cal would love nothing better than for Perry's book to expose some kind of scandal at the Church of the Open Door.

Frankly, though, Perry didn't think Theodore Hawthorne was the type to be embroiled in a scandal. Of course, he didn't know the man—really know him. He tried now to visualize Brother Hawthorne in a compromising situation, but the only woman whose image he could conjure up in the same picture was soft, round, red-haired Edna. He wondered what they were doing right now. It was getting on toward suppertime. Was Brother Hawthorne in the kitchen now helping Edna? Did he put on an apron like Mister Rogers? He wondered if the Hawthorne children watched Mister Rogers on television.

Mister Rogers was back in the kitchen now rolling out dough on a floured cutting board. An assistant, dressed in a dog costume, was helping him cut out shapes—stars, fish, hearts, etc. Another helper, this one a cat, was helping to sprinkle each cookie with sparkles and tiny colored beads. It all went so smoothly that Perry wondered if they had practiced all of this beforehand with a different batch of cookies.

Perry sat up suddenly as the door buzzer sounded, followed by several loud knocks. A pizza delivery car idled in the driveway, and a teenager wearing a Pop's Pizza Palace cap stood at the door holding two large cardboard boxes. Perry pushed open the screen door, frowning slightly.

"It comes to fifteen twenty-five, sir," the boy said cheerfully.

"Uh—I didn't order anything," Perry said. The boy's smile vanished.

"Not again," he groaned. "This is the third time in an hour." He stood there staring helplessly at the boxes he was holding. "I can't believe this is happening," he said. Perry liked the kid, though he didn't know why. Teenagers as a rule usually annoyed him. This one had on a well-worn gold and black letter jacket with a big "D" on one side and a huge hornet on the other—probably an athlete of some kind at Derby High School. Too little for football, though, and basketball, too, most likely, unless he was incredibly quick and wily. Track was a possibility; he could be a sprinter or maybe the anchor on a relay team. He had an angular jaw and deep-set brown eyes—a youthful Clint Eastwood kind of look about him. But for all his good looks, he had a vulnerable, almost childish expression in his dejection. As the boy started back down the steps, Perry saw the name "Darrell" emblazoned across the back of his jacket. He wondered if Darrell knew Joe Leonard at school.

"Wait a minute, Darrell," he called. "What are they—I mean, what kind?"

The boy turned back, his eyes hopeful. He quickly glanced at the paper taped on one of the boxes. "One's double pepperoni, sir, and the other's ham and mushroom."

"Hang on," said Perry. "I mean . . . I'll take them, I guess." He held the door open and motioned the boy inside. "Wait here. I need to . . . well, my money's right over here. Just a minute."

"Both of 'em?" the boy said.

"Well, sure—I guess so," said Perry. He got his wallet from his coat pocket and returned with a twenty-dollar bill. He saw Darrell staring at the television screen. The boy quickly glanced away as he handed Perry the boxes and reached into his belt-pack for change.

As Perry closed the front door a minute later, he was sure he heard Darrell say, "All right!" The thought struck Perry that maybe Pop over at the Pizza Palace sent Darrell out to different neighborhoods around this time every afternoon with unordered pizzas, counting on the boy's winsome looks and good acting to sucker people into buying. As he watched Darrell back out of the driveway and take off in an old red Chevy, he could almost hear him boasting to Pop: "And then the guy gets this *real* sympathetic look on his face and stammers around and says 'Hey, listen, uh, I'll take 'em both.' And then he gives me back two of the dollars I hand him in change, for a tip, and then just stands there like some kind of statue or something not saying a word till I finally just turn around and leave." He could see Pop and Darrell hanging onto each other as they laughed. "And wait—here's the funniest part," Darrell would gasp. "Guess what the guy is watching on television? *Mister Rogers*! A grown man watching Mister Rogers!"

Perry set the pizzas on the kitchen counter. He heard the Blanchards' kitchen door open and saw Joe Leonard carrying a large plastic bag toward the two garbage cans sitting next to the house. Without stopping to think, Perry opened his own door and called to Joe Leonard.

"Hey!" Joe Leonard looked over and waved. "Is your mother cooking supper?" Perry asked.

"She's in the kitchen," Joe Leonard called back, "but I don't know if she's cooking yet. You need something?"

"Well, not really," said Perry. "I was just wondering . . . well, does your family like pizza?"

Joe Leonard set the bag of garbage down. "Yes sir, we do," he said.

"Well, ask your mother if you'd like to share some with me." Joe Leonard looked confused. "I mean, I ordered two—well, I didn't really order them exactly," said Perry, "but that doesn't matter; I have them anyway and thought maybe you all could help me eat them."

"I'll ask," said Joe Leonard. He quickly deposited the garbage inside one of the cans and bounded back up the steps.

The telephone rang almost immediately, and thirty minutes later Perry watched as Jewel, Joe Leonard, and Eldeen walked in a slow procession across both driveways to Perry's front door. Joe Leonard was carrying a bowl of tossed salad.

Eldeen spoke as soon as Perry opened the door. "I was just telling

Jewel that this has got to be the *nicest* surprise anybody's ever treated us to! How you could ever know that my mouth was just watering for some pizza I can't for the life of me figure out! It's true—I been hankering for some pizza for over a week now! I'm one grateful person, that's what I am. Yes sir, I'm grateful with all my heart. We all are!" As she stepped across the threshold, Perry saw the lampshades sway. The snow inside the music globe stirred lightly and resettled.

Chapter 12

Several nights later, on Friday night, Perry found himself seated beside Jewel and Eldeen in the Derby High School auditorium. The room was dim and cavernous with its dark wooden rows, the high ceiling, the heavy gold curtain across the stage. Perry could hear muted metallic thumps and could see the curtain rustle as people moved behind it. Then someone on stage hissed a loud "shhh!" and the curtain grew still.

The school was old; Jewel had already told him she had attended high school here, and Perry had noticed the year 1946 engraved into the stone portal as they entered the building. A long black crack zigzagged diagonally across one wall of the auditorium, Perry noticed, and the cement floors were pitted with wear. The small folding wooden seats creaked badly as the audience settled in. Had people been smaller back in 1946, Perry wondered, or were the postwar manufacturers of auditorium seats urged to conserve wood? Eldeen grunted as she lodged herself in one of the narrow seats, her knees touching the seat in front of her.

Perry saw pale wads of gum stuck to the bottoms of several upturned seats in the unoccupied row behind them, and it occurred to him that every single wad of gum represented the history of Derby High; the pinkish one had perhaps been chewed and snapped by a perky cheerleader wearing saddle oxfords, the smaller white one maybe by a popular boy voted Most Likely to Succeed, the light green one by a captain of the debate team. Maybe the cheerleader was a grandmother by now, warning her grandchildren that gum could cause cavities. The one predicted to succeed could have ended up a casualty in Korea or Vietnam; the debater might be struggling through a midlife crisis. They had probably never dreamed when they sat here in student assemblies, Perry thought, that life would turn out as flavorless and sticky as the used gumwads they left behind to harden.

"Don't you?" Eldeen asked, reaching over Jewel to touch Perry's arm.

"I'm sorry—don't I what?" Perry said.

"Love to see young people perform!" Eldeen said enthusiastically. "It's just so wonderful that there's so many things the young folks can do in school nowadays. I keep telling Joe Leonard he's *got* to take advantage of all these chances! I didn't have them, but if I had of, I'll guarantee you I'd of sure been busy taking them all on. Why, to learn how to play a instrument and be in a *band*—I can't think of what a thrill that must be!" Eldeen went on to recite all the extracurriculars available to the Derby High students.

A young couple slouched in the row in front of them had turned around to stare at Eldeen during this speech, then ducked their heads and laughed hysterically. Perry heard the boy's mimicking voice, low and throaty, and watched as the girl leaned her head back and emitted a long, drawn-out, breathy giggle. He was surprised at how suddenly and violently they aroused his anger. They couldn't be older than junior high, and here they were jammed against each other like Siamese twins—two stringy-haired, gum-smacking pubescent punks. Sometime during the concert they would probably spit their gum right out on the floor for other people to step on, not even bothering to stick it to the underside of their chairs. And who could tell, Perry thought, what they planned to do after the concert?

He watched as the boy ran his index finger along the girl's lower lip. She licked his finger sensuously, after which he withdrew it, touched it to his mouth, and wet it with his own tongue. He whispered something, and the girl nodded coyly. Perry stared in disgust. Did their parents have any idea that these children—that's exactly what they were, children—were trading saliva?

The curtain began to open, first just a few inches, then a long pause, followed by several swift jerks—and there in full view was the Derby High School Concert Band. The audience grew quiet.

"Joe Leonard is so tickled you could come with us tonight," Eldeen whispered loudly. The girl in front of them gave a tiny snort, and the boy slapped her knee, then slid his hand a little higher and kept it there.

Perry couldn't imagine Joe Leonard being tickled about much of anything. The boy had in fact looked uncomfortable when his grandmother had brought up the subject to Perry on Monday night while they were eating pizza together. When Perry had said he'd be glad to come, Joe Leonard had reddened and flashed him a quizzical look. The truth was Perry would have welcomed any invitation to fill up a Friday night. Friday nights were as bad as a whole week of afternoons put together.

It was the band's winter concert, Jewel had explained, but it was later than usual this year because the conductor, Mr. Beatty, had taken suddenly ill back before Christmas and had been hospitalized for two weeks. "The chorus teacher tried to fill in," Eldeen had added, "but she was mostly just treading water, Joe Leonard says, and not making a bit of headway." So the December concert had been postponed till the end of February.

The band members sat motionless now, holding their instruments in their laps, staring intently at the man who stood before them. Mr. Beatty was tall and spindly. With his dark hair and loose-fitting black suitcoat, he could have been Abraham Lincoln standing up there. Perhaps he had filled out the coat more before his recent illness, Perry thought. Perry wondered what Mr. Beatty was doing right now with his back turned to the audience. Was he mouthing last-minute instructions to the students? Was he making faces at them? Maybe reciting the "Gettysburg Address"? Several of the flute players were trying to hide smiles and cutting their eyes over at one another.

Then Mr. Beatty stepped up on a small platform and raised a slender baton. The players immediately lifted their instruments in military unison, and Perry saw two large round tuba bells rise above the back row. Mr. Beatty gave a swift downward stroke of the baton, and the auditorium was filled with sound. Though the room was old, the designers back in the forties had obviously put some thought into acoustics. Or else somebody knew how to place microphones strategically. Maybe the big freestanding wooden panels behind the band helped direct the sound. Anyway, Perry was surprised at the volume. He counted sixty-two players, and this surprised him too. He had been assuming it would be a much smaller group, more the size of the choir at the Church of the Open Door.

Mr. Beatty turned to face the audience when the opening number ended. Amid the applause, he bowed several times and swept a long arm backward to encompass the players in the audience's show of approval. He was an angular man with a thick, uncooperative bush of hair falling over his forehead. Probably around fifty, maybe even a little older, Perry guessed. He couldn't help wondering if Mr. Beatty had done this all his life—conducted a high school band. Perry couldn't imagine doing that for a living.

When the clapping ended, Mr. Beatty spoke. His voice was resonant, almost stentorian, but with a deep drawl. Perry could well imagine him debating Stephen Douglas and giving speeches from the backs of trains.

"That was *Spitfire Fugue*, composed by William Walton, a British composer born in 1902," Mr. Beatty announced. He spoke slowly, his head thrust forward on his shoulders and nodding slowly as he scanned the audience from right to left. He reminded Perry of one of those small flocked dogs people used to set in the rear windows of their cars, whose heads would bob and swivel slowly. "You can tell Mr. Walton had a fine imagination and a sense of humor to match," Mr. Beatty continued. "His music's always fun to play. The *Spitfire Fugue*—or the 'Spitfire Fudge' as a few of the band members like to call it—is one of my personal favorites."

Mr. Beatty paused and smiled a slow, private sort of smile. Then he resumed. "Mr. Walton was more or less a self-taught composer, whose early teachers saw his potential and let him develop his own style." He paused again to indulge in a leisurely, silent chuckle before continuing. "I'm afraid neither Walton nor the composer of our next piece is a very good example for the young people behind me, who are all too eager to prove their teachers an unnecessary encumbrance."

Perry couldn't shake the thought of Mr. Beatty's resemblance to Lincoln—the same deliberateness of speech flavored with a dash of humor. He saw Mr. Beatty splitting logs and studying law by a kerosene lamp, swapping tales at the general store and wrestling boastful yokels.

Mr. Beatty was announcing the next piece, composed by a Brazilian named Heitor Villa-Lobos, who, he said, "was a brilliant musician in spite of his lack of formal academic training." Again, that slow smile and the momentary pause. "Of course, my students have suggested to me that it was probably *because of* his lack of education rather than in spite of it that his creativity flourished."

A ripple of soft laughter swept across the audience, punctuated by Eldeen's throaty, sustained rumble. The junior high couple turned and stared at her, poker-faced, then turned around and collapsed on each other in helpless giggles. The band members on stage grinned good-naturedly as if pleased that their director was eliciting chuckles at their expense.

The Villa-Lobos piece began, and Perry was instantly struck by its exciting rhythms. It reminded him of something, but the memory was slow in coming. When it did come, the Villa-Lobos number had almost ended. Relieved to have cornered the memory, Perry wondered how he could have forgotten it—even though it must have been close to twenty years ago now.

He had gone with a fellow he had met in one of his literature classes to a weekly event called "Underground Arts." It was held in the basement of a dilapidated Victorian-style house near the University of Illinois campus. When they had walked in, a pony-tailed guitarist was sitting under the single lightbulb suspended from a dangerous-looking frayed cord in the center of the room. The room was cold, and everyone wore coats and caps, except for the performer, who wore overalls over what looked like the top to a pair of red thermal underwear. Many of the listeners held candles, Perry noticed. He wondered if the city fire marshal knew about all this.

In the small circle of lighted faces nearest the guitar player, Perry saw a girl he had observed often. Finding her here was a happy surprise. He stood watching her, noting her expression of awe as she gazed at the guitarist's fingers. Before, he had always seen the girl sitting beside a small fountain near the quadrangle, her eyes always on a book in her lap. He had seen her there first during the early fall and then on into winter, her small white face framed by bulky layers of wool scarves and caps. Never on a regular schedule, though, so that he had to make numerous inconvenient trips past the fountain, hoping to find her there.

Perry's friend—the one he had come with anyway—had found a seat against the basement wall on part of an old bed frame, and he motioned Perry to join him. But Perry hadn't. He had stood by the basement steps watching the girl, who was enthralled by the guitarist's performance. He remembered clearly the sudden ache of longing, wishing he could be the one sitting there in the center of the room with her eyes fixed admiringly on him.

And what if he did find himself suddenly thrust upon that stool under the hazardously wired lightbulb? What would he perform? As a boy, he had always had a fear of being shoved out onto a stage during a performance or being coerced into competing in a sporting event at the last minute. It had gone so far as to become a recurring dream: Finding himself onstage with a ballet troupe performing *Swan Lake,* suddenly feeling himself spotlighted. Or standing on top of a diving platform, hearing the announcer's voice: "And now Perry Warren, America's last hope in this most difficult of all dives—the reverse quadruple-flip, flying-twist, cyclone-spin." He hated water and had never even completed the swimming lessons his mother had paid for the summer he was seven.

He swallowed and told himself to calm down. This wasn't the sort of place where performers were dragged out of the audience. Whenever one person finished, according to his friend, whoever wanted to could take his place and do his thing. But then another fear arose. What if Perry suddenly found himself making his way to the stool, unable to stop himself, excusing himself as he stepped over people, then sitting down under the lightbulb and finding a hundred or more expectant faces staring up at him? He knew how tenuous a person's hold on reality and propriety was; what if he suddenly forgot himself and went forward on his own—just for the brief prize of the girl's close attention?

He sometimes, even now in college, held his breath during class lectures, afraid he would suddenly stand up and walk to the podium to argue a point the professor had just made. Thankfully, he never had, but he couldn't help fearing that it was only his constant vigilance that had prevented it.

What if it happened now in front of the girl? Suddenly an idea came to him. He could recite something—that was it. The girl would love the passages he had memorized from *Walden*. He could almost imagine himself looking deep into her eyes, blocking out all the others, and speaking with religious solemnity:

> I wanted to live deep and suck out all the marrow of life, to live so sturdily and Spartan-like as to put to rout all that was not life, to cut a broad swath and shave close, to drive life into a corner, and reduce it to its lowest terms.

He wondered if he should credit his source outright; surely, artistic types like these students would recognize Thoreau. He wouldn't want to insult them.

He caught his friend's repeated gesture to come sit beside him. Several others looked back at him curiously. Perry suddenly grew worried. Had he perhaps said something aloud without intending to? He moved quickly to the wall and sat down. He could still see the girl. She had her eyes closed now and was swaying to the music. The guitarist was now playing and singing—and here was the key to the memory—a Brazilian folk tune. The rhythmic complexity was astounding, and the poetry was lovely. The man sang it first in Portuguese, then in English. One phrase Perry still recalled: "the pale, dappled luster of twilight's opaled skies." He had always been fascinated by the art of translating poetry; how could the Portuguese line possibly be as lovely as the English?

After the "Underground Arts" had ended that night, Perry had hung around the basement steps as people pushed past him. His friend left—and never again asked him to go anywhere with him as Perry recalled—and finally the girl had stood to leave. She came toward him, walking slowly by herself, squinting at the steep, dim steps.

"Hi," Perry had said. She looked up at him and frowned. A light-colored woolen cap was perched sideways on her head, covering one ear but riding on top of the other. Perry wondered if it meant she was careless about details—or maybe she did it on purpose, preferring an asymmetrical look. A thick wool muffler was slung loosely around her neck, with a silk paisley scarf tied tightly above that. Perry was filled with admiration at the unstudied charm of these details.

"I don't know you—do I?" she said, stopping to look closely at him. He wished it weren't so dark over by the steps. He wanted to see what color her eyes were.

"Not yet," he had said. For months afterward, she was to tease him about that reply. "Pretty sure of yourself, weren't you?" she would say.

It had been so unlike anything he had ever done that he surprised himself thoroughly. But it worked. He walked her ten blocks to a house she shared with six other girls, lecturing her mildly about the dangers of walking by herself so late at night. "But I'm with you," she had said. "But you don't even know me," he had replied. "Not yet," she had answered.

Her name was Dinah, of course. And eventually he had quoted Thoreau to her—Emerson too. And, it had turned out, her eyes were green.

Perry wasn't sure how many more numbers the Derby High School Band had played during his mental lapse, but when he came back he found himself clutching the hard wooden armrests of his seat as if strapped to an electric chair. He even felt hot, as if the button had just been pushed and the electrodes were sending their deadly energy through his body. He saw Jewel glance over at him, puzzled. He breathed deeply and released his grip. The band was in the middle of a medley of tunes from *The Music Man*. Joe Leonard had a solo part in "Marian, the Librarian"—a clever, loping line of bass notes under the trumpet melody. During the applause that followed, Mr. Beatty had the soloists stand, and Joe Leonard rose awkwardly, his face flushed crimson. Perry couldn't tell if it was from pleasure, embarrassment, or simply the exertion of blowing so hard.

He lost track of time again during the second half but faded in and out as Mr. Beatty interjected droll comments, then turned, his lanky arms aloft, to launch a new piece. It was funny how a single memory set off others; how quickly they flashed and shimmered and changed shapes, like a kaleidoscope, each slight movement producing a new burst of color that spread into a different design. By the time the concert had ended, Perry felt that he had relived his entire four years of college in Urbana, the period of time he had always considered his rite of independence, both dreaded and relished, from the stark frame house in Rockford where he had lived with his mother and Beth.

The band closed the program with Sousa's *Washington Post March,* and the audience applauded wildly. Even the junior high boy in front of them leaned forward in his seat, scrunched up his mouth, and whistled a series of shrill blasts as he beat his hands together. The girl stared at him, amused, and then began examining her fingernails.

Mr. Beatty bowed several times, then made the whole band stand and bow. He walked offstage, then returned almost immediately and went through the bowing procedure again. The next time he came back out, he held up his hands for silence; when the applause stopped, he smiled and said, "All right, all right, you talked us into it. We've got an encore for you, but it might be a little out of the ordinary for this time of year." He stopped to pucker his mouth, trying to erase his smile, but the smile crept back. The band members were rustling through the music on their stands.

"We had some Christmas numbers all picked out to play for you back in December," Mr. Beatty said, "but then I decided to take a little vacation in the Dickson County Hospital for a couple of weeks, and when I got out, to my amazement Christmas was almost over and done with." He put the side of one hand up to his mouth as if confiding a secret. "But it did provide certain advantages, such as saving me the trouble and expense of shopping for gifts."

Everyone laughed and Mr. Beatty continued. "We thought we'd play as our encore one of the little Christmas pieces we worked up for the December concert—and, really, it's not so much Christmas as it is winter. And since winter's not officially over for another few weeks, we can't be faulted too much." He turned back to the band, stepped up on the platform, and lifted his arms.

The piece was "Winter Wonderland." Of course, thought Perry. The perfect finale for an evening of reminiscing. Nobody could have planned it better. The band played the piece briskly, and people in the audience even started clapping in rhythm toward the end. Perry only faintly heard it all, however; inside his head the sounds of diabolical laughter reverberated. He sat perfectly still, wondering whose laughter it was and envisioning a swirl of snow inside a glass ball, with a small plastic figure tumbling over and over.

Chapter 13

The following Tuesday was Jewel's birthday. Perry looked at the clock: five more hours before they would leave for dinner. He still had the afternoon to make it through. He cinched the bread wrapper shut with a twistie, deposited his plate in the sink, and headed back to the computer.

The surprise party on Sunday night had gone off successfully, with a larger-than-expected turnout due in part to several visiting families in attendance that night. They had run short on the paper party cups Eldeen had bought at Wal-Mart and had to supplement with some flimsy, cone-shaped ones from the ladies' rest room. Birdie Freeman, the organist, had made three large chocolate sheet cakes, each one frosted a different color—pale pink, green, and yellow. In the corners of each cake she had fashioned a cluster of flowers in contrasting colors. Marvella Gowdy brought several dishes of mixed nuts, and Trudy Gill furnished small cups of Dixie Dairy vanilla ice cream. Eldeen supplied all the paper goods and Hi-C.

Jewel had seemed surprised and pleased. Perry had admired her poise when she entered the big room called Fellowship Hall and was met by the astonishing outcry: "Surprise! Surprise!" Willard Scoggins had detained her in the auditorium after church to discuss the music for an upcoming choir special, and Eldeen had told her she'd be back in Fellowship Hall looking for a casserole dish she'd left at the last social. Still, Perry thought, Jewel must have suspected something when everyone cleared out of the auditorium so fast.

Standing in the doorway of Fellowship Hall, with Willard beaming behind her, Jewel smiled serenely through "Happy Birthday"; it was a different version from any that Perry had ever heard: "Happy Birthday to Jewel, we hope it will bring, A new year of service to use for the King." Brother Hawthorne led in prayer, expressing thanks "for this faithful servant of the Lord's, whose life so beautifully reflects her name." Then Jewel was escorted to the long serving table to lead the line for refreshments. They had lit the candles, only a token few for looks, and Jewel bent gracefully to blow them out, smiling and pretending to pant when she finally got them all. After she was served, she was escorted to a metal folding chair that had been draped with a white sheet and set under a latticed arch decorated with artificial flowers; here she sat like a queen holding court while everyone stopped at the end of the serving line to wish her a happy birthday. Joe Leonard and Eldeen pulled up chairs to sit beside her, and when Perry filed past, Eldeen gestured broadly with her plastic fork.

"Here, pull you up a chair with us, Perry! After all, I got you to thank for helping me plan all this!"

Perry glanced apologetically at Jewel. "All I did was drive her to Wal-Mart," he said, but he wasn't sure she heard him.

Joe Leonard set his cake and Hi-C down and dragged another chair over beside Eldeen. Eldeen hooked a foot around it and pulled it closer, then patted the metal seat firmly. "Here you go, we saved this one just for you!" As he sat down, Perry was glad to note that his chair was situated behind one side of the white arch and thus mostly hidden from the sight of the people filing past.

All the children sat at two tables against the wall, and the adults milled around a while, then arranged their chairs in a loose semicircle in front of the seat of honor. The visiting families were taken in, absorbed into the happy community, plied with friendly questions and offers of more punch. People had brought cards and gifts of all kinds, from knitted house slippers to ceramic figurines, and Jewel opened them all, softly praising each one.

By the time it was all over—including a Bible quiz game Eldeen had made up and a chorus sing led by Willard Scoggins—it was almost ten o'clock. Levi Hawthorne was asleep, Perry noticed, his curly head heavy on Edna's shoulder. People began leaving, and the ladies cleared off the tables. Joe Leonard and the Chewning twins started folding up chairs and setting them in rows against a wall.

All the way home Eldeen had declared it the best party she'd ever been to. "It just went off so nice!" she exclaimed. "That was the tastiest cake Birdie's ever made, and them mixed nuts Marvella brought—why I'd forgot how much I liked them! And the Hi-C and Trudy's ice cream—mmmm! It was all sure a heap better than that fancy shower of Rhonda Tribble's over at the Assembly of God church last week. Remember that cake, Jewel?" She turned back to talk to Perry. "The Tribbles don't believe in sweets, so everything was health food. Why,

I never saw the likes—carrot juice and oatmeal and bran fiber—at a *shower!*" She smiled over at Jewel again. "And all them gifts and cards people brought you—why, I never saw anything to beat it! And to think, I never told a soul to bring presents, they just did it on their own, because they think so much of you, Jewel. You should feel proud. And the game—it went over big, too, didn't it? Why, that little Bonita Puckett surprised me to no end with all those quiz answers she knew! Isn't it funny how you never hear a peep out of some people, and then all of a sudden they just pop up and shock you to pieces!"

No one else had said much, but Jewel's profile had looked calm in the faint glow of passing streetlights. The empty Hi-C jars made a hollow clanking sound as they bumped against each other inside the grocery bags at Joe Leonard's feet.

When they had turned onto Blossom Circle, Perry suddenly had an idea, and before he could reconsider he had found himself talking.

"I'd like to invite you all out for dinner on Tuesday night," he said. A moment of silence had fallen, and for a while Perry wondered again if he had really spoken or only thought he had.

But then Eldeen gasped and looked over at Jewel. "Out to dinner! Why, we haven't done that for—how long's it been, Jewel? I can't even remember."

Jewel shook her head. "I don't know, Mama. I really don't. Of course, Perry had us over for pizza last week, don't forget."

"Well, I should say not. We couldn't any of us forget *that!*"

They pulled into the driveway, and Jewel turned around to face Perry. She didn't speak right away but finally said, "That's awful nice, Perry, but please don't feel like you have to take us out for dinner." Joe Leonard turned his head quickly and looked out his window.

"Have to?" said Perry. "Well, I know that. It's just that . . . it came to me that Tuesday's your real birthday and . . . well, I'd like to do it. If you want to, that is."

"Well, yes," said Jewel, "we'd like to." She looked over at Eldeen. "Is that all right with you, Mama?"

"All right? Well, I guess that's one way of putting it!"

"Joe Leonard, does that suit you?" Jewel looked at her son through the rearview mirror.

"Sure," said Joe Leonard. He shifted his feet nervously and accidentally kicked one of the bags; the glass jars clamored briefly.

"We'll plan on Tuesday then," Perry said as he opened the car door.

"If it doesn't snow like they're predicting!" Eldeen called after him.

On Monday Perry had phoned around and finally settled on a place called the Purple Calliope. They didn't need reservations, the woman on the phone had said, but Perry told her anyway that a party of four would be arriving Tuesday night at six-thirty. "Call us tomorrow in case of bad weather," the woman had said. "We might not be open if it threatens snow."

The weather forecast had been suggesting the possibility of snow for three days now, ever since Sunday morning, but Perry was skeptical. He had heard about the snow mania in the South. Cal had told him about schools being canceled at the sight of a single snowflake, about multicar pileups because of the ineptitude of Southern drivers on ice, about runs on bread and milk in all the grocery stores when the temperature dropped to below freezing.

The computer was still on in the guest room. Perry started shuffling through several handwritten sheets, looking for the notes he had taken at prayer meeting the week before, but stopped suddenly and walked over to the window. The sky was a hazy white but brindled with low clouds. As far as snow skies went, it looked remotely possible but certainly not likely. Recalling the weather report on the local news the night before, Perry shook his head and smiled. The forecaster, a man with a rubbery face and a toupee, had sounded theatrical in his intensity: "A winter storm of historic proportion has spawned in the Gulf and appears to be headed full speed toward the coast of Louisiana, where it will collide with a cold air mass coming down from the Midwest and then rip across the Southeast, leaving a path of poorly equipped towns buried by snowfalls up to fifteen inches." For South Carolina, it was hard to tell, the man said, exactly where the snow line would fall, but most likely at least half of the state, from Columbia southward, would be crippled by the storm, with other regions getting significant flurries and high winds. Perry had smiled at the dramatic word choices: "historic proportion," "spawned," "full speed," "collide," "rip," "buried," "crippled." "Get a grip on yourself," he had wanted to tell the man. "Let me tell you a thing or two about *real* winter storms."

He turned back to the computer and once again searched through the papers spread out beside it. He had been to three complete rounds of Sunday activities at the Church of the Open Door now, including Sunday school, morning worship, Training Union, choir practice, and the evening service. Besides that, he'd attended prayer meeting for two Wednesdays. Last week instead of going with Eldeen, Jewel, and Joe Leonard to Peewee Powwow, he had stayed with the adults for their prayer session in the sanctuary. From the pile of notes, he at last pulled out four small sheets torn from his Daytimer; there they were.

For now he was typing up his notes in chapters with unimaginative titles like "Sunday School" and "Choir Practice." He opened a new file and named it "Adult Prayer Session."

Once the children had left the auditorium, Brother Hawthorne had opened the floor for prayer requests and testimonies. Perry tried to get down as much in writing as he could; almost everyone else was writing also, he noticed. It intrigued him as the request session wore on that these people were so unabashedly open and detailed with the personal information they shared. A woman named Nina said her sister in Birmingham had a cyst on one of her ovaries and would be having surgery on Friday, and a man named Bernie requested prayer for a brother-in-law who had lost his third job in a row because of his addiction to alcohol, which he still refused to admit. Hoyt Bagwell asked prayer for his granddaughter who was attending Michigan State University, that she'd be able to "keep her testimony."

An elderly woman named Marjorie stood and spoke in a whispery voice about her niece who had left her husband a week ago with their Pontiac and the thousand dollars they had in their savings account; the niece, whose name was Felicia, was seven months pregnant and didn't leave any word about where she was headed. Harvey Gill requested prayer for his unsaved son, who although financially prosperous was "living a life of blatant sin far away from the Lord out in Los Angeles."

Perry wrote them all down, a whole list of depressing human burdens. He wondered as he was writing down the one about Grady's medical insurance being canceled whether it ever disturbed anybody in this church that this God they claimed to be so loving and so powerful allowed their lives to be so fraught with problems. He wondered how Jewel dealt with that, how she could reconcile the idea of a loving God with a God who had permitted her husband to die—perhaps even *ordained* it if he understood the theology of these Christians.

Maria Pyle spoke up and asked everyone to keep praying for Crystal Kahlstorf's husband, Lowell. He had pawned Crystal's sapphire ring, which had belonged to her grandmother, and then spent the money on whiskey. An audible murmur of sympathy swept across the assembly at this news, and Brother Hawthorne asked the deacons to stay for a short meeting after the service to discuss additional financial aid for Crystal and her children. Woody Farnsworth told about spraining his ankle falling off the ladder from the attic and asked for prayer that it would heal quickly because he needed to shingle his roof as soon as the weather warmed up a little more. He went on to say how thankful he was that he'd been able to break his fall with the bag of old baby clothes he was carrying or it could have been a lot worse.

Among the prayer requests were interspersed some happy stories that Brother Hawthorne called "praises." Frankly, some of them sounded suspicious to Perry. A woman named Myrt claimed that her car's brakes had gone out on Monday and she'd had no idea how she was going to pay for the repairs. Then just today, Wednesday, before she had gone to get the car, she had found a letter in her mailbox from an aunt in Idaho she hadn't heard from in over three years, and in with the letter was a check for $300. The car repair bill had come to $282, and Myrt praised the Lord that she had eighteen dollars left over for a new pair of windshield wipers, which the mechanic had said she desperately needed and which cost $16.98. Myrt was crying by the time she finished, and so were others. Several people simultaneously declared "Amen!" or "Praise the Lord!" when she sat down.

Sid Puckett said his father had been diagnosed with prostate cancer two months ago, but last week his mystified doctor told him there was no sign of the cancer now.

Deus ex machina—that was the term for it in fiction. A writer churned up some complex series of problems to grab the reader's interest and then simply wiped them all away with some contrived twist of plot, like a surprise inheritance or the winning number of a billion-dollar jackpot or—the most reprehensible—a sudden awakening to realize it had all been only a bad dream.

But Myrt's and Sid's stories weren't fiction; they were real life. So, Perry asked himself, how could the $300 check and the mysterious healing be explained? The answer came immediately. It was simple—it was all chance: lucky timing, honest mix-ups, the kinds of things that happened every day. These people just credited it all to the power of God, that's all. There was no such thing as "fate" in their way of thinking.

When prayer time actually started, people began standing to rehearse, with eyes closed, the inventory of needs. That was another thing Perry would like to ask somebody one day. If God was everywhere and knew everything and always opened the door when you knocked and filled your cup to overflowing as these people seemed to believe, then why did they think they had to *repeat* their needs over and over as if God were a slow learner or hard of hearing? Why did they even have to verbalize them for that matter?

He began listing phrases common to many of the prayers: "if it be thy will," "unsaved loved ones," "thy throne of grace," "the privilege of prayer," "the blessings bestowed upon us," "strength and comfort," "work in a special way," "guide and direct us." Perry wondered how many of the people praying were really thinking about what they were saying; or had their prayers become rituals, comforting in their familiarity but devoid of meaning?

When Brother Hawthorne stood at last to end the prayer session, Perry listened carefully. The man fascinated him. Not one of the catch phrases Perry had copied down on his list was repeated in the pastor's prayer. Perry raised his head and looked up. Brother Hawthorne stood with his arms crossed in front of himself, as if trying to protect himself from arrows. His eyes were tightly closed, and his face looked pained as if the arrows were finding their mark. He held no script in his hands, but the words poured forth fluently, warmly, wrapping themselves easily around the thoughts and almost convincing even Perry that these things would indeed come to pass. How could God resist such a moving plea?

Perry stopped and glanced up from his computer. The wind had kicked up outside. He could hear its low whistle and the scratchy sound of dry leaves scuttling across the driveway. He turned off the computer and went to the window. The daffodils in the neighbors' yard across the street were standing sideways, leaning evenly like a row of chorus girls. A teardrop-shaped tree, already flecked with early white blossoms, was quivering like a pom-pom. It was almost three-thirty, he noticed on the clock. He saw two schoolchildren bending into the wind, slowly moving toward the house across from the Blanchards'. Some papers blew out of the hands of the smaller one and went whipping down the street behind her. Her brother took her hand and pulled her ahead, shouting something over his shoulder. The door of the house opened, and a woman came out, calling and beckoning to the children as she scanned the sky.

Perry was entranced. He couldn't remember ever watching a storm brew so rapidly—and ominously—as this one was doing. He saw Jewel's station wagon coming down the street at the same time he saw the first snowflake whirl past the window. They must have encouraged the teachers to get home early. He saw Joe Leonard jump out of the car before Jewel reached the house and stop a garbage can lid that was clattering down the driveway toward him. Thirty minutes later the sky was swirling with snow. It surprised Perry to see some of it begin almost immediately to whiten the ground. How could it stick, he wondered, with such powerful wind gusts? There was a steady roar like a powerful jet hovering overhead.

It was snowing thickly now, large flakes spiraling and lifting—a wild, confused type of storm unlike the slow, steady drifts that dropped straight down from the sky in pictures. Perry watched it blow off the eaves of the houses across the street, blurred wisps circling upward then eerily flying apart like ghosts. Along the rooftops little whirlwinds of snow flew up in a rampage, blew sideways, and then disappeared swiftly like smoke.

It came to him again that he ought to study photography. There were prizewinning photographs out there on a day like today. A writer ought to make a good photographer, he had often told himself. The ability to see the world from unique angles, to capture details others overlooked, to create magic out of the mundane—he ought to be able to do that as well on film as on paper. But Dinah used to laugh over his shoulder as he studied with disappointment each new set of prints he had developed. It was always the same. By the time he found the background setting he wanted and positioned Troy and Dinah perfectly, their smiles would have congealed or the sun would have cast shadows over their faces. Troy had begun groaning every time he saw Perry unzipping the camera case. The best picture he had of the two of them was one Dinah's mother, who couldn't even see well enough to get her driver's license renewed, had snapped in her front yard with a Kodak Instamatic.

At 4:40, the electricity went off. The phone rang a few seconds later.

"It's a freak spring storm, that's what it is!" cried Eldeen. "And now we've gone and lost our power, haven't we? You doing all right over there by yourself?"

"I'm fine," he said, "but it doesn't look good for going out to eat."

"No, there's no chance of that, Jewel says. That's one reason I'm calling. She says we'll have us some sandwiches for supper a little later on. We was wondering if you could come over and join us. Think you can make it across the driveway without getting picked up and carried off like little Dorothy and Toto? Maybe we better throw a rope out to you!" She broke off to laugh huskily, then stopped abruptly. "My, that wind's making a racket. I'll be if it *doesn't* sound like a cyclone. Or a tornado—I always get them two mixed up; maybe they're the same thing. Anyway, I lived through one of them a long time ago when I was still in Arkansas, and it's something I'll sure never forget." Perry heard Jewel's voice in the background; then Eldeen spoke again. "So will you come over in about an hour? Jewel says to tell you it's only baloney sandwiches, but we'd be honored to have your company. Won't this here be some birthday party to remember? We'll eat our baloney sandwiches by candlelight!" She sounded as excited as a child.

It was darker than usual when Perry left the house an hour later. The neighborhood looked unfamiliar, surreal, as if he were looking at it through a trick lens that distorted shapes and angles. The snow was still falling heavily, and the ground looked pearly blue in the twilight. The power was still off, but Perry had located the few half-burned candles left over from the night he had arrived in Derby and had laid them all out, along with some matches, on the kitchen table. He carried a small flashlight in his coat pocket, and in his right hand he held a broom. It was a brand-new one that he had bought at Wal-Mart the day before. It wasn't the most elegant gift, but it was practical; besides, he felt he should give Jewel something after all those gifts the others had brought to church Sunday night, and he knew she needed a broom.

As he came down the steps by the kitchen door, he saw the man across the street pull into his driveway in his green pickup. The two children he had seen earlier opened the front door and leaned out, shouting and waving eagerly as their father opened the door of his pickup. The boy lunged forward and met his father in the yard. The woman appeared at the door now, shouting and gesturing, putting her hand to her mouth as the boy lost his footing and fell onto the snow. The man shifted his thermos to the other hand and reached down to pull the boy up. The whole scene—the house, the family, the snow eddying wildly—reminded Perry suddenly of the music globe. He half expected to see the little boy float up into the sky. But he didn't. His father had him by the hand now, and together they were quickly sucked into the dark house.

A weak beam of light wobbled at the Blanchards' side door. Perry looked up to see Eldeen holding a hurricane lamp and motioning to him. The candles on the table inside flamed cheerily. "Come on!" Eldeen called, pushing the door open a crack. "Watch your step! I got the way lighted for you!"

Part 2
FIRELIGHT

And who shall stand when he appeareth? For he is like a refiner's fire.

Malachi 3:2

Chapter 14

This is just the prettiest drive up along here," Eldeen said, pointing to the mountains ahead. "Look at them different shades of green all dotted together that way. It gives the hills a sort of tweedy look." She fanned herself with a folded newspaper.

They rode in silence for a few minutes. Perry switched the air conditioner to high and adjusted the vent to aim more cool air toward Eldeen. Maybe South Carolina had limited experience with winter, but it sure knew how to do summer, he thought. At least they were headed north, though. Maybe the mountains of North Carolina would provide some relief. He glanced in the rearview mirror at Jewel. She was gazing out the window, her blue eyes half-closed against the sun. Her hair was pulled up away from her neck in a short ponytail, but a few stray curls had worked themselves loose around her face. It looked pretty in a girlish sort of way, and if he didn't know Jewel better, he might think she had stood in front of a mirror for a long time arranging the effect.

"This sure is some picture, don't you think?" Eldeen said. Perry thought at first she meant the view of the mountains, but then he saw that she was digging a postcard out of her purse. She held it out for him to see. It showed a few hikers along a mountain trail; a waterfall tumbled over the rocks behind them, and sunlight fell in shafts through the trees. In the corner of the picture were stamped the words "Wilderness Gospel Camp, King's Peak, North Carolina."

"I can't believe how much I've missed Joe Leonard," Eldeen said, turning the postcard over to the other side. "Seems like he's been gone a month instead of just a week. My, but they keep 'em busy there. Just listen to this:

Our cabin won the raft race and the tug-of-war too. Tomorrow is the soccer play-off game. If we could win that, we might get Cabin of the Week. Mr. Brent Geyer has been the speaker for all the services. He's been the best ever. Talent Night is tonight, and I'm singing in a quartet. We're doing a funny song called "Dirty Dan's Dungarees." My counselor's name is Andy. I've been down the Serpent Slide a hundred times at least but don't worry, I am still in one piece. Last night was the Giant Ice Cream Sundae Trough. It was twenty-five feet long. I think I ate a ton. See you on Saturday, Joe Leonard.

"Now didn't he write a good letter?" said Eldeen. "I told him he better not just write us one of these little old cards that says, 'Hi, everything's just fine, bye.' Told him what we wanted was details, details, and he sure did come up with them, didn't he? Yes sir, he really packed that card full—but you can still read his writing just fine. He's got a real nice hand, don't you think?" She studied the message a while longer, laughing softly, then handed it back to Jewel. "Here, you want to see it again, Jewel?"

The Church of the Open Door had sent its members to Wilderness Gospel Camp for over twenty years, Perry had been told. Brother Hawthorne had frequently praised the camp from the pulpit, several adults had given testimonies in church after attending a Couples Retreat in May, and two fifth graders had been saved during Junior Camp two weeks before. Joe Leonard had ridden up with the Pucketts six days ago for Senior Week; he had been saving his money for a year, Eldeen had told Perry, to be able to attend.

Since it seemed to play such a significant role in the lives of the church members, Perry had decided he would include something about the camp in his book, and he had readily accepted Jewel's invitation to go along to bring Joe Leonard home, even offering to drive his own car since the air conditioner in the station wagon hadn't worked for years.

The road was full of sharp turns. Perry hoped neither Jewel nor Eldeen was prone to car sickness. He saw Jewel bend forward and knew she must be holding on to the back of his seat to brace herself.

Eldeen opened her purse again and began rummaging. Finally she extracted a tiny spray can, popped off the lid, and aimed the nozzle inside her mouth. She gave two brisk squirts, then smacked her lips. "Breath-o-peppermint," she explained. "I'd offer you some, but I'm afraid I'd spread my germs." She snapped the lid back on. "My, this road's not for the fainthearted, is it?" she gasped, as a convertible whizzed past them going the other way. "That mister better just watch it if he wants to get home alive." She jabbed the air with the Breath-o-peppermint can for emphasis. "If he only knew how dangerous it is to drive that way, he'd slow down. Why, he could kill hisself faster than a snakebite and drag a lot of other folks to their deaths right along with him! Fast driving is something that just doesn't make a lick of sense."

She sighed and dropped the breath spray inside her purse. "But then neither does a lot of other things folks make a habit of doing."

Eldeen unfolded the newspaper in her lap and started turning pages. "Oh, that Janice Boone, if she isn't a card. She gives the funniest answers! Listen to this one." For the next several minutes Eldeen read the advice column aloud—letters from a beleaguered housewife whose husband never rinsed out the bathtub, a mother whose grown children never wrote thank-you notes for gifts, and a college student whose roommate's pet toad drove him crazy. "She just thinks up the cutest answers, doesn't she?" Eldeen said. "Listen here: *'Dear Toad Hater, Speak up! Get the frog out of your throat and have a talk with your roommate. Don't let such a little thing stick in your craw. Hop to it before you croak!'*" Eldeen threw her head back and laughed so hard that she snorted. Wiping her eyes, she said, "How she comes up with them answers beats me!" Perry noticed that Jewel was smiling as she looked out the side window.

From the advice column Eldeen went on to a column called "Ask Dr. O'Nealy" and read aloud several questions and answers concerning psoriasis, premature balding, and goiters.

They continued to climb higher. Coming around a hard curve, they passed a small picnic clearing set against a backdrop of kudzu. With a sudden flutter of iridescent wings, a flock of starlings rose en masse from the stone tables and dissipated into the trees like the trail of a dark meteor. All except one. He stood on one of the stone tables, one foot raised, his small eyes staring toward the road. Maybe he was the patriarch of the flock, Perry thought; maybe he scorned the timidity of the others, self-assured as he was from his long experience in the poaching of picnic leavings. Or maybe he was the slow one of the family. Maybe he was standing there now, wondering, "Now where did everybody go? They were right here a minute ago."

"Oh, we disturbed their lunch," observed Eldeen. "Speaking of which, I hope they serve that chicken noodle dish for supper after the service like they did last year." She suddenly put both hands over her ears. "There, it happened again—my ears popped! That was the best-tasting casserole! Remember, Jewel, it had them little green peas in it, and they served them big biscuits with strawberry jelly?"

Jewel nodded. "I remember, Mama. You and Joe Leonard couldn't get enough of those biscuits."

Eldeen went back to her newspaper, reading aloud an article about a recent carjacking near Greenwood. "That was some smart gal to outfox that man that way by running her car into that plate glass window and setting off the burglar alarm," she said. "I've done decided what *I'm* gonna do if anybody ever tries carjacking me. I read somewhere that if you start acting real crazy, like you're having some kind of a mental fit, that it'll scare the crook to pieces and just sort of paralyze his thinking. So *that's* my plan." Perry nodded as she looked to him for approval. It occurred to him that anybody who tried to carjack Eldeen had no idea what he was in for. She needn't go to all that trouble of acting crazy; just being her normal self would incapacitate the carjacker's thought processes.

Jewel spoke up. "I don't think you need to worry about being carjacked, Mama, since you don't drive anymore."

"Well now, that's true," Eldeen said thoughtfully, almost sadly, as if her hopes had been dashed. "But then I could be a passenger in a car that got waylaid. I think I read one story where it happened that way. The man got in the backseat and aimed a gun at the two ladies in the front and told them to drive him to—I think it was Myrtle Beach where that happened. They did it, too, and he took all their money and made a clean getaway, and there they was, stuck in Myrtle Beach miles from home with a empty gas tank. Looks like to me with two of them, they could of thought of something to do."

They passed a sign that read "Wilderness Gospel Camp 6 miles." Perry checked his watch. The closing service for Senior Week started at three o'clock, so they should make it in plenty of time. He remembered his week of camp with Uncle Louis's church group when he was a teenager. Were the campers here in North Carolina as bouncy and happy as the ones in Wisconsin? he wondered. Were the counselors as pushy? He sincerely hoped they didn't circulate among the visiting adults and prod them to go to the prayer room at the end of the service.

Eldeen read several of the comics aloud, then some sale ads, and then arrived at the obituaries. "Oh, Jewel, looka here, that woman Mayfield Spalding told us about at church must of died. The one over in Filbert, whose car was hit by a ice cream truck on Highway 25. I believe this is her—Sally Willis Farmington. I remember because when Mayfield mentioned that woman's name I right away thought of my aunt Sally that used to live on a farm when I was a girl in Arkansas. I can remember names that way, by making pictures out of them. Now isn't that a shame? I believe Mayfield said she had a husband in a wheelchair. Wonder what'll happen to that poor soul now that his wife's dead. I need to pray for him. But praise the Lord, Mayfield said *she* was saved and ready to meet Jesus. It says right here, 'Mrs. Farmington was a longtime member of Community Baptist Church in

Filbert, where she faithfully served as president of the Ladies Lending Love Society and taught the Joyful Juniors Sunday school class.' Oh, just think what it must be like to be singing praises in glory right now! But we sure need to pray for her husband left all alone now, poor soul."

Eldeen folded her hands on top of the paper and sat silently for a few minutes. Perry knew what she was doing without even looking over at her. Presently she opened her eyes and read aloud an obituary poem in memory of a man named Bart Gosnell, whose picture showed him to be a strapping man in his forties but whose dates revealed that he had died two years ago at the ripe age of ninety-two. The poem explained the picture, though:

> *We think of you like you were in your prime,*
> *Handsome and strong and always on time.*
> *A man admired by folks far and wide,*
> *And especially to us who knew you inside.*

Eldeen had known Bart Gosnell before he died, and she paused after the poem to tell about how he used to lead the Independence Day parade as the oldest veteran, still wearing his World War I uniform, which was actually too loose on him in his old age.

She turned at last to the sports section and spent the next several minutes expounding on the assets and liabilities of the Atlanta Braves.

"Gettin' Greg Maddux was sure a bonus," she said, "but I tell you if them fielders lets one more ball drop through their fingers, I'm gonna write Bobby Cox a letter and say send them back to the Little League!" It had surprised Perry to discover Eldeen's love for baseball. Once in April when she had asked him for a ride to the G.O.O.D. Store to drop off some sets of pillowcases, she had added a qualification: "But it can't be between two-thirty and five 'cause I'll be listening to the Braves on the radio." He had been puzzled at first, thinking he had misunderstood her. Maybe the Braves were a singing group, older brothers and sisters of the Peewee Powwow children at church perhaps, who were giving a program on the local religious station. But for two and a half hours? "I hope Smoltz smokes the Dodgers' socks off!" Eldeen had added, and then Perry had put it all together.

Joe Leonard was looking for them as they drove up to the big building called the Tabernacle, situated in the center of the camp-grounds. He was standing with two other boys but broke away as soon as he saw the car and came toward them smiling shyly.

"Hey," he said, stopping awkwardly beside Perry's door. Stepping out of the car, Perry noticed immediately that the air was fresher and cooler up here in the mountains. He breathed in deeply. The flag in front of the Tabernacle was fluttering lightly.

Jewel got out of the backseat and gave her son a one-armed hug and patted his shoulder. "We missed you," she said, smiling at him. Perry had never noticed before that Jewel and Joe Leonard were almost exactly the same height. Had the boy grown over the past week?

Joe Leonard extended his hand, and Perry shook it. "I hear you've had a busy week," he said, and Joe Leonard nodded, grinning widely. His freckles looked darker, and his hair, not slicked down as usual, stuck up in little tufts on top. He wore khaki slacks and a royal blue camp T-shirt.

Eldeen finally made it around the car and approached Joe Leonard with her hands outstretched, her smile gleefully contorting her face. "I didn't think this day would ever come!" she cried. "You can't begin to know how long this week has been—and so quiet, why, I thought I was living in a graveyard!" Perry couldn't see how a boy as reserved as Joe Leonard could possibly make such a difference in the noise level at home, but maybe it was because Eldeen had had one fewer person to address her comments to. She hugged the boy enthusiastically, and Perry noticed that while Joe Leonard didn't exactly return her hug, neither did he pull away.

Someone rang a large bell beside the flagpole, and teenagers came from all directions, heading for the Tabernacle. They all wore the same royal blue camp shirts and carried Bibles. Inside, Joe Leonard went to sit with his cabinmates, and Perry followed Jewel and Eldeen to a section marked off for visiting parents and friends.

Brent Geyer had been a missionary for twenty years but had returned to the States when his wife grew ill in Kenya. His closing sermon to the teens was entitled "Down from the Mountaintop" and blended together two ideas: first, the difficulty of returning to normal life after a week of what he called "spiritual mountain climbing" at camp and, second, the descent of Moses from Mt. Sinai, when "his face shone with the glory of having communed with God."

During the course of the message, Brent Geyer told about having climbed Mount Kilimanjaro with a group of native Kenyans and tourists. The trip had taken five days, the first three being moderately paced to acclimatize themselves to the change in altitude, then the rigorous fourth day during which they pushed to the summit and started back down, then the last day of completing the trip down. He told about an old woman who lived in a hut at the base of Kilimanjaro, who cautioned every group of climbers about the importance of taking the ascent slowly, and about two young men, brash, cocky athletes from Europe, who saw themselves as the exception and pushed too hard. "One of them died right there in Africa at the age of twenty-six," he said, "and the other was hospitalized for several weeks. They thought the rules didn't apply to them, but they were wrong. Dead wrong." He paused a moment and rapped his index finger loudly against the wooden podium.

"Now we've had some changes this week in *spiritual altitude*," he continued, "and the results have been some important changes in *attitude*." He looked across the audience and then draped himself over the podium so far that Perry worried that he would lose his balance and tip forward. "You have heard some things this week," Brent Geyer said, pointing his finger at the campers, "things that can make a difference for the rest of your life. We haven't pushed you too fast, but we've challenged you. You can either take the principles you've heard and apply them to your lives—or reject them at your own risk." A man moved to the piano and began playing softly. Perry saw two other young men bending over the fireplace. Soon a small fire was burning.

Brent Geyer asked the audience to bow their heads. "Many of you have already made life-changing commitments this week," he said. "Others are on the brink of doing that, and we want you to have the opportunity today before you leave." He paused and removed the microphone from the stand; holding it, he went to stand beside the fireplace. "In a few moments, as the piano plays, I want you to decide whether you're serious about following God. If you are, then I'll ask you to step forward, take a small stick from this box, and throw it into the fire as a sign of your surrendering your life to burn out for Christ."

Perry glanced around. Burn out for Christ? What was going on here? This went a step further than the harmless candlelighting ceremony he recalled from the Baptist camp. It brought to mind all those gruesome stories of martyrs being torched alive. Combining fire and religion seemed dangerous; it reminded him of occult ceremonies he'd read about, the ones where unidentified charred remains were left behind. He thought of the Buddhist monk years ago who had immolated himself; the news coverage had shown the event over and over. "Take it easy," he wanted to shout now. "Douse the fire!"

But one by one the teenagers began leaving their chairs and slowly, calmly filing to the front, plucking sticks from the cardboard box, and tossing them into the fire, then returning to their seats, their heads bowed as if in deep sorrow. Was this for real? Perry wondered. Were these kids' brains in operation throughout this procedure? Or were they just playing a slightly more sophisticated version of Follow the Leader, all the while itching to return home to normality? Joe Leonard had joined the procession, and Perry watched as he walked forward and took a stick. He knew it was only his imagination, but the flames seemed to leap a little higher as Joe Leonard dropped his stick into the fire.

He remembered Cal's words: "Keep your eye on the kids. That's where you can prove the failure of the system." Perry studied the teens as they slowly filed back and forth. None of them wore jeans with holes ripped in them; there were no shorts, no spiked hair, no tank tops or baseball caps worn backwards. The boys wore no jewelry, and most of them had short haircuts. The girls wore skirts that came to the knee. And everywhere he looked he saw the royal blue camp shirt. Even Brent Geyer had one on. What were these kids like, he wondered—*really* like? They all seemed so compliant. Was it fear? Had the camp leaders threatened them? Browbeaten and brainwashed them—taken away all their gumption? Surely there weren't this many teenagers who truly wanted their lives to "burn out for Christ."

All the adults seemed to understand that the appeal to participate in the fire ceremony was only for the campers, but as Perry felt a rustling beside him, he saw that Eldeen was moving out into the aisle to join the teenagers. No one tried to stop her, though, and she finally made her way to the front, at the end of the line. Perry watched her lean over the box, feel around inside, then remove several sticks. She examined them all and then selected one—a small forked stick—and tossed the others back into the box. She stood motionless for several moments, pointing her stick toward the fire, clutching it with both hands as if it were a divining rod, and moving her lips in silent prayer, then threw the stick into the flames quite forcefully and nodded with satisfaction. As she returned to her chair beside Perry, she was audibly singing the words to the song the piano was playing: "I surrender all, I surrender all, All to Thee my blessed Savior, I surrender all."

Perry looked around, but no one was reacting. He could imagine one of these teenagers later, hanging out at a drive-in somewhere, laughing about all this: "And then, this old lady, I mean, like, *really old and really big*, comes tottering out and gets her a stick and hurls it into the fire like Nolan Ryan or something, and then she lumbers back to her seat *singing out loud* in this *bass* voice." Then after everybody had laughed uproariously, Darrell from Pop's Pizza Palace would chime in, "Yeah, well, let me tell you about this retard I suckered into buying

two pizzas off me one time. He was the *dumbest* guy you've ever seen."
Teenagers could be so heartless. Perry moved closer to Eldeen. She had
stopped singing and was swinging her head slowly as if suffering from
a deep, incurable wound. He had a sudden urge to put his arm around
her protectively and offer comfort; in spite of her bulk, she seemed so
pathetic and vulnerable. But he stood still, his arms hanging rigidly by
his side.

The piano played through several more stanzas and even switched
to a different song finally. Brent Geyer asked everyone to sit down but
to keep praying. People were moving back and forth, some headed to
a smaller room in the back, others approaching the front, talking in
intimate huddles with adults stationed close to the fireplace. Perry
marveled that the temperature in the room seemed so tolerable with a
fire blazing in the middle of summer, with the closely packed rows of
metal folding chairs, with the pressure put to bear on all these young
souls to "get things right with God."

It must be the cool mountain air. Or maybe he was just experiencing
another of his retreats from real life. It was odd, though. Sometimes,
like in Eldeen's living room that first time or during Joe Leonard's band
concert, he became so feverishly hot that he thought he would pass out.
It was funny how unpredictable things were. He felt perfectly calm now;
seeing the counselors occupied so wholly with the teenagers, he no
longer feared being cornered about salvation. No troubling memories
about Dinah were brewing at the present. He was simply observing,
having emotionally distanced himself to a cool hilltop to spy on the
encampment below.

Then it was over. Everyone seemed to be breathing more easily.
The campers all smiled cheerfully and turned around in their chairs,
talking excitedly. Brent Geyer had yielded the microphone to another
man, this one so stocky and jolly, with his enormous bulbous nose and
white hair, that Perry was sure he must be in great demand around
Christmastime. "That there's Carl Chastain," said Eldeen. "He's the
camp director and a real crackerjack too."

Carl Chastain proceeded to announce the awards for the week.
"Cabin of the Week" went to Andy's cabin, number 8. Perry watched
in surprise as Joe Leonard leaped to his feet and cheered along with
seven other boys, all of them pummeling each other on the back and
slapping hands. He'd never before seen such an open display of emotion
from Joe Leonard.

Then came "Campers of the Week." Carl Chastain announced the
"young lady winner" first, reading off her accomplishments during the

week, her hometown, church, school, and finally her name: Gina Simons. Everyone broke out into applause, and a girl stood and was pushed forward, covering her face with both hands. At first Perry thought she was crying, but when she took her hands down to receive the plaque of honor, he saw that she was laughing. "I can't believe it!" she kept saying, and then she'd burst out laughing again as if she'd just caught the punch line to a joke.

The "young man winner" had won something called the Devotional Award, had scored highest in the individual free-throw contest, had earned four hundred points for Scripture memory, two hundred for hiking to the top of King's Peak, and a hundred for winning his cabin's Ping Pong tournament. "He's a member of the quiz team at Calvary Bible Church in Helman, Georgia, and will be a senior this fall at East Valley Christian School," said Carl Chastain, beaming toward the section where the boys were seated, where one boy—a solidly built blond—was already being assailed by the others. Carl Chastain's voice thundered over the din: "Jonathan Macintosh, come on down!"

Perry gave a short bark of laughter, but to his relief no one noticed in all the noise. He wondered if Jonathan Macintosh had ever been to Rome and whether he lived with his Granny Smith near an apple orchard. Evidently the humor of the name hadn't escaped the others, for someone started up a chant as the boy strode forward: "Applesauce! Applesauce! Applesauce!"

Supper was served at five o'clock, and Eldeen seemed to forget her earlier wishes when she saw the table spread with hamburgers and macaroni and cheese. "Now doesn't this look good?" she exclaimed. "Looka there, Joe Leonard, they got green Jell-O and lemonade too." Turning to Perry, she said, "Them's two of his favorites."

Perry studied the campers as they ate. They looked like typical teenagers as they took huge bites out of their hamburgers, filled their forks with macaroni and cheese, and poured seconds of lemonade. They used their napkins and passed dishes in the normal fashion. The dining hall was noisy, with the constant scraping of silverware across plates, the hum of a large ceiling fan, and the animated voices of the campers. Perry caught snatches of their conversation, which included a variety of subjects ranging from the Chicago Bulls to white-water rafting. "He's such a goofball!" he heard one girl say, and then "You know what he said to Amanda?" Several heads bent together before an explosion of laughter. Perry glanced away quickly when one of the girls looked over at him. What had the goofball said to Amanda? he wondered.

"Isn't that the truth?" asked Eldeen, bending near and shouting into Perry's ear. He flinched.

"What's that?" he said.

"I said it's just a joy and a blessing to see so many young people on fire for the Lord!" She swept her spoon back and forth in front of her like a flashlight.

"Hey, give that back!" yelled a boy at another table, and a photograph quickly exchanged hands. Someone shoved it at Joe Leonard. "Here, Blanchard, pass it on!" Joe Leonard handed it to Perry. Looking down at it, Perry saw the picture of a teenaged girl, a pixieish smile on her pink lips and an aureole of light brown hair circling her smooth, untroubled face. Would she end up marrying the boy who was still wailing "Give it back"? he wondered. In sixty or seventy years, would the two of them be shriveled and scarred, their lives having burnt out for Christ?

Chapter 15

I hope you got your music," Jewel said to Joe Leonard as they backed out of the driveway the next morning. Joe Leonard was holding just the mouthpiece of his tuba, blowing into it with his eyes closed, as if trying hard to remember something. He released a huge gust of air.

"Yes, ma'am, I did," he said. Then taking a deep breath, he blew another series of notes into the mouthpiece, producing sounds that junior high boys would laugh over but which no one in the car seemed to think funny.

"It's sure a nice day to be celebrating July the Fourth," said Eldeen. "I've heard lots of folks say they don't like it when a holiday falls on a Sunday, but me, I like it just fine. It makes it all the more special to my way of thinking. I hope you won't think I'm rude," she said, waving her hand over her head toward Perry, "but I need to study my piece a little bit. Don't think just because I'm not talking that I'm settin' up here sulkin'."

As they rode along the familiar streets, Perry studied Joe Leonard. The boy's hair was combed back smoothly from his face, slick furrows running in small, neat parallels above his ears. There was a tiny knick along his jawline; he must have started using the razor Jewel bought for him at Revco back in the spring. He wore a white shirt and a navy sportcoat that looked too snug; instead of his usual brown bow tie, though, he wore the red necktie Jewel had given him for his fifteenth birthday the week before camp. He was wearing his light blue slacks—one of the few pairs, Perry had noticed, that were long enough.

The boy's face flushed as he exhaled slowly into the tuba mouthpiece—an ascending string of arpeggios this time. Holding his breath that way, with his face scrunched into a scowl and his eyes closed, Perry was suddenly reminded of a young child throwing a temper tantrum. He wondered if Joe Leonard had ever done things like that. He thought instantly of Troy and wondered if he'd thrown a tantrum lately or held his breath until he got his way. Surely he was outgrowing that. He should have outgrown it years ago.

Troy's fits of temper had always been a source of disagreement between Perry and Dinah. Dinah's response was always swift and fierce; had Perry not intervened each time, physically blocking her way, she would have done bodily injury to the boy—he was sure of it. One of Perry's worst fears during those earlier years had been that she would seriously hurt Troy in her anger. He couldn't imagine what would have happened if he hadn't been around each time to protect him. Over the last year or two she had given up, simply stalking away and calling back over her shoulder, "Go ahead, Perry, give him what he wants so he'll shut up."

"Can't you see," Perry had wanted to shout after her, "he's inherited his passionate nature from *you?* Can't you try to *understand?*" But he had never shouted anything in his whole life and couldn't bring himself to do so now. He always remained calm, bending over Troy and talking soothingly. And invariably the boy had calmed down. All it took was a little patience.

Perry wondered what Dinah and Troy would do today. The last few years they had all gone to Pierce Lake on July Fourth. Troy liked to fish from the bank of the lake with a Teenage Mutant Ninja Turtle rod and reel they had bought him, and Perry always shadowed him, cautioning him about slipping into the water, secretly horrified of the possibility of Troy actually catching a fish, which, fortunately, he never did. They always ate a picnic lunch by the lake later in the day and let Troy splash in the shallows with dozens of other children. Dinah usually stretched out for a sunbath, but Perry never took his eyes off Troy. He wondered if Dinah would take Troy to the lake today; he felt a tightness around his heart.

"This program Willard's got planned sure is gonna to be a thrill." Evidently Eldeen had finished studying. "And just think, all four of us get to help out in it. Ever since I first woke up this morning I been thanking the good Lord for the United States of America. Oh, sure, it's got its problems, there's no disputing that, with all those spendthrifts in Washington squandering our taxes on a bunch of foolish nonsense, but I can't think of anywhere else in the world I'd rather live than right here! And anybody who's not going to stand up and be a loyal American should just hightail it to some of them other countries for a little while and see all them little babies with runnin' sores and bloated bellies and nasty flies all over theirselves, and drink water that's got germs and infection crawling in it and see their bones sticking out through their scabby, oozin' skin and feel their intestines all twisted up inside of 'em from starvin' to death!" Perry felt something shift in the pit of his stomach. He glanced at the Corning Ware dish filled with spaghetti on the seat between Joe Leonard and himself and quickly looked out the car window, focusing on the clear blue sky overhead. They drove along in silence for several blocks. Joe Leonard once again blew into his mouthpiece, a few halfhearted notes, and then stopped and stared out his window.

When Willard had asked Perry to sing in the choir for the patriotic special, he hadn't known what to say. "I need some basses like everything," Willard had said. "Isn't that what part you sing?"

"Well, yes, I guess, but . . . I don't generally sing much really." The last time Perry could remember singing in a group was in general music class in seventh grade. The teacher had been a delicate little woman past the prime of beauty but still feminine and pretty like antique bone china. Perry wondered now what the teacher—Mrs. Fairfax was her name—had done to make a class of twelve-year-olds so willing to sing. He couldn't imagine children of that age singing so unreservedly today. They'd be cutting glances at each other, reading off-color meanings into innocent song lyrics, and drawing satanic designs on the soles of their hundred-dollar sneakers with blue ballpoint pens. Well, maybe at Wilderness Gospel Camp they wouldn't. He still didn't know what to think of those youngsters.

While Willard reviewed a list of the numbers they'd be performing in the patriotic program, Perry suddenly remembered with absolute clarity the seventh-grade school program in which he'd sung a solo line. He could hardly believe he had ever done such a thing. It was a question-and-answer song called "The Dandelion," in which the entire chorus sang all the questions, while the answers were assigned to three different soloists. His solo came in the second stanza after the chorus sang, "O dandelion, yellow as gold, what do you do all night?" He had answered, "I wait and wait till the cool dew falls and my hair grows long and white." He wondered now how it had ever come about that Mrs. Fairfax had chosen him for a solo and how she had convinced him to actually do it. His mother and Beth had been sitting in the audience, six rows back, and he could still see his mother's pallid oval face with her brooding eyes gazing above his head. She had never said a word about his solo afterward. He always wondered if she'd even heard it.

That all seemed so long ago, far removed in time and space from the world today—a distant time when seventh graders sang wholesome songs and scrubbed their faces for school programs, drank milk at all three meals, and recited the Pledge of Allegiance regularly. Even the Beatles, a sensation when he was in elementary school and junior high, seemed sedate in comparison to the cacophonous metallic racket he heard today. Perry still recalled with a sick feeling the time he had walked into Troy's school a year ago and seen a fourth grader swinging his fists at a teacher and screaming obscenities that Perry had never even heard at that age. He remembered looking down at Troy, at that time a second grader, and wondering if he knew what those words meant. But he wouldn't have dreamed of asking him.

Willard had stopped talking and was looking at Perry as if waiting for an answer.

"Well . . ." Perry halted. Was Willard expecting a commitment now?

"Five-thirty Sunday nights, okay?" Willard tilted his head and pulled at his earlobe. His fingers were the size of frankfurters, Perry noticed. "The music's not hard, and we could sure use you. Besides, you're always here by then anyway, aren't you?"

So he had noticed. Perry wanted to believe he had been sitting unobserved in the back row during choir practice, as he listened and jotted notes, sometimes even getting down a few good paragraphs of text which he would later type into the computer at home. But no, somehow Willard, who always had his back to the darkened auditorium, had known he was there. Had Jewel told him—or Eldeen? Eldeen usually spent the hour during choir practice back in Fellowship Hall hearing children recite memory verses in a program called S.M.W., which stood for the Sincere Milk of the Word, Perry had learned, and of course Jewel was always playing the piano for choir practice. Maybe Joe Leonard had suggested to Willard that Perry could help out the men.

Anyway, Perry had ended up agreeing to practice with the choir for a few weeks in preparation for July Fourth and had become the fifth member of the bass section, sitting between Phil Spivey and Sid Puckett. Joe Leonard sat a few seats down from him, one of eight in the tenor section, and Perry could hear his voice above the others.

Pulling into the parking lot, Eldeen said, "Good gracious, I'm nervous as a kite! I sure hope Marvella doesn't forget in the middle of all the excitement that she's supposed to help me into my costume. Maybe I ought to speak my lines again, just for practice."

"Mama, you know that poem backwards, forwards, and sideways," said Jewel. "It'll go fine, just calm down." Jewel was wearing a white dress, one Perry had never seen before, with navy beads and earrings, and she had a red scarf draped loosely around her neck and tied in a little knot that gave the effect of a rosette on one shoulder. The choir members had all been urged to wear red, white, and blue today, and from the looks of everyone Perry saw getting out of the cars in the parking lot, the whole congregation—not just the choir—had cooperated. Perry was glad he had gone downtown to Carson's Menswear and bought a new tie for the occasion—navy and red striped. With his navy suit and white shirt, any visitors in the audience would think he was a longtime member of the Church of the Open Door.

This morning Willard had scheduled the choir for an extra rehearsal during the Sunday school hour. Eldeen sat in the front pew observing it all so that she would know when it was her turn to stand and say her poem, but they didn't have time to actually hear any of the speaking parts. Perry felt a growing dread as the hands on the large clock above the double doors swept closer to program time. Not that he was insecure about the music; it was all fairly simple. But he knew the program would be a great, corny show of sentimental patriotism, and here he would be sitting in the choir facing everybody; what if something struck him funny—something that wasn't supposed to be funny? This was going to be a test of self-control, and he wished now that he had anticipated the problem and resisted Willard's urgings to join the choir. This was exactly the kind of thing anyway—getting involved in the church—that he had intended to avoid. But it was too late now, he thought as he looked at Mayme Snyder's ponytail in the row ahead of him. How did she get it to do that? he wondered. It looked as if it were turned inside out somehow.

To open the service, the choir marched in from the side—actually marched. Willard had drilled them repeatedly, shouting, "Left, right, left, right!" until they could all stay together. Leading their procession were two youngsters in Boy Scout uniforms, carrying the American and Christian flags. As they marched in, the choir sang "The Battle Hymn of the Republic." Perry held his black choir folder down by his side, as they had been instructed, and stared at Sid Puckett's back. Behind him he could hear Phil Spivey's rumbling bass: "He is trampling out the vintage where the grapes of wrath have trod."

It had never dawned on Perry, as many times as they had sung the hymn during choir practice, that this line of text must have been the source for the title of Steinbeck's novel. He wondered now, as they started the chorus, filing into their choir rows and turning to face the audience, whether Steinbeck had had the title in mind all along or if he had wrestled with a thousand possibilities as Perry himself usually did, until one day—perhaps attending an Independence Day ceremony among migratory fruit pickers out in California—he had heard "The Battle Hymn" sung and had wept with relief and joy, crying, "I've got it! I've got it!"

He thought suddenly of a quotation of Steinbeck's he'd once read: "What we have always wanted is an *unchangeable.*" If that's what he'd really wanted, thought Perry, Steinbeck should have moved from California to Derby, South Carolina. He should have come to the Church of the Open Door. He should have embraced this religion of fundamentalist Christianity, with its tenets of the immutability of God, the inerrant inspiration of Scripture, the universal applicability of the Ten Commandments, the rigorous standards of separation and sanctification, and Jesus Christ, the same yesterday, today, forever.

Brother Hawthorne was reading a passage of Scripture now. "If my people, which are called by my name, shall humble themselves, and pray, and seek my face, and turn from their wicked ways, then will I hear from heaven, and will forgive their sin, and will heal their land." In Perry's opinion, this didn't seem like the most cheerful verse the pastor could have chosen to read on such a peppy national holiday. But everyone was nodding in agreement in the pause that followed, before Brother Hawthorne cleared his throat and began a prayer, emotional and ardent in its plea for God's hand of revival on a sinful nation.

The choir sang three numbers in a row, during which Perry had disturbing visions of Dinah lying on a large beach towel, her eyes shut, while Troy romped in the water with the children of strangers. In one song, as they sang "For He chastens whom He loves," a picture emerged in Perry's mind of Troy throwing a tantrum and Dinah lifting her hand to strike him. After each number an appreciative chorus of amens rose from the congregation.

Birdie, the organist, played "God of Our Fathers" during the offering, and Joe Leonard slipped out of the choir to get his tuba. Perry noticed for the first time that Eldeen was no longer sitting on the front row; she must have gone back to change into her costume. He had no idea what it was she was going to do. He wished more than ever that he wasn't sitting in plain view of everybody. The church was more crowded than usual this morning. People he had never seen were interspersed among the regular members. Where had they all come from? Perry wondered. He thought he saw Belinda, the bank teller, sitting near the back.

After the offering Joe Leonard played "My Country 'Tis of Thee" on his tuba, and after that Edna Hawthorne walked to the pulpit to sing a solo. It was a song Perry had never heard before, called "Christ Our Hope," which was full of requests in the imperative mode for God to "rouse feeble spirits to lift high the cross" and "lure us with the fire of Thy love from sin's darkness" and "make of our land a prospering kingdom of light." Perry still marveled that these people never let an opportunity pass to push their religion to the front. They acted like every holiday was made especially for them. He wondered what they would do with Labor Day.

Suddenly Perry noticed that Eldeen had begun mounting the steps to the platform—slowly, like a giant toddler, lifting one foot to a step, then pulling the other one up to stand a moment before tackling the next step. Brother Hawthorne jumped to her assistance before she reached the second step and stood beside her, supporting her arm the rest of the way. The auditorium fell silent. Probably from shock, Perry guessed. Eldeen was swathed in a white sheet that was probably supposed to signify a classic Greek or Roman robe of some kind but which could also be interpreted as burial swaddling. Sitting on top of her head was a small circlet of greenery. Reaching the platform, she turned to face the audience and lifted her right arm. Perry heard a dull click and saw a beam of light wobbling across the ceiling. It was only then that he realized she was holding a large lantern-type flashlight wrapped in aluminum foil. Jewel began to play the piano softly, and Eldeen began her recitation.

Perry wondered if others caught on faster than he did that she was supposed to be portraying Lady Liberty. "Give me your tired, your poor," she declaimed, "your huddled masses yearnin' to breathe free." No one laughed, no one even moved. "The wretched refuse of your teemin' shore," she continued. "Send *these*, the homeless, tempest-tost to me. I lift my lamp beside the golden door." By the time she finished the short poem, her right arm had begun sagging and the flashlight was shining into the faces of the audience. Several children put their hands over their eyes. Eldeen clicked the light off, put her hand down by her side, and stood straight, gazing out at the audience, smiling faintly like a stage actress receiving the silent awe of her admirers. Her deep, phlegmy voice still echoed in Perry's mind, and he knew that her image, a thick tubular shape wrapped in white, would be brightly imprinted in his memory for the rest of his life. He thought of the sausages wrapped in white butcher paper his mother used to bring home from the corner grocery.

Mayme Snyder and her mother, Vonda, came to the platform to sing the words to Emma Lazarus' poem Eldeen had just recited. Perry wondered if they had made up the music themselves or if it was a real song they had found in a book somewhere. It wasn't bad, really, and at least they harmonized well. Mayme's pretty inverted ponytail swished ever so slightly as she sang. He had heard that Vonda used to sing in Nashville in the sixties before she was saved. Eldeen had told him the story once of how Vonda had met her husband, Walt, at a gas station when her group, the Red Embers, had an engine fire in their tour van.

Perry could hardly concentrate during Brother Hawthorne's sermon later, though he tried to take a few notes since the title interested him: "Liberty in Bondage." The general idea was that conformity to Christ afforded freedom in ways the world could not understand; he got that much. But each time as he lowered his head to write, he kept seeing Eldeen standing with proud dignity while Vonda Snyder and her daughter, Mayme, sang. Then the picture of Eldeen as Lady Liberty would begin to recede, and, inexplicably, Perry would see an endless, depressing trail of Okies leaning into the wind, stumbling along dirt roads pulling little wagons—old black-and-white photographic images of whole families strung out in single file, with long, sad faces, scanning the parched fields beneath the hazy sky, the sun blotted out by the grit of swirling dust.

Then the Dust Bowl scene would vanish, and once again Perry would see Dinah in her purple and teal bathing suit, lying beside the lake, asleep, while Troy bobbed up and down in the water, drifting farther and farther from shore.

Chapter 16

Perry sat on the couch and stared at the telephone on the end table. It looked just like the one he remembered from the narrow, dark house where he had grown up. Not yet old enough to be labeled an antique, but give it a few years and it might be worth something. Now that he thought about it, he was quite sure it must be the one from his boyhood home in Rockford. Beth had probably taken it at some time—practical, frugal Beth, for whom fashion and design meant nothing as long as her columns of numbers worked out right. Perry reached for the telephone, then glanced at the clock. No, not yet; ten more minutes. He put his head back and closed his eyes.

He never remembered July Fourths lasting this long when he lived in Rockford. It had been a full, bombastic day with all the stops pulled out. His ears were still ringing. After the morning service, there had been a big, noisy church-wide dinner in Fellowship Hall. Everybody sat jammed together at long metal tables; there was a continual jostling as people kept getting up for seconds, returning with their paper plates soggily weighted down. Next to Perry, Bernie Paulson ate four amazing platefuls, talking all the while.

Bernie had no method of eating, Perry noticed; he just troweled in forkful after forkful of whatever he scooped up. Once Perry watched him take a single bite that consisted of five different foods—rice pudding, zucchini squash, green beans, and coleslaw, all coated with melting strawberry Jell-O. Seated between Bernie on one side and Eldeen on the other, Perry nodded his way through the dinner and wondered if he was the only one who thought that people were talking five times louder today than usual.

Brother Hawthorne's family sat across the table and several seats down from Perry. He watched Brother Hawthorne get up three times before taking his first bite of food—once to get a napkin for Esther, once to get a spoon for Levi, who dropped his on the floor, and again to bring Edna her sweater and place it around her shoulders. How anyone could be too cool on a day like today was beyond Perry's understanding, even in the air-conditioned Fellowship Hall, but he noticed quite a few women wearing shawls and sweaters.

While Bernie Paulson recounted a story about running into the tail gunner of his World War II bombing crew while he was at Six Flags with his grandchildren, Perry watched Brother Hawthorne and Edna. How could a man seemingly as intelligent as Theodore Hawthorne be content in a place like this? Perry wondered. What secrets were behind that calm, sincere exterior? Was the man just biding his time here in Derby until something bigger and better opened up? Most of all, Perry wondered if Brother Hawthorne really believed in his heart and consistently lived all the things he preached from the pulpit. Did Edna ever get exasperated with him and flounce out of the room as Dinah used to do?

He watched as one of the little Hawthorne girls, the one named Hannah, tipped over her cup of Kool-Aid. Someone appeared with a stack of paper towels from the kitchen, and Brother Hawthorne moved plates and cups as Edna sopped up the spill. Then Brother Hawthorne leaned close to Hannah and whispered something. Perry wondered what he had said. "You're going to get it when we get home"? Or "It will cost us seven dollars to take this suit to the cleaners"? Or "Don't expect anything else to drink, young lady"? Whatever it was, Hannah looked up at her father and stopped crying. She gave him a weak smile and buried her face against his sleeve for a brief moment. Then Brother Hawthorne kissed the top of her head and left the table for the fourth time.

". . . and I says, 'Your name isn't by any chance Freddie Lopez, is it?' There he was, imagine it, sitting on a bench down by the Mind Bender eating a corn dog, and I looked at him and knew in a flash who it was." Perry nodded at Bernie and watched him take an enormous bite of spaghetti, carrot and raisin salad, and lima beans.

On the other side of him, he heard Eldeen telling Nina Tillman about the blueberry bushes Jewel's husband, Bailey, had planted in the backyard four years before he died. "You don't normally think of growing blueberries here in South Carolina, but it sure can be done, that's a fact! Yes sir, ours are prosperin' up a storm!" Brother Hawthorne returned with a new cup of Kool-Aid and sat back down.

Bernie gave Perry a soft dig with his elbow. "To think we hadn't seen each other for almost fifty years and I knew him without batting an eye. 'Course, the scar all the way acrost his forehead helped some. He'd got it as a kid playing swords with his cousin—with garden spades."

". . . and they's covered right now with nets that Ginger Coker gave me that used to belong to her uncle who raised tobacco 'cause if you don't keep 'em covered the birds'll have theirselves a feast and you won't get a single berry for all your hard work!"

Brother Hawthorne was leaning forward as Myrt Silvester shouted something from across the table. He smiled and replied, then took a bite of food and leaned over to Edna. They both laughed and looked down at Levi, whose mouth was outlined with dark chocolate pudding.

". . . for a dollar a pint," Eldeen said to Nina, "and he's getting phone calls now from folks all up and down the street and all over Montroyal wanting to buy some more. Some of 'em's as big as grapes—and sweet, oh, you just never saw the likes, although we got some bushes that bears the tart kind too."

Bernie was gazing steadily at Perry. "I'm sorry, did you say something?" Perry asked.

"I asked you what you thought the odds were of meeting up with somebody you knew fifty years ago, when you hadn't laid eyes on each other in all that time and you lived in South Carolina and he lived in New Mexico and was out visiting his daughter in Atlanta and he was supposed to be there a month earlier instead of then but had gone and changed his plans at the last minute because his wife took sick and *you* were supposed to be there a week *later* but had decided to go on and take the kids a week early since one of them was playing baseball and their team had made it into the championship game that was the next week."

Perry slowly shook his head to gain time, wondering at the strange things that happened in the lives of these people and thinking how much fun it would be to try to break Bernie's sentence into its component parts, to diagram it on the blackboard as they had done every day of the school year in Miss Whitcomb's English class in tenth grade. He heard Eldeen erupt into laughter on the other side of him—deep, bass chuckles tumbling over each other. "Yes, sir, burned them muffins crisper than a cornflake!" she said, slapping the table with her large palm. "And them berries on top was blacker than coal pellets!"

"Not very likely I'd say," Perry said to Bernie.

Bernie threw his head back and laughed. "I like that! Oh, I like that a lot! 'Not very likely'—I like that. You got a way with words, Perry."

Down the table Brother Hawthorne was smiling again at something

Esther had said, and Edna was shaking with laughter, her mouth covered with her napkin. Across the table from him on the other side, Perry heard Wally Grimes telling Joe Leonard and the Chewning twins about hunting raccoons when he was a boy: "And we run that hunk of barbed wire up inside that tree holler till we run up against that 'coon, and then we twisted it around in a circle, gittin' it all tangled up in his fur, and then we yanked us out a 'coon!" Wally was half standing, acting out the feat over the top of the table using his fork to represent the barbed wire. The three boys laughed appreciatively, and Josh Chewning imitated the sound of a wounded, enraged raccoon. Archie Gowdy called from farther down the table, "Give that hongry boy some more food!" It seemed to Perry that the whole room was combustible, and, ignited by this one remark, it was soon engulfed in hot flames of laughter.

Perry felt like jumping up onto the table, stepping right on top of plates of chicken pot pie and brown-and-serve rolls, knocking over paper cups of tea and Kool-Aid, and shouting, "Stop it! Stop all this laughter and chatter! Stop it, stop it right now! Talk one at a time!"

He had been greatly relieved when the dinner was over. Everybody had helped clear the tables and fold them up out of the way; then with a great clanging of metal and more laughter, they all pulled their chairs into rows for the next activity, which had been talked about for weeks, printed in the bulletin, and announced in every service—the annual Church of the Open Door Needlework Auction. Half of the proceeds went to the Lena Lansford Home for Girls over in Mount Chesney, South Carolina, and the other half went into the Missions fund.

Willard Scoggins was the auctioneer, though it was obvious to Perry that Willard had never attended a real auction. The event moved along without haste, with Willard holding up every article, reading aloud the printed tag attached to each one, and then making some general, unfocused remark such as "Now isn't that nice?" or "This would look real pretty in somebody's house." The bidding would then start, with a great deal of friendly teasing back and forth, and finally Willard would pound his fist on top of the piano and say something like, "Well then, I guess that's it. Come on up here and pay your money, Earl."

Perry was sitting in the second row, close enough to see the detail of the needlework. The variety and beauty surprised him. He had imagined that the auction would consist of rough, slapdash pieces. He wasn't prepared for Birdie's pink appliqued place mats with a white border of something called "tatting" or for Dottie Puckett's pale yellow crocheted baby's blanket with the tiny matching sweater. Edna Hawthorne had made and framed a cross-stitched sampler in bold primary colors, evidently for a child's room, with a verse stitched below the alphabet: "Thy word is a lamp unto my feet, and a light unto my path." Small pictures of children's toys formed the border of the sampler—a ball, a pail and shovel, a toy soldier, a rocking horse. Brother Hawthorne bid heavily on this one and finally got it after some good-natured rivalry with Harvey Gill. Little Hannah Hawthorne clapped her hands with delight when her father went forward to pay for it. Perry wondered if Edna had already promised Hannah that the picture would be hung in her bedroom.

It seemed that every woman in the church had made something. Even Jewel contributed a set of seven embroidered dish towels, with a day of the week and a picture of some kind of kitchen-related item handstitched on each one. Perry saw that on the one for Thursday was sewn a picture of a basket of produce and Saturday's held a mixing bowl and spoon. Perry could have predicted what picture would be on the Sunday towel, and he was right: a large black Bible with a red cross stitched on its cover. Willard Scoggins himself bid on Jewel's dish towels and in the end outbid Martha Joy Darrow. Perry couldn't help wondering what Willard would want with seven embroidered kitchen towels.

When Willard held up the last item in the auction, Perry recognized it immediately as Eldeen's. It was a set of pillowcases. Willard read the card aloud: "Two pillowcases, all cotton, washed and pressed but not starched of course. Embroidered by Eldeen P. Rafferty. Get ready to count sheep. These woolly lambs will make you sleep good. Ha ha." Perry hadn't realized before this that the women must have written their own descriptions on the cards.

No one spoke for a moment as everybody studied the light blue pillowcases. The lambs frisking about in various poses on a green hillside were stitched in bright pinks and reds. The pattern must have slipped as Eldeen was ironing it onto one of the pillowcases because the hill was slanted sideways and the colorful little lambs appeared to be toppling headlong over it.

"Five dollars!" Harvey Gill called out. Brother Hawthorne followed swiftly with "Six dollars!" Bernie Paulson went up to seven, and Marjorie Eckles went to seven-fifty. Harvey bid again and so did Marjorie. Perry could see Willard getting ready to pound his fist during the long pause that followed Bernie Paulson's bid of nine dollars. Perry glanced behind him, where Eldeen was sitting, smiling with pleasure. He imagined her sitting in her living room amid the bright clutter of ceramic owls, afghans, and suncatchers. He saw her adjusting the radio dial, then bending over her pillowcases. He saw her lips moving as she prayed for Mr. Hammond and Belinda and Flo between innings of the Braves games, and he saw her large, rough hands slowly pushing the needle in and out, painstakingly forming the outline of a fuchsia lamb.

"Thirty dollars!" He must have shouted it, from the looks on the faces that turned to stare at him.

He heard Eldeen gasp behind him and felt her hand on his shoulder. "Why, Perry Warren, do you know what you just said? You musta meant thirteen, but even that's way high for just a set of pillowcases! Bless your heart, biddin' on my embroidery like that."

Willard Scoggins had a look of confusion on his face. He stepped closer and spoke in a hushed whisper over the front row. "Did you say thirty or thirteen, Perry?"

From a steady hum of conversation and laughter, Fellowship Hall suddenly fell silent. Even the Chewnings' new baby, who had been crying off and on all during the whole auction, was quiet. All eyes were turned on Perry. It was the kind of moment he had always feared. Something from one of his bad dreams started taking shape in his mind. He was coming out into a brilliantly illuminated circus arena; someone was holding out a flaming sword to him as the ringmaster's sonorous voice reverberated throughout the big top: "And now, ladies and gentlemen, Perry Warren, filling in for Farouk the Fire-Eater, who has taken ill." With a sense of foreboding he remembered all his old fears of standing up suddenly to babble incoherently in the midst of large audiences.

Perry blinked several times and forced himself to look hard at the blue pillowcases Willard still held aloft. You're here, he reminded himself, here in Fellowship Hall at the Church of the Open Door in Derby, South Carolina. Stop thinking stupid thoughts.

And it worked. After a brief moment, he swallowed and said evenly, "Thirty—I said thirty dollars." He was already rising from his chair and reaching for his wallet. For an instant he worried that he might not have thirty dollars in cash. What if he didn't? Would Eldeen unsnap her purse, dig around inside a zippered pocket, and produce the difference? But he did. As he paid his money, he thought about the girls at the Lena Lansford Home. He wasn't sure why they lived there—if they were incorrigibles or orphans or maybe even unwed mothers. It sounded like a good cause, though, and, besides, he was now the possessor of a set of unique handmade pillowcases.

The day had gone on and on. There had been a two-hour break

after the auction, during which people went home to change clothes and take a brief rest if they wanted to. Then at five o'clock they met again for an informal evening service in Fellowship Hall. Willard Scoggins sang "God Bless America," and the choir gathered around the piano and sang "The Church in the Wildwood," after which Brother Hawthorne preached a short sermon entitled "Our Spiritual Heritage" and Fern Tucker, who had once worked as an announcer on the Christian radio station up in Charlotte, told a story about a weak young soldier named Jimmy during the Civil War who fell asleep on patrol and was ordered to be whipped, but was spared by the mercy of a stronger soldier who offered to take the lashes in Jimmy's place.

Eldeen groaned faintly and bowed her head as Fern concluded the story with a Bible verse, dramatically delivered: "Who his own self bare our sins in his own body on the tree, that we, being dead to sins, should live unto righteousness: by whose stripes ye were healed." Perry had never heard of soldiers in the Civil War being *beaten* for failing in a duty; surely the story wasn't based on fact. Whoever wrote stories like that should be ashamed, he thought—giving all these people a false view of history just to provide a sentimental allegorical vehicle for a Bible verse. But then, maybe it was based on truth after all; duty had been highly revered in earlier times. He would have to look it up sometime.

Following the service, there had been a softball game in the open field behind the church. The teams consisted of all ages of boys and girls, men and women. Those who didn't want to play carried out folding chairs and sat in the shade under the stand of sweet gum trees along the side of the property bordering the road. When the sides were divided up and Brother Hawthorne's team was short by one player, Eldeen stood up waving her orange straw hat, her enormous culottes ballooning around her calves, and cried out, "Here, get Perry to play! He'll make it come out even!" So Perry had played and had made a run in the second inning and again in the fifth, which Eldeen had loudly pointed out as significant. "See, the preacher's team beat Willard's by *two* runs, and how many did you make? Yes, sir, you made the difference, Perry! You made a plain old ordinary team into a winnin' team!"

There had been hot dogs, lemonade, and homemade ice cream back inside Fellowship Hall at eight o'clock, and at nine-thirty everyone drove over to the stadium at Derby High for the community fireworks display, which had lasted ten whole minutes. With his eyes closed now, Perry could still see the vivid bursts of color exploding against the dark sky. His favorite had been a shower of gold droplets twinkling like topaz as they spread symmetrically over the sky. "It looks like little drizzlets of honey!" Eldeen had exclaimed. And later, during the finale, she had cried, "The whole sky's on fire!"

Perry opened his eyes and looked again at Beth's old black telephone. He checked the clock again. It was three minutes after ten o'clock. In Rockford it would be three minutes after nine. He was three minutes late for his weekly call.

As he dialed the number, he tried to think of things to say if Dinah answered the phone this time as she had last week. He had made a fool of himself stuttering and halting and finally asking if he could speak to Troy.

"Don't you even wonder how I'm doing?" Dinah had asked, her voice low and tense. And Perry had tripped over his words assuring her that yes, he did, and how was she anyway and how were things going and was it hot there and . . . then he thought he heard a man's voice in the background, and he had stopped cold. Wait a minute, Dinah had said, let me turn the TV down, and then Troy had picked up the phone when she set it down, and Dinah never had come back to answer his questions.

The rotary dial spun off the last number, and Perry heard a small voice before the second ring. "Dad, is that you? How come you're late?"

Chapter 17

The sound of Troy's voice over the telephone never failed to fascinate Perry. My son, he always thought, this is *my son* I'm talking to. At the first sound of his voice each week, Perry started dreading the end of the conversation, and at each good-bye he began looking forward to the next week's call.

"I've had a *full* July Fourth, how about you?" Perry said. "Your old dad played softball today."

The whole idea of calling Troy every week had come up two months ago, on Mother's Day, when Perry had taken Eldeen, Jewel, and Joe Leonard to the Purple Calliope after church.

"To get to come here two times in only two months is more than a body deserves," Eldeen had said to Perry as the waiter seated them. Then to the waiter she had said, "*He*"—pointing at Perry—"he brought us here back in March for my daughter's birthday, that one there"—pointing at Jewel—"right after that big snowstorm we had. We had to put it off for a few days till everybody could get situated again, but we finally got to come, and now here he is treatin' us *again*." Eldeen wrinkled her face as if preparing to laugh but didn't. "I guess he's doin' like the Bible says and taking care of the widows and the orphans!" She grinned up at the waiter, who cocked his head and clasped his hands under his chin, looking slightly dazed as if wondering whether this woman was using her normal voice or just playing a joke on him.

Jewel opened the menu and lowered her head to study it. Joe Leonard frowned at his plate as if trying to figure out if he really qualified as an orphan. Soft organ music was playing over the intercom.

Perry watched the waiter fill their water glasses. The man held the pitcher like a woman, with his pinkie extended and daintily curved. All his movements were close to the body, and as he told them about the specials of the day, he pursed his lips between sentences. He wore a small diamond earring in one ear, and the nametag on the lapel of his short purple waiter's jacket read STANLEY AT YOUR SERVICE. He had the kind of looks that could go either way; without the mannerisms, he could be the sensitive, reticent artist-type, the lover of painting and poetry, but with a solid core of manliness—actually, the kind of man Perry fancied himself to be. As it was, Stanley looked—well, as Dinah used to say, more like one of the cheerleaders instead of the quarterback. This should be interesting, thought Perry: Fundamentalist Christians Confront Stereotypical Homosexual. He saw Joe Leonard watching Stanley but couldn't read the boy's expression.

"Those people preach love," Cal had told him months ago, in one of his phone briefs before Perry had even moved to Derby, "but what they're really good at is *hate*. You wait and see if I'm not right. You have to watch for it because they try to decoy you with all their pious talk and little acts of kindness, but underneath it all they've got a deep, dark well of meanness."

The way Cal remembered it, they hated anybody who didn't do things their way—"especially anybody that looks like they're making a lot of money and having a good time while doing it. And I'm not just talking about a little mild distaste either; I'm talking about out-and-out hatred. Why, if somebody like Michael Jackson walked into one of their church services, he'd never know what hit him." And, according to Cal, they not only hated individuals, like the Kennedys or Madonna, they hated whole groups in general—all liberal Democrats, the N.O.W., the A.C.L.U., the N.A.A.C.P., and most of all, homosexuals.

Stanley had left the table, Perry noticed, and the others were reading over their menus. Eldeen was reading hers aloud. "'Beef brisket marinated in our own special herbal sauce.' Now that *might* be good, but then you never know. They's all kinds of herbs in the world, and some of 'em's good and some of 'em's not fit for hound dogs to eat, much less human beings."

It was at that moment that Perry noticed the family seated at a table over by the calliope—he guessed that's what the big purple hulk was supposed to be. It had a yellowed keyboard and steam whistles of varying sizes rising from the back. The cabinet was painted with purple gloss, although surely it hadn't come that way originally. Perry wondered if paint stores kept that shade of grape-purple in stock or if it had to be custom-ordered. He could imagine the paint mixers at the paint plant joking over the order and wondering who in the world would want such a garish shade of paint and why.

Perry was facing the calliope, and from his side of the table, right between Eldeen's and Jewel's faces, he had a straight view of a family—or at least that's what he assumed they were at first—sitting at a table across the room. There were three of them—a man, woman, and child. The first thing that caught his attention was the woman, who was seated with her back to Perry. She had long, caramel-gold hair that swayed when she moved her head—hair exactly like Dinah's before the awful haircut. The man had blond hair too and lean, chiseled features like a California surfer; he sat across from the woman and couldn't keep his eyes off her it seemed. The boy, probably only five or six years old, was partly hidden from Perry's view.

As he pretended to study the menu, Perry kept glancing toward the woman. Once she bent forward and appeared to be writing or drawing something on the boy's paper place mat while both the man and boy watched her hands with fascination. Perry wished she would turn around so he could see her face. Maybe he could feign interest in the calliope, walk all the way around it for a closer look, and then peer over the brass pipes at the woman. He was chagrined to see a waiter pick up the woman's plate; they must be almost ready to leave.

He was beginning to realize that the man and woman probably weren't married. They didn't act married. When she spoke, the man fixed his eyes on her face. He touched her hand, he smiled, once he reached his hand forward toward her face. He had that openly devoted, attentive behavior not common among husbands. Besides that, they talked a lot more than most married couples. Perry shifted his gaze to a couple seated to his right—late forties maybe; they were both eating, silently lost in the buttering of rolls and cutting of meat. The husband and wife of a family over by the window were talking but not to each other; the woman was wrangling with a toddler, and the man was pointing to the menu, apparently negotiating orders with the two older children.

He looked back to the woman with the long hair. She reached down to pick up something from the floor, and he watched her hair swing out like a shining silk fan. The boy must be hers from a previous marriage, Perry decided. The man seemed to take very little notice of the boy, which wasn't a smart move in Perry's opinion. If the man was serious about wooing the mother, he'd better pay attention to the kid; that seemed only logical. A dark thought suddenly began to take form in Perry's mind—was Dinah going out to dinner with other men? He looked back at his menu and breathed in sharply. Glancing up, he caught Jewel's eyes on him, perplexed. She turned around quickly to look behind her, then dropped her gaze to her lap, as if she understood and was sorry for him.

He realized that Jewel and Joe Leonard must have already given their orders to Stanley, and now Eldeen was giving hers. "But give me the dressing separate in a little cup or else bring me the whole bottle if you don't mind 'cause I like to dribble it on a little at a time instead of all of it at once. Last time the lettuce got all limp at the bottom from settin' in a puddle of dressing." Stanley stood rigid and unblinking, his pen poised in midair as Eldeen continued. She was fingering the folds of the large pink gauzy scarf arranged around her shoulders; it was anchored with a huge rhinestone peacock that, she had explained to Perry, had been a gift from her secret pal at church.

"And when I said white meat on that chicken, that includes wings. Fact is, I like wings more'n I do the breast meat of chicken, although there's not as much meat on them, of course. So maybe you could bring me a breast *and* a wing or two and that'd be just fine—I just wanted to make sure that was clear 'cause some folks don't consider wings white meat even though it's right up there beside the chicken's breast." She tucked one hand up close to her side to signify a chicken's wing and flapped it just slightly. Stanley's puckered lips relaxed for the briefest moment into a small, tight smile, and he wrote something on his order pad with a flourish.

"There, I guess that's it for me," Eldeen said, closing the menu firmly and handing it to Stanley. "I don't believe you were here last time we came, but you're doing a real good job, so don't be nervous." She patted his hand lightly. Stanley looked bewildered and said nothing. He moved nimbly around the table to Perry and stood beside him, his legs close together, the toes of his feet pointing in opposite directions. Perry had seen ballerinas stand that way.

Perry ordered quickly and then noticed with disappointment that the woman with the long hair was getting up to leave. The man was standing too, reaching inside his back pocket and taking out his billfold. The little boy was over by the gum machine next to the cash register. Why it was so important for him to see the woman's face Perry couldn't say, but he couldn't stop to think about it now. Even while he scoffed at himself—"You idiot, get control of yourself, it's not Dinah"—he heard another voice retorting, "Lighten up, I know it's not, but I just want to *look*, for Pete's sake," and he knew he couldn't stop what he was about to do.

"Excuse me," Perry said, standing suddenly. "I'll be right back." The men's room was off a little hallway right behind the cash register. He strode to it briskly. As he pushed open the door, he turned and looked back at the woman. She was pointing to the antique musical instruments displayed on the wall behind the cashier, and at first Perry thought she was pointing straight at him. "See that?" she said to the boy. "It's a lyre."

If he had been a different kind of person, it would have been a good moment for a witty bit of playacting. "I beg your pardon," he could have said with a broad, comical sweep of the arm, letting go of the restroom door and stepping toward her. "I'm *not* a liar, and I highly resent being slandered by a total stranger. I demand an apology." But he didn't do it, of course.

As he turned the faucet on full force inside the rest room, he closed his eyes and saw the woman's wide-set eyes, her wide smile, her high, white forehead—none of it at all like Dinah, but still pretty in its own way. He also heard Brother Hawthorne's fervent reading during to-day's Mother's Day sermon of a quotation by a seventeenth-century theologian named Jeremy Taylor: "A good wife is Heaven's last best gift to man—his angel of graces, his gem of virtues; her smile, his brightest day; her kiss, the guardian of his innocence; her arms, the pale of his safety. . . ." As he watched the water gushing from the faucet, he noticed how easy it was to imagine that the water was flowing in the opposite direction, being drawn upward from the drain back into the faucet by a powerful suction.

Another man entered the rest room, and Perry quickly rinsed his hands and turned off the faucet. He hit the knob of the dryer and stood for a moment kneading his hands beneath the warm current of air. It occurred to him again, as it often had during recent months, what pitiful creatures men were—not humankind in general, but males.

As he walked back toward the table, he scanned the faces of all the men he saw. They were pathetic in a way. Sitting there with their muscles and their deep voices and their powers of intellect and their male hormones; eating with male appetites and then going home to belch on the sofa and watch boxing and baseball on television and then getting up tomorrow to charge into the workplace and earn a living. All their posturing and swaggering and windy boasts—all of it at the mercy of women. How funny, how very, very funny—none of it was worth a plug nickel without the attention of a woman. He saw a man just exiting the restaurant behind his wife, trying to fit his wallet back into his hip pocket; he was overweight and the seat of his trousers looked uncomfortably snug. For some reason Perry felt a wave of pity sweep over him at the sight.

He arrived back at the table, and as he pulled out his chair to sit down, he saw Stanley approaching with their salad plates, taking small, light steps. He took note of Stanley's fair, rosy cheeks and the damp curls around the curve of his pink ears. Perry felt himself recoil and immediately rebuked himself. He was supposed to be the kindhearted social libertarian, wasn't he? He had studied homosexuality in depth in one of his graduate courses, had even written a paper on it. These other people—the hatemongers at the Church of the Open Door—were supposed to be the ones repulsed by someone like Stanley. Maybe, he told himself, Stanley should be praised for his independence from women. Then again, maybe Stanley was the ultimate example of dependence on women.

"Well, looka here," said Eldeen, "both our men is arriving back at the very same time!" She beamed up at Stanley as he set the plates around, and while he was refilling their glasses, she said, "Joe Leonard can say the blessing for us today if it's all right with you, Perry." Stanley's eyes darted around the table, and he pivoted swiftly and left.

It was right after Joe Leonard's prayer, during which he thanked God for this special day and for his mother and grandmother, along with the food, that Eldeen attacked the subject of Troy. Perry wondered if Jewel had said something while he was in the rest room about his interest in the people at the other table or if Eldeen had just come up with the idea by herself.

Ordinarily Perry would have deflected any discussion about his personal life. Shrugs, nods of the head, faraway looks, and silence— they were all useful in discouraging further questions. Most people got the hint easily. But not Eldeen. She never tiptoed toward a subject anyway; and once she lunged in, she apparently had no intention of climbing out.

"When was the last time you talked to your little boy, Perry?" she said abruptly, spearing a cucumber. Then she locked her attention on his eyes as sternly as a schoolteacher on a troublemaker in the back row.

No one spoke as Perry moved his salad greens around with his fork for a while. He could feel Eldeen still looking at him. He shrugged a little and stabbed at a cherry tomato but didn't eat it. He rolled the tomato around in the dressing for a few moments, then sighed. "Oh, I guess—let's see, it was . . . in February I guess."

"You mean before or after you came to live at Beth's?" The cucumber must have been very fresh, for Perry could hear the crisp crunching as Eldeen chewed it.

"Well, before. It was, I mean I . . . well, I said good-bye, you know, before I left."

Eldeen grunted, then poured some white dressing onto her salad. Perry quickly put the cherry tomato into his mouth and hoped she was finished. But she picked her fork back up and waved it at him. Her thick eyebrows bristled as she scowled at him.

"Do you mean to sit there and tell us you haven't heard the sound of your own child's voice for all this time? That's a crime! I tell you, it's a crime!" Jewel reached over and placed her hand on Eldeen's lap.

"Mama, you're attracting attention," she said softly.

Eldeen snorted. "Well, somebody sure *needs* to attract attention to this sad, sad situation," she said. "Here sits a man who's not even allowed to talk to his own flesh and blood! His own little boy! Why won't she let you talk to him?" she asked, jabbing her fork into her bowl. Perry remembered seeing thin, stooped men along highways poking at pieces of litter that same way. Part of him tried to focus on what Eldeen was saying, and another part wondered if those men ever came up with something valuable on the nails at the ends of their sticks—maybe a gift certificate or a twenty-dollar bill.

"She must be a hard-hearted woman not to let you speak to your boy, that's as much *yours* as *hers*! 'Course I know I don't know the whole story, and I shouldn't be sittin' here passin' judgment, but it just riles me, that's all. Does *she* always answer the telephone when you call?" Eldeen asked.

"Well . . . yes—yes, she does," said Perry. How could he admit that he had called her only three times since he'd been in Derby? And all three times he had broken out in a sweat and been unable to utter a word when he had heard her voice. And all three times she had repeated, "Who is this? What do you want? Who is this?" before she finally hung up.

"That rankles me good," said Eldeen, chewing energetically. "That's not fair—not one bit fair."

Jewel spoke up. "Isn't there an agreement on paper about that? You could ask your lawyer, couldn't you?"

All three of them stared at him, waiting for his answer. Joe Leonard picked up a package of Ritz crackers and opened them without ever taking his eyes off Perry.

There didn't seem to be any way out of this. Perry set his fork down and looked up at the ceiling. A wavery organ rendition of "Moon River" was playing in the background. "There's no written agreement," he said, shrugging, "because I never got a lawyer."

"Well, that still doesn't give her any right to . . ." began Eldeen, but Perry interrupted.

". . . and it's not that she won't *let* me talk to him," he said. He realized how weak and spineless this was going to sound. "I just . . . well, I was afraid that . . . no, not really afraid, but just . . . well, it's been hard to know what to do. I thought maybe it would be better for them if I . . . oh, it's too much of a mess to explain." He stopped and picked his fork back up and stared at it. He couldn't force himself to look them in the eye.

"You thought it would be easier to just walk away than to fight, didn't you?" Jewel spoke quietly, and when he lifted his head, he marveled again at the piercing blueness of her eyes.

"Well, go home today and *call* her," Eldeen demanded. "And tell her plain out that you want to talk to your little boy—what's his name?"

"Troy."

"Tell her you want to talk to Troy—and not just for today but regular. Set it up! Set it up today."

Perry nodded. "I should. I really should."

"You *want* to, don't you?" asked Jewel, and he nodded again.

"Then do it!" said Eldeen, pouring the rest of the dressing onto her salad. "Pick up the telephone and call her and tell her. Joe Leonard here doesn't have a daddy, bless his heart, but your little boy does and he needs to know it." They all grew quiet as Stanley returned with their entrees.

Afterward Perry couldn't say how it had happened, but before they left the Purple Calliope, he had told Jewel, Eldeen, and Joe Leonard things about himself that he had almost forgotten. He wasn't sure if it was Jewel's low, musical voice and easy manner or Joe Leonard's silent, sympathetic interest or Eldeen's frank questions; anyway, it all worked together to loosen his tongue. Dinah would have been amazed if she could have heard him—he was sure of it. She would think he'd been on some kind of mind-altering drugs. Maybe the muted organ music and the sibilant conversation of the other diners had something to do with it. Maybe even Stanley with his delicate glidings around the table somehow diverted his attention, eventually dulling his natural wariness and loosening his reserve.

Whatever it was, Perry was astonished to hear himself talking about his last memory of his father—the dark night he had awakened, terrified, and stood at the top of the staircase looking down at the front door standing wide open in the middle of January, his father sprawled across the threshold and his mother sobbing on the floor in the hallway, surrounded by shattered crystal figurines—her prized collection swept from the shelf and lying like chipped ice on the hardwood floor. He could still see the tiny glass antlers of the deer lying on the bottom step as he crept down.

He told them about his mother's remoteness, her tendency to forget important dates and lose track of a conversation. He even told about her failing to show up for his high school graduation. She had been taking a pie out of the oven when he left home that night—lost as always in her private world of cooking—but she had stopped to watch him walk across the kitchen in his cap and gown. She had called after him, distractedly, promising to follow shortly. But Beth had come to the ceremony alone, looking distressed and apologetic, and later they discovered that their mother had taken off walking toward the civic auditorium and had waited outside on a bench for over an hour, even though Perry had told her repeatedly that the graduation ceremony was being held in the school auditorium.

"Well, now, that there's a sad story," said Eldeen, shaking her head slowly. "People like that can be real funny sometimes—like a uncle of mine that kept wandering out in the middle of the highway totin' a big bag of dirty clothes and then spreadin' them all out on the median, thinking he was at the Wash-a-teria—but then they can also be a real heartache and trial—like when they don't even come see their own son get his diploma." She reached over and patted Perry's shoulder.

Perry thought later that maybe this was exactly the kind of thing he had always dreaded—forgetting himself and blathering on and on. But whenever he thought about it in months to come, he felt no humiliation, only a sense of wonder that such a thing had actually happened. He realized, of course, that this was due to the collective compassion of his three listeners. If any one of them had glanced over at another one with the faintest flicker of disbelief or amusement, it would have ended the whole thing.

Perry looked around the restaurant and noticed all of a sudden that most of the other diners had left. He felt his face flush as he realized how talkative he'd been and how much he had revealed of himself. Maybe he ought to lighten the mood now by saying something flippant like, "Okay, everybody, on the count of three, say, 'Poor, poor Perry.' All right, here we go—one, two, three. . . ." But Stanley was there with the check now, and Eldeen was assuring him that no, they didn't want *or need* dessert because Jewel had just made a blueberry cobbler yesterday and they could heat that up at home and put a little Cool Whip on top of it.

Then she pinched the cuff of Stanley's purple jacket, tugged at it actually, and said, "Stanley, I'd like to invite you to come to our church. It's over close to Montroyal—the Church of the Open Door, it's called. You've probably passed right by it dozens of times, 'specially if you do your grocery shopping at Thrifty Mart. It'd please us more'n we could tell you if you'd come visit." She gave his hand a teasing swat. "And if you came tonight, we'd even invite you over to our house for some of that cobbler I was telling you about."

Stanley looked at her for a long time and then bent forward in a rapid bow. "That's nice of you, ma'am," he said, "but I'm afraid I won't be able to make it." He laced his long, smooth fingers together in front of him and took a small, neat step backward.

As he turned to leave, Eldeen opened her purse and extracted a packet of leaflets secured by a rubber band. "Here, wait a minute, Stanley!" she called. "I got something for you to read. This here'll tell you some mighty important things if you'll just take a minute to read it after you finish up here at your job." She handed him a tract with a question printed in bold red on the front: "WHERE WILL YOU SPEND ETERNITY?" Stanley took it and fled toward the kitchen.

Getting into the car a few minutes later, Eldeen had gazed sorrowfully at the front door of the Purple Calliope. "I need to put that young man on my prayer list," she said. "I can just tell from watching him that Satan's got him under his foot and is stomping down real hard. Real, real hard. Inside, he's a sad, sad man." She clucked her tongue loudly and steadily, like a metronome. "I sure want him to see how much Jesus loves him."

Chapter 18

As it turned out, though, Perry had decided to approach Dinah first by means of a letter instead of by telephone. He knew it was cowardly. He knew that when Dinah read the letter, she would say to herself, or maybe even out loud, something like "That's right, Perry, put it all down on paper like the chicken you are and then go back and stick your head in your shell." It would never occur to her that the wording was all wrong.

All his life Perry had taken refuge in writing; if some communication couldn't be ignored, he would write it rather than tell it face to face or even over the telephone. Early in his marriage, however, he had found it easy to talk—or at least he thought he was talking, although Dinah had informed him two years ago that he had never been able to look her in the eye and talk, *really* talk. What was it, though, he wondered, when he told her he didn't like the way her mother tried to organize everybody else's life, for instance, or the time he described to her the passionate altercation he had witnessed between a Lithuanian man and his daughter's Armenian boyfriend or when he shared with her Cal's troubles with his children? What was it if it wasn't talking? He wondered if she would have called it *talking* had she heard him in the Purple Calliope, divulging all his family secrets.

After several days of deliberation and two rough drafts, he had simply written, finally, that he would like to call Troy every week, and he had decided that a good time might be at nine o'clock every Sunday night, which would be ten o'clock here in Derby; at least that might be a good time now that school was almost out, and then when it started again in September, they could reconsider if she thought it was too late. He had said that his first call would be in two weeks, on May 30, and if she had any questions or comments she could write back before then. He had closed it with "Sincerely" and neatly signed his first name. She hadn't written back, of course, as he knew she wouldn't, but he had called anyway on May 30, Troy had answered, and so the weekly phone calls had started.

Tonight's call was the sixth one.

"Did you get any hits?" Troy asked after Perry told him about the softball game that day.

"Sure did," said Perry. "Even scored two runs."

"We're going to see fireworks here," Troy said, "soon as I hang up."

Perry couldn't tell if that was a hint to cut the phone call short or not.

"We just got back from seeing some here," Perry said, "but yours will probably be bigger."

"Did somebody go with you?"

"Oh, just the people at the church and the next-door neighbors— nobody in particular, really."

"Do those people have any boys?"

"Who?"

"Those neighbors next door."

"Well, yes, they have a boy about—let's see, he's a little more than six years older than you. And that reminds me of something. Doesn't somebody have a birthday next month?"

"Are you coming home for my party?" It was the first time Troy had mentioned such a possibility. Perry had begun to wonder if the boy had even missed him. Their talks had been so—surface, really, just polite questions about everyday things going on and brief, unembellished answers.

"Well, I . . . I'm still working down here in South Carolina, you know, and . . ."

"Can't you take a vacation? It's summer." There was a brittle edge to Troy's voice, an upward inflection at the ends of words—the same tone he used to adopt right before throwing a fit.

It sounded so simple. To Troy it was just a matter of getting in the car and driving. He couldn't begin to comprehend all the complexities of the situation—the awkwardness of seeing Dinah, and of course *that* couldn't be avoided if he went to see Troy; the weight of a thousand memories that would fall on him anywhere he turned; all the hurts from childhood hanging over Rockford like a heavy cloud; the regrets, the self-loathing, every tongue-tied blunder he'd ever made; even the sight of Troy and the immense burden of knowing that he, the boy's own father, hadn't been able to hold his child's world intact.

"But I'll call you and find out all about your party—and I'll send you a present, of course." Perry's words rushed together. "Is there anything special you're wanting? I can start looking now and make sure it's the best one I can find, and I'll have it all wrapped up and mailed in plenty of time—even if it takes a moving van to get it there, and . . . Troy? Are you still there?"

"Yes."

"How about it? Any ideas for a birthday gift?"

"No."

Neither of them spoke for a few moments. Perry heard a sound in the background like dishes clinking against one another.

"Sounds like you and Mom are getting ready to eat something."

"No. Mom's unloading the dishwasher is all." Troy's tone was flat now. Maybe he wasn't sure how to go about throwing a fit over the telephone—or maybe he really was growing out of his tantrums finally.

"Did you go swimming today?" Perry asked.

"No, it rained."

"No fishing either?"

"No, I said it rained. I can't find my pole anyhow." He was back to whining now.

"It's in the garage, remember, on the wall over by the lawn mower. It's lying across those two big nails." Silence. "Has it stopped now?"

"What?"

"The rain."

"Yeah."

Perry was stalling now. He knew the conversation was over.

"Is . . . is your mother all right? Is she working much?"

"Uh-huh."

"Are you still going over to Grandma's when Mom is working?"

"Yes." Troy sighed, and Perry wondered if he was impatient to get to the fireworks or if he was just bored with talking—or maybe disgusted with the poor excuse of a father life had furnished him with, a father who played softball and went to fireworks displays with other people now, a father who wasn't home to help him find his fishing pole, who wouldn't even come to his birthday party.

They hung up a few minutes later, after Perry had made a feeble effort to describe the Derby Independence Parade that had been held downtown the day before. Troy showed no interest, though, and at one point Perry even suspected him of setting the receiver down and leaving, but when he said, "Troy?" the boy had mumbled, "What?" Maybe he was reading a book or playing with his Game Boy. When Perry had promised to call again next week, Troy had said, "Okay" and hung up abruptly.

Perry placed the heavy black receiver back in its cradle and then let himself flop back onto the couch. Maybe he would just sleep here all night; he didn't feel like tackling the details of bedtime. He focused his eyes on one corner of the ceiling, then slowly traced the perimeter of the room. Four walls—a small room probably only twelve by fifteen. It needed painting; the nailheads on the studs were beginning to show through. What had gone on inside these four walls over the years? Perry wished he knew. He wished he knew if a family had lived here and been happy. It wouldn't surprise him to find out it had always been inhabited by sullen bachelors, tight-lipped spinsters, childless couples. He couldn't imagine a child in these cheerless rooms, banging doors and tumbling on the floor.

He looked around. Beth had no decor as such. It was not the kind of living room that would be written up in *House Beautiful*. Amid the brown throw rugs, black-and-white photographs, tan drapes, and cheap end tables, the couch provided the only splash of color. Where had Beth ever found such a hideous plaid anyway—lime green, junk-yard rust, Halloween orange, and mustard yellow? It reminded Perry of a combination of nasty things—stagnant ponds, spoiled food left in refrigerators, infectious diseases, noxious weeds.

He ran his hand across the stiff, rough fabric and wondered what kind of person would go to a furniture showroom and actually choose this couch. Knowing Beth, he was certain that she had bought it through the want ads. Maybe it was among the household goods being sold after a death, or maybe a divorce. Perhaps it had even been the source of a long-running argument between the husband, who had bought the couch for his bachelor pad before his marriage and was attached to it, and his wife, who loathed the sight of it and nagged him to haul it out to the curb. Maybe she had finally declared an ultimatum: either the couch goes or I do. Maybe in the nanosecond during which the husband was considering how to phrase his reply, she had exploded: "Okay, if that's the way you want it, buster, you got it!" If only women weren't so quick to take offense, so ready to leap to conclusions. Of course, the man should have had better taste in the beginning and not chosen such an unsightly plaid. Perry shook his head to clear his mind.

A tall bookcase of unfinished wood stood against the wall by the door. Perry had already looked through the books and even read parts of two or three. One night he had browsed for several hours through a copy of the *Guinness Book of World Records,* filled with disbelief that somebody had thought of collecting all that remarkable data—the highest price paid for a lock of hair, the largest number of piglets born in a single litter, the greatest distance for spitting a watermelon seed, the longest kiss in a movie—and then not only had *thought* of it but had gone to all the trouble to actually *do* it. The thought had come to Perry that many people would consider the book he was writing now—the one about the church here in Derby—to be just as pointless as this one. Or worse, what if they considered it *cute?* After all, what was the difference, really, between recording that the Sparkies Sunday school class had collected fourteen dollars and thirty-two cents to send to a Navajo mission and listing Snowball as the oldest caged guinea pig?

And on the bottom shelf of Beth's books, he had come across a Bible a week after moving in; he had been taking it to church ever since. It still surprised him that Beth had kept a Bible. Inside the front cover was an inscription written with a dark blue fountain pen that had bled through to the other side of the tissue-thin paper. *To Catherine from Mother and Daddy,* it read, and underneath, the date *September 15, 1939.*

He had figured it up immediately. The Bible would have been a gift to his mother from her parents on her sixteenth birthday. It appeared never to have been used. He tried to picture his mother reading a Bible but couldn't. He couldn't picture her reading anything for that matter. Though he had often seen her sitting in her green armchair with a book or magazine open in her lap, her eyes had always been staring through the page or at the printed design on her dress or at the armrest covers on the chair; she had rarely turned a page. Only once could Perry recall his mother reading him a story, when he had dragged out an enormous book of illustrated fairy tales. He must have been only four or five, and he remembered sitting in her lap. He didn't remember the story itself, though, only the traumatic effect of her sudden and violent embrace as she broke into sobs halfway through it. Then she had released him abruptly, looking at him as if she wasn't sure who he was, and stood up; he had almost hit his head on the hardwood floor when he toppled off her lap.

His eyes traveled over Beth's shelves of books. He had never known his sister's interests were so varied. There were books about orchids, Etruscan art, the U.S. Naval Academy, labor unions, Erma Bombeck's breast cancer, and Martin VanBuren. He couldn't imagine her keeping books unless she really liked them; Beth wasn't the pack rat type. They were all neatly stowed, arranged by height and pulled out so that they all rested exactly one inch from the edge of each shelf. Now he noticed that the top shelf held tall, thick volumes—catalogs of some kind—and what looked like several photo albums. He had never looked up that high before.

He rose from the couch, crossed over to the bookcase, and pulled down the four photo albums. A little flurry of dust motes sifted toward the floor.

Two of the albums were old—a dusky maroon color, with the corners of the pictures tucked inside trim little triangular tabs—and two were newer. Perry settled himself back on the couch and opened one of the old ones first. Though he couldn't remember ever having seen any of the pictures, he recognized the main characters immediately. His mother had been quite pretty as a girl, with a pale, fine, aristocratic face and small features. In contrast, her hair had been dark and abundant. In most of the pictures she was smiling, and in one she had her head thrown back in laughter. Perry stared at that one a long time. She looked to be thirteen or fourteen. She wouldn't have laughed, he thought sadly, if she had known what lay ahead of her in life.

In another picture a few pages over, his mother's whole family was gathered on the wide front porch of their house; her parents—who by this time would have already given her the Bible—were standing on the top steps, looking unprepared for the taking of the picture. Her mother was pointing downward at one of the younger children, it must have been Uncle Joel, who was examining a scab on his knee. Her father was gazing off to the side—perhaps toward a cornfield about which he was worried. Perry's mother, Catherine, had been the only daughter, with two older brothers, then Uncle Joel and Uncle Louis, both younger. In the picture she was sitting on a step with her hands encircling her knees, looking straight into the camera with a coquettish smile. She wore a wide, light-colored ribbon in her dark hair. Perry realized that all the people in the picture except Uncle Louis were dead now; it was an oppressive thought.

He flipped over several pages. His father began showing up in pictures—sitting in the porch swing twirling a hat on his finger, half-lying on the hood of an old Studebaker, standing in a victory pose under a banner that read "Class of '40," grinning out the window of a bus. It was easy to see how charming he had been and how completely a girl could have fallen for those charms, especially if she had grown up on a farm and he had moved to their small community from the big city of Chicago. It wouldn't have even mattered to her that she was two years older than he was. One picture of him in a uniform had a message scrawled across one corner: "Catherine, Yours until the sand in the hourglass of Time runs out, Allen."

But it had taken Catherine nine more years of sand trickling through the hourglass of Time to get Allen to marry her. He must have been a genius at thinking up excuses, one after another—first, the horrors of war, of course, then a lengthy and complicated recovery from the horrors of war, then finding a suitable job after recovering from the horrors of war, then . . . on and on. Finally, Perry supposed, his father had given in from exhaustion and married her. Perry wondered how many good years they'd had before his mother stopped laughing, then smiling, then talking—until the hourglass had run dry. He felt a flash of irritation at her. She should have been suspicious of the words his father had written on his army picture. The sand in an hourglass doesn't last long—an hour to be exact. But maybe she had thought she would never tire of turning the glass over to start another hour.

Beth must have taken the two older photo albums when she had gone through their mother's things. The two newer ones, however, were clearly her own. Perry had never seen these either. He opened one of them and was surprised to find a chronicle of pictures detailing Beth's life from her high school years until quite recently. On second thought, he wasn't surprised at all; anyone who kept a Daytimer would go in for this sort of thing. He had no doubt that she also kept an updated address book and careful service records on her car. Each picture in the albums had a caption handwritten in Beth's meticulous, bold print with a fine-nibbed black marker—the kind of humorous captions they used to put in old yearbooks, like "Whoa there, Gracie, not so fast" or "Tea for two" or "Anybody need a lift?"

He flipped through the pages swiftly but then stopped suddenly at a picture with the caption "Big brother makes a catch." At first Perry had no recollection of posing for the picture. He was standing on the lawn of the house in Rockford where he had grown up, wearing a pair of plaid bell-bottom slacks and sporting a bushy head of hair with an amazing pair of sideburns, and beside him stood Dinah, her long, straight hair covering half her face as she looked down at her left hand. He bent down closer to the snapshot, and all at once he remembered clearly.

It had been spring break, and they had driven to Rockford to show his mother Dinah's engagement ring. Beth had ridden with them and studied calculus in the backseat the whole way. It was the first time his mother and Dinah had met each other, and Dinah's high spirits had seemed to pain his mother. She had spent the whole three days exiting whatever room Dinah entered. Beth had snapped the picture in the front yard right before they left to go back to college. In the background Perry could see the faint outline of his mother standing in the threshold behind the screen door with the decorative grillwork of an iron flamingo—the same doorway across which his father had fallen, disheveled and out of his senses, years earlier.

Chapter 19

Shhh, listen! Stop!" cried Eldeen, waving both hands. Perry stopped in mid-swing, and the badminton birdie fell at his feet.

"It sounds like it's coming this way," Jewel said from the other side of the net. Eldeen stood up from her lawn chair and cocked her head at different angles. Her floral turquoise muumuu flared about her like a gaudy tent, and she wore large pink canvas sneakers. Joe Leonard leaned forward in his chair as the sound of the siren grew louder.

Then through the dogwood trees along the back fence, they saw the spinning light and the gleam of red as a fire truck sped past on Lily Lane, then turned onto Daffodil Street. Slowly the siren's wail diminished.

Eldeen sat back down, arranging the folds of her muumuu, and Perry stooped to pick up the birdie.

"My heart near about stops whenever I hear one of them sirens," said Eldeen, fanning herself with both hands. "You just always think, 'Maybe it's my very own house on fire and I don't even *know* it! Maybe a neighbor spotted the smoke billowin' out the front door, and here I am a'settin' in the backyard just as trustin' as a baby.' I heard once of a deaf man who was hoeing turnips back behind his garage, and his wife had a grease fire in the kitchen and the whole house practically burned up before he was even the slightest bit aware of anything going on. He did say later in the newspaper that he kept catching a whiff of something that smelled peculiar, but he thought it was the neighbor's compost."

"The score's still nine-ten," Joe Leonard said. He balanced his racket across both knees and folded his arms.

Perry halfway hoped Jewel would win this game so he could sit the next one out. But it was only during the brief lulls before a serve that he hoped that; in the middle of each point, he surprised himself at the lengths to which he would go to win the point. He had never considered himself very competitive before now. Although sports had always come naturally to him, he had generally held back just a little, even as a child on the school playground, never sure if he could really pull it off. Dinah used to tell people she had married an avid spectator.

When Jewel had first invited him to play badminton with them one night after supper back in June, Perry had approached the game with a somewhat condescending air, assuming it to be a genteel pastime for people who liked to pretend they were getting some exercise. He envisioned Victorian ladies in long white dresses and enormous, veiled hats taking dainty, feather-soft strokes with their slender racquets while another group played croquet in the background.

He had been thoroughly trounced that first day by both Jewel and Joe Leonard, had felt his heart pounding with exertion, had perspired heavily, and had awakened the next morning with sore muscles. He wondered how he had ever gotten the idea that badminton was a sport for sissies. Since the first match, he had begun trying in a way he couldn't remember ever doing before. *He* knew now how strenuous a good game of badminton was, but not everyone did; he'd hate to have it known that he routinely lost to a woman and a boy.

"Earl Vanderhoff was telling me last Sunday that every last scrap of his family's earthly possessions went up in smoke in a house fire when he was a boy," said Eldeen after Jewel won a point by lightly flipping the birdie just inches over the net.

"Ten-ten," said Joe Leonard.

"And his family had to live out in the barn for a whole summer with the cows and horses and what have you. Imagine what *that* must've been like"—she fluttered one hand in front of her nose as if fending off a bad smell—"and his mama had to do all the cookin' in the farmyard over a open fire."

Jewel served the birdie, and Perry returned it low and hard to her backhand side.

"They all slept up in the hayloft," Eldeen continued, "and Earl says them was some of the happiest memories of his whole childhood."

Jewel swept the birdie back across the net, but it was high and short—the perfect setup for what Joe Leonard called a "zinger." Perry raised his racquet and watched the birdie fall in a plumb line toward him.

"Don't you just know that scratchy old hay made 'em itch all over ever' inch of their bodies, though!" said Eldeen.

Perry swung and hit the birdie with the metal rim of the racquet. It went over the net feebly, and Jewel responded with a brisk upswing that sent the birdie behind Perry. He backpedaled swiftly and with a long arch of his body contacted the birdie and sent it back.

Eldeen clapped her hands loudly, apparently at an insect. "Get away, you pesky feller! At least we can thank the Lord the mosquitoes aren't as troublesome this July as usual. 'Course, I coated myself good with Bug-Off before we came outside too. Anyway, all the neighborfolk pitched in that whole summer and helped 'em build a new house, Earl said, and it was a heap nicer than the old one too. So I guess that's just another good example of how the Lord uses trials and tribulations to give us something better in the end, just like the story of Job all over again."

After the point was over, Jewel looked over at Eldeen and shook her head. "Mama, it's awful hard to concentrate on the game with you telling a story."

Eldeen laughed and laid both hands over her mouth. "Oh, I know it, I know it! I'll try to be good, I promise I will!" she said. But as Jewel served again, Eldeen began shaking with silent laughter. All during the next point Perry could hear her stifled chuckles, often erupting into low snorts.

"I couldn't help it," she said after Perry won the point finally. "I got to thinking about something else Earl said. His great-granny was living with them at the time, he said, and she got so mixed up after the fire that she'd wander all around the inside of the barn looking for a particular room in the house or a pincushion she thought she'd misplaced or her favorite rocking chair, and once in the middle of the night they found her curled up in one of the cow stalls, stroking a calf and singing to it like it was one of her babies." Her smile suddenly froze and she stopped laughing. "Bless her heart," she said. "I feel real mean gettin' a kick out of a poor old crazy woman's misfortune." She looked around at them all soberly. "I hope you'll all forgive me. What a low-down thing to laugh about."

Perry felt embarrassed. Eldeen looked like she was about to cry. Joe Leonard looked at Jewel uncomfortably.

"Oh, Mama, it's all right," Jewel said. "You didn't mean any harm. What's the score now, Joe Leonard?"

"Eleven-ten, your favor. Perry's serving."

"I know I didn't," said Eldeen tartly, "but careless, thoughtless remarks is the worst kind of hurt. I been stung by words before—I know how it feels."

"Well, Earl's great-granny can't be living anymore, so I don't think you've hurt her feelings." Jewel bent forward, holding her racquet with both hands as Perry prepared to serve the birdie.

"But I been settin' a bad example for Joe Leonard here, talking that way," Eldeen said. Perry swatted the birdie firmly. "And also," Eldeen continued, "it's been a bad testimony in front of Perry."

"Shhh, Mama, it's *okay*," said Jewel. She returned the serve with a low backhand stroke. Eldeen said nothing more until the point was over.

"What a sad, sad thing not to even know where you are!" she said. "To go roaming around lost and befuddled! And then to set yourself down next to a cow and think it was somebody you loved—mmm, mmm, mmm." She closed her eyes as if the thought had grown too weighty to bear.

"Still eleven-ten," said Joe Leonard. "Mama's serve."

Jewel served and the birdie sailed low across the net. "But at least she didn't *know* she'd lost her mind," said Eldeen. She had dropped her voice, apparently addressing her words just to Joe Leonard now. "That's one blessing of that kind of a sickness I guess," she said. Perry hit a high, deep return, and Jewel fired it back with a forceful overhand. Perry managed to get his racquet on it and loop it back over.

"Although you know that teacher you had back in first grade," he heard Eldeen say, "the one whose mind just suddenly *snapped* after they retired her three years ago? They say she just meanders around the nursing home crying all the time now, and when anybody talks to her or asks her what the matter is, all she does is just cry the harder. Miss Perpetuo, that was her name, wasn't it? I always liked that name—Miss Lydia Perpetuo. I thought it had a real important ring to it, like some kind of a famous millionaire. She was one of your best teachers I thought."

Joe Leonard murmured something in response. Perry hit the birdie into the net.

"Twelve-ten," said Joe Leonard.

"I've wondered if Miss Perpetuo isn't always crying because she *knows* her mind's not like it used to be and she's grievin' over what she's lost. So maybe some people *do* know they've gone crazy after all. Oops, you hit that one too far, Perry." Eldeen pointed to the short piece of rope laid on the grass to mark the back boundary.

"Thirteen-ten," said Joe Leonard.

"I been meanin' to go to the nursing home someday and visit her, the poor old soul. She's too young to be in such a fix as that. She can't be seventy yet."

Jewel finally won the game, and Perry sat down next to Eldeen. With both hands he smoothed his hair straight back off his forehead. The humidity here in South Carolina made it feel like it was always ten degrees hotter than it was.

"At least Lydia Perpetuo is born again, though," Eldeen told Perry, turning to look him full in the face. "She taught the ladies' Bible study at the old Methodist Church down off Derwood Street. We had us some good talks back when Joe Leonard was a pupil of hers in the first grade." Watching Joe Leonard playing badminton now, Perry could hardly imagine him ever being a first grader.

"So she might be a little deficient up here"—Eldeen tapped her forehead—"but she's rich right here"—and she pointed to her heart. "And I believe with all my soul that the good Lord's preparing her a mansion in heaven right this minute—to live in *eternally.*" Perry didn't reply. He was used to it by now.

Eldeen never pressed him directly, but neither did she let an opportunity pass to remind him of the benefits of salvation. Eldeen fished a Kleenex out of the pocket of her muumuu and brought out with it a small box of Milk Duds. "Why, I forgot all about these. I wonder how long they been in there. Here, have some." She poured several into Perry's hand, then popped one into her own mouth. "Mmm, I do love these!" she said. They watched Jewel and Joe Leonard for a while in silence except for munching sounds. The Milk Duds were a little hard. "Joe Leonard's had some of the most *interesting* teachers!" Eldeen said at length and then spent the next several minutes telling Perry about a fifth grade teacher who used to raise and harvest herbs for medicinal purposes.

After Jewel won the game with a zinger Joe Leonard couldn't return, she handed her racquet to Perry so he and Joe Leonard could play. When Perry finally won 17-15, Eldeen said, "Well, I was beginning to think we'd have to drive the car back here and turn the headlights on to finish up! That was some close game." Joe Leonard took the racquets and birdies to the shed, and Perry folded up the lawn chairs and set them against the side of the house.

"Come on in for some ice cream, Perry," Jewel said.

"And we can garnish it with some berries on top!" added Eldeen. "Joe Leonard did a big picking this afternoon, and they're as pretty as plums!"

They looked at Perry expectantly.

"Well, all right," he said.

Eldeen clapped her hands and laughed. "Well then, come on, everybody, let's don't stand out here and let the bugs get us!"

As they walked toward the side door, Joe Leonard loped past them and bounded up the steps.

"Yes sir," said Eldeen, "it all comes down to *giving up* is what I think about that poor, pitiful man." Perry had no idea what man she was talking about. He tried to think back to what he had last heard her talking about, but it was no use. Maybe the comment was in reference to Joe Leonard's herb-growing teacher. But when had he given up—and why?

No one spoke as they slowly filed up the side steps behind Eldeen. When she reached the top, she turned around and pointed her finger at Jewel and Perry. In her floral muumuu, she looked like some formidable Samoan matriarch. "Nobody who's got a deep-down feeling in their heart that they're fearfully and wonderfully made is going to lie down in the dirt like a little mewling crybaby like that man's done and just *quit!*" she said emphatically. At the same time he was wondering if she could possibly be talking about *him,* Perry hoped he could remember her exact words later; he'd thought for a long time what a fascinating study Eldeen's speech would make. He'd like to unravel it all someday and examine it systematically—syntax, grammar, diction, and then of course the enormous category of content. Once he'd heard her use the words *rigamarole, pip-squeak,* and *underdrawers* in a single sentence.

"Set yourself down," said Eldeen, motioning Perry to the kitchen table. "I got to go wash the skeeter juice off my hands." Joe Leonard opened the freezer and got out a half-gallon carton of vanilla ice cream, then took a huge bowl of blueberries out of the refrigerator. Jewel handed him the colander, and he measured out two handfuls of berries into it and began rinsing them at the sink. Jewel was getting out bowls and spoons when the door buzzer sounded.

"I'll get it!" called Eldeen from the bathroom, and Perry heard her humming to herself as she walked heavily down the hallway toward the living room. He got up and ambled after her. Two separate instances of vandalism had been reported over on Tulip Court recently, and one woman on Daffodil Street said she caught some teenagers rummaging around inside her car late one night but they ran away when they saw her at the window with a flashlight. Perry knew Jewel's house could be marked as an easy target if anyone knew the neighborhood. Two women and a fifteen-year-old wouldn't pose much of a threat to whoever was doing these things.

The draperies were still open in the living room, but it was growing too dark outside for Perry to identify the car parked at the curb. A slow draft of air from a large box fan sitting in the doorway between the kitchen and living room stirred the suncatchers hanging from the window panes so that they trembled ever so slightly. The DePalmas's porch light across the street shone directly behind the newest one—a small lead crystal butterfly one of Jewel's piano students had given her this summer; its fractured blues and purples shifted softly in the lazy, sultry breeze.

"Why, just looka who's standing here at our front door!" cried Eldeen, throwing open the front door and unlatching the screen before Perry even saw who was there. "Wait a minute," he wanted to urge her, "let's make sure it's somebody we trust." But it was too late. "Come on in, come on in!" Eldeen said, and Willard Scoggins stepped across the threshold. When he caught sight of Perry, his smile faded a little.

"Oh, I didn't mean to interrupt anything," he said.

"Not at all, not a bit of it!" said Eldeen. "Come on in the kitchen. We just came inside ourselves and are fixing to have us some light summer refreshment. You're welcome to join us."

Perry and Willard shook hands, and Perry led the way back to the kitchen.

"Look who's come to see us, Jewel!" called Eldeen. Perry couldn't make sense out of Jewel's expression when she looked up and saw Willard. Was it gladness or dismay? Or shyness? Amusement? Or maybe just plain surprise?

Willard had on a bright green knit shirt with a tiny penguin stitched on the pocket. The shirt was tucked tightly into his gray pants, which appeared to be hiked up a little too far above his waistline. His face was shiny, and what little hair he did have was wet and neat. He reminded Perry of a little roly-poly inflatable man Troy used to have. "Mr. Pop-up" was weighted down at the feet somehow so that when you punched him, he'd rock back up ready to take another blow. Perry suddenly felt unkempt and sweaty. He saw Jewel trying to stuff her blouse down inside her baggy blue slacks.

"Well, let's don't just stand here grinning at each other," said Eldeen. "Come on, Willard, sit down here at the table next to Perry."

"I really just came to bring you these," Willard said, looking at Jewel eagerly and holding out some sheets of music. "I told you on Sunday, remember, that I'd written out an arrangement for the choir, and I thought you'd like to see it and maybe play through it."

Suddenly something clicked in Perry's mind. He couldn't believe he hadn't figured it out sooner; it all made such perfect sense now: Willard's expansive smiles from the platform over to the piano, his bright-eyed attention as he bent near Jewel each Wednesday night to whisper the song selection, his childlike excitement at her surprise birthday party, his determined bidding on her set of embroidered dish towels. Willard Scoggins clearly had his sights set on Jewel, and here it had taken Perry nearly five months to piece it together.

Dinah would have seen it the first Sunday and would have pointed it out immediately. Perry had watched her assessments and predictions prove valid the whole fifteen years they had been married. At first he had accused her of snap judgments, but then as they kept coming true, he had attributed it to luck, only later realizing finally that it was a fundamental difference between them—maybe between all men and women for that matter. With unerring instinct, she could size up people and their intentions in an instant; she could read nuances of facial expression, tone of voice, and body movement and come up with amazingly detailed—and accurate—character analyses.

Once in the last year or so, well after their marriage had taken its wrong turn, she had said to him, "The supreme irony of it all—Perry Warren, the *sociologist,* the writer, the famous reporter of human behavior, has no clue about what's underneath a relationship." She had been standing in the doorway of his study eating an apple. He still remembered the furious crunch each time she took a bite. He had refused to look up at her, so she had finally spun on her heel and left, calling back over her shoulder, "See Perry. See Perry observe. See Perry write. See Perry miss the whole point of it all."

She had come back a few seconds later, having finished her apple. "I just thought of something," she said. "You're as clever with words as a juggler, but you're a clown when it comes to knowing what they *mean* when you put them all together." That was so like Dinah to be so close to a cunning analogy but fail to clinch it. The circus idea had lots of potential, but she had stopped short. Perry had written her statement down after she left again and had spent the next half hour developing it into a complete, well-shaped, tightly expressed paragraph. He had even included a ringmaster and an acrobat in the little composition.

Eldeen had told Perry once that Willard used to court Myra Gresham, who ran a daycare center over in Pelzer, but that it had ended and he had never married, as if it had been his choice. Perry's first assumption was that no one would have the man, but after he joined the choir, he rethought the matter. Willard was overweight, true, and he was probably considered a religious wacko by the people he worked with at the public library, but he had a lot going for him too. He was unfailingly courteous, well organized, and obviously intelligent. He had a quick wit too; once in choir practice Edna Hawthorne had mentioned that her husband used to play the violin, and Willard had asked her if he'd played pastoral symphonies. He was always playing with words and mispronouncing musical terms on purpose. "Let the fermata ferment a little longer!" or "I want to hear that crash-endo now!" or "Shhh! That *dim.* abbreviation means dim your headlights."

So Willard Scoggins had his eye on Jewel Blanchard. Perry was sure she must be several years older than Willard, although she didn't look it. He watched the two of them as they went into the living room and spread the sheets of music out on the piano. He could see them from where he was sitting, Willard standing behind Jewel and leaning over her shoulder, singing the melody close to her ear, his broad backside hiding all but her head from view.

While Joe Leonard dished out the ice cream, Eldeen got out paper napkins, folded them in half, and set a spoon on top of each one. "I sure hope nobody got hurt in that fire," she said earnestly. "I can still hear that siren inside my head. What a awful thing it would be to die in a fire!"

Chapter 20

So *that's* what Eldeen meant. There it was, right in the book of Deuteronomy. Perry had heard her say it at least a dozen times and had always wondered what she was talking about. The last time had been only a week before, on their way home from Wilderness Gospel Camp. She had been looking through a teen magazine distributed to all the campers before they left and was reading aloud a true story about a boy named Doug Salmani who had been addicted to drugs since the age of twelve but had gotten saved when he was seventeen and now gave talks in junior high and high schools about the harmful effects of drugs.

Eldeen had read the words distinctly and slowly, clearly intending everyone in the car to pay attention. "'Without Jesus,' Doug says today, 'my life would be totally messed up. I might not even be alive if that man hadn't cared enough to stop and see if I needed help that day. I didn't know what to say the first time he asked me if I knew what would happen to me if I died, but now I can answer that question. If I die today, I'll be in heaven!'" Eldeen closed the magazine and smacked the dashboard with it.

"Thank the Lord for sending that faithful Christian man along to witness to that boy Doug!" she said. "But, oh, just think, just *think* of all the youngsters like Doug who're still drug addicts! Where are the mamas and daddies of all them children? Why don't they *see* what's happening in their very own homes?"

"Lots of them are in the same fix as their kids," Jewel said from the backseat. "The children just act like they see their parents acting."

Eldeen sighed. "That's the honest-to-goodness truth. Even Christian parents don't always see what little copycats children are. Oh, how important it is to *live right* in front of your boys and girls!" And that's when she said it again, pitching her voice slightly deeper, as if she were a radio announcer: "Bind them as frontlets and write them upon thy doorposts and gates when thou sitteth and when thou lieth and when thou walketh and when thou riseth up!"

Perry saw now that she had misquoted it a little, but at least he would understand the allusion from now on. After reading the rest of the chapter in Deuteronomy, he turned to the book of Acts and read about Paul and Barnabas on their first missionary journey. It interested him to see how frank the Bible accounts were. Whoever wrote it could have left out so much and made the people seem far more saintly. But no, there it was, reported bluntly: "And the contention was so sharp between them, that they departed asunder one from the other." Imagine, two missionaries involved in a big argument over who was going with them on their next trip and then having it recorded for all succeeding generations to read.

When Perry had mentioned to Brother Hawthorne in privacy that he thought it would be a good idea for him to familiarize himself with the Bible in order to write his book more knowledgeably, the pastor had nodded gravely but, Perry thought, had also looked deeply satisfied, as if he were marking the progress of some building project. Perry had opened his mouth to assure Brother Hawthorne that his interest in the Bible was merely professional and academic, in conjunction with his research, so he could understand his subjects better—but he had stopped. He hated to squelch somebody's hopes. Let the pastor think whatever he wanted to, he had decided.

Brother Hawthorne had suggested that Perry begin reading in both Genesis and Matthew, working his way through the Old and New Testaments at the same time. He said that reading several chapters at a time like that would give a broader picture and would also reveal the unity of Scripture. He further suggested ending each day's study with a chapter or two from the book of Psalms.

Perry turned now to Psalm 111. He loved the beauty and simplicity of the psalms; he could see how people could feel rested, even transported after reading parts of the Bible like this. He liked the poetic flow of the verses, the repetitive refrains and elegant clarity. Even though the agitated chapters, in which the speaker was crying out for vengeance, didn't seem quite in keeping with the others, they still had a certain purity and dignity about them.

He had just read "the LORD is gracious and full of compassion" when the telephone rang. He got up from the kitchen table, taking his Daytimer and pen with him. He had been expecting the call. Cal often called him from his office at home on Saturday mornings.

"So *what* are you doing down there, Perry? What's this stuff you just mailed me? I send you down there to write a book about a church, and what do I get? Nothing like what I was expecting, I'll tell you!" Cal's voice was friendly underneath the blustery complaints, so Perry let him continue. "Got the envelope yesterday and tore into it, thinking, 'Must be the first few chapters from my good pal, Perry, the writer our publisher is counting on to send us a manuscript ready to go by the first of the year.' Couldn't wait to see something in writing finally. So I start reading and I say, 'What *is* this? Has Perry flipped out or what?' Hey, maybe I'm thinking of somebody else, huh? I sure thought you were the one writing the thing about fundamentalists." He paused for a moment, then laughed. "So what is this you sent me, Perry?"

"It's a short story and a poem," said Perry.

"But you don't write short stories and poems," said Cal. "You write kids' novels and sociological research, the latter being what you're presently under contract to do. Or have you forgotten?"

"Take a deep breath, Cal. Calm down, it's all right." Perry began doodling on a blank page in his Daytimer, scribbling a series of circles and loops. "I haven't forgotten about the book. I'm working on it, I really am. I write every day. I've got tons of notes. It's coming, I promise. There's no reason to send you anything yet. Or have you forgotten how I work?" He stopped scribbling and started looking for a pattern in the jumble of lines.

"No, I haven't forgotten—but a story and a poem? You've never done this before, Perry, especially not right in the middle of another project."

"Have you read them?"

"Yeah, I did."

"And?" Perry saw the profile of a face emerging from the network of scribbles. He began retracing the lines to make them darker. The forehead was flat, but the nose was an enormous, inflated sac. The lips were puckered in a heart shape, and the chin protruded to a long, narrow tip.

"And what?"

"Come on, Cal. You're my agent, sometimes even my editor before the real one sees the stuff—I've listened to you more than once, you know I have. And once in a great while you're my friend. Don't play with me now. You think you can sell them?"

"Oh, maybe—probably, at least the short story," said Cal, sighing, "if you're not picky about where." Perry could hear him tapping something against a hard surface. "Perry?" Cal's voice became serious. "You all right, really? I mean, this story is—well, it's just so *different* from anything you've written before. This man-woman business—it's not like you. I'm not even sure I catch it. I mean, I started out thinking it was supposed to be satire, just knowing you. Then I finished reading it, and I thought, 'He's not kidding.' And then I thought, 'Naaah, he *is* kidding.' Is there something here I'm missing? I can't put it all together—this story and what you've been through in the past year. Are you . . . are you okay, Perry?"

"Sure I'm okay. You're making more out of this than you need to. So I try something new—so what? Give me some leeway here, Cal."

"Now see, that's what I mean. If there's anybody I can count on to be consistent, it's you—or at least that's the way it's always been before. But now all of a sudden you're talking about change and leeway and trying something new. Perry, remember when I suggested a couple of years ago that you try writing an adult novel next, and you didn't even let me get the whole sentence out of my mouth? No, you said. If you've got something that works, stick with it, you said. If you sell adolescent books, then write adolescent books, you said. Remember?"

Perry didn't answer. Above the flat forehead he began creating a pompadour that gradually worked into a beehive of ornamental curls.

The tapping sound stopped, but Perry could still hear Cal's heavy breathing.

"Okay, I give up," Cal said at last. "I can take a hint. But, listen, if I hear you jumped off a bridge, I'm not feeling guilty, I'll tell you that. I tried. If they call me up and say, 'What can you tell us about this guy who just flung himself in front of a moving train?' I'll say, 'Not a thing. You know as much as I do.'"

"Fair enough," said Perry. "What about the poem? Can you send it somewhere?"

"Poems are crappy to market," said Cal. "You must've known that or you'd have sent it off yourself like every other writer of the stuff does. Agents don't bother with poetry, Perry. It's not even worth the postage."

"Try," said Perry. He drew a conversation balloon coming out of the heart-shaped lips. Inside he printed, "*Agents don't bother with poetry!*"

"I've never wasted my time with anybody's poetry before. I hate poetry."

"Yeah, well, just stick it in an envelope and mail it somewhere, okay?"

"You lazy bum," said Cal.

"Right—I'm down here in the trenches, and I take a little break, just a little one, and what do I get?"

"Who's the kid in the poem anyway? Is he yours?" Cal asked.

"Cal, you don't look for real people in literary art. How many times have I told you that? But no, he's not mine. Definitely not. Maybe he's what I wish mine would become." Perry immediately wished he hadn't said so much. He heard the rustling of paper over the telephone.

"I like the old lady in the story," Cal said. "I won't ask you who she is, though, since she's in a work of literary art."

"She just fell onto the page," Perry said. "She was easy." He heard Cal turning more pages.

"Well, you never know till you try," Cal said after a few moments. "I send off things all the time that I don't think have a snowball's chance, and they get snatched right up. But then a lot of the stuff I think is great gets turned down over and over. Like the thing about the zoo doctor that Breshkin wrote. Fascinating story—and true too. But nobody'll buy it. Strange how it works."

"Guess I should feel encouraged, huh?" said Perry. He made a small ear out of a squiggle and began drawing an elaborate earring on its lobe.

Cal laughed. "I'll see what I can do, Perry, but don't cross your fingers. In the meantime, get back to your book. No more experimenting for now, okay? They want a manuscript by January, you may recall."

"They'll get it," said Perry.

"And how are you getting along with the brethren at the church?" Cal asked. "Any new developments?"

"Oh, fine. Everything's going fine. They . . . they sure have their own view of life, their own little world really. It's been an interesting experience." Actually, though he couldn't tell Cal this, he woke up most mornings feeling like he had started out on a normal, predictable journey but somehow had gotten lost along the way. He had even dreamed one night that he was crawling on all fours, slowly traversing a vast expanse, having lost his sense of direction. He saw people standing far above him, as if at a scenic lookout point, watching his labored movement and motioning wildly, shouting individual words he recognized but arranging them in sentences he couldn't understand, like "Darkly feed irrelevant tailgate march!" But all this was too much to try to explain to Cal.

"Ha! An interesting experience—that's one way to put it," Cal said. "I don't see how you can keep your sanity. To be honest, that's the first thing I thought of when I opened this envelope of yours. I said to myself, 'Oh, no, they're getting to him. Perry's losing his grip.'"

Perry smiled. "Well, my sanity may be a matter of question, but I don't think *they* have anything to do with that. That equipment has always been prone to malfunction." He held his picture at arm's length and studied it. "The people at this church are all . . . so *different*," he said. Suddenly he noticed that a small figure eight above the curls would make a perfect butterfly preparing for a landing. He added two long antennae and began shading in the wings.

"Different! Hey, you don't have to tell me!" Cal broke off for a hearty laugh.

"No, I don't mean that way. I mean they're all so different from each other," said Perry. "Just take the way they look. Dottie Puckett could be on the front of a fashion magazine, and Louise Farnsworth wears lumpy knit dresses she must've pulled out of a rag bag. Some of them wear dime-store jewelry, and some of them don't wear any. And then there's Marvella Gowdy, who wears a string of real pearls with the polyester sweaters she buys at the Dollar Store."

"Well, that's true anywhere, Perry."

"But it's everything, not just their clothes. Harvey Gill could lecture on geology at Yale, but Grady Ferguson just learned to read and he's sixty-seven. And Mickey Freeman is forty-eight and works at a mill, but Curtis Chewning, who's the same age, is a pediatrician." Perry knew he was talking fast, but he couldn't stop himself. He had to get it out, he had to prove his point. "And Burton Finley is almost always sick but laughs and smiles like he's having the time of his life, and Mayfield Spalding hardly ever even speaks to anybody, much less smiles. And the pastor looks like an aerobics instructor, but Willard Scoggins . . ."

Perry stopped. He could feel Cal's response hovering almost palpably between them: a deafeningly loud but unspoken "So what?" Perry knew there was no way to describe the diversity of the church members—and maybe it didn't matter anyway.

"Well, I'm glad it's you doing this book and not me," Cal said. "I can't cope with those Bible zanies." He emitted a harsh woof of laughter. "Everything that comes up, they say it's either the Lord's judgment or the Lord's blessing—I mean, sometimes the same thing can even qualify for both! And they're always *talking* about it all, even advertising it with bumper stickers. My grandmother had one on her car that said, 'Jesus is my copilot.' The woman drove like a maniac too. I tried to get the thing off after she died so we could sell the car, but it must've been *welded* on. I finally got it all off but the *Jesus,* and I just finally gave up."

Then Cal plunged into a story about a great-uncle of his in Georgia who used to send half of his social security check every month to an evangelist who claimed to use all donations to print Romanian Bibles. Perry had heard Cal tell the story of the scam before, though he thought in the original version it was a grandfather instead of a great-uncle.

He kept wanting to break in, to say that Eldeen and Jewel and the others weren't like the people Cal had known growing up in Georgia, but he didn't. He couldn't help thinking, though, of Eldeen's reaction a few weeks back when they had pulled up to a stoplight behind a car with a "Honk if you love Jesus" bumper sticker. "That makes me madder than a hornet's nest!" she had said, shaking her finger with every accented syllable.

"What are you talking about, Mama?" Jewel had asked her.

"That sticker on that fender in front of us!" Eldeen had said. They were too close to the car now for any of the rest of them to see what it said, but Eldeen didn't stop to explain. "It's disrespectful is what it is! Like our Jesus would be pleased by a noisy, blaring hullabaloo like that! My Bible tells me Jesus is somebody to stand in worshipful awe of, not toot at! He's the Alpha and Omega, our High Priest, with eyes like a fiery flame and a voice like the sound of many waters. He carries seven stars and the keys to victory over death in his right hand, and his face shines brighter than the noonday sun! He's the Son of God, not somebody to have a pep rally for!" No one had spoken after this surprising outburst, and Eldeen had scowled disapprovingly after the car when it made a left turn a block later. Perry finally saw what the bumper sticker said and wondered what Eldeen would have done if he had leaned over the seat and beeped the horn.

He remembered being confused over the whole incident. Just when he thought he had figured these people out, they went and did something like this. If anyone had asked him, he would have guessed that Eldeen would be thrilled over a bumper sticker that said "Honk if you love Jesus." He would have said she would be the first to honk and would honk the loudest and longest. But no, it turned out that she was highly offended. The thought slowly settled over him that he still had a lot to learn; these people had some quirks that defied a predictable pattern. Just like the comment Eldeen had made another time about Rush Limbaugh. Perry would have expected her to extol the man's conservative political views, views he knew she shared, but instead she had said, "He rides a mighty high horse, that man does, and he's profane, and I don't like the way he cuts people down either."

When Cal finally wound down and said good-bye several minutes later, Perry hung up the phone and stared down at the profile he had drawn. During Cal's story he had filled in several warts and moles and darkened in a lush, hairy eyebrow. The figure looked like a sexual mutant, neither distinctively male nor female. He neatly tore the page out of his Daytimer and walked over to the refrigerator, where he secured the drawing under a pineapple magnet. There, that added a homey touch. A stranger walking through the house would see that and think there was a child living here. Well, maybe not. Children were rarely ambiguous about the sexual orientation of the people in their artwork.

He picked up his coffee cup and emptied it into the sink. For a long moment he stood at the window over the sink and looked out into the backyard. Someone before Beth's time had planted a number of flowering trees and bushes, all of which were in various stages of bloom now. The mimosa was still covered with what looked like the feathery pink puffs on a pair of frivolous acrylic heels Dinah had once bought as a joke and worn around the house with a frilly yellow robe. The hydrangea blooms were heavy and lush—a rich lapis blue—and a row of tall plants Eldeen had identified as hollyhocks boasted tall spikes of showy purplish flowers.

Toward the back of the yard stood a lone crape myrtle with a slim, gnarled trunk and white lacy clusters just beginning to bloom. A large fig tree took up one whole corner of the yard, its wide leaves spread out like flat green mittens to shield the ripening figs. If the person who had planted all this had taken any time to do a little preliminary planning, the effect might have been quite attractive. As it was, it looked accidental. The hedge along the side fence was in need of a trim, but Perry quickly dismissed the thought of working outside in this weather. Yard work held no appeal for him anyway.

He leaned closer to the window and found that he could see most of Jewel's backyard too—the small storage shed, the badminton net, the blueberry bushes partially sheathed with white gauze netting. To his surprise, as he watched, one of the bushes trembled slightly and the white netting slipped down farther on one side. Joe Leonard stood up suddenly in the middle of the bushes and looked up at the sun. He was wearing a white T-shirt, Perry noticed, and he had a handkerchief tied around his forehead. He stepped out from among the bushes and set a small bucket on the ground, then busied himself recovering the bushes with the net.

Watching Joe Leonard now, Perry felt the sudden transfer in time that he often did when observing his neighbors. If he weren't standing in a house cooled by three air-conditioning window units with a 1991 Toyota sitting in the driveway, he could easily believe it was around the turn of the century. Joe Leonard, with his freckles and rolled-up denim jeans, picking up his pail of berries, could easily pass for Tom Sawyer. He could imagine the boy walking on a rail fence and rafting down the river. Of course, he couldn't imagine him sneaking out of the house at night or telling bald-faced lies, but then Tom Sawyer hadn't lived with the likes of Eldeen either. He started wondering how differently Mark Twain's book would have shaped up if Aunt Polly had been Eldeen instead. That would have changed things from the outset. Huck Finn would have gotten saved in the second or third chapter, and his drunk pappy would have sobered up and become a traveling preacher.

Joe Leonard stopped at the storage shed and set his pail down. Perry saw him lift a brick beside the door and remove the Zip-loc bag that held the key to the shed. He unlocked the door, then carefully slipped the key back into the plastic bag, ran his thumb and index finger along the seal, and set it back between the two bricks. He swung open the shed door and rolled out the lawn mower. Turning it over, he examined the blades, then set it upright again. He stepped back inside the shed and brought out a small red gasoline tank. It was hard for Perry to see Troy ever reaching this level of responsibility—regularly tending a dozen blueberry bushes, handling gasoline, keeping up with the yards of eight or ten neighbors. He even did housework; Perry had been paying him for over three months now to vacuum and dust Beth's house every Saturday.

He thought of a line of the poem he'd just sent Cal: "The lean hand, the slow swell of sinew." He had watched Joe Leonard's hands last Sunday when he had played his tuba for the July Fourth service at church. He had studied him afterward as he gingerly set the tuba on its large bell beside the piano and stepped back into the choir. He saw Joe Leonard's long fingers nimbly open his black folder and smooth the pages of the next choir number they were preparing to sing. He wondered what those hands would do in years to come. Then the choir rose, and though Perry knew he should be watching Willard for the cue to begin singing, he couldn't take his eyes off Joe Leonard. The boy's lips parted and he came in confidently: "O beautiful for spacious skies, for amber waves of grain."

Now, as he watched Joe Leonard tightly rescrew the lid to the gasoline can and take it back into the shed, he remembered the last line of the poem he had typed out and sent to Cal: "The steady eye, the scanning for bottles washing into port."

Chapter 21

Look at them big old poofy white clouds!" Eldeen said later that day as she and Perry walked across the gravel parking lot toward the church. "What a pretty day for a wedding!" Perry nodded in assent, although his idea of a pretty day was one about twenty degrees cooler and without the oppressive humidity. Why two people would choose to be married during the hottest month and in the hottest part of the afternoon was a mystery to him.

But he was glad for the wedding. He had told Cal in an earlier phone conversation that he was hoping he would get in on a wedding and a funeral during his year here. He had already witnessed several baptismal and Communion services and had typed them up in detail in a file labeled "Ordinances," although he had omitted the part about little Micah Spivey losing his footing in the baptistry and splashing water onto some of the choir members.

Now for the wedding. He couldn't remember the last time he had gone to a wedding; it could have been the one he and Dinah had attended at the biggest church in Chicago. The bride was a distant cousin of Dinah's, and the wedding was a flashy, spectacular affair, with ten attendants, all of whom looked like Barbie clones. If he remembered correctly, the marriage had lasted only a little longer than it had taken the bridesmaids to get down the aisle.

"I'm so glad Pat found her such a nice young man to marry," Eldeen was saying. "It was just the Lord's timing that brought them together that way." The story of Pat Tillman's meeting Marty Chest had been repeated many times among the churchfolk, but Eldeen still loved to talk about it. On the first day of classes back in January at a Christian college in Alabama, Pat had been looking for a blue pen she'd dropped during chapel. She was running her hand up under the seats when she felt another hand all of a sudden. She had drawn back immediately and looked behind her, and there sat Marty Chest, blushing bright red, she said. She leaned down again and peered under her seat, and there she saw her blue pen lying right beside a gold one. She picked them both up and passed the gold one back to Marty, and then after chapel he had thanked her and apologized for the trouble.

They had discovered the next day that Marty was sitting in the wrong place, when the girl assigned to that seat showed up. He moved to his right seat two rows back, but he and Pat continued to say hello and smile at each other.

"But Pat couldn't get the sight of them blue and gold pens out of her mind!" Eldeen said now as they started up the four wide steps to the church. "Said it reminded her of a husband and a wife going through life side by side. And I guess Marty couldn't either 'cause he started writing Pat little notes and asking her to go places with him. To think they *both* dropped their pens at the same time and they landed right smack next to each other! The Lord sure uses curious ways to bring people together!" Secretly, Perry suspected Marty of manipulating the whole thing—of seeing Pat drop her pen and then quickly reaching down to place his own beside hers, then pretending to grope around in search for it. But to the church people, it was all a divinely orchestrated moment that had set in motion the romance that culminated now in this happy occasion.

Perry wondered if Pat had regrets about changing her last name from Tillman to Chest. Pat Chest was the kind of name people would make wisecracks about. Besides, how would anyone know from hearing their names—Marty and Pat—which one was the husband and which was the wife? He started thinking of humorous names Marty and Pat could choose for their children but could come up with only two: Harry Chest and Hope Chest. It struck him that Marty Chest would have been the perfect addition to his high school geometry class in Rockford. It had been the joke of the school; four of the class members were Bob Hand, Phyllis Head, Larry Bone, and Kelly Foote. Everyone used to say it would have been perfect if only Sam Butt and Twan Wong Chin had taken geometry that year.

Now that he thought about it, though, he supposed it was no less a coincidence to think that Pat and Marty had both dropped their pens at the same time or that Myrt Silvester had received an unexpected check to pay for her car repair or that Bernie Paulson had run into his old army buddy at Six Flags than to believe that four students with body parts for last names had ended up in a single geometry class.

As they walked into the church, Perry was startled at the transformation. The pulpit was gone, and someone had draped the long choir panel with a filmy, off-white fabric, over which streamers of dark green ivy were arranged in scallops. Large masses of roses in vases of various sizes flanked the platform—donated by church members especially for the wedding. For several weeks there had been an announcement in the bulletin asking for roses to be picked fresh and brought to the church by noon on July 10 for the wedding of Pat Tillman and Marty Chest at two o'clock.

Tall white candles surrounded by rose petals sat on each windowsill along both sides of the church. Big yellow bows were fastened onto the end of each pew along the center aisle, with a sprig of ivy tied into each knot. Birdie sat at the organ, softly playing "Savior, Like a Shepherd Lead Us." Perry saw Joe Leonard, looking neat and scrubbed after his morning's work outdoors, sitting beside Jewel on the front row. Surely Joe Leonard wasn't going to play his tuba for a wedding. He hadn't thought to ask any questions when Eldeen told him Jewel and Joe Leonard both had to go early. As they moved into the pew indicated by the usher, Perry began imagining Pat, who was quite a large girl, walking down the aisle to a tuba rendition of "Here Comes the Bride."

As they sat down, Eldeen must have seen him smiling because she reached over and squeezed his arm. "It *is* pretty, isn't it?" she whispered. "They sure did some fancy decoratin' job! And it looks like there's going to be a real good turnout." She craned her neck toward the back, where people were still filling the small vestibule.

Presently a quartet assembled around the microphone beside the piano: Joe Leonard, Sid Puckett, Edna Hawthorne, and Vonda Snyder. They sang a song with the repeated phrase "make of our home a mirror of heaven." "A nice thought," Perry wanted to tell Pat and Marty, "but don't get your hopes up, kids." He felt a sudden stab of sorrow for the young couple, knowing that the realities of married life would eventually crack and chip away at all that rosy idealism.

Just yesterday he had seen a large heart with two names spray-painted on a concrete balustrade outside the Derby Public Library: "Tyrone + Sheela." He could tell it had been there a good while when he bent closer to examine it, and he had stood there for a while staring at it and wondering what had become of Tyrone and Sheela. Had they had an argument and broken up the day after they had sneaked down here with their can of red paint? Or had they gone on to marry and raise a family? Maybe they were divorced and remarried by now. He knew one thing—if they *had* married, they had no doubt learned the sad truth about love and marriage. But then, as he watched Edna Hawthorne's round, radiant face during the final stanza of the quartet's number, he wondered what *she* would say about love and marriage. Did she really consider it a "mirror of heaven"?

He thought back to an interchange he had observed between the Hawthornes several weeks ago. He had gone to Wal-Mart one Friday evening to buy washers for Beth's drippy bathroom faucets and had pulled into a parking space in front of an ice-cream shop next door called Darlene's Kreamy Kones. There at a booth beside the window, right under a large red sign announcing KREAMY KONE'S NEW FLAVOR: KRANBERRY ALMOND KRUNCH, sat Edna and Theodore Hawthorne facing each other. Edna was wearing a wide plaid headband in her red hair, and Brother Hawthorne had on a short-sleeved sport shirt. For several minutes Perry had sat in his car watching them.

Brother Hawthorne was licking his ice cream from a cone, and Edna was eating hers from a small cup with a plastic spoon. Then Brother Hawthorne must have asked Edna something because she tilted her head and bit her lip as if thinking of an answer. After she spoke, Brother Hawthorne laughed and shook his head, then reached over and patted her hand and said something in return. Edna lifted her eyes then and looked at her husband; neither of them spoke for several long seconds but just sat and smiled at each other. Perry watched in amazement; why didn't one of them *say* something? He couldn't imagine staring at someone for that long.

Finally Edna broke the spell and pointed to Brother Hawthorne's cone; he licked a neat ring around it. Perry got out of his car and closed the door softly, hoping not to attract the Hawthornes' attention. As he headed toward Wal-Mart, he wondered where Levi, Hannah, and Esther were. The Hawthornes had left Darlene's by the time he returned to his car, but all the way home he couldn't get the thought of that long, intimate look out of his mind.

Birdie played another number on the organ, and then Fern Tucker recited a poem entitled "A Wedding Rainbow," in which a mother questioned why God had allowed it to rain on her daughter's wedding day. Then as the mother complained, the storm passed and a rainbow spanned the sky, spreading its bright bands; as Perry could have predicted, the mother immediately turned to sentimental didacticism and joyfully proceeded to draw an application to marriage from each of the colors—blue speaking of the faithfulness of husband and wife to each other, green of the eternal youth of their love, yellow for the bright hope of tomorrow, and so forth.

Perry wished the poet had been scientifically correct and put the colors of the spectrum in the right order, starting with red and ending with purple, instead of mixing them all up, but he knew the order was probably determined by which words the poet could wrestle into rhyming. Anybody who ended two consecutive lines with *dearth* and *mirth* was obviously more concerned with rhyme than with optical physics. He saw Eldeen wiping at her eyes with a large man-sized handkerchief as Fern spoke the last lines of the poem: "'No rain, no rainbow,' she said with a nod;/ 'Yes, all things—e'en rainstorms—are presents from God.'"

The annoyingly cheery iambic platitude echoed in his mind as the mothers of the bride and groom were ushered in. How could Christians buy that? He still couldn't figure it out. He had heard that verse repeated over and over since he had been here—"All things work together for good to them that love God, to them who are the called according to his purpose"—and as far as he could tell, all these people really seemed to believe it. He heard the poem again in his mind: "'No rain, no rainbow,' she said with a nod." He imagined children chanting it as they jumped rope. He might have missed the solemn spectacle of Pat's maid of honor and the one bridesmaid moving down the aisle in pale yellow dresses carrying bouquets of multicolored roses if Eldeen hadn't poked him and whispered, "Oh, don't they look like precious little fairies?"

Perry intended to ask Brother Hawthorne sometime how he explained the verse in Romans in light of certain recent developments in the lives of church members. Marjorie Eckles's niece, for example, had had a baby with Down's syndrome a couple of months ago. She was the one, Perry recalled, whose husband had run off. And Louise Farnsworth, who taught the junior girls' Sunday school class, had lost control of her car on the way home after visiting her sister in Columbia and had run into a highway worker mowing the median. The man, who had a wife and five children, was still in a coma. Grady Ferguson didn't have medical insurance yet, and Emory and Maria Pyle's youngest son out in Texas had lost a foot in an explosion. How could anyone interpret these things as *good?*

On the other hand, Harvey Gill's reprobate son in California had recently landed a high-paying job as senior editor with a motion picture studio. It surely didn't sound to Perry as if all things worked together for good in the lives of Christians. But here they were, still smiling and reciting lines of poetry like "Yes, all things—e'en rainstorms—are presents from God."

People were beginning to stand up now. Birdie had pulled out all the stops on the organ. Perry stood quickly and turned to watch Pat and her father walk down the aisle. Jarvis Tillman held out his arm stiffly; one side of his mouth twitched nervously. Beside him, Pat was smiling broadly as she clutched her father's arm and looked adoringly at Marty, who returned her gaze from the front of the auditorium. The firm, straight planes of her face were softened and her skin was peachy-pink behind the layers of white netting. Her dress was of a delicate, swishy material, and the lines were long and simple, not full and fussy; it looked to Perry like something Ginger Rogers would have worn in a ballroom scene with Fred Astaire, except Ginger Rogers's dress would have been a much smaller size.

"My, she does make a sweet little bride!" Eldeen whispered loud enough for several rows to hear. There were murmurs of agreement. Pat was an inch or two taller than her father and a solid, big-boned girl. Perry never would have used the word "sweet" or "little" to describe her, but she looked sturdy and healthy and even-tempered—and, he thought, Marty would most likely find those to be qualities that wore well over the long haul. Marty himself would win no prize for good looks; he reminded Perry a little of his elementary school principal, Mr. Hal Mack, whom the boys had called Halloween Mask behind his back.

Brother Hawthorne was asking, "Who giveth this woman to be married?" and Jarvis Tillman started to speak, then had to stop and clear his throat, then cough and try again before he got it out: "Her mother and I do." Several people smiled sympathetically.

Perry remembered this exact moment in his own wedding, though he hadn't thought of it for years. Dinah's father, who had been twenty years older than her mother and who would die of a heart attack four months after the wedding, had answered loudly, "*I* do." Dinah's mother had drilled him repeatedly at the rehearsal to say "Her mother and I do," so whether he had forgotten or was simply testing his wife to see if she would correct him in public as usual, no one ever knew. Perry could still hear his mother-in-law's sharp inhalation as her husband spoke the words. During the reception afterward she had kept her back rigid and her lips pressed together in a thin, frosty smile. Perry had never known whether it was because of her husband's mistake or because she felt Dinah was marrying beneath her.

Marty's face flushed as he stepped forward to take his place at Pat's side. He was built like a lumberjack but moved awkwardly; Perry could see him getting trapped beneath trees and toppling off logs. His whole face looked lopsided, and his nose was a large wedge slightly off-center, the kind that would become decidedly hooked the older he got. Still, his countenance glowed, as if he couldn't believe his good fortune in winning the hand of the winsome, robust Pat.

Brother Hawthorne was using an old-fashioned script for the ceremony; he even included the line inviting any man who knew any reason why these two should not be joined to speak up or "forever hold his peace." Perry wished he knew how many times in the history of weddings someone had taken the preacher up on that offer. What kinds of things had been presented as reasons? Had anyone ever shouted out something preposterous as a prank? Something like "Don't marry him! He's already got six wives in six different states!"

As Marty and Pat repeated their vows, Perry felt a sense of panic on their behalf. Listening to the first few promises, uttered so glibly by Pat, he began frantically working out a homily in his mind, admonishing Marty and Pat to reconsider it all. How could they know what they were saying, what enormous commitments they were making? When he heard Marty's husky voice declare, "Till death do us part," he wanted to grip him by his massive shoulders and say, "How can you possibly stand there and promise all that to someone you barely know?"

Soon, Marty and Pat were kneeling at a small white prayer bench, their heads touching as Brother Hawthorne blessed their union. The quartet stood again after the prayer and sang "Take My Life," changing all the *my*'s to *our*'s. Then Marty and Pat rose and Brother Hawthorne addressed them directly, looking up at them both but speaking earnestly and kindly as a father giving last-minute instructions. His final words were for Marty: "Pat is your treasure. Love and cherish her. Her happiness, the success of your marriage, the spiritual prosperity of the children God may choose to give you—all these lie at your feet, Marty. Consider your responsibility gravely and execute it faithfully."

Perry hardly heard the rest; he was aware that Brother Hawthorne said something else that made everyone smile and laugh softly, and he knew that Marty and Pat turned around at some point to face the audience. He vaguely remembered Marty's fumbling at Pat's veil, then finally bending to kiss her—clumsily, as if he had never practiced it. He saw them bound down the aisle hand in hand while Birdie played "Praise Him, Praise Him." He began filing out with everyone else, nodding mutely in response to Eldeen's enthusiastic summary of the ceremony's many charms. He even ate a piece of white wedding cake and drank a cup of lemony punch in Fellowship Hall, and he saw Marty and Pat emerge later from separate Sunday school rooms, Pat now wearing a soft blue dress and Marty a dark gray suit. He watched Pat throw her bridal bouquet and saw Mayme Snyder catch it and flourish it above her head victoriously.

Perry stood at the back of the crowd watching Pat give her parents one last hug before taking Marty's arm again and running with him toward the old mail Jeep he had bought and painted deep maroon that summer. Marty opened the door for her, and before she got in, Pat turned and waved back at everyone, shielding her eyes from the birdseed being thrown. Perry saw the tin cans tied to the back bumper, heard them begin to rattle and clank as the Jeep lurched forward, saw the words "FAITH HOPE AND CHARITY" written in shaving cream across the back windshield—but over and over he kept remembering Brother Hawthorne's words to Marty: "Her happiness, the success of your marriage, the spiritual prosperity of the children God may choose to give you—all these lie at your feet."

Here he had been, all these months, assuming the failure of his marriage to be an equal partnership. He was willing to take his share of the blame, but Dinah was the one who had changed, not him. How could Theodore Hawthorne lay a woman's happiness—the *success of the marriage,* of all things—at the feet of her husband and let her off scot-free?

"There they go!" he heard someone say, and he noticed as the Jeep turned the corner that the shaving cream words were already melting away.

Chapter 22

Perry tried to look casual as he fingered the clasp of his life jacket again. The aluminum boat was rocking gently as the waves of a passing motorboat slapped its side.

"There," said Willard, sighing contentedly, "this is the time of day when the fishing starts getting good. The big boats go in and things quiet down." Perry slowly reeled in his line, studying the pink blush of the sky above the shoreline. If anyone had told him that before July was over he would be in a boat on a lake with Joe Leonard and Willard Scoggins, *fishing* of all things, he would have laughed in disbelief.

He had never considered going on the father-son outing for several reasons. First, and most obviously, he didn't have a son or a father here to go with. Besides that, it was a water activity and he preferred dry ground. Then, too, part of it was simply the idea of being around a whole group of men for that long without the easy talk of women to fill in the silent gaps and blend things together. As a clincher, it was a fishing excursion and he hated the smell of fish.

But when Joe Leonard had knocked on his door one morning last week, had stammered his request in embarrassed politeness, then had finally looked up at him with an almost wounded expression, Perry found himself powerless to turn him down.

"Well, I'm not a fisherman," he had said, shrugging and raising his hands in a helpless gesture. "I . . . to be honest, I've never really been fishing before in my life." Joe Leonard appeared to be holding his breath to brace himself for Perry's answer. They stood silently, Joe Leonard shifting from foot to foot in the doorway, until Perry thought to invite the boy inside.

Joe Leonard sat stiffly on the edge of the sofa, his long arms resting on his knees. He was wearing blue jeans with patches on both knees, Perry noticed, and his royal blue camp T-shirt. His eyes darted about, taking in every detail of the room, but his head never moved. Obviously he didn't intend to say anymore, so Perry tried again, leaning forward in the chair he had taken.

"I guess it's hard to believe that somebody my age hasn't ever been fishing." He stopped and gave a feeble laugh. Joe Leonard was squinting hard at the bookcase. "And what's even funnier, I guess," Perry continued, "is that I never even learned to swim." Joe Leonard raised his eyebrows and glanced quickly at Perry. His mouth was open as if he were about to speak, but instead he licked his lips and looked toward the door.

It came to Perry again that Joe Leonard lived a lonely life in many ways. No brothers or sisters, only his mother and grandmother at home. He worked by himself, methodically tending the blueberry bushes—watering them, checking the nets, picking the ripe berries, delivering them to people up and down the streets of Montroyal. He mowed lawns just as methodically. Perry had watched him several times guiding the mower in careful lines, cutting clean swaths, trimming along driveways and sidewalks afterward, sweeping up after himself.

The only young people Perry ever saw him with were at church, and there were really only six in what was called the Youth Group: the Chewnings' thirteen-year-old twin boys; Fern and Roy Tucker's fourteen-year-old daughter, Marilee; Joe Leonard; sixteen-year-old Bonita Puckett; and Mayme Snyder, who was going away to college this fall. It was odd to Perry how a church could have such disproportion in its age groups; there must be fifty children under the age of ten but only six teenagers.

He knew Joe Leonard liked to read. Books, in fact, were about the only subject Perry and Joe Leonard had ever discussed together. The boy liked basketball too. The Jelliffs, who lived in the house next door to the Blanchards on the other side, had an old basketball goal bolted to their carport. Their sons were both grown and married, and they had told Joe Leonard he could use the goal anytime he wanted. Almost every day, at odd times, Perry heard the dull, steady bouncing of Joe Leonard's basketball against the Jelliffs' driveway. If he looked out the corner window of the living room, he could see down to the Jelliffs' driveway; he had watched Joe Leonard several times, dribbling, pivoting, shooting from various angles. The goal itself was hidden from view, however, so he never saw whether the ball went in. The boy also played tennis with Jewel sometimes and Chinese Checkers or badminton after supper, but still it couldn't be a life of much excitement for a fifteen-year-old. They didn't even have a television, a phenomenon Perry hadn't discovered until a month or two ago.

Joe Leonard was picking at a thick thread around the edge of one of his knee patches. The silence was heavy. Perry didn't know what else to say. He realized that he hadn't really given a definite answer to Joe Leonard's invitation, although he had clearly implied a negative one, but now they were stuck, neither one sure of the next step. Perry wished Eldeen were here to take things in hand and lay it all out plainly.

Perry thought of Joe Leonard's father—Bailey Blanchard, the hapless fisherman. Joe Leonard would have been twelve or so when his father died. Perry wondered suddenly how the boy had handled the tragedy. *"A boy abruptly bereft of the strongest male influence in his life."* The words came to his mind in an instant; he had heard the phrase somewhere recently—or maybe read it—but he couldn't place the source. And immediately he saw the link between himself and Joe Leonard. Perry had lost his own father as a child, he was lost in a sense to his own son, and now he was offered a chance to substitute for Joe Leonard's missing father. Not that it would change any of the sad circumstances, of course—but it came to him that maybe this was one of those things you had to do.

"I'll go," Perry said, louder than he meant to. There was a sharp snap as Joe Leonard broke off the denim thread. He looked at Perry self-consciously and grinned, then stood to his feet and moved toward the door.

"Well, good," he said, "I'm . . . well, thanks a lot," and he ducked his head and was out the door. Perry stood at the door a moment watching the boy walk quickly toward the driveway. Then from somewhere, an open window probably, he heard Eldeen's deep voice: "What did he say, Joe Leonard? Is he going?"

Willard Scoggins rose partway from his seat and reached for his tackle box. The boat began swaying again, and Perry looked wistfully toward the shore. He could still see the glow of the fire from their wiener roast earlier. Several younger boys were leaping about it, cupping their hands over lightning bugs. Two or three men were fishing off the dock.

"Think I'll try this new lipless crankbait I got," Willard said, turning around and holding up a chartreuse lure. "See, it's a half-ouncer, two treble hooks and the tie on top. You ever tried one?"

Perry shook his head. He wished Willard would quit moving around so much. With his weight, one slight misstep and they could all end up in the lake. Willard turned back around again and rummaged through his tackle box. Perry studied the breadth of his Levi jeans, noting the "42" waist size stamped on the back tag. Perry wondered if he had ever considered removing the tag; it shouldn't be hard to do. There was no need to go around advertising your waist size.

"Oh, that's right, I keep forgetting," said Willard, lifting one leg and swinging it over to straddle the seat. "You said you didn't fish much, didn't you? Well, these little fellers"—he jiggled the lure and Perry heard a metallic rattle—"they're great. See, they're sinkers. You let them fall, and when you start reeling, they waggle around like a live minnow. See how flat it is on the side here and how the head's down at a little angle like that? Well, coming through the water they vibrate like this, see"—he stood up again to demonstrate the motion of the lure, and Perry felt the boat tip to one side—"and the fish hears the racket and sees the little guy zipping by and—chomp!—he takes a bite he probably won't live to regret!" Willard laughed quietly and sat back down hard. Perry grabbed the side of the boat. "Lots of people don't understand crankbaits," Willard said, turning serious. "They don't get a whole lot of respect."

Perry looked down into the water and felt a twinge of fear. The lake was murky, with little bits of something yellowish floating all over the top. He ran a hand along the hard padding of his life jacket. How did these things work anyway? Were they good for only a certain amount of time? After all, a sponge would hold only so much water.

Perry saw Joe Leonard look back at him anxiously, so he smiled and tried to look relaxed. From somewhere on shore he heard a bird with an insistent, wheezy call, like the sound of a little rubber squeeze toy. He breathed deeply and looked intently at the spot where his line intersected the surface of the water, feeling grateful that the day had gone smoothly so far. Earlier, he had ventured into the roped swimming area in an old pair of denim cutoffs, and no one seemed to question his staying in the shallow part with the little boys. He had helped to organize a little game of water basketball with a Nerf ball and a coat hanger he rigged up to a low tree branch and had even supported Levi Hawthorne and some of the others while they tried to learn to float on their backs. He and Joe Leonard had gone out in a paddleboat for more than an hour later on and had talked at length about *The Lord of the Rings,* which Joe Leonard was presently reading.

Then before they ate, when everyone had gone over to the volleyball nets to get a couple of games started, Joe Leonard had motioned Perry to the dock and had shown him how to cast. He had brought along an extra rod for Perry to use, already baited with something he called a spinner. It was easy, really, and Perry soon had the knack of releasing his thumb at just the right time so that the line could play out. He had thanked Joe Leonard, and they had gone to join the others.

Perry could understand the attraction of fishing, not for actually catching fish, of course, but for the leisurely drifting along in outdoor solitude. He finished reeling in again and recast, wondering if there were some way to make sure no fish would be attracted by his spinnerbait. He wished it weren't such a bright, shiny turquoise.

Willard was still expounding on crankbaits. ". . . in shallows or out deeper, it doesn't matter. You can pump it, or jig it up and down, or let it zigzag, or just reel it in fast. But the hooks on these things"—he broke off and hunched over, his huge fingers almost hiding the lure he was working with—"they're never sharp enough for me, and I don't like these old curled-in ones. I always change them to round bend trebles," and he held one up for Perry to see. "Gamakatsu—they're the sharpest—cuts bone clean."

On shore another bird was calling over and over—sweet, liquid notes: *too-roo-a-lee, too-roo-a-lee!* The inflection was more like a question, though: *Do you agree? Do you agree?* Perry reeled in very slowly. It occurred to him that maybe he could get the fish to think his spinner was a sick minnow, not fit to eat, if it moved lethargically. He began studying the sky, the bank, the grassy shallows, formulating descriptions he could use in a story sometime—"the dark range of steep pines silhouetted against the deepening coral of sunset," "ribbons of mauve and gray," "the bass choir of bullfrogs," "the sun slipping like a burnished medal beneath the horizon," "the moon rising like a porcelain saucer," "the reeds set ablaze by the sun's last flame, like slender gold torches." He brushed at a mosquito around his ear. "The whine of mosquitoes searching for a landing strip."

He felt a light jerk on his line but was immensely relieved to see that he had only reeled in too much line and the turquoise spinnerbait had run up against the tip of his rod. It appeared to be choking, one tiny dot of an eye fixed sternly on Perry. He quickly loosened some line and then recast far out toward shore. Thankfully, neither Willard nor Joe Leonard had noticed.

"Now then," said Willard, "let's try this little baby." He leaned back and cast off the other side of the boat. Perry was beginning to get used to the swaying of the boat now; he thought maybe he could come out here by himself sometime under the pretense of fishing and try doing some writing. He could borrow a rod from Joe Leonard, rent one of these same boats, and drift all over the lake; a change of scenery might energize his writing. If he came close to anyone else, he could quickly pick up his rod. And if anybody shouted anything to him—like "Catching anything?"—he could shout back, "No, these hooks on my lipless crankbait must not be sharp enough!"

Zebco—that was the name imprinted on the rod he was holding. He wondered all of a sudden if it could possibly be the same rod Joe Leonard's father had used on occasion. Joe Leonard had said it was one "we've had for a long time." Perry wondered if this could even be the very lake where Bailey Blanchard had drowned. On second thought, he doubted that Brother Hawthorne would do that—plan a church activity at the scene of a former tragedy. Anyway, now that he thought about it, he was sure Eldeen had said it was a small lake, and this one was definitely not what he'd call small. They hadn't even come within shouting distance of any of the other boats.

Suddenly Willard lunged sideways, then immediately straightened and leaned back. The boat rocked crazily. "I got something!" he yelled. Perry and Joe Leonard watched as Willard fought to keep the fish. "Oh, no, you don't," he said, clenching his teeth and snapping the rod tip up. "Come on out of that brush pile, big guy." Perry watched Willard strain backward and forward, heard him grunting and chuckling. "Come on, there, brother, come see me." At last he sat back down and quit reeling but still kept the line pulled taut. "That's what's good about a rod like this, see," he said to Perry. "It'll give just enough so the fish doesn't throw the lure. Now I've got him out in the open, see, and I'll just let him wear himself out."

Later, after Willard had accomplished what he called "pulling that head over" and had swung the fish into the boat, clamping its lower jaw with his giant thumb, Joe Leonard sprang forward to help him remove the hook. "When he starts to jump, see, you've got only a second to do it!" Willard said, breathing hard. "Now that's a fine fish there," he said, then emitted a war whoop and lifted his eyes heavenward. "Thank you, dear Lord, for what you did on the fifth day of creation!" He held the fish within inches of Perry's face. "Must be a four-pounder, wouldn't you say?"

Perry suddenly remembered Dr. Holland holding Troy up in the delivery room almost nine years ago. "Bet he's an eight-pounder if he's an ounce!" the doctor had said. Looking at the fish now, Perry wondered if Dr. Holland had been a fisherman. He could still picture Troy wriggling and arching his back, his small face livid with passion, his tiny chest heaving with every outraged gasp of air. Perry narrowed his eyes and focused hard on the fish; it writhed and flipped its tail wildly. Willard was looking at Perry like a proud father, as if expecting a compliment.

Perry smiled and nodded. "Oh, at least four pounds," he said.

An hour later, after they had fished all around a little island, they heard the whistle signal to start for shore.

Willard took a series of short, choppy breaths, then exhaled loudly with a satisfied "Ahhh!" He pounded lightly on his chest and looked toward the sky. "It doesn't get much better than this—fishing on a summer night!" He took the oars and expertly swung the boat around, then began rowing swiftly toward shore. "I appreciate you two taking me in," he said jovially. "It's never as much fun going fishing by yourself."

"I imagine," said Perry, though he wasn't so sure about that.

"Yep, when I called Joe Leonard and asked him if he was going with anybody today, I was one disappointed angler, I'll tell you. Then when he called back later and suggested we make it a threesome, I jumped at the bait—just like my buddy here," and he nodded toward the bass on the stringer.

Perry looked back over the lake. It looked smaller now with the tall pines reflected like a velvety fringe around the edge of the water. Up on shore he could see the others climbing out of boats, could hear their laughter and the gentle thumping of the boats being chained to the dock. The campfire was burning brighter now in preparation for the marshmallows and the devotional time. Brother Hawthorne was bending over Levi, unfastening the boy's life jacket. *"Abruptly bereft of the strongest male influence in his life"*—all at once Perry remembered where he had heard it. It was from a radio talk Brother Hawthorne had given a couple of weeks earlier. He had been telling the story of a missionary child in Uruguay whose father was killed in a plane crash.

As Willard eased the boat up to the dock, Perry saw in his mind the face of a little boy crying for his father. At first it was a face he didn't know—some nameless, grieving child. Then he saw it change into his own face as a small boy, withdrawn and frightened—a little boy left to grow up in a house with two women. Then into his mind came the image of Joe Leonard's face—a younger version, his hair in ragged tufts about his freckled face, large tears swelling in his blue eyes. Little boys "abruptly bereft" of their fathers; it was a sad thought. As Perry stepped out of the boat onto the solid dock, he saw another face: that of Troy—his own son—crying out in the night, his eyes wide with terror.

"Here we are, Perry," said Willard, touching his elbow. "Hey, you all right? You look a little—well, *worried* or something."

"No, no, I'm . . . I'm fine, really," said Perry, forcing a weak smile. He released the clasp on the front of his life jacket.

"Well, don't feel bad," Willard said, clapping his back and throwing a heavy arm around his shoulder, "I didn't catch anything either the first half-dozen times I fished this lake." Together, they walked off the dock toward the campfire, Joe Leonard following behind.

Chapter 23

Thank you for coming," Brother Hawthorne said the next night, shaking Perry's hand at the door. "Edna and I have been talking about having you over ever since you came. We're ashamed it's taken this long."

Perry shook his head. "Don't be. The time's gone fast, and we've all been busy. And anyway," he said, waving his hand back toward the dining room table, where the plates were already scraped clean and stacked on one corner, "this was worth waiting for." There, that wasn't bad, he thought. The words hadn't gotten blocked up as they often did between his mind and his tongue. Edna smiled at him from behind her husband, and the three children peered at him around Brother Hawthorne's legs.

"I'll walk you to your car," said Brother Hawthorne, stepping around Perry to open the screen door. Perry thanked Edna again, patted Levi's head, and followed Brother Hawthorne down the steps.

"Oh, here, let me show you something first," Brother Hawthorne said, motioning to the side of the house. Inside the garage, he pointed upward and aimed a pocket flashlight toward one of the crossbeams. In the dim light Perry could barely make out what looked like a small thatch of grass.

"A nest?" he asked.

Brother Hawthorne nodded. "Doves—it's been fun for the children."

As Perry's eyes adjusted to the darkness, he could see the outline of a bird in the nest, a vigilant mother twisting her head. Or he supposed it was the mother; if it was, where was the father? It was late to be out flying around. Maybe male doves were notoriously inconstant, wandering about seeking new mates after every new batch of eggs. But surely not. They seemed too genteel and peaceable for that sort of lifestyle. Maybe the father was out gathering provisions for the next day. Or perhaps the female had thrown him out of the nest with some shrewish complaint—"Why don't you *coo* to me more?"

"How's your book coming?" Brother Hawthorne asked.

"Oh, it's taking shape," said Perry. "Thank you for tonight—letting me sit in on the deacons' meeting before church, I mean. That was . . . well, I know you don't usually allow that."

Brother Hawthorne laughed quietly. "Well, they're not very exciting, are they?"

Perry didn't answer. Standing there in the dark, he heard the weak cheep of a baby bird. That must be it; the father dove was out finding food. But didn't birds do that during the day?

Brother Hawthorne imitated the low triple coo of the dove's call. "That's how they sound. You hear them all the time around here. Those and Carolina wrens"—he whistled a brilliant trill followed by a shrill falsetto "Tea kettle, tea kettle, tea kettle." The bird in the nest didn't stir. The thought came to Perry that he ought to ask Brother Hawthorne about the birds he had heard at the lake. But he would feel silly trying to imitate their calls.

"Well . . ." Perry took a step backward. "I'd better head home."

"I'm glad you agreed to let me tell the people about your book," Brother Hawthorne said as they started toward Perry's Toyota. "I know it was better for you at first the other way, but once you started visiting all the Sunday school classes and other activities with your notebook and pen, people did start to get a little curious."

Perry nodded. "It was time to let them know. Anyway, Jewel had it figured out months ago."

Brother Hawthorne smiled. "Well, it made it easier to get you into the Ladies' Bible Circle. They would have really wondered about you if they hadn't known what you were up to."

Perry nodded and laughed. "Well, everybody has been very kind about it all," he said.

"They can't wait to read it," Brother Hawthorne said. "Or I should say, *we* can't wait. It's not every day you get to see yourselves from an outsider's point of view."

Actually, Perry hadn't expected to keep his book a secret for so long. After he had told Eldeen, Jewel, and Joe Leonard about it back in May at the Purple Calliope, the day he had let himself get so carried away, he thought it would soon leak out to everybody at church. But evidently it hadn't. The people had seemed genuinely surprised when Brother Hawthorne announced it in a Sunday evening service in June.

Brother Hawthorne stooped and pulled out a small clump of

something among the geraniums lining the driveway. "You can't do much gardening," he said, holding up the handful of weeds, "before you start thinking of Scripture." Perry wondered if Brother Hawthorne ever did anything without thinking of Scripture. Once in a sermon he had heard him draw a spiritual parallel from a can of Edna's hairspray that had gotten clogged. And another time while accompanying the pastor on Thursday evening visitation, Perry had heard him explain the process of sanctification to a new convert by using the illustration of an Easter egg dye kit. "The more times you dip the egg into the dye," he had said, "the brighter and purer its color becomes." The convert had caught on quickly. "And the more time I spend in the Bible, the more like Christ I'll become," the man had said. "Absolutely," Brother Hawthorne had said, his eyes shining.

As they reached the car now, Perry realized this was the perfect time to ask a question that was on his mind. He wished there was a way to lead into it gradually, but he needed to get home for his phone call to Troy. He opened the car door but didn't get inside.

"The wedding last Saturday was interesting," he said. Brother Hawthorne cleared his throat but didn't respond. "I was wondering . . ." said Perry, "well, at the end you said something to Marty that I—I really didn't follow." Perry put one foot inside the car but kept the other on the curb. Brother Hawthorne raised his eyebrows.

"It was the part," continued Perry, "about the success of the marriage being Marty's responsibility." He shook his head. "Do you really mean that? Somehow it just doesn't seem . . . altogether fair."

Brother Hawthorne tossed the clump of weeds into the gutter. He answered slowly. "I know—it doesn't *sound* fair, does it?" Somewhere on the next street a car horn blared suddenly. Brother Hawthorne folded his arms and looked up at the night sky, then sighed and looked at Perry. "I've counseled so many married couples who were having trouble that I couldn't begin to count them," he said, "and all I can tell you is that in almost every case, *almost every case,* Perry, the husband's attitude was wrong."

"What about the wife's?" Perry asked.

"Many times it was wrong too," Brother Hawthorne said, "and I'm not saying there might not be cases in which the woman is mostly to blame for a marriage gone sour." He smiled at Perry and laid a hand on his shoulder. "I have only my experience to back me up, Perry, and I'll say it again—in almost every case of marital counseling in which *I've* been involved, the fundamental problem was the husband. If a man loves his wife as Christ loved the church and if he loves her as his own body, well—that's a level of love most of us never reach." He removed his hand from Perry's shoulder and stepped back. Perry wished there were something he could argue about.

Brother Hawthorne spoke again, more slowly now. "Men are by nature insensitive and selfish . . ."

"And women aren't?"

"Women are *sensitive* and selfish," Brother Hawthorne replied quickly. "We all have a healthy dose of selfishness all right, but if the husband is the man he ought to be, he can set the whole tone for . . ."

"I gave her every single thing she wanted!" Perry said suddenly. He felt his face grow warm and was glad it was dark.

"Maybe what she really wanted wasn't things," said Brother Hawthorne quietly. Perry opened the door wider and slid behind the steering wheel.

"I can't think of what it was I did that made her . . ." Perry broke off, then tried again. "I wasn't doing anything that . . ." Again he faltered.

"Oh, but there are so many things a husband must do," said Brother Hawthorne. The faraway sound of a telephone ringing made them both glance toward the house, where the front door stood slightly ajar.

Perry inserted the key into the ignition and turned it. He needed to get home. Troy would be expecting his call in a half hour.

"Would you like to talk more about this?" asked Brother Hawthorne, leaning forward as Perry pulled the door shut. He squatted down on the curb beside the open car window, like an agile Bolshoi dancer. "You know, Perry, a man can never be the husband he ought to be—the kind we've been talking about on Wednesday nights—unless he's born again. There's no magic formula, and it's too hard a job without the help of the Holy Spirit."

"Well, maybe . . . I don't know," said Perry. He looked into Brother Hawthorne's searching eyes briefly, then turned away. "It's all still so confusing." He waved his hand. "Thanks again for tonight," he said. As he eased the gearshift into place and pulled away, he saw Edna come to the front door and call to her husband. In his rearview mirror he saw the pastor rise slowly and start toward the house.

Perry turned on the radio. He recognized the woman's voice as the childcare expert on a nationally syndicated call-in program. The station was probably replaying an earlier broadcast. "And if it can't be flushed out with water," she said, "try licking the child's eye." Licking the eye? What was she talking about, Perry wondered. The mother calling in evidently wondered the same thing.

"*Lick* the eye?" she asked.

"Yes, your tongue can't injure the eye, but a handkerchief or rough finger might. Just gently hold the eyelids apart with your thumbs and run your tongue right over the eyeball. The eye is so sensitive that . . ."

Perry turned it off. He didn't want to hear the word *sensitive* again, and he didn't want to hear advice about licking somebody's eyeball.

Sensitive. These Christians had a pat little answer for everything. As if men couldn't be sensitive too. As if men were so busy thinking their cold, complex, logical thoughts they could never spare the effort it took to feel. He remembered one of Dinah's last comments to him before she had left the house that last day, the day when he was packing up the things he was taking with him.

"If you could just once in your life let down and show me that you really *care*," she had said. He had been standing beside the kitchen counter drinking a cup of coffee, and she was at the back door, one hand on the doorknob and the other clenched in a tight fist at her side. Troy was already in the car.

"Care?" he remembered thinking, as he had turned to pour the rest of his coffee into the sink. At that moment he could have written a whole compendium on caring, a comprehensive lexicon of all the gradations of the word; he could have written an encyclopedia—an entire multivolume set of them—about that single word: *Care*. But giving a speech, saying anything aloud at that moment was inconceivable. So he had said nothing, had kept his back to her, and Dinah had left, slamming the door behind her.

He remembered standing there for a long time, watching her shove the car into reverse and rocket out of the driveway. He could still see Troy's look of alarm as he was jolted forward in the backseat. And he could still feel the hurt and frustration—the helplessness of losing something irreplaceable, the disgust over his own failure to act decisively, and finally the cold fear of being alone again. Oh, yes, he knew all about being *sensitive*.

Driving home now, he passed Thrifty-Mart. It was still open. A huge banner hung in the front window: DOUBLE COUPONS EVERY-DAY. He remembered suddenly that he was out of milk. If he didn't stop now, he wouldn't have any for his cereal in the morning. He'd have to hurry, though, or he would be late for his phone call to Troy. He pulled into the parking lot and swung into a space in front of an ancient-looking Ford. As he was about to open his door, he saw an old man and woman, both of them creeping along behind a shopping cart, making their way toward the Ford. Perry's hand rested on his door handle, but he waited, watching the couple. Now here was a man who should have some valuable insights on how to go about keeping a wife. Perry rolled down his window.

The man guided the cart to the rear door of the Ford while the woman shuffled forward to open it. Silently the husband lifted a single bag and carried it to the backseat. Perry could hear his low grunts of exertion. The woman took another bag, and so they went, back and forth like large toys winding down, until all six bags were safely deposited in the car. The woman pushed down the lock on the back door, closed the door, then tested it. The man then pushed the cart away from the car, and the two of them stood, one behind the other, watching it roll toward the concrete base of a lightpost, where it banged with a jingly clatter and came to a halt.

They turned back to the Ford then. Still neither one had spoken. The woman opened the driver's door and gingerly seated herself behind the steering wheel, then with both hands lifted each leg one at a time and swung it into the car. Then she reached out, pulled the door closed, and locked it. Meanwhile, the man was tottering around the back of the car toward the passenger's side. Something fluttered from his hands as he started to get in—a long white strip of paper; probably the receipt of their purchases, Perry thought—and the old man had to stoop over to retrieve it, then scoot a few steps forward, then a few more as a breeze caught it. He finally grasped it as it flattened itself against the front tire; then he stood up and slowly wound it around his fingers before turning back to the car. Perry felt like he was watching a silent movie in slow motion, or an old comedy routine with Carol Burnett and Dick VanDyke as two elderly people, exaggerating every movement, milking it for humor. He wouldn't have been surprised to hear a great outburst of canned laughter.

The passenger door was still open, and the woman inside was watching her husband impassively, her mouth slackened. As he approached the car, however, the woman suddenly took on new life and issued an ultimatum, incongruous for the whiny, plaintive tone in which it was delivered. "Come on hyere or I'm a'leavin'! And lock yor door when ya git in, too," Perry heard her say. The old man made a great production of getting himself into the car and settled, then reached out and caught hold of the door handle. Right before the door swung shut, Perry heard the man say distinctly and quite venomously, *"Shut up, woman!"*

The woman had to start the car several times before it caught, and then she revved the engine mightily. And still they sat there. She turned to the man and said something, pointing to the dashboard, and they both stared hard at whatever it was. Perry tried to imagine what life would be like at this pace, where even the simplest action required great concentration.

He glanced at his watch. The milk would have to wait until tomorrow. He needed to get home; it was almost ten o'clock. But he felt sluggish, infected with despair by the scene he had just witnessed. Finally the headlights of the Ford flicked on, and both the woman and man looked in both directions behind them before the car backed up and then crept slowly toward the parking lot exit.

Well, so much for instruction in enduring marriages, Perry thought. He started his car and pulled out behind them. He watched them turn left and disappear down the road, two old people chugging along at twenty miles an hour, looking straight ahead, scanning the road for hazards, a great dark space between them.

What would it be like, he wondered, to be old and married? Would an old woman still have her moods? Would she still badger her husband to *talk* to her or would she be ready finally for silence? As he approached Montroyal, Perry tried to imagine the Hawthornes as an old couple, Theodore with springy white curls and Edna still plump but her hair faded to a pale apricot. His mind flashed back to tonight, both of them carrying in the serving dishes, sitting side by side at the round table, answering each other courteously, touching without embarrassment. He saw Brother Hawthorne's attentive expression as Edna told a story he must have heard many times, about an old Mexican woman in their apartment building when they lived in Florida, who made tortillas from scratch every day. Perry remembered a recent Wednesday evening, when Brother Hawthorne had made the statement, "Your respectful attention is one of the best gifts you can give your spouse."

It would be easy to write the Hawthornes' relationship off as public show if it hadn't been for seeing them at Darlene's Kreamy Kones that time. And who could tell? Maybe even that night had been staged; maybe they went somewhere every weekend and acted affectionate just in case one of their church members happened by. Maybe right now back at their house they were arguing vehemently: "You put too many spices in the taco sauce again!" "Last time you said it was too bland!" "And the tea tasted like swamp water!" "Well, why don't you go find somebody who can make tea to suit you?" But the scene lacked realism.

As Perry pulled into his driveway, he saw the porch light switch on next door. Eldeen stepped outside in her floral muumuu, fanning herself with a magazine. "Well, did you have yourself a good time?" she called. "Did Edna fix you some tacos?"

"Yes," said Perry. "Tacos with all the trimmings."

"Mmm, mmm, she does make the best tacos," said Eldeen. "That's one of her specialty dishes, along with Chinese chicken dumplings and zucchini pie. Did she tell you they used to live in a apartment building with a Mexican lady down in Florida who taught her how to cook the real authentic Mexican way?"

"Yes, she did," answered Perry.

"Well, well," said Eldeen, "it's sure hot—and it's my bedtime." She turned abruptly to go inside. "We sure missed you riding with us tonight. It just wasn't the same. Good night now, I know you got you a phone call to make so I won't keep you." And the front door closed and the yellow light turned off.

Perry unlocked his front door and went swiftly to the telephone. According to the digital clock on the bookshelf, it was one minute before ten o'clock.

Dinah answered. No hello, no formalities. Just "Troy's not here."

Perry felt betrayed. Troy knew he called at this time every Sunday, and so did Dinah.

"Where is he?" Perry asked.

"Spending the night with Chad, camping out in their backyard."

Perry frowned. "Sleeping outside? But . . . isn't that . . ."

"Dangerous? Is that what you were going to say?"

"Well, isn't it?"

"Kevin and Mark Kline are there too."

Perry thought suddenly of the three little boys who had disappeared in Charleston the week before. They had been together, riding their bikes, but they never came home. The police had arrested two sleazy-looking men in connection with the crime, but neither of them would talk. Perry had studied their pictures in the newspaper, feeling certain that he could easily strangle both of them barehanded without a pang of remorse.

"Are the Hudsons home tonight?" Perry asked.

Dinah sighed. "I checked it all out, Perry. They've got a Doberman, remember. And, yes, Jeanie and Tom are both home. If you're so concerned about it, you . . ." She stopped without finishing.

You what? thought Perry. What was she going to say? He gripped the receiver tighter. This had been the pattern of their conversations during the months before he had left: Dinah blurting out thoughts in a great rush, then cutting off in the middle of a sentence that could go in so many different directions, and Perry standing mutely, trying to fill in the long, empty blank.

Did all men have to tread through this minefield of conversing with an unpredictable woman? Perry wondered. If he had been able to talk with the old man at Thrifty-Mart, would he have admitted the same problem? He could almost hear him: "They's all like the dang wind, sonny. You never can tell whichaway they're a'gonna blow." Did Edna Hawthorne ever break off without finishing a heated remark, leaving Theodore to guess at where it was headed?

At last Perry spoke. "How's your work going?"

"Okay." At least she hadn't shot back with "Fine," which usually carried with it a caustic implication that she didn't want to talk about it.

"Any big sales lately?"

"A couple."

Again there was a long pause.

"Dinah, what . . ." He wasn't even sure at first what he had started out to say.

"What *what?*" she asked finally.

"What . . . what did I ever do?" There was a reverberation to the silence that followed, as if it were growing more intense—a locomotive of sound and light bearing down on him. Why was the lamp next to the sofa suddenly so bright—and so hot? And why didn't Dinah answer?

She finally did, with a short, scornful laugh. "What did you ever *do?* Oh, Perry, that's priceless, that's really priceless. You honestly want me to tell you the answer to that?"

"Well, yes. Yes, I do."

"Well, let me tell you then. You did *nothing,* Perry. Absolutely *nothing.*" From her tone, Perry knew it wasn't an exoneration.

And without even meaning to, he heard himself repeating the words Brother Hawthorne had spoken earlier that evening: "Oh, but there are so many things a husband must do."

"What? What did you say?" asked Dinah. "Are you being . . . ?"

Perry stopped breathing for a moment. "Nothing," he said at last. As he carefully hung up the receiver, he heard what sounded like a low moan from somewhere outside, then realized it was a police siren starting up in the distance. He thought of the mournful call of the dove and remembered the lone mother bird sitting on her nest.

Part 3
STARLIGHT

For we have seen his star in the east, and are come to worship him.

Matthew 2:2

Chapter 24

Perry reread the sentence he had just typed into the computer: "Though the tag *legalism* has been affixed to fundamentalist Christians in general, Pastor Frazier of the Gospel Lighthouse regularly preaches more about freedom than restrictions." Perry knew he was approaching a touchy subject in this chapter; one of Cal's favorite harangues centered on the "narrow-minded, rule-listing, hellfire-and-damnation legalists" that had stifled his normal development as a human being.

"You want to know what I did on prom night back in 1959 in Sand Flats, Georgia, Perry?" Cal had once told him. "While everybody else went to pick up their girl in their dad's car, old Cal was at—drum roll, please—*church!* Yep, we had a Youth Club Banquet that night, one that was supposed to make us all forget what we were missing out on. They had a lasagna dinner—all our mothers showed up to serve it on fancy tablecloths, with candles, flowers, the whole works. Then for two hours we played stupid games—all twelve of us dressed up in the same clothes we'd have to put back on the next morning for Sunday school—and then we had a film. And you want to know what the film was about? It was called *Decision Countdown,* and it was about"— here Cal dropped his voice to a lower register—"a rebellious teenager who failed to heed his parents' warnings, got involved with the wrong crowd, and ended up in a gruesome car accident, from which he eventually recovered of course, but now he was a changed boy who carried his Bible to school and prayed before lunch in the cafeteria."

Cal had guffawed afterward, then quickly sobered. "I can laugh about it now, but it sure wasn't funny back then. I was so mad that . . ."

"That you vowed not to make the same terrible mistakes your parents made in bringing their kids up," Perry had interrupted. He regretted his words instantly. How could he have been so thoughtless?

Cal's children were the great disappointment of his life. Perry felt mean; he had stabbed his friend—with the truth, to be sure, but a stabbing nevertheless. It had always annoyed him, though, that Cal griped incessantly about his upbringing yet had failed so abysmally to improve upon it with his own family. One of his sons had been arrested numerous times for drug possession, the other one was presently in a rehab program for teens with suicidal tendencies, and more recently his seventeen-year-old daughter had left home with the bass guitarist of a rock group called Fields of Dung.

Perry read the opening sentence of the new chapter once more, then shoved back his chair and reached for a folder; he hadn't told anyone about his new filing system, but it had worked beautifully. On the double bed in Beth's guest room were spread out all his manila folders, fanned out in groups of eight or so, like oversized playing cards. Beth would have a fit if she saw how he had taken over this room. He had been delighted when she had called in August and said she wasn't coming home as she had originally planned but was spending her summer break instead with a friend at Cape Cod, a woman who, according to Beth, was writing test bank questions for graduate courses in statistical analysis.

He selected the folder labeled SEPARATION and began riffling through his handwritten pages. What he needed was in here somewhere.

Now that his book was progressing and he was actually writing drafts of chapters, Perry had begun reading what others had written about fundamentalists. In the early stages of a study, he liked to observe and record without the clutter of other people's research in his mind, but once the project was taking a clear form, he found it valuable to compare his findings with those of others. When the term *legalism* kept appearing, he had concluded that it wasn't just a pet word of Cal's and had confronted Brother Hawthorne with the issue in one of their private talks.

There it was. Perry removed from the folder a sheet of ruled paper and read through it front to back. On it he had written categories, then had left space after each one to record Brother Hawthorne's responses: MOVIES? SLACKS? DANCING? DRINKING? MUSIC? HAIR LENGTH? DATING? HOMOSEXUALITY? Looking over the sheet now, he was surprised at how little he had written down. He would have to check the cassette tape to see if he'd omitted anything significant.

He had just typed the first three words of the next sentence when the telephone rang.

"Perry, I need your help." It was Jewel.

"Sure. Where are you?" He realized that in all the months he had lived here, he had never heard Jewel's voice over the telephone. It sounded soft and charmingly Southern, like Melanie Wilkes's voice in *Gone with the Wind*.

"I'm at school," she said. "I've got five minutes before the last class of third graders comes in, and I just now realized I forgot my recorder and left it at home along with the lesson I'd planned out for today. I don't need it for another half hour or so, but that's what I'd counted on doing with my fourth graders this afternoon, and . . ."

"You want me to bring it to you?" said Perry. "It won't be any problem. Where is it?"

"Well, first, you'll need the key. Mama's not home, you know. It's her day to work at the G.O.O.D. Store; I dropped her off on my way to school. But there's a spare key to the house hanging on a little string inside the storage shed right by where the badminton racquets are. You know how to . . ."

"Yep, I know how to get into the shed, and I think I can get past the monster in the backyard. Where's the stuff you need in the house?"

"Well . . ." Jewel gave a frustrated laugh, "that's the problem. I *know* I left it at home, but I'm not sure exactly where. I was sitting at the piano practicing the recorder last night after church, remember?"

"Right." Perry remembered clearly. He had watched the two of them closely, Jewel swaying slightly as she played and Willard sitting beside her, flipping through the pages of the hymnbook for songs in the key of C. He remembered staring at the slender legs of the piano bench, worrying every time Willard shifted his weight forward to point to a new hymn.

"Well, I *think* I set the recorder down on the piano when we stopped, but I might have carried it back to the bedroom later and set it on the dresser. I just can't remember. We ate right after that, you know, and then I didn't play it anymore."

Perry tried to recall if he had seen where she laid the recorder, but then he remembered that the smoke alarm had interrupted the concert, followed by Eldeen hooting from the kitchen, "Why, just looka here what I've gone and done!" And they'd all rushed into the kitchen to find her convulsed in laughter at having burned one of the grilled cheese sandwiches to a blackened crisp. Jewel had taken over and finished up, with everybody else pitching in, and then after they had eaten, they had sat around talking for about half an hour before they'd played a game of dominoes, which Willard had brought over. Perry didn't remember noticing the recorder on the piano when he left around nine forty-five.

"Well, I'll look around," he said. "It can't be too hard to find."

"And the lesson plan—I really need that too," Jewel said apologetically. "It was one I'd written out on Saturday. I think I set it on the desk in the hallway, but it might be on the nightstand in my bedroom too—or maybe on my dresser. It's on a sheet of typing paper. I was looking at it again before bed last night."

"I'll find it," Perry said. "Don't worry. Is that all?"

"Yes. I'm so sorry, Perry. I don't usually do things like this, but lately . . . well, it must be from getting older." She laughed weakly.

"It must be from getting besieged by Willard the Conqueror, you mean," Perry wanted to say, for recently Willard had made his intentions quite clear with a flurry of public gallantries. Jewel seemed dazed by it all.

"I'll be there soon," Perry said. "It's no problem, really, so don't feel bad. I needed to go out anyway."

"I could've run home at lunchtime if I'd realized it," she added. "But I never thought of it until a minute ago." She had such a pretty voice—so fluid and light, like a pleasant tune. Perry almost wished he could keep her on the phone. "Thank you, Perry," she said. "This is sure sweet of you."

"Forget it," Perry said. He could hear children laughing in the background as she hung up, and someone called out, "Hey, Miz Blanchard!"

Hormel rushed forward yipping madly as Perry unlatched the gate to Jewel's backyard. Perry stooped and offered the dachshund an Oreo, the only thing he could find as a quick substitute for a dog biscuit. Hormel sniffed it suspiciously, then dispatched it in one gulp and wagged his tail at Perry. Perry smiled down at him. Of all Willard's gifts to Jewel, this was his personal favorite, although the sewing cabinet Willard had made out of a section of tiny drawers from the library's old card catalog was nice too.

"Sorry, no time to play, hot dog," Perry said to Hormel now, striding past him to the shed. He had no trouble finding the key and letting himself into the house.

He went in through the side door, and as he stepped into the kitchen he could still smell last night's burnt sandwich. He glanced at the table and at the bookcase by the telephone. No sign of the lesson plan or the recorder there. On the little chalkboard beside the refrigerator was written in Eldeen's uneven printing "CALL FERN TUES.! BIRTH-DAY!" along with what must be a grocery list: TUNA, RAISINS, DOG FOOD, TOILET PAPER, CORNSTARCH. The box of dominoes was on the kitchen counter; Willard must have left them last night.

Perry went into the living room but saw nothing on the piano except the sheet music for a tuba solo Joe Leonard was working on. On the end of the couch where Eldeen always sat, next to the old radio, he noticed a new pillowcase in progress, stretched into an embroidery hoop; half a lamb was already outlined in lavender. Beside it lay Eldeen's large Bible open to the book of John. At the large front window, the suncatchers shone warmly, like mellow gems, in the early afternoon light of autumn.

He walked into the hallway and searched the top of the little metal desk crowded against the wall. There lay a stack of assorted maga-zines—*Modern Maturity, Reader's Digest, U.S. News and World Report*—along with a vitamin catalog, a telephone bill, an old issue of *Grit,* and a bank statement for a savings account in the name of Jewel R. Blanchard. Even while he was staring at the amount under "Current Balance," Perry's mind was saying, "Don't look; this is none of your business." But he had already seen it, and as he stepped from the hallway into Jewel's bedroom, he was wondering if $2,018.38 was the total sum of her lifetime savings or if maybe she had several accounts in other banks.

He had never been in any of the bedrooms, and he felt like an intruder as he stood at the doorway at the end of the hall and looked at Jewel's bed, with its nubby white bedspread and high, curved headboard. The furniture struck him as 1950s, maybe earlier; all of it was blonde wood—big and chunky, with rounded corners and recessed drawer pulls. He saw some papers on top of the chest, but they turned out to be handwritten scripts for Peewee Powwow puppet shows. Jewel's bedroom slippers lay on a small dark green rug beside the bed, and for some reason Perry's heart ached when he saw them. They were light blue terry cloth slippers, the washable kind with elastic around the top and little pink rosettes; lying there, they were curled up at the ends, the elastic puckered tightly. They looked like little empty pouches. He thought of Jewel lying here alone every night and rising every morning to get dressed and leave for school, and he felt strangely sad. He tried to imagine Willard in here, but the room seemed too small.

He turned his eyes away from the long pink nightgown hanging on a hook inside the open closet door; he even pushed the door closed a little. He found the recorder easily; it was on the dresser beside a black padded jewelry box, the top of which was open. Most of the jewelry was inexpensive—bright strings of colored beads, imitation pearl earrings, an old Timex watch, a bracelet of coppery links. Perry wondered where she kept the cameo pin Willard had given her; maybe she was wearing it again today.

He picked up the recorder. The sheets of paper on the corner of the dresser didn't include the lesson plan; they appeared to be another piece of music Willard had arranged for the choir, this one entitled "Manger Star." He had told the choir yesterday that he had some ideas in mind for the Christmas program and they would start rehearsing soon. Perry wondered if Jewel had been singing the melody to "Manger Star" as she brushed her dark hair in front of the mirror before bed.

He turned to scan the rest of the room. Seeing a paper on the nightstand, he quickly stepped around to the other side of the bed to see if it was the lesson plan. He read just enough to see that it was: "Show students recorder—point out 8 finger holes. Play 'Hot Cross Buns' to demonstrate sound. Play scale. Give brief history—use chart. Distribute student recorders. Introduce G."

At the doorway he paused a moment and looked back into the room, taking in the whole scene—the thin curtains, mint-green and ruffled, the kind you usually saw in kitchens or bathrooms, not bedrooms; the old picture above the bed of Jesus sitting on a hillside, with the blue rooftops of Jerusalem spread out behind him in the twilight; Jewel's worn Bible lying on a white doily beside the electric clock; a snapshot of Joe Leonard in a tarnished frame on the dresser; the oscillating fan perched on a corner of the chest, aimed toward the bed; and, again, the small blue slippers beside the bed. The bed was situated close to the window; Perry wondered if Jewel ever lay awake at night, with the venetian blinds open and the curtains pulled back, gazing out at the stars, dreaming. What would a woman like Jewel dream about?

He glanced into the other two bedrooms as he passed through the hall. He thought the one with the poster of Tom Glavine on the wall was Joe Leonard's at first until he passed the other room and saw the music stand, the tennis trophy, and Joe Leonard's penny loafers beside the bed. The night light was still on in the dark little bathroom, casting a rosy glow against the walls.

He was at Derby Elementary School exactly twenty-two minutes after Jewel had called. He remembered where the music room was from the spring program he had attended in May, and he walked toward it briskly, his sneakers making rubbery squeaks against the polished floor. Around the corner he encountered a group of older children, probably fifth graders, spilling out of a classroom and arranging themselves against the wall into a line of sorts. One boy, his hair sticking straight up in stiff spikes, grabbed the back of a girl's shirt and yanked. A loud snap followed, and the girl—a pretty brunette, the kind who would grow up to be a popular Mary Tyler Moore type—though she tried to act grossly offended, looked secretly pleased while the other children laughed and pointed. A short, dumpy teacher emerged from the classroom, and the laughter subsided a little as the line straggled off toward the rest rooms.

Perry stood outside the door of Jewel's music room and watched her through the small pane of glass. The third graders were singing "Oh, Where Have You Been, Billy Boy?" But these were stanzas Perry had never heard:

> Can she pick a bale of cotton, Billy Boy, Billy Boy?
> Can she pick a bale of cotton, charming Billy?
> She can pick a bale of cotton
> even though her teeth are rotten,
> she's a young thing and cannot leave her mother.

> Can she count from one to ten, Billy Boy, Billy Boy?
> Can she count from one to ten, charming Billy?
> She can count from one to ten,
> then go back to one again,
> she's a young thing and cannot leave her mother.

The children broke down into giggles between stanzas.

> Can she chop a pile of wood, Billy Boy, Billy Boy?
> Can she chop a pile of wood, charming Billy?
> She can chop a pile of wood
> like Paul Bunyan wished he could,
> she's a young thing and cannot leave her mother.

Jewel stopped playing the piano and stood up and smiled. She gestured to the chalkboard with one hand, fingering the cameo at her neck with the other; she said something and laughed, and all the children laughed too. Perry wondered if maybe they had made up the words they had been singing. While Jewel played through the song two more times, the children filed from their chairs by rows, marching in time to the music, and stood in front of the door. Two of them stayed behind to collect books from the chairs and put them away. When Jewel opened the door and saw Perry, she clasped her hands and closed her eyes. "Oh, thank the Lord, you found them! I've been praying all during this class period that you wouldn't have any trouble."

The words to her prayer leaped to Perry's mind: "Can he find the things I need, dear Lord, dear Lord? Can he find the things I need, oh dear Lord? He can find the things I need if you will only lead . . ." The last phrase didn't come to him until he was almost out the front door of the school: "He's a poor man who has no wife or mother."

As he pulled away from the school, he looked at his watch—almost 1:30. He needed to stop at Thrifty-Mart for bread; then he'd try to write another three or four hours before taking a supper break. *Legalism:* He thought again of the three criteria Brother Hawthorne had laid out in response to his questions about movies, dancing, and the other "no-no's," as Cal called them. Perry had recorded all three on the sheet of paper. In fact, that's about all he had written down: *(1) Does the Bible expressly forbid it? (2) Would I feel uncomfortable telling someone about Jesus while I was doing it? (3) Will it in any way harm my relationship with Christ and other believers?*

"This is how we approach these things with our people," Brother Hawthorne had said. "You don't hear me harp on specifics that much from the pulpit, but I cover the principles regularly." And it was true. Perry had heard it all before. He knew that someone like Cal could probably find a dozen loopholes in the reasoning, but to himself Perry had to admit that it seemed perfectly consistent with everything he'd observed at the Church of the Open Door. "I see the standard for Christian conduct as being that which will please God most and offend others least," Brother Hawthorne had added. Then he had smiled and said, "Love the Lord your God with all your heart, soul, mind, and body—and then do whatever you want!"

Perry felt certain that an exposé was what Cal was secretly hoping for—or at least a study with subtly sarcastic overtones. Though he had recognized and praised Perry's objectivity in the earlier research projects, Perry knew Cal had a deeper personal interest in this one—and a longtime grudge that yearned for gratification. He recalled a recent phone conversation when Cal had verged on sullenness: "Good grief, you sound like you're starting to *like* these kooks!" he had exclaimed at one point.

"I always get interested in the people I study—you know that," Perry had answered. But he knew it was more than that really; it was more than being interested in them. He *liked* them, especially Eldeen, Jewel, and Joe Leonard.

"What do the fundamentalists do for *fun* these days?" Cal had asked another time. And Perry had been so overwhelmed with an abundance of memories that for a few seconds he hadn't been able to speak. He saw the church people singing, eating potluck dinners, playing softball, sitting around in folding chairs laughing and talking; he saw Jewel and Joe Leonard playing tennis and badminton, he saw Eldeen's look of glee after a quadruple jump in Chinese Checkers, he saw Willard's luminous, round face as he pulled in a fish. He remembered the Hawthornes eating ice cream and Fern Tucker reciting poetry and Joe Leonard playing his tuba and Jewel leading the Peewee Powwow children in "Jesus Wants Me for a Sunbeam." At some point over the last eight months he had ceased to doubt that these people truly enjoyed themselves; they in no way matched up with the "long-faced sourpusses" Cal had described.

"The best argument against fundamentalism," Cal had declared, making a gagging noise, "is *fundamentalists.*" He always pronounced the word with the greatest contempt, as if these people were on the same level with serial killers, whoremongers, or pedophiles.

And now, as Perry pulled into a parking space at the grocery store, he looked up at the clear, translucent blue of the October sky and was struck with another thought: "And maybe the best argument *for* fundamentalism is fundamentalists, too, not in general but in specific—like Eldeen, Jewel, Joe Leonard, Edna, Theodore, Willard, Sid, Bernie, Harvey, Nina . . ." His thoughts trailed off as he opened his car door.

A rusting red Pinto pulsating with rock music jerked into the parking space next to his, and a teenager bounded out of the passenger side and went running toward the entrance of the grocery store. There was a huge ragged hole torn in one leg of his jeans. The driver yelled after him, "Hey, get *two* packs!" Why weren't these kids in school? Perry wondered. As he passed the Pinto, the driver turned the volume of the radio up even louder and sat whacking the steering wheel with the heels of his hands in time to the pounding beat. Perry couldn't begin to decipher the words of the song, but he thought he heard "baby" several times in a row. Walking across the parking lot, he matched his steps to the beat of the song. Words formed in his mind: "Can they dance to rock-and-roll, Billy Boy, Billy Boy? Can they dance to rock-and-roll, charming Billy? If they danced to rock-and-roll, could they touch a sinner's soul? They are Christians; they live for God and others." As the automatic door opened and then closed behind him, the beat subsided and then ceased.

Chapter 25

Perry certainly hadn't started out with the intention of looking in people's windows, but it just happened. It was after nine o'clock the next night, Tuesday, when he pushed his chair back from the computer keyboard and realized he hadn't eaten anything since the ham sandwich at noon. He rubbed his eyes, then tilted the oval mirror up to study his face. He needed to be careful; this was the point in a project when he always became driven. He remembered Dinah fretting over his health during the writing of his other research studies, and usually for good cause. Near the end of the Lithuanian project, he had been consigned to bed for two weeks—a sentence he had fudged on, he recalled. Once when Dinah had run out for an hour, he had sneaked out of bed just to reword a paragraph that had haunted him since the onset of his illness; but one thing had led to another, and before he knew it, there was Dinah gasping as she came into the room and saw him typing. Her mouth constricted and tears sprang to her eyes. "Perry, how could you?" she had said, and he had meekly returned to bed.

He turned off the computer now, and out of habit walked into the kitchen. Then he saw the pan he had almost ruined during last night's supper preparations still sitting in the sink, filled with rust-colored water on which little islands of whitish scum were floating, and he knew that the thought of cooking something now—at 9:15 at night—was not to be considered. He slipped on his windbreaker and headed to Hardee's.

At first he meant to drive as he always did, but when he stepped outside and breathed in the fresh October night and heard the wind sifting through the tree branches and saw the starry canopy of sky, he decided to walk. He made his way across the front yard, his feet scuffling softly through the newly fallen oak leaves, then crunching the tiny acorns scattered over the driveway.

Next door Hormel came to life, barking frenetically and leaping against the gate with his stubby legs.

"Cork it, short stuff," Perry called softly, walking over into Jewel's driveway. "See, it's just me, your buddy, the Oreo man." Hormel stopped barking and jammed his pointed snout through the chain-link fence. "Pipe down and I'll give you another one when I get back," Perry said, and when he reached the street and looked back, Hormel was still sitting there, as if prepared to wait indefinitely for the fulfillment of the promise.

A snatch of an old poem came to Perry's mind: "The faithful collie watching at the meadow gate,/ His boy, no friend to time, was ne'er before so late." It was a sappy little poem he had learned in ninth grade, and he couldn't recall the rest of it; he only remembered that the boy never came home—he had gone off to war, he thought—but the dog kept his vigil beside the gate, a picture of undying hope and loyalty. Funny how dogs seemed to have more powers of steady devotion than most people had.

Perry stepped out into the street then stopped again. In all the months he had lived here, he had never really examined his neighborhood at night. He looked around him now.

Joe Leonard's bedroom light was on next door as well as the living room light, and Perry tried to picture what they were all doing. Maybe Joe Leonard was studying for a history test; or maybe he needed to, but Eldeen had his history book tied up for the evening. They had all discussed the American Revolutionary War on the way to church Sunday night because Eldeen said she'd been reading about it in Joe Leonard's history book and announced that she wasn't "so sure that was the right thing for them colonists to do—rise up in arms like that and charge out shootin' right and left at the redcoats!" She had gone on to say that "if the good Lord had of wanted 'em to be free"—and she believed he did—"then he sure could of worked it out another way if only they hadn't been so hotheaded and bloodthirsty."

Perry wondered what Jewel was doing tonight. Maybe she was thinking up more stanzas for "Billy Boy" or practicing her recorder again—or maybe even talking to Willard on the telephone.

There were only nine houses on the cul-de-sac of Blossom Circle, plus an empty lot between Beth's house and the next one, which belonged to the Musselmans, a couple in their fifties who both worked third shift at the bottling company. Perry was sure there must be a story behind the empty lot, but no one seemed to know for sure what it was. Eldeen said she thought she had heard once from the Musselmans that the Montroyal developers had originally put a gazebo on the lot with plans to form a little community band to give open-air concerts, but that the gazebo had been burned down by some teenagers and never rebuilt. The lot had become a tangle of weeds and tall grass, with a few pecan trees. Eldeen said she was sure she had seen raccoons scuttling back and forth in the undergrowth.

The Musselmans' house was dark now, but the Whittingtons'—the next house over—was ablaze with lights. Gerald Whittington drove a green pickup truck and worked for the power company. Perry couldn't help wondering as he noted the lights at every window whether the employees got a discounted rate on their electric bill.

Unlike the other streets in Montroyal, Blossom Circle had no sidewalk, so Perry walked slowly down the middle of the dark street, studying the houses. Joanne DePalma lived next to the Whittingtons; she was a divorced woman with two teenaged girls. A steady motorcade of low-slung cars with loud mufflers cruised the circle regularly, honking and idling their engines until one of the DePalma girls, both of them skinny blondes who were partial to spandex bodywear, came running out barefoot, squealing something like "Hey ya, Chuckie, sweetie! Whatcha doin'?"

Right now there was an orange Karmann Ghia parked in front, and one of the DePalmas was squatting down beside the window, talking to the driver, stopping to screech with laughter between exchanges. As Perry passed, he heard her say, "It was like *totally* wild! I was going, 'Okay, man, whatever you say, no problem.' I mean he was, like, ready to . . ." She broke off as she noticed Perry; he quickened his pace, then heard her burst out laughing. "My word, I thought that was *him!*" she said.

The St. Johns, who lived next to the DePalmas, were a young couple with a baby. Perry knew Eldeen had embroidered a miniature pillowcase for them when they brought the baby home from the hospital, and Jewel had made a turkey casserole and taken it over. They had visited the Church of the Open Door a few times recently too.

It was the St. Johns' open window, with the shade pulled up, that started it all. It was a bedroom, he supposed, for he could see what looked like a large framed mirror above a dresser. A woman passed in front of it, wearing something loose and flowing. Perry glanced away quickly, conscious of the DePalma girl behind him, but then looked again. The woman had come back to the mirror and was bending over, her hair falling around her head like a skein of fine yarn. Perry slackened his pace and watched her till he could no longer see her. She wasn't a pretty woman; in fact, the first time he had seen her, her face had made him think of a small weasely animal like a badger or ferret. But the vision of her supple movements as she brushed her hair over her head reminded him again of all the different forms feminine beauty could take.

When he looked across the street, back toward his own house, he was surprised to see, through a clearing in the treetops, the moon, suspended like an enormous misshapen pumpkin.

The Jelliffs lived in the house next to Jewel; it was their driveway where Joe Leonard shot baskets. The Jelliffs were a retired couple, Roman Catholics and avid golfers. Their front door was open now, and Perry saw their large white poodle, Mozelle—short for Mademoiselle, Eldeen had told him—lying beside the couch inside. Curt Jelliff sat in a recliner beside the couch, aiming the remote control toward the television, and his wife sat on the couch writing something.

Perry saw a shadow pass in front of a window back at the Whittingtons'. Mrs. DePalma came to her front door and hollered to her daughter: "Telephone, Andrea!" Tim St. John pulled down the shade in the bedroom, and as the wind gusted, Perry heard the faint clinking of the pipe chimes on the corner of the Musselmans' house. He stopped in the middle of the street and turned in a slow circle.

At the Bushongs' house, next to the Jelliffs', Perry heard a sudden wail, like that of a frightened child, and saw a light go on in a corner room. And, ironically, as he turned to the last remaining house on the circle—the Fullers'—he saw a light go off.

Slowly the thought impressed itself on Perry's mind that tonight was unique; never again would things be repeated just this way. Whatever went on inside these little brick boxes tonight would never happen exactly that way again. Some small act performed tonight could cause a response, which in turn could lead to another act, which could in some subtle way alter the course of someone's whole life. The ordinary details of life suddenly seemed to be laden with importance. That telephone call, for example, at the DePalmas' house could change their lives somehow. The child's cry at the Bushongs' could signal the genesis of some lifelong fear. Whatever it was Emily Jelliff was writing could end up terminating the way things *used* to be.

It had always intrigued Perry to think of dividing lines and starting points. As a child during a thunderstorm he had always wondered where the exact point was that the rain stopped falling; there had to be a place, a geometric plane, where on one side it was raining and the other side it wasn't. He used to wonder what it would be like to stand in that spot, arms stretched out on either side, one hand wet and the other dry. Other dividing lines weren't so distinct; he still thought of his music appreciation professor in college saying, "Don't think that on the day Bach died, people ran through the streets yelling, 'Finally! We can get out of the Baroque Era and start writing classical music now!'"

He also used to wonder when certain ideas had first begun. When he was nine, he remembered asking his mother where bread had started. She had been kneading dough at the time, scowling into it as she stretched and pounded, when it suddenly occurred to Perry that someone must have *invented* the whole process of making bread. But how would anyone ever come up with something like that? When he had asked his mother, she evidently hadn't understood his question, for she had merely replied distantly, "Oh, my grandmother taught me how to do this."

In high school biology he had pondered over the inception of life—not just the point at which something was born, but the moment at which matter became, say, a potential *being*. He had heard a radio talk-show host argue the issue of abortion once, asserting that a baby was not an entity, thus not a *person,* until the moment it emerged from the mother's womb; therefore, the host had concluded, abortion was not the same as killing a living person. A fetus, he had told the caller, had no identity, therefore no rights. "Not until the moment I was *born,*" he had said, "did I become Dale Halston."

"Then when your mother was carrying you," the caller had responded, "who *was* that inside her—Peter Pan?" Dale Halston had immediately cut the caller off and said wearily, "Let's screen these callers a little more carefully; we should at least make *marginal intelligence* a criterion for getting on the air." Perry had been disappointed. He had wanted to hear Dale's answer to the caller's question.

The Bushongs' front door opened suddenly and someone stepped outside. "*What the*—you mean you never even checked the mail today?" a man's voice from inside asked. "What did you do all day anyway?" As Perry started walking again, he heard part of the reply, a woman's shrill voice: "Well, for starters, I cleaned up two bucketfuls of puke after breakfast, then . . ." The voices were cut off by the slamming of the door.

Marriages had their dividing points, too, Perry thought as he turned onto Lily Lane and took to the sidewalk. Over the past months he had tried to analyze his life with Dinah—put it on some kind of graph with the fifteen years laid out across the bottom and a scale from one to ten along the side, with corresponding descriptors ranging from "ecstatically happy" to "hellishly miserable." When had the first hairline crack occurred? How long had it gone on before that dark, wide fault of Dinah's afternoon pronouncement: "I want out"? What had he done— or failed to do, as Brother Hawthorne would have him believe?

As he looked back over it, he was ready to admit he hadn't been a good listener. In recent years, that is. During the early years he remembered soaking up Dinah's words thirstily, astounded at her openness; he had grown up thinking all women were closed up as tightly as his mother or were as tiresomely unimaginative as Beth.

Listening—this was a subject Brother Hawthorne had drummed on repeatedly in his Wednesday evening talks. But how was a man ever supposed to know how much that meant to a woman? Or to kids either. Brother Hawthorne frequently took a break from harping on the subject of listening to your wife and said things like "It's imperative, parents, for us to *attend* to our children when they talk to us. We must lay aside our work and look at them while they speak. Otherwise, the day will come when we long for the closeness of their talk but hear only silence, for we figuratively closed the door on them years ago." Perry remembered all the times he had nodded absentmindedly when Troy had run into his office to show him a picture or a rock or—what *were* all those other things?

But how did Brother Hawthorne know? Maybe he was just guessing. Maybe listening had nothing to do with it; however, Perry had to admit that it *had* been included in Dinah's complaints of recent years.

Dinah had always been a talker. In the good years of their marriage, she would burst through the front door talking, and at night when Perry fell asleep she would still be talking. Details, always details—what color a friend's new sofa was, how many ounces of formula Troy drank, how much down to the penny a new pair of shoes cost, what so-and-so *said*, which wasn't at all what she *meant*. On and on. It was only natural that he had become selective in his listening. "You didn't hear a word I was saying, did you?" she began to ask him. Sometimes he could fake it, retrieving a few key phrases from his short-term memory bank, but more and more in the last few years she wouldn't even bother to ask the question; she would merely stop talking, fix him with a withering glare, and leave the room.

Did the husbands in these Montroyal houses listen to their wives? In how many houses right now, Perry wondered, were husbands actually doing that? The notion of conducting an informal survey came to Perry's mind. Maybe he would just see how much listening was going on. And of course, talking. In how many houses were a man and woman actually engaged in a conversation in which the man was actually listening attentively part of the time?

It was surprising how many people in Montroyal left windows and doors wide open at this hour of night. All up and down Lily Lane, light spilled out into the tiny front yards. October had been mild so far; although the nighttime temperatures dropped, the daytime ones still climbed into the low eighties. By nightfall everyone seemed to remember it was autumn again and opened up their houses to the cool breezes.

Once again Perry slowed his steps and turned his attention to the houses. He wasn't sure why the Bible story of Sodom and Gomorrah came to mind, but he found himself thinking, "Peradventure ten shall be found there." The piquant, archaic phrasing had appealed to him immediately the first time he had read the passage in Genesis about Abraham's bargaining with God to spare the city of Sodom. Then sometime later Brother Hawthorne had preached a very dramatic sermon entitled "The Sin and Sorrow of Sodom." Of course, Sodom had nothing to do with Montroyal; God didn't consume cities with fire just because men didn't listen to their wives. Still, Perry couldn't shake the analogy from his mind, and he felt certain that, like the wicked cities of old, Montroyal wouldn't produce its quota.

It was eight blocks to Hardee's, but Perry stretched it to eleven by taking a few detours. From Lily Lane, he turned onto Rose Street for three blocks, then took a side trip down Tulip Court, then Violet Street and from there to Fredericks Road, one of Derby's main thoroughfares. When he arrived at Hardee's, the teenager who was mopping the entryway looked at him unenthusiastically and sullenly motioned him to come on in. Perry tiptoed through, then quickly placed his order inside and sat down in a booth by the window.

Two houses—that was the result of his survey. Through an open window on Tulip Court, he had seen a middle-aged couple sitting together at the dining room table. The man was the only one eating, but as he lifted each forkful to his mouth, he kept his eyes on the woman, who sat in a chair to his left but facing him. She had one arm propped on the table, but the other was moving freely, almost wildly as she talked. Perry had stopped and watched them only long enough to verify that they really qualified, then had continued on his way.

He hadn't come across the other house until he was almost at the end of Violet Street, near the large brick marker overtaken with vines and bearing the faded old signboard that read "MONTROYAL, TEXTILE MERCHANT OF THE SOUTH." It was a small house, one of the two-bedroom variety Perry guessed from the outside, but at some point an occupant had extended the front stoop to a porch, and it was here, in the porch swing, that Perry saw the second couple. He had slowed his steps. They were sitting close together on the swing, and the man had his arm around the woman, who was talking in that rapid, breathless way that younger women often have. She was holding a book in one hand, gesturing with the other. Perry caught a few phrases as he drew nearer: "actually got *pictures* of it," "like a giant sea slug," "probably forty feet long," "as deep as Loch Ness," and "tracking it by sonar." The man watched her fondly, smiling indulgently, interrupting once to ask something, at which the woman laughed and waved her hand impatiently before she went on talking. They both looked up at Perry as he walked by, and the woman stopped in mid-sentence, then continued after he had passed by. Perry heard her say, "But it *could* be true, you see! And there have been all kinds of reports about creatures like that in the African Congo, too. Natives have *seen* them, Ray! Really! It's all right here in this book if you'd only read it."

So a grand total of two husbands were found to be listening—and he wasn't even sure he should count a man listening to a book report on the Loch Ness monster. Of course, he hadn't been able to see into every house. Maybe in the ones that were dark the husband and wife were whispering in bed; maybe in the ones with the blinds closed, the wives were talking intimately while their husbands listened with rapt expressions. On the other hand, maybe the husbands were snoring in front of the television.

Perry was halfway through with his hamburger when two women came in and sat in the booth behind him. They were both heavy women in their forties, he guessed, and they both wore colorful neon warm-up suits that swished loudly as they moved. Perry wondered if they had been out walking for exercise and had decided to reward themselves with fries and large drinks. Perry's booth wobbled violently as they settled in.

"Yep, he's one sorry man," one of them said.

"Well, if you ever find one that's not, let me know," replied the other one. As they both laughed, Perry felt the booth shake again and imagined them craning their necks to look at him and point derisively.

"Doctor says Lorena's dilated four centimeters," he heard the first one say. "If that baby don't come on, she's gonna die, poor thing. She's not as big as a gnat."

Perry started eating faster.

"Didn't she have a hard time with her first one?" the other one said.

"Oh, Lord, honey, she was in labor for *thirty-seven* hours . . . look, isn't that Eddie pulling into the Texaco?" The booth shook again, and Perry found himself looking out the window at the Texaco station next door, where a man was just getting out of a red Honda.

"That's him all right, that low-down . . ." They were both silent a few moments as they watched Eddie yank the lever on the gas pump, then shove the nozzle into his tank.

"He sure thinks he's God's gift to the female population, don't he, though? Look at the rooster strut!" the first woman said. Perry agreed that the man did look pretty self-satisfied swaggering toward the station attendant with his money extended, rolled up like a long cigarette between two fingers.

Suddenly the other woman guffawed. "Oh, listen, *listen!* See that car wash there? Charlene told me the funniest thing today! You gotta hear this! You know, she takes her granddaddy to all his doctor's appointments and things—well, yesterday—oh, honey, this is the *best* story—on the way back from their trip to the doctor, Charlene decides to get her car washed, okay, 'cause Joe's been telling her how cruddy it looks. So she pulls into this drive-through place—I think it was that one right there—and anyway she tells her granddaddy what she's doing and all, only he's mad at her for leaving him at the doctor's twenty minutes after his appointment was over, so he doesn't answer her. And Charlene—you know how spacey she can be—she thinks she's pushing the button to roll the back windows *up* when really she was rolling them *down.*" The woman broke off with a loud yap of laughter, and when she finally resumed the story, she kept having to stop after every few words before she could go on. "Her granddaddy never said a *word* the whole time they was going through that car wash! And Charlene said she didn't even catch on to what was happening at first because she was just sitting up front enjoying the view and thinking, 'My, that water sounds awful loud,' and then she all of a sudden felt some spray on the back of her neck, and she looks around and"—she broke down again in a paroxysm of laughter—"there sets her granddaddy just lookin' like he wanted to *murder* her and the water just *shootin'* at him from both sides!"

The booth vibrated with the women's laughter. "And after they finally got through to the other side, old gramps says to Charlene"— and the woman gasped out the punchline a word at a time: "'Please—be—so—good—as—to—provide—me—with—a—bar—of—soap—next—time—Charlene.'"

As the women broke into a fresh round of laughter, Perry stuffed the rest of his hamburger into his mouth, slid across the vinyl seat, and headed for the door, dropping his trash into the large bin stamped THANK YOU. Walking past the Texaco station, he glanced into the square opening at the end of the car wash and felt a twinge of sympathy for the indignity Charlene's grandfather had suffered—and a flash of anger at the two fat women in Hardee's. Who did they think they were criticizing all the men of the world, calling them sorry and low-down, laughing at the mishaps they endured at the hands of careless women?

Perry hardly noticed the houses on his way home. The couple on the porch had gone inside, but the swing was still moving like a small, steady pendulum. He still caught glimpses of the yellow moon through the treetops, but it was hazy now, out of focus, for the wind had shifted and clouds were blotting out the stars, covering them like wispy cobwebs.

When he arrived home, he went directly to the kitchen cupboard, got a handful of Oreos, and walked over to Jewel's backyard. At the sound of Perry's low whistle, Hormel came scooting out of his little house. So he hadn't waited faithfully beside the gate after all. "Didn't think I'd keep my promise, huh?" Perry chided, dropping three Oreos through the fence.

Chapter 26

Well, would she like something dressy, do you think, or something like this—more casual?" the saleslady asked, pulling out a pair of western-looking jeans with a red bandanna-print belt threaded through the loops. "See here, we have this whole line, with all these different tops and even some little vests and these fun little skirts." She was whipping out garments faster than Perry could respond, holding them up briefly, then returning them to the rack and grabbing something else. "Look at this little sweater that goes with the pants—aren't those little cowboys the cutest things? And this little shirt—if you don't want to spend quite that much—see, it has the same little cowboys and broncos stitched on the collar and down the front? These little things are all just real popular with the ladies this season. Actually, it was a summer line, but we reordered it for fall because it went over so big."

Perry wished he had gone ahead and ordered something from the L. L. Bean catalog as he had started to do—even if he couldn't figure out what colors "mesa sage," "forsythia," and "mango" were. This woman was confusing him with all her distracting "little's"; she looked so eager to please yet at the same time somehow slightly sinister, batting her incredibly long, dense black eyelashes and fluttering her hands with their shiny vermilion fingernails in front of his face. Her little white teeth glinted with every swift smile, and she moved entirely too fast, jangling and tinkling with silver jewelry. She couldn't possibly be a native Southerner, Perry decided; Southern women weren't this high-strung as a rule. As she straightened from picking up a wide-necked cotton top that had slipped off a hanger, Perry was embarrassed to find himself staring straight at her ample bosom. He looked away quickly.

"So, what do you think?" she asked. "Can I fix you up with one of these nice little ranch ensembles?"

"Oh, well, I . . . I'm not really sure," Perry said. He knew Dinah liked clothes—there was no doubt about that—but she was also particular; only once before had he bought her anything to wear. He remembered her holding it up for a long time and finally shaking her head: "It's just not me, Perry," she had said, kissing him. "It reminds me of something my mother would wear." And sure enough when her mother had come over the next day, she had pounced on the dress with uncharacteristic ebullience, saying, "Oh, Dinah, that's exquisite! What I'd *give* to have a dress like that!"

Perry looked back at the salesclerk. She was still smiling, but he saw her cast a sideways look at a woman browsing through another nearby rack. She looked back at Perry and widened her smile. "Can I show you something in a particular size?"

Perry took a deep breath. "I like the sweater and the skirt—that denim one with the buttons down the front," he said.

"Oh, you mean this one with the darling little oval buttons?" the saleswoman said excitedly, pulling out the skirt. "And which do you like—the cardigan sweater or the pullover?"

Perry suddenly remembered something and felt immensely proud. A few months before he had left home—in fact, about a year ago exactly—he had heard Dinah say to one of her friends, "I'm going to take that black sweater back. I'm getting tired of pulling everything on over my head."

"The cardigan," he told the saleslady.

"Oh, that's a good choice," she replied cheerfully. "What size can I get you? We have several left."

Thirty minutes later he was sitting on a bench by a small fountain in the center of the mall, eating a chicken sandwich and watching the Friday crowd. His packages were in an enormous bag beside him. He wasn't so sure about the outfit now—or rather, the two outfits, for the saleslady had talked him into the blouse, too, and then had pointed out that he could buy a vest for only sixty-eight more dollars, and "then your wife can have two different little ensembles." He could picture Dinah in the clothes. The long lines would suit her height, but now he worried that she'd think they were silly. "What's this?" he could hear her saying. "Don't you remember how I always hated those old John Wayne movies?"

The afternoon sunlight flooded in through the angled panes of the mall's center skylights, throwing brilliant bands of colors across the floor. A toddler at a bench across from where Perry sat pointed gleefully from prism to prism and struggled to get down from his mother's lap. She finally gave up and snapped a stretchy cord around his wrist, then set him down on the floor. He waddled to the nearest spectrum and tried to pick it up, clawing at the floor with his tiny fingers, then looking back at his mother peevishly. Abandoning that one, he crawled to another one and again scratched at the floor, a look of bafflement crossing his face as the colors tinted the back of his small hand.

Several people had stopped to watch, and when the toddler finally screamed in fury and lay down thrashing his chubby legs, everyone chuckled and one woman said indulgently, "Isn't that precious?" The mother came quickly, with reddened face, and scooped up her little boy, who swatted her with one flailing arm and then grabbed a fistful of her hair. The laughter died as she bore him off. Perry hadn't laughed; he knew too well how she must feel. He finished his sandwich then headed toward the card store at the opposite end of the mall.

The clothes were already gift-wrapped, but now he picked up a long tube of brown mailing paper, then looked around for an appropriate card. He was surprised at the variety of occasions represented; he passed by the Halloween and Thanksgiving cards, the anniversary and wedding cards, and then turned to the next aisle. These were all humorous, with pictures on the front of gorillas wearing clothes in domestic settings or questions like "Know what you get when you cross a penguin with a birthday candle?" One had the picture of a voluptuous blonde hitchhiker in short shorts, one high-heeled shoe perched on top of a small suitcase. The message said, "How about a little birthday pickup?"

He walked past baby cards, then another section labeled "Unique Remembrances," with cards for "A Fine Young Man's Baptism" and "Now That You're Retired" and "Congratulations on the Promotion!" He even saw one that said "Let's Forget Our Quarrel." He stopped briefly and wondered what Dinah would say if he sent a card like that to her. It would probably throw her off balance; was he trying to be funny, she would wonder, or was he spitefully trivializing what they had been through? Or was he still so addle-brained that he thought a trite apology would erase it all?

When he finally found the serious birthday cards, he realized he'd have to make it one of the friendly, impersonal kind since "Ex-wife" wasn't one of the categories included. At last he settled on one that said "A Special Birthday Wish." On his way to the cash register, he passed a display of clothbound books filled with blank pages. On an impulse he picked up one and added it to his purchases.

Outside the card shop, Perry dug into his pocket and pulled out the list he had made before leaving home. There were still six errands left on it—unimportant things, all of them, but not totally unnecessary. At least he hadn't come to that yet—filling up his time with "piddling" as Dinah called it. One of her friends named Shelley had been married to a man who was the worst piddler of all; Paul spent Saturdays doing things like polishing the underside of his car hood and going to estate auctions, though he never bought anything. Dinah—and Shelley, too, apparently—had nothing but contempt for Paul; he and Shelley had divorced several years ago.

Perry looked at his watch. This was working out well; the worst part of the day would be used up before he finished. There wasn't a World Series game on television tonight, but he could watch the Perry Mason movie; those weren't bad. He had always liked watching another man named Perry handle so competently the challenges of his job. He stuffed the list back into his pocket and headed for the mall exit. He couldn't help thinking of Beth. She would be so proud of him if she knew he had made a list of errands and was proceeding through them one at a time, even marking them off as he went. Lists were one of her passions, right up there with filing her receipts in alphabetical order.

It was after seven-thirty when he finally arrived home. Willard's car was parked in Jewel's driveway, and her front door was open. He saw Joe Leonard come to the door and look out, then disappear from sight. As Perry started up the steps to the side door, Jewel opened her kitchen door and called to him.

"Perry, we're fixing to start a game of Monopoly and wondered if you'd like to join us. It's Willard's birthday and we're going to have some cake and ice cream later." Joe Leonard was standing behind her, listening for Perry's answer, and it struck Perry again that the boy was getting taller.

Perry Mason or Monopoly—he couldn't remember the last time he had had a choice of what to do on Friday night. It didn't take him long to decide; those movies were on every month or so. "Sure, I'll play," he told Jewel. "Just let me set these things inside." Chinese Checkers, dominoes, Monopoly—what will it be next, he wondered, Old Maid? He set his packages on the kitchen table next to the two bags of groceries he hadn't bothered putting away yesterday. At the top of one of the bags sat a two-pound can of special-blend coffee. He took it out now, carefully removed the large gold bow the giftwrap girl had taped to Dinah's present, and stuck it on top of the coffee can. He found the card that said "A Special Birthday Wish" and signed his name, then wrote "To Willard" on the front of the envelope. There—never let it be said that Perry Warren came to a party empty-handed. He'd have to get another card for Dinah—or maybe he wouldn't even bother with a card. This one really hadn't seemed suitable anyway. And the bow would have had to come off, too, before wrapping the gift to mail.

When he looked in at Jewel's open kitchen door a few minutes later, no one was there. He saw the Monopoly game board spread out on the dinette table, the chocolate layer cake on the counter beside the stove, and a two-liter bottle of 7-Up beside it. One cupboard door was standing open, and several glasses sat upside down in the dish drainer. The dish towel was slung carelessly across the countertop. Where was everybody? Perry wondered. There was no sound whatsoever from inside the house. He paused a minute before pressing the buzzer. It's not *that,* he told himself, remembering Harvey Gill's recent Sunday school lesson on what the church people called "the Rapture." Eldeen had once described what she thought it would be like after this momentous event: "And just think of all the things left at loose ends! The airplanes without pilots and the patients on operating tables without a doctor and the mamas in rocking chairs all of a sudden without their little babies—and everybody wondering and wondering what's happened. And then somebody saying, 'Oh, now, could it be that thing all them Christians kept talking about? Maybe it really was true after all! Maybe they've all been *raptured!*'"

Standing here outside the empty kitchen, Perry suddenly thought of all the vacancies in Derby's everyday activities if these people really did disappear into the heavens someday. Annoyed at himself, he pushed the button forcefully and heard the buzzer inside. There was no response; no one came hurrying to the door to welcome him. He knocked loudly, then opened the screen door a crack and called, "Anybody home?" Still nothing. He felt a chill down his back. They had been here less than fifteen minutes ago. Where were they now? Hormel wasn't even sitting at his normal post beside the gate.

All at once he heard a startled cry—low and raspy: "Well, I *never!*" It was coming from the backyard. Perry hurried down the steps and unlatched the gate. Hormel came racing toward him, barking furiously, then stopped and wagged his tail. Then Perry saw them—all four of them were huddled together behind the house, and Eldeen was sitting in a lawn chair peering through something mounted on a tripod. In a flash it came to Perry what it must be. Jewel had talked recently about Willard's interest in buying a telescope; he must have gone ahead and done it. Willard was the first to notice him. "Hey, Perry, come on over here and take a look through this thing," he said.

Perry felt a wave of relief wash over him. Eldeen looked up and motioned to him excitedly. "I seen all kinds of wonders in nature," she said fervently, "but I never, *never* did see anything to match this! You just got to come see this, Perry." She got up slowly, shaking her head. "What is man, that thou art mindful of him?" she said, her voice tremulous.

A few minutes later they were back inside. "Thank you, thank you, for sharing your new telescope with us, Willard," Eldeen said. "That's some wonderful piece of equipment. Wait till I tell Inez and Juanita and the rest of 'em at the G.O.O.D. Store about *this.*" She sat down heavily at the kitchen table as if exhausted by the marvels she had witnessed. "Which token you want?" she asked Perry. He set his gift and card down on the counter. "We already picked ours," Eldeen continued. "I got the thimble, Jewel's got the shoe, Joe Leonard's got the ship, and Willard's got the cannon." She held each piece aloft as she named it "That leaves the hat, the iron, the racecar, the locomotive, the dog . . ."

"I'll take the dog," Perry said, taking the empty chair at the end of the table. He wondered if anyone had ever done a study in which a player's personality was analyzed based on which Monopoly token he chose: *"The person who chooses the little terrier is intelligent, warm-hearted, and loyal. Though he is often shy and appears to be aloof, he earnestly desires affection and approval from those he loves. He enjoys the outdoors but is also artistic and . . ."*

"Did you hear that, Perry?" Eldeen said. "And it says here in this little book that when the doctor examined him at the hospital, he wrote out a prescription that said, 'Go directly to jail.'" She doubled over in laughter and pounded the table with both hands so hard that all the little tokens bounced straight up and toppled over. Perry looked over at the booklet Eldeen had spread open on the table. The page, entitled "Monopoly Mania," was full of zany facts about Monopoly tournaments held in prisons, in a huge aquarium, on a peak in the German Alps, and during a train robbery.

"Well, let's put the book back in the box, Mama, and get started or else we won't have time to finish," Jewel said, setting the tokens back up. As Eldeen closed the book, Perry saw a list of "Marathon Records" at the bottom of the page. One of them said "Longest game in a moving elevator: 384 hours."

It occurred to Perry as he studied the Monopoly board that the colors were at least arranged a little more systematically than in Fern Tucker's rainbow poem, but still not as precisely as those of the skylight prisms spangling the mall floor earlier today. He was glad the Monopoly board designers had chosen such rich, vivid shades of color. He thought suddenly of writing the L. L. Bean Company and suggesting they use Monopoly street designations for their catalog; everybody would instantly recognize the colors: Baltic Avenue Purple, St. Charles Place Magenta, Illinois Avenue Red, Boardwalk Blue.

"I read somewhere that there's a national Monopoly tournament every year," said Willard, "and the winner even goes on to the World Championship. One year the prize was a free trip to anyplace in the whole world, all expenses paid."

"Oh, just imagine that!" cried Eldeen. "Why, if I won a prize like that, I would be mighty hard put to make up my mind. I've always wanted to go someplace Oriental—I can't say just why exactly, but them pagodas and kimonos and rickshaws and all just fascinates me. I like chop suey a lot too, like Marvella can fix. But then, I think it'd be real interesting, too, to visit Egypt and Israel and all them Middle Eastern places close around where Jesus lived. Just think of walking through the Garden of Gethsemane! My, my. And *France*—the Jelliffs next door went there and lived for a whole year when Mr. Jelliff was in the army, and Emily said . . ."

"Mama, go ahead and roll. We're seeing who goes first," Jewel said. Eldeen rolled a four.

". . . that all them little French cafes was just the quaintest things. They just fell in love with France and have all kinds of souvenirs settin' around their house—you should just see 'em all. They got this heavy iron doorstop in the shape of the Eiffel Tower. And, of course, Mozelle, their French poodle—although she's not a souvenir . . ."

"And the race is on!" said Willard, who had rolled an eleven. He cupped the dice in his huge hands, pretended to whisper to them, then tossed them across the board. He got all the way to Pennsylvania Railroad on his turn.

"I know them folks up in Pennsylvania must be about to *bust* rooting for their home team," Eldeen said. "I wouldn't mind seeing the Phillies win myself, even if they did beat out the Braves. They better hop to it, though, 'cause they sure are in a hole right now." As Willard slid the dice over to Perry, Eldeen told about seeing a Braves sponge tomahawk sitting in the backseat of a car two days earlier. "It looked so faded and limp and lonesome it almost made me cry," she said. "It just reminded me all over again how fleeting fame is—and life too! One day a ball team's all the go, and the next thing you know they been beat and left in the dust."

Perry picked up the dice slowly. He wondered if Eldeen was going to talk through the whole game as she had done during the dominoes game last week. He remembered how hard it had been to concentrate, how the dots had seemed to leap up off the dominoes and dance around devilishly every time he tried to count them.

"Did I tell you, Jewel, what Emily told me about Mozelle's back?" Eldeen asked. Jewel shook her head as Perry rolled the dice. "Looking at Perry's little dog there on GO made me think of it," Eldeen continued. "They'd noticed that Mozelle was walking real stiff and painful-like, and she'd stopped jumping up to greet them like she usually did—oh, looka there, Perry rolled hisself double fives! Aren't you glad you're just *visitin'* and not behind bars?" She slapped at his hand playfully as he picked up the dice to roll again.

"So anyway, Emily took Mozelle with her next time she went to the chiropractor and snuck in the back door so the regular customers wouldn't see—well, I'll be! If he didn't roll double fives again! You sure you shook 'em around, Perry?" She grinned trollishly. "Too bad there's not a lick of money on Free Parking or you'd be sittin' pretty. So, anyway, the chiropractor like to fell over when he saw Emily come in carrying Mozelle. But he was a good sport about it, Emily said, and asked her to help him hold Mozelle on the table while he felt around."

"It's your turn now, Mama," Jewel said.

Eldeen rolled a seven and landed on Chance. "Oooheee!" she hollered when she picked up the card. "Bank pays me a dividend of fifty dollars it says! Pay up, pay up!" she cried, holding out her hand to Joe Leonard, who was the banker. He gave her a fifty-dollar bill, then picked up the dice for his own turn.

"And so that chiropractor *did* feel something out of line in Mozelle's little old back, and he grabbed her real quick-like before she had a chance to turn skittish and he gave her a jerk, like that!" Eldeen clapped her hands. "Now that's a discouragin' way to start out, Joe Leonard—landing on Income Tax right off. And you know, Emily said she actually *heard* something crack in Mozelle's back—a little tiny pop—and Mozelle gave a little yelp and just leaped up from there a new dog!"

Perry glanced at Willard, who was following Eldeen's story attentively. "And is the dog walking better now?" Willard asked.

"Oh, you should just see her!" Eldeen exclaimed. "Yesterday she was in the Jelliffs' backyard just chargin' at Hormel on the other side of the fence, like she was ready to tear him up! I watched her with my mouth hangin' open, thinkin' 'Is this the same dog I saw mopin' around a few days ago, hardly able to squat down?'"

"Look, Mama, I landed right here with you on Chance," Jewel said. She studied her card, wrinkled her nose, and said, "Only mine isn't as good as yours was. I have to pay a poor tax of fifteen dollars."

"I sure hope that chiropractor washed his hands before he called in his next customer!" Eldeen said.

Two hours later they pushed the game board carefully to the end of the table and set about getting ready for refreshments. Jewel started arranging candles on top of the cake, and Joe Leonard got out plates and a half-gallon of ice cream. Eldeen trundled down the hallway to one of the back rooms and returned with several small gifts.

Willard smiled broadly as Jewel walked to the table bearing the cake, its forty-two candles aglow. "Better call the fire department," he said, and Eldeen whooped with laughter. Jewel led out with "Happy Birthday" and everyone joined in.

Just as Willard was inhaling to blow out the candles, he straightened and pointed to the counter. "Oh, I forgot something. Grab my camera there, would you, Perry, and snap a picture of this happy occasion. Push that button on the back of the flash first. Come on, I want all the rest of you in the picture too."

As he held the camera up to his eye, Perry realized he hadn't done this for almost a year. "Hold it just a second," he said, adjusting the focus, then checking for the ready signal on the flash. "There now, everybody, get in closer around Willard. There you go. Now Eldeen, lean over toward Joe Leonard more. All right, now . . . Jewel, could you turn more to your right—no, not quite that much. And look up this way a little more. Okay, now hold it right there, everybody. Let me see . . . where's the . . . oh, here it is." Just before he clicked the shutter, Perry studied the smiling foursome through the camera lens— Eldeen on the end, her lips spread wide so that her dentures gleamed like miniature Chiclets; Joe Leonard wedged between Eldeen and Willard, looking embarrassed; Willard, smiling beatifically, hunched forward toward the cake sparkling with its galaxy of candles; and Jewel, sitting on the end next to Willard, her chin lifted, a chaste, contemplative smile lighting her face.

"Can't you find the button, Perry?" Eldeen asked, her smile still stretched taut.

"Here we go, everybody," Perry said. The flash expelled a burst of light.

"You better blow out the candles before they drip on the cake," Jewel said quickly, and Willard took in a mighty breath.

"Wait! Wait! Wait! Did you make a wish? No use blowing out candles if you don't make a wish!" Eldeen said.

"Oh, I made forty-two of them," Willard said. He inhaled again and then held his breath for a moment, scanning the top of the cake as if planning his strategy.

Wouldn't it be nice, Perry thought, if that's the way life worked? Make a wish, blow out the candles, and your wish would come true. Make a wish, throw a penny in the well. Make a wish, wave a magic wand. Make a wish, pull the wishbone. Make a wish, stroke the genie's lantern. No, he was getting things out of order now. You rubbed the lantern first *then* made the wish.

"Well, well, well, you got 'em all but three," Eldeen said admiringly. "I guess that means you'll get thirty-nine of your wishes. Here, open up your cards and presents."

The Monopoly game finally ended at eleven-thirty when Joe Leonard rolled doubles and landed on Ventnor Avenue; he was able to pay Perry the $1150 after selling all the houses on his green property, but then he rolled a ten and landed on Park Place.

"That's it!" Eldeen exclaimed. She had been out of the game almost an hour and had already changed into her long flannel bathrobe. "Perry's the big millionaire of the night! He cleaned us all out of cash! That little old dog of his just hightailed it around the board and hardly ever stepped in anything he shouldn't of!" She threw her head back and laughed at her joke.

Willard thumped him on the back. "Congratulations, Perry. I thought I'd included the Monopoly game in my list of wishes a while ago, but it must have been one of the candles I didn't blow out." Everybody laughed.

"Here, Joe Leonard, I'll help you put away all the filthy lucre," Eldeen said. She held up a five-hundred-dollar bill and waved it around. "Just remember, everybody, this here won't buy you happiness. Godliness with contentment is great gain." By the time she had finished, her smile had died and she had grown suddenly solemn.

Perry and Willard left together a few minutes later. In the driveway Willard extended his hand. "Thanks for the coffee. I'm flattered that you remembered how much I like it. I'll take a thermos of it to work with me in the morning. It'll help keep me awake while I put bar codes on the new bird books we got."

"Bird books?" Perry asked.

"Yeah, some man over in Berea was this big bird aficionado, and his widow just donated his whole library to us."

Suddenly Perry thought of something. "Do you know much about birds?" he asked.

Willard's head was lifted, and his eyes searched the small gems of stars dotting the night sky. "Well, some . . . not really much, though. Why?"

"I was wondering about . . . well, doves. Do you know anything about the ones we have around here?"

"Oh, nothing much except that they're in the same family as pigeons and the male and female take turns incubating the eggs and . . . oh, yes, I believe they mate for life. Why? You including the native flora and fauna in your book about us local yokels?"

Perry felt relieved, as if some small, irritating rattle had quieted. "No, no . . . it's nothing really, I was just wondering—that's all."

"Well . . ." Willard looked up at the sky again and sighed contentedly.

"Well, good night," Perry said. "And . . . I hope those thirty-nine wishes come true." He started off toward his house.

"I'll settle for just one," Willard called after him, laughing. "Look at those stars, would you? Star light, star bright . . ."

Perry stepped inside the kitchen and saw Dinah's present on the table. He picked up the little book with blank pages and ran his hand over the cover. He imagined Willard, cheerfully starting his car and backing out of Jewel's driveway, heading off down Blossom Circle toward Lily Lane, finishing the rest of the little rhyme: "I wish I may, I wish I might, Have the wish I wish tonight." Perry walked back to his bedroom with the book in his hand.

Chapter 27

Good grief, where were you yesterday?" Cal said when Perry answered the telephone the next morning.

"Oh, I was in and out," Perry said.

"Mostly out, I'd say. I must've tried calling you a dozen times or more. Started about four o'clock—and finally gave up at eleven."

"You were making phone calls on a Friday night?" Perry said. "Must be a real exciting life you lead."

"Not nearly as exciting as yours obviously," Cal said.

Perry wondered what Cal would say if he knew he'd spent the whole evening playing Monopoly with his neighbors, that the last time he'd tried calling, at eleven, Perry was just forcing Jewel to liquidate all her holdings and turn over all her assets to him. Or if he knew Perry was spending most of tonight at the Palmetto Miniature Golf Course and Batting Range with the church youth group.

"Got your first three chapters," Cal said.

"I thought you probably had," said Perry.

"You said there are three more coming?"

"Yep, probably in a couple of weeks. I've got drafts of the next nine, but I'm revising in groups of three. And I've started my first draft of the 'Cast' section. It'll actually probably end up as Part Two, but I wanted to write it last."

"*Stage Right: The Drama of a Fundamentalist Christian Church*— clever title, but I wonder . . . I mean, I *like* the organizational idea of the five parts—the setting, the conflict, the theme, and all that. That's good. But well, you don't think the first impression of the whole thing might look too *cute,* do you?—like we've forgotten we're serious researchers."

"Have you read the chapters? Is that what you think—they're cute?"

"Oh, Perry, no, for the love of—you know they're good. You

haven't lost your touch, not a bit. I'm not talking about the actual content, although it's sure not what I was . . . expecting."

"Or maybe hoping?"

"Well, all I can say is that your Gospel Lighthouse is nothing like the fundamentalist churches I know about down there. I can't help but worry a little. I mean, it just doesn't sound . . . well, representative of fundamentalist churches in general."

"You mean it doesn't reinforce the stereotype some people are so fond of."

"*Fond of*? You think I'm . . . ? Oh, come on, Perry. What's gotten into you? I hope you know me better than that. I just want this thing to be on target, that's all."

"You want to come down here and validate my research? You're welcome to. You don't do a sociological study just to perpetuate a bias, Cal; you look at the group the way it *is*. I'm sorry it's not to your liking. But I'm not making up anything."

"Oh, stop being testy, Perry. What's wrong with you? I'm giving you my opinion, my *response* to what you've sent me. That's what I always do, remember?"

"Right, but you usually don't already have your mind made up about the group I'm studying. Maybe I should have gone to Sand Hill, Georgia, and done the whole thing on—what was it, Beulah Tabernacle? Maybe it was *your* church that wasn't representative of fundamentalist churches in general—ever thought of that?"

Cal didn't say anything for a few seconds. When he spoke, his voice was tight. "Between visiting aunts and uncles and grandmothers and third cousins, I must've been in a dozen different churches down there until I left home and escaped to college. From what I can tell, this Gospel Lighthouse of yours isn't like *any* of the fundamentalist churches I got dragged to."

"Well, it doesn't matter, does it? You don't choose a subject based on how typical it is. I don't remember you even mentioning it in the other projects. Nobody ever asked if the preschool was *representative* of all preschools for handicapped kids. Or if the Lithuanians I studied were like the ones in other parts of Illinois or over in Pittsburgh."

Perry heard a muffled bang. Was Cal pounding his desk in frustration? "I'm just thinking of *you*, Perry. You've got me worried. Here you are stuck in a little one-horse town during a low point in your life, with a bunch of very persistent, abnormal people who would love to pour you into their little mold. They're experts at preying on people's weaknesses and laying a guilt trip on you every time you loosen your

necktie. I *know* these people, Perry. And I know you. Or I used to. You
. . . well, whenever I talk to you now, you just don't seem the same.
You make this place sound . . . well, perfectly sane and reasonable,
almost like . . ."

"Like what?"

"Well, like they've gotten to you or something. Like you're starting
to think they're onto something good. I can't put my finger on it, but
there almost seems to be a tone of *approval* in a lot of what you
say—and even in what you've written in these chapters."

"Approval? Cal, I'm writing social science research. I've got a Ph.D.
in the field. I *thought* I was a professional researcher, but you make it
sound like I'm writing copy for a promotional brochure. Look, I've
been here eight months and have attended every function of this
church—observed, listened, taken reams of notes, written drafts, all the
same stuff I did on my three other books. I'm writing what I *see*, Cal.
I have no agenda; nobody here's paying me to make them look good,
and I don't . . ."

"Hey, wait a minute. Here's something else I can't figure out." Cal
sounded genuinely perplexed. "I can't *ever* remember you getting so worked
up over anything. Never in all the twelve years I've known you."

"And I can't ever remember you questioning my objectivity! Read
me one sentence that carries this 'tone of approval' you mentioned."

Perry heard Cal turning pages. "Okay, here's one. 'The first-time
visitor would no doubt admire the new burgundy carpet in the sanctuary,
but he might take a closer, more appreciative look if he understood the
lesson of brotherly harmony behind its purchase and installation.'"

"Well? That's it? Didn't you read the paragraphs after that?"

"Oh, sure."

"And you don't think the details of the incident prove the assertion
of brotherly harmony?"

"I didn't say that."

Perry had actually wrestled over the question of whether to include
the carpet purchase in the "Setting" section or to save it for the "Cast."
That was the problem with organizing the chapters—everything overlapped. You couldn't isolate the church setting from the people from
the activities from the purpose. But he had decided to put it with the
setting since he knew he had plenty of material to round out Eldeen in
the "Cast" section without describing her role in the carpet contro-
versy.

It had started at a Wednesday evening business meeting back in
early August when Brother Hawthorne had asked the members to vote

on authorizing a committee to shop around, select samples, and present a recommendation to the congregation for replacing the bargain-quality blue-gray carpet that had been laid in the sanctuary twenty years ago.

When the committee had compiled and presented its findings to the congregation two weeks later, Bernie Paulson had opened the discussion with a speech Perry had written down verbatim: "I think we should go with the dark brown; it's practical and economical both. Face it, who looks down at the carpet when you're in church anyway? All we need is something to put our feet on, nothing fancy."

It had been a muggy evening during the hottest week of the whole summer, and the air-conditioning was laboring. Eldeen was fanning herself with an old bulletin she had pulled out of her Bible, and someone behind them had whispered, "I think we need to get the air-conditioning checked before we talk about new carpet!"

Trudy Gill had risen and stated a preference for the moss green carpet because green was such a restful, versatile color and would always look nice with any flower arrangement. It would cost a little more than the brown but not as much as the burgundy, she had pointed out, so they would be hitting a happy medium.

But Mayfield Spalding, who usually sat morosely in the back pew and never said a word, had agreed with Bernie: "Buy the brown and put the extra money in the missions fund!"

Willard had expressed an interest in the burgundy. "I'd like to see us dress our sanctuary up a little," he had said. "The burgundy has an elegant look, I think, and would provide a nice contrast with the light paint on the walls."

"The dark brown sure wouldn't show dirt," Marjorie Eckles had offered.

"The burgundy is dark too," Willard had added.

"But look how much more it'd cost!" Emory Pyle had said, rising to his feet. "I don't know about the rest of you, but I was raised on plainness. Plain food, plain clothes, plain old hard work, the plain gospel, plain hymns—I say we get the plain brown. We don't need to get mixed up in all this high-falutin' decoratin'!"

Jarvis Tillman had agreed. "We gave Pat a real nice wedding in this very room, and nobody even noticed that the carpet was old and worn-out. You can make a church look nice without having to bust the budget on things that don't really matter. As long as we got something on the floor, I don't think we need to worry about how many threads per square inch it's got and all that. Just get something that'll wear a decent amount of time and'll hide the wear and tear. I think the dark brown is the way to go."

Curtis Chewning thought the dark brown looked too "industrial and depressing." He said he thought the decor of a church shouldn't be showy but should certainly uplift the soul. "I know the Bible tells us we're made of dust and to dust we shall return," he said, smiling, "but I don't think God necessarily expects us to forgo beauty just to remind ourselves of our temporal, depraved condition."

"Of course, a *doctor* wouldn't be as concerned about the cost of something as the rest of us with a regular-size income," Perry heard Woody Farnsworth say under his breath.

Not even during the business meeting when the subject of paving the parking lot had been discussed had Perry witnessed such dissension. Nobody was really angry—not yet—but he noticed that people were fanning themselves faster.

Myrt Silvester reminded everybody that the church carpet didn't get as much wear as a normal carpet since they weren't using the sanctuary every day. "So it doesn't seem like we need to be all that worried about buying the very best quality or else we'll all be sick of it by the time it finally wears out." A few people tittered politely, but most of the faces remained set in uncompromising lines.

"I don't know about that," Grady Ferguson said. "It might not be used every day, but when it is, it gets a lot of wear. I'd say a couple hundred people tramping around on it six hours a week or so might average out the same as a family using it every day. Phil, you've done cost efficiency studies for different companies—you can figure that out for us, can't you?"

"But everybody doesn't walk in the same places," Martha Joy Darrow said. "Like Burton and me—we come in and sit back here in this same spot every service. We never even go up front as a general rule. In a house the wear is more evenly spread out, don't you think?"

Somebody behind Perry said, "Maybe if we had an invitation at every service, more people *would* go up front!" Perry couldn't tell whether the person was serious or was just trying to lighten things up.

"We're getting off track!" Bernie Paulson declared. "The point is which carpet will meet our needs—not exceed them but *meet* them."

"The Lord does expect us to use our money wisely," Phil Spivey said. "There's no use being extravagant. Maybe we don't even need to buy it right now. This carpet doesn't look all that bad to me. Why not wait till after the parking lot is done next spring?" There was a stirring of bodies and a swelling undercurrent of responses to this remark.

So far Brother Hawthorne had remained silent on the front pew, rubbing his jawline thoughtfully as if considering whether to grow a beard. As he tried to keep up with his note-taking, Perry kept looking up at Brother Hawthorne, wondering what he was thinking and when he was going to take over and smooth things out. Usually the discussions at business meetings were far more leisurely than this.

Perry had just written down "P. Spivey—suggests postponing purchase" when he felt a ponderous movement next to him and realized that Eldeen was standing to face the rows behind them. On the other side of him, he sensed Joe Leonard tensing, probably in dread of what was coming. Jewel, sitting next to Willard, glanced over toward Eldeen anxiously.

The room grew silent. Brother Hawthorne cleared his throat and started to rise, then saw Eldeen standing and slowly sat back down. Perry couldn't tell whether his expression was one of relief or resignation. Someone in back whispered something, and someone else hissed, "Shhh!" The air conditioner emitted a low moan and seemed to shift gears. Perry heard a large insect bat against the window and then flutter its wings, producing a faint, rhythmic clicking.

At last Eldeen's thick voice broke the stillness. "When I was a little girl," she said slowly, "I went to a church called the Sweet Fields of the Promised Land over in Cloverdale, Arkansas, just fifteen miles from Chester, where I was born. The preacher was named Brother Farley Whitehead, which I always thought suited him just right since his hair was snowy white." She stopped and pulled the large button-like red earring off her right ear. "There—that feels better. It felt like a lobster had a hold of my ear! Anyway, Mr. Whitehead was a man of God, bless his heart, and one time he said something that I never ever *ever* forgot. I guess I couldn't of been more'n eleven or twelve that summer. I know I wasn't as old as Joe Leonard here." She paused and squinted her eyes almost closed as if trying to see back through all those years.

Perry was seized with a sudden curiosity about the Eldeen of long ago. What would she have been like as a *child?* His imagination, usually so agile, was unable to produce the slightest inkling of an idea. But she was already talking again, he realized, and he couldn't dwell on the matter now. He vowed to ask her sometime if she had any pictures of herself as a child. There was so much about her background that he didn't know; he wasn't sure why had he never thought to ask. Maybe it was because the Eldeen of *now* was so overpowering that it was all he could do to keep up with her, without the task of trying to develop her history. Most likely, though, it was because he had known all along that he would feature Eldeen in the "Cast" section with a personal profile—along with three or four other church members—and had simply postponed delving into her past until he scheduled her official interview.

"And so he did," Eldeen was saying. "He invited this Mr. Esperando, who just had one arm, to lead the singing for the summer tent meetings that year. Oh, you just should of heard the clashin' and fussin'! 'What do we need a *opera* singer for?' folks was saying. 'Why doesn't he just get Freddy Showalter over in Pikeville to do it like always?' Freddy was this little man who never had grown right and was just shy of being what you'd call a dwarf. But, oh, he was the *friskiest* little man—just hopped around the platform like a toad frog! Sometimes he'd even stand up on a chair and holler, 'Is that all the louder y'all can sing? Come on, let's shake the rafters of heaven on this next verse!'" Perry heard Sid Puckett slap his knee and guffaw, then break off suddenly.

"Well, anyway," Eldeen continued, "Mr. Reginald Esperando accepted Brother Whitehead's invitation and came to Cloverdale that summer and was the songleader for Mr. Samson Warwick, who was the travelin' preacher Brother Whitehead had engaged for our annual tent meetings. Some of you've probably heard tell of Samson Warwick. He was a real famous preacher in the South back in the twenties and thirties. I can remember clear as it was yesterday how I just purely walked around in a *trance* that whole week. Mr. Warwick was one ball of fire as a preacher, I'll tell you what—but the *real* bang for me, spiritually speakin', came from Mr. Esperando, that one-armed opera singer. He had a voice clear and true as a pitcher of mountain spring water. It just *flowed* out like sparklin' liquid. When he opened up his mouth that first night and led us out in 'I Would Be Like Jesus,' every person under that tent just *gawked* I'll tell you. Our singin' just fizzled out—we was dazed by Mr. Esperando's voice! He was left singin' all by hisself. Freddy Showalter was always good enough before, and he'd sure done the best he could, bless his little heart, but next to his little old thin, nasaly voice, Mr. Esperando sounded like the wind and the waves and the rollin' thunder! I can still feel the shiver that went all over me that night—and not just because Mr. Esperando had such a powerful voice but also because he sang the words so that you were forced to think about the wonderful *meanin'* of it all!"

Joe Leonard had lifted his head, Perry noticed, and was staring at his grandmother. Jewel was gazing into her lap, a placid smile playing around her mouth. Willard ran his thumb back and forth across his lower lip. All around him Perry saw eyes wide with interest as Eldeen told her story. It was impossible to tell where she was headed, of course, but she had such a colorful style of speech that apparently no one thought of questioning the relevance of what she was saying.

"And I can still hear every word Brother Whitehead said plain as a church bell when he rebuked us all in his gentlemanlike way the Sunday after the revival meetings was done: 'God doesn't mind us enjoying *quality*,' he said. 'The Bible doesn't command us anywhere to settle for tackiness!' Oh, he was a wise old man, Brother Whitehead was. He sure ruffled some feathers around Cloverdale, but the point was he was *right,* and my little old girl's heart told me so. 'Some of you thought I was way out of line,' Brother Whitehead told us, 'bringing a man of Mr. Esperando's credentials here to little backwoods Cloverdale—I know you did. I heard reports of some of the talk. But I wanted you to see something,' he said. 'I wanted you to see for yourself that beauty and art and music and elegance, when it all comes from a pure heart, can *elevate* a Christian's soul and make him more tender to the truth of God. It cost us a little more to get Mr. Esperando's services,' Brother Whitehead said, 'but what we got in return was well worth it.'"

Eldeen paused a moment and reached up to remove her other earring, then stood with her head cocked, rubbing her earlobe and staring down at the carpet. "My mama had Mr. Esperando for supper one night during the revival, and I sat across from him at the table just soakin' up every word that man said. He had this little tiny black mustache and just the most refined manners I had ever seen! I never knew if he was really left-handed or had only taught hisself to be on account of losing his right arm, but he was so smooth and *resourceful* with that one arm that you almost forgot he didn't have another one, until you noticed the empty sleeve pinned up out of the way. When he led the singing, he just moved that left arm around so graceful; it just floated like a bird!" Here she stopped and gave a brief demonstration, holding her right arm behind her.

Eldeen dropped her left arm abruptly and craned her neck forward, narrowing her eyes. "God loves beauty!" she said, pointing her finger and moving it slowly across the congregation. "Think of the names he gives his Son in the Holy Bible: the Rose of Sharon and the Lily of the Valley and the Bright Morning Star! I think he wants his house to be a *beautiful* place. He didn't tell his people to make the curtains of the tabernacle out of some old rags—he said they was to be made of fine linen, purple and scarlet and blue—*not dark brown so it wouldn't show the dirt!* I been readin' in the book of Exodus how God tells 'em down to the *teeniest* detail how he wants his house to be built and decorated—with gold and silver and brass and fine needlework and sweet-smellin' spices and soft animal skins. And he didn't tell the priests to sling just any old burlap sack over theirselves either—he gave 'em a big old list of instructions about their holy garments that must've weighed a ton after they got 'em all on, with all them jewels on the breastplate and them solid gold chains and the pomegranates and bells on the hems of their robes and all. But, see, the point of it all wasn't just to flaunt all them *things*—it wasn't just show-off beauty, it was beauty that was a testimonial to the *holiness of the Lord!*"

The air-conditioning unit gave another clunk and began humming in a lower, steadier key. Perry saw Brother Hawthorne turning the pages of his Bible. No one else moved.

Eldeen shifted her weight and shook her head sorrowfully. "I sure didn't aim to hurt anybody's feelings," she said. "Something just came over me all of a sudden-like. I just now remembered too that after the children of Israel followed all them instructions, it says that the glory of the Lord filled the tabernacle. That's what we want here at the Church of the Open Door—we want God's spirit to hover over us and surround us and fill us and send us out to be saints in circulation!" She stopped and turned around to face Brother Hawthorne. "I want to go on record in favor of the burgundy carpet, and I mean to give some extra in the offering plate to help out." She looked back at the people uncertainly, then crinkled her face into its painful-looking smile, and said, "Amen! The end!" and sat down.

After Eldeen sat down, the room was deathly still. Perry never knew who started it first, but someone—maybe it was Willard—began singing softly: "Holy, holy, holy, Lord God Almighty." As others joined in, Perry recorded in his notes: "Eldeen—speaks at length about relationship of beauty and holiness of God; supports purchase of burgundy carpet."

Chapter 28

You think you can get all the guys in your car, Perry?" Sid Puckett asked. "Dottie and I can take the girls in our van, and we'll just meet out there."

"Sure." Perry looked over at the boys standing in a loose circle under the maple tree in the church parking lot. One of the Chewning twins was throwing rocks at a telephone pole over by the empty field next to the church and yelling "Gotcha!" every time he hit it. Joe Leonard had both hands balled up inside his jacket pockets and was nodding at something Howie Harrelson was saying. The other three boys—Caleb Chewning and the Chewning boys' two guests—had their backs to Perry, looking up at a low-flying airplane in the sky.

The six girls were already climbing into the Pucketts' van. One of them looked back at the boys and shouted, "We're gonna beat y'all there!" and there was a chorus of laughter as the van door slid shut.

"You're all riding with me," Perry called to the boys.

Joshua Chewning dropped his handful of gravel onto the parking lot and dashed for the station wagon. "Last one there owes the first one a hundred dollars!" he said. Caleb took off after him, and the two brothers scuffled good-naturedly getting into the car.

Joe Leonard and Howie got into the front seat with Perry. Joe Leonard had already introduced Howie when they had picked him up at his house earlier, and Howie had talked nonstop all the way to the church. It was odd to Perry at first that Joe Leonard had chosen someone like this to invite to the Each-One-Bring-One activity, but maybe he had wanted to relieve himself of the burden of having to make conversation. Perry could certainly understand that. Or maybe Howie reminded Joe Leonard of Eldeen and made him feel like he was at home. Howie played percussion in the band, Joe Leonard had explained, and that's how they knew each other.

As soon as Howie had gotten into the car, Perry had started trying to think of who it was the boy reminded him of, and it wasn't until they had pulled into the church parking lot that he thought of it. It was Wally Cleaver's friend on the old *Leave It to Beaver* TV show—Eddie Haskell, that was the kid's name. Howie had the same smile that was a little too ingratiating, the same courteous tone of voice with adults that was a little too deferential, the same placid eyes that blinked a little too fast. This was a kid who would shred you to ribbons behind your back, Perry decided.

". . . probably doesn't get very good gas mileage, though, does it, Mr. Warren?" Howie was asking now.

"Probably not," Perry replied. "Joe Leonard would know more about that than I do, though, since it's his mother's car. She offered it for tonight since mine's pretty small."

"Oh, I see," Howie said politely. "That was nice of her." He turned to the boys in the backseat. "Any of you guys play basketball?"

"I do," one of them said.

"You're Brian, right?" Howie said.

"No, Kent—that's Brian there."

"Well, Kent, you ought to get me and my buddy Joe Leo here to give you some tips. He's going out for basketball this year, isn't that right?" He gave Joe Leonard a friendly dig with his elbow.

"Maybe," Joe Leonard said, looking straight ahead.

"Yeah, him and me's gonna be the backbone of the team, aren't we?" Howie laughed so hard and long that Perry wondered if he was making fun of Joe Leonard or just celebrating prematurely. Joe Leonard smiled but didn't reply.

"Tryouts are next week, you know," Howie said to Joe Leonard. Then he began a lengthy story about a boy named Huron DeLacey, who had moved to Derby from Delaware during the summer and was reportedly such a good basketball player that he had carried his team to the regional finals last year in Delaware, rallying them to win the championship game with only four players on the floor during the last ten minutes.

"We *might* let him play on our team, huh, Joe Leo?" Howie said, and Joe Leonard grinned but said nothing. As they neared the miniature golf course, Howie started describing a game he himself had played in the year before as a sophomore, subbing for a senior who fouled out. "I scored twelve of the last fifteen points," he stated proudly.

"Wow," one of the boys in the backseat said.

"I'll bet you played a little basketball yourself in school, didn't you, Mr. Warren?" Howie said to Perry as they got out of the car a little later at the Palmetto Miniature Golf Course and Batting Range. But before Perry could answer, Howie sprinted away, pretending to dribble forward for a layup, then leaped and turned, extending one arm and flicking his wrist. Perry suspected that his performance was for the girls, who were standing beside the Pucketts' van.

"Think we can all stay together?" Sid Puckett asked Perry.

"Oh, probably—we can try," Perry replied. "It doesn't look all that crowded."

"They said six would be a good time," Dottie Puckett said. "I just hope everybody had time to eat a bite at home so they can make it till we eat our subs back at the church afterward."

"They have vending machines over by the batting cages, ma'am," Howie pointed out.

A few minutes later they were all clustered around the first hole. Sid filled in six names on his scorecard, and Perry took the other six.

"Okay, Josh, you go first, then Brian," Sid said. "We'll keep all our young people with their guests all the way through but alternate who goes first. Go ahead, Josh, start us off right and show us how to do it."

Joshua Chewning stuck his tongue out the side of his mouth in a goofy smile and crossed his eyes. "Duh—okay, everybody, watch this!"

Perry saw the girl who had come with Marilee Tucker raise her eyebrows. Marilee whispered loudly, "He's a nut!"

Hole 1 was a straight stretch of green between red two-by-fours, but at the very end was a short, sharp slope with the hole situated at an angle. Joshua's first putt was so hard that his ball hit the end board and bounced out onto the concrete. Everybody laughed, Joshua loudest of all. By the time he negotiated his ball into the hole, he had taken seven shots. His friend Brian fared a little better with only five.

"Who's *she*, Joe Leo?" Perry heard Howie ask when Trisha Finch stepped up for her turn.

"Her name's Trisha," Joe Leonard said. "Her family just started coming to our church."

Perry thought back to the day in early September when he was taking Eldeen to her afternoon shift at the G.O.O.D Store. Spotting a moving van pulled up in a driveway over on Geranium Lane, Eldeen had grabbed his arm and pointed. "Stop! Pull in there! Now I know why the Lord laid it on my heart to leave a little early this afternoon." And he had watched her in disbelief as she got out of the car and walked over to the moving van. She grabbed a floor lamp sitting beside it and then marched purposefully up the front steps to the door, which was standing open.

"Yoo-hoo!" she had called, and a petite woman about half her size had shown up at the door. Perry had watched them standing there together on the small porch, Eldeen towering over the other woman like an Amazon warrior, wielding the floor lamp like a spear as she talked. The other woman had stood there, her hand against her forehead like a visor, gazing up at Eldeen as if confronted with some rare museum specimen. Shortly they both disappeared inside, and when Eldeen came back out, she was no longer carrying the floor lamp.

"You wait right here just a minute, Glenda. I got something for you in the car," he heard Eldeen say as she started down the steps from the porch. The woman stood at the door watching Eldeen curiously; Perry knew just how she felt. He remembered well the first time he had met Eldeen. Glenda was probably standing there thinking, "Is she for *real*—or is there a hidden camera somewhere?" He thought he even saw her glancing toward the eaves and then down to the bushes beside the steps, then out toward Perry's car, as if searching for the Candid Camera crew.

Perry got out of the car and met Eldeen on the sidewalk. "Did you want these?" he asked, holding out the plastic Thrifty-Mart bag that contained her latest two sets of pillowcases.

"Oh, you're a mind reader, you are, Perry! You can just see right into my brain!" Eldeen cried. "I told Juanita at the G.O.O.D. Store that I was bringing in two sets today, but I'll tell her something came up." She reached inside the sack and pulled out both sets. "Which one do you think is the prettiest?" she asked, lowering her voice and drawing her thick eyebrows together.

"I like the lavender," Perry said after studying them both. "But the red is pretty too."

Eldeen dropped the red set back into the sack and took Perry's arm. "Come on up here and meet the new lady in the neighborhood! Her name's Glenda Finch, and she's just the sweetest little thing. They got a teenage daughter and a ten-year-old boy, and her husband's already been here a month findin' 'em a house—this one right here—and gettin' all set up to teach at Derby High. He's a science teacher—isn't that interesting? Biology and chemistry and all them kind of things—and I'll just bet you Joe Leonard's in one of his classes. He's signed up for biology this year, and he said he had a new teacher from Alabama—and that's where the Finches moved from—Boaz, Alabama. Isn't Glenda sweet-looking? Doesn't she remind you of a little china doll?" Eldeen spoke loudly, beaming up at Glenda, who looked temporarily disconcerted at hearing herself described in this way. "I got a welcome-to-Derby present for you!" Eldeen called.

Glenda met them at the bottom of the steps. She looked up at Eldeen, still uncertainly, then darted a glance toward the moving van. Perry wondered if she thought the camera could be hidden in there. Or maybe she was just eager to get back to her work.

"Here you go," said Eldeen. "This here's a set of pillowslips I embroidered just for you. 'Course I didn't *know* you when I was working on 'em, but I just had me a feeling inside here"—she thumped her chest—"that somebody *special* would end up gettin' 'em." Glenda took them and held them in her hands as if they were breakable, staring back and forth between them and Eldeen. From the look on her small, heart-shaped face, Perry couldn't tell if she was about to cry or laugh. Maybe she was thinking, "*Purple* lambs on a *blue* hillside?"

Eldeen reached forward and patted the embroidered lambs. "There now, little fellers, you got you a new home! Y'all be nice and soft and quiet when Glenda here goes to lay down her pretty little curly head at night. Don't you be bleatin' and baa-in'!" And Eldeen shook with laughter. "I got to go now, honey," she said to Glenda, then looked over at the moving van. "Maybe we can come back later, after Joe Leonard gets home, and help you get some more of your things moved inside."

Glenda finally spoke. She had a frail, whispery voice—or maybe it was just that way, Perry thought, because she seemed to be all choked up with emotion. "You don't know what this means," she said with a sharp intake of breath. "It's been really hard these last few months, and . . . now everybody's off at school and I'm by myself all day trying to . . . well, I was inside before you came, just sitting in the kitchen . . . well, *upset*. And . . . oh, thank you for coming. I won't *ever* forget this."

Howie nudged Perry's arm. "Me and Joe Leo both got three's, Mr. Warren. Are you keeping score? I'd be glad to do it if you don't want to."

"Oh, sure, sure," Perry said. "I'm doing it." He took the short pencil from behind his ear and marked down the scores. The first group of six had already finished Hole 1, he noticed, and had started on the second one. Perry heard someone say, "There goes Josh again," and he looked up in time to see Josh's blue ball plop into the narrow pool under a tiny bridge on Hole 2.

Joshua stuck his club into the water and fished the ball out. "Look what I caught!" he shouted, holding it up and shaking the water off. "It's a slimy bluegill puffer!" He laughed uproariously, and Bonita Puckett's friend—a sophisticated Polynesian-looking girl named Rochelle—turned her back to Joshua and spelled aloud, "I-m-m-a-t-u-r-e."

Undaunted, Joshua grinned and drawled, "I heard tnat. She done called me a name. But I ain't never larned to spell. It started with i-m-, though . . . hmmm, now what was it? I know!" He stuck his index finger up in mock inspiration. "Im-portant!"

"Imbecile," his brother, Caleb, called out, and everybody laughed.

"Immobile," Joshua countered, bending to replace his ball on the little rubber mat and then stiffening as if frozen.

"Impaled," Caleb said, pretending to stab his brother. Josh fell over and writhed around briefly, then stood up and took another shot, swinging more carefully this time but still too hard. The ball passed safely over the bridge but hit the hole on the other side too fast and flew over it. It hit the end board, then rebounded briskly and once again landed in the water.

"Immersed!" groaned Joshua, and everyone laughed again, even Rochelle. The next time he aimed carefully and hit the ball gently; it stopped just inches from the cup, and he putted it in easily.

"Improved," Caleb said.

"Impressive," said Joshua, flexing his muscles and striking a winner's pose. Then he moaned loudly, faked a cramp in his biceps, and hobbled off clownishly to sit beside the Pucketts on the bench. These Chewning twins were quick, thought Perry. He would hate to try to keep up with them.

"How old is he—*eight?*" Perry heard Rochelle ask Bonita, but she was smiling this time.

"Did you get Marilee's score?" Howie asked. Perry looked at him blankly. "She got a four," Howie said. "And Vicky's on her seventh stroke." Perry quickly recorded a four and a seven and made up his mind to keep track of his six players more closely.

"I'd be glad to help if you want me to," Howie offered again, but Perry shook his head and smiled.

"Caleb, you're next," Howie called, looking at the scorecard over Perry's shoulder. Caleb and Kent jogged back to take their turns on Hole 1.

"You know where she lives?" Perry heard Howie ask Joe Leonard. Howie was watching Trisha Finch take her turn on Hole 2.

"Sure. We helped them move in a month or so ago. It's not far from my house. Her dad is . . ."

"Hey, wait! He's that new teacher, right? Finch—yeah, that's his name. Dan Simpson says he's gonna be the assistant basketball coach this year."

"Maybe, I don't know about that. He's my biology teacher."

"Yeah?" Howie watched Trisha bend to retrieve her ball from the cup. "What is she—a sophomore or what?"

"No—a senior. She's seventeen, I think."

"And she goes to your *church?*" Howie whistled low and shook his head in disbelief, as if unable to picture someone so pretty attending church regularly.

"Yes. The girl with her lives a few houses down from hers I think—Jill somebody. She's a senior too."

"Uh-huh . . ." but Perry could tell Howie had no interest in Jill or her place of residence.

Two hours later they were all back at the church eating submarine sandwiches that Sid and Dottie had ordered earlier and picked up on their way back from the Palmetto. All twelve of the young people were sitting at a long table, and the three adults sat at a card table over by the kitchen.

"That fellow with Joe Leonard seems to be such a nice young man," Dottie Puckett said, nodding toward Howie, who had just stood up and was approaching the kitchen window, where the potato chips and bottles of pop were sitting.

Howie looked over at the adults' table and smiled angelically. "It's all delicious," he said. Perry was surprised the boy could eat anything after devouring two bags of corn chips, a Dr. Pepper, and a package of Hostess twinkies at the batting range. He noticed Howie had managed to get seats at the table across from Trisha and Jill, and he had to admire the kid for being so resolute; he knew that he himself would never have dared to pursue a girl a year ahead of him in school. But then, Dinah was the only girl he had pursued, and he hadn't even meant to do that; it had just happened.

After they ate, Sid and Perry set up the Ping-Pong table and the young people played several games of what they called a "round robin blitz"; they lined up six on a side, and after the first person in line hit the ball, he laid the paddle down and ran around to get in line on the other side. When someone missed a shot, he had to sit out. In the last game, Caleb Chewning, Howie, Rochelle, and Joe Leonard were the last four left. When Rochelle fumbled the paddle and hit the ball with the palm of her hand instead, Josh Chewning wagged his finger and spelled out, "I-m-p-r-o-p-e-r!"

"Oh, hush!" Rochelle shouted back and kept playing. But a few minutes later only Howie and Joe Leonard were left.

"Okay, Joe Leo, are you ready?" Howie said. Perry saw him cut his eyes over at Trisha before rapping a swift, rhythmic tattoo on the table with his two index fingers. To determine the winner between the two players, each boy had to stay on his own side of the table. After hitting the ball, he had to lay his paddle down, spin around, pick the paddle back up, and be ready to make the next return. Howie wiped his hands down the sides of his jeans, picked up the paddle, and bent forward in a wrestling stance. Before long both boys were making shots, slinging their paddles down, spinning around, and fumbling for their paddles to return balls. When Joe Leonard finally hit one across the net before Howie could grab his paddle and return it, everyone clapped and cheered.

"I-m-p-o-l-i-t-e!" declared Josh, grinning and pointing at Joe Leonard.

"Well, I didn't know old Joe Leo here would turn so vicious," said Howie loudly, laughing a little too brightly, obviously chagrined over losing. "But I invite everybody to watch me take him on in a regular game. How about it, Joe Leo? Not afraid to get beat, are you?" Howie picked up a paddle and ball and poised as if ready to serve.

But Sid Puckett stood up then and corralled everybody over toward the piano. Marilee Tucker accompanied while Sid tried to lead a few choruses, but the words on the chart he had written out were hard to read and only the six members of the youth group knew the tunes anyway.

"I'm not going to preach to you tonight," Sid said after the third song, "but I did ask our young people to be ready to give a few words of testimony before we have prayer and eat dessert." He looked around hopefully. "Who'll go first?"

Bonita Puckett stood up, twisting her hands. "I just want to say thanks to my mom and dad for planning all this for us and for starting the youth group activities this fall because we never used to do anything like this just for us. And I want to thank Rochelle for coming with me since Dad told us all we couldn't come unless we brought someone with us." Everyone laughed nervously as if to help Bonita out. She cleared her throat, took a deep breath, then said, "I'm glad I'm a Christian, and I'm thankful to God for the way he directs us. I prayed that he'd show me who to ask tonight, and the very next day Rochelle stopped by my locker and asked if I had a pencil she could borrow. So we made this trade—she got the pencil and I got her to come with me tonight . . . and I'm just thankful for a good church like this and a good family and good friends . . . and I guess that's all." She shrugged and giggled, then sat down.

"Bet she never gave the pencil back!" Josh called out.

"Did too!" Rochelle shot back.

"Okay, you two," Sid said, laughing. "We're going to make you sit by each other if you don't learn to get along."

"She started it!" Josh cried, pointing at Rochelle and pushing out his lips in a fake pout.

"Let's get back to our testimonies," Sid said. "Who wants to go next? Josh, how about you?"

Josh sprang to his feet. "At your service, sir!" he exclaimed, saluting crisply. Perry expected a comedy routine, but instead Josh sobered and delivered a short speech that he had obviously thought about before-hand. Perry had already heard from Eldeen that the Chewning twins were bright, but Josh's testimony proved it. Remembering the stub of a pencil behind his ear, Perry jotted down a few of Josh's points on a paper napkin so he could remember them later. "I always wanted to be a star" was how Josh led into his testimony. Two or three of the visitors started to laugh but stopped when no one else joined in. The church young people somehow seemed to know Josh had switched from silly to serious.

Josh proceeded to develop three ways he had decided he could be a star. The first was "to shine *wherever* God puts me," and he talked briefly about being willing to go to the mission field if that's where God led him someday; he said he thought maybe God wanted him to go to Peru or Chile but his family was praying about it. The second way he could be a star, he said, was "to radiate light in a dark world," and he quoted the verse from Matthew: "Let your light so shine before men, that they may see your good works, and glorify your Father which is in heaven." The third way was "to shine *all* the time," and he pointed out that the stars were always up there, even in the daytime, even on cloudy nights; they never quit shining just because they weren't on display.

After Joshua sat down, Perry looked back over the short outline he had written down. Surely the boy hadn't come up with this on his own; had he read it somewhere? The kid was only thirteen or fourteen years old; where had he learned to speak like that—so fluently, so convinc-ingly, so sincerely, so *maturely*? Perry looked over at Rochelle. She was staring at Josh with a puzzled expression, looking almost rebuked, as if wondering, "Is this the same kid I called immature earlier?"

Marilee Tucker was speaking now, but Perry could hardly concentrate. It came to him that this whole concept of the youth activity was a pretty good one for accomplishing the church's objectives. It wasn't a dating thing, yet there was the fun of boys and girls being together. There were alert chaperones and no dangerous dead time. It fulfilled the principle Brother Hawthorne was so adamant about: "reaching out to others." There was friendly competition, besides good food and lots of laughter—and now an opportunity for the church teens to tell a captive audience about their Christianity. And they were all doing it too—standing up one by one to say their piece. How did these fundamentalists do it? How did they raise kids like this? It had to take constant effort.

He recalled a Wednesday evening talk Brother Hawthorne had addressed specifically to fathers, in which he had spoken about the subject of discipline. "Part of my love for Hannah, Esther, and Levi," he had said, "includes my saying things like 'No, you may not play in the street, and if you disobey, you will face my judgment.' My love goes hand in hand with my chastening. I wouldn't fully love my children if I didn't take the time to discipline them. In that way we fathers are to our earthly children what God is to his spiritual children."

Brother Hawthorne had paused, then continued. "You cannot bring your children up properly, fathers, if you fail to correct them—lovingly yet consistently. Even when your favorite football team is on television. It can't wait till halftime; you have to be willing to get up and take care of first things first." Perry had felt uncomfortable as the pastor's words sank in. He thought back to all the times he had overlooked Troy's fits of temper, had given in to him, had intervened when Dinah had wanted to take a firm hand. Maybe part of the fundamentalists' success with their children—at least the six here at the Church of the Open Door—had to do with the fathers. Perry wished he knew for sure.

". . . and for Perry too." Joe Leonard was talking now, looking first down at his feet, then up to the ceiling. Perry wished he had been paying attention better. "I know God sent him to us," Joe Leonard continued. "He's . . . well, he's been an awfully good neighbor . . . and a friend, too, and I guess in a lot of ways like a . . ."

In the short space of time it took Joe Leonard to form his thoughts, Perry hoped earnestly, almost frantically, *Don't, please don't say that I've been like a father to you. You know it's not true. Fathers teach their children, they guide them, they provide them with confidence to face life, they encourage them, they . . . do so many things that I don't even do with my own son, much less you, don't say it, please don't say it.*

". . . well, he's like a . . . big *brother* to me, and I always wanted one of those," Joe Leonard concluded. Dottie Puckett looked over at Perry and smiled warmly. Joe Leonard paused again and even from behind him, Perry could tell the boy was blushing by the way his ears pinkened.

Chapter 29

A*nd those are some of my memories,*" Perry wrote on the last page of the little book he had bought at the card shop. He twisted his gold Cross pen, retracting its ball nib, then set it down neatly beside the book. There. He was finished. He picked up the book and thumbed back through the pages, surprised at how easy it had been to fill them all. He had actually written something in ink without a rough draft. He had started late Friday night after he had come home from Jewel's, added a few pages on Saturday and more last night after talking with Troy on the telephone, then finished it this morning. Now as his eye caught phrases he had written, something inside him said again, "You'll never mail this to her. It's too revealing. You'll intend to, say you're going to, maybe even wrap it up and address it. But in the end you'll choke. When it comes to releasing it to the care of the United States Postal Service, you'll snatch it back."

Looking back over his own written words, he was troubled by a strange sensation, somewhat like that of studying his own face in a mirror. Is this really me? he often found himself saying as he shaved in the morning. Am I really standing here shaving? He wished he could remember the name of the ancient Chinese philosopher who had had a dream about being a butterfly but posed the question afterward: "Was I a man dreaming I was a butterfly, or am I a butterfly dreaming I am a man?" During his first two months here in Derby, Perry had frequently looked around in Beth's house and asked himself, "Am I *really* here—or is this something I'm *imagining* for a book I'm writing?" He often felt like he had somehow managed to transfer himself to some past time and was simply remembering a place he had once visited.

He usually printed his notes, but he had written the words in the little book in cursive. Dinah used to say his penmanship belonged on the Declaration of Independence, that he could easily forge the original document if he ever wanted to. Studying the ruled pages now, he found it hard to believe he had really written these words, slanted so uniformly, set down so boldly. But who else would have written phrases like "your wide-brimmed straw hat tipped rakishly, your amber hair spilling out beneath its circle of summer flowers," "the delicate, swift curves of your tapered fingers—the ballet of your hands as you talk," "the grace of your classical features, the glow of your romantic eyes"? Certainly not Thomas Jefferson or John Hancock. The founding fathers would surely blush at such sappiness.

He turned back to the first page. *"These are some of my memories,"* he had started out a few minutes before midnight on Friday. He had just seen Willard's wistful, shining eyes searching the skies overhead, had just heard his whimsical entreaty "Star light, star bright," had sensed the plaintive urgency behind it, had felt a tug of desire in his own heart as he stepped into his empty kitchen and saw Dinah's birthday gift wrapped in its shiny gold paper sitting beside his bags of groceries on the table.

In recording his memories in the little book, he had reached far back—to the first time he had seen Dinah sitting beside the old stone fountain in a shady, secluded alcove outside the Student Union. She had been reading, but from time to time she looked up toward the little naked cherubs spewing water from their stained copper mouths.

He had been pretending to read himself—excerpts from William Bradford's *Of Plymouth Plantation,* John Winthrop's *Journal,* and the poetry of Anne Bradstreet. Vivid phrases jumped out at him, but none of the prose passages held together with the least bit of cohesion—"a hideous and desolate wilderness full of wild beasts and wild men," "riotous prodigality and profuse excess," "took a rapier and ran him through," "she did frequently abuse her husband, setting a knife to his breast." Only Bradstreet's poetry made any sense whatsoever, but even then only a single line here and there—"The earth reflects her glances in thy face," "I prize thy love more than whole mines of gold," "There's none on earth can parallel." He had been forced to reread the entire twenty-page assignment later that night, at which time he saw that he had completely missed the overall meaning in his earlier reading.

Having begun writing on Friday night, committing on white, lined pages in unequivocal black ink his memories of Dinah, Perry had compiled an amazing assortment of specifics. And Dinah had always scolded him for being in a daze. This would show her that he had been paying a lot more attention all those years than she had given him credit for—if he decided to send it, that is. He even surprised himself at some of the details he had poked out of the corners of his memory.

He was hoping in his handwritten chronicle to run across some memory that might unlock the mystery of Dinah's disaffection, but the last page was now filled and nothing had come to light. One detail disturbed him, though, and he wasn't sure why it hadn't signaled danger the first time he observed it. Probably because he wasn't looking for danger.

It had happened about two years earlier. He had driven to Chicago to meet with Cal about several matters. It had turned out to be a setup, however, with a former sociology professor of Perry's who had left Urbana for a teaching job at the University of Chicago. This professor had wanted to collaborate with somebody on a book about a street gang called the Scorpios, and Cal had suggested Perry, then lured him to lunch with Professor Jernigan. It hadn't worked, of course; Perry was deep into a science-fiction trilogy at the time, with plans for a second series after that one, and had no intention of returning to academic writing anytime soon.

He had gotten home earlier that night than he had expected to and had entered the house without Troy or Dinah hearing him. He wasn't *trying* to sneak up on them, but once inside, hearing the sound of their voices in Troy's bedroom, he had walked quietly down the hallway and stood outside the door, observing them around the corner. They had been playing the Memory Game, a simple little matching game with rows of pictures turned face down, a game that Dinah insisted on playing regularly, holding to the theory that it would increase Troy's attention span, which had been a problem in second grade.

"I *knew* it was there!" he had heard Troy say triumphantly, adding a pair of cards to his small stack.

"You get to go again," Dinah had prodded, followed by a moment of silence.

"Where was that other train?" Troy had said. "I think it was . . ."

"Sorry," Dinah said. "You were close; it was right next to it. See?"

"Mo-o-o-om." The inflection was one they heard often, stretching out the word and weighting it with exasperation, blame, whiny protest.

"Oh—the banjo," said Dinah. "Now that other one was up here somewhere, maybe here?—I thought so." She ignored Troy's high-pitched objection as she gathered up the matching pair and then turned up another card to continue her turn. Perry had always admired her tough playing in these little games; whenever he played with Troy, he tried hard to remember where the cards were only to keep from choosing a match; his goal was always to avoid the spectacle of his son in the throes of defeat.

"The book—the book—now where did I see it?" Perry saw Dinah's head bent over the cards, her finger running back and forth above the rows. She turned up a card. "Nope—wrong choice. Okay, your turn."

Troy raised up on his knees and reached over to the last row. "It was right there!" he said, gloating. "You shoulda remembered the *book,* Mom. That's what Dad writes." He added the pair to his stack.

"Yes, Dad does write books, doesn't he?" Dinah said, but her voice had a sharp-edged sound. "That's about all he *does* do." Troy was busy deliberating over the location of the other chair card and didn't respond, but Perry remembered wondering at the time what Dinah had meant—if she had meant anything at all. He puzzled over it only a few seconds, however, and then gave up. Wasn't it a funny verb construction, he thought, to use the helping verb *does* with the verb *do? Does do, does do, does do*—the phrase kept repeating itself. So much so that he almost missed Dinah's next equally mystifying remark.

"Look at these two chairs, Mom. One of 'em's a different color—they used to be exactly alike, didn't they?" Troy held the two cards up for Dinah to see.

"I bet that's the card that got lost that time," Dinah said. "We found it in your windowsill, remember? It probably got faded by the sun." Then she looked over to the window and sighed. "Lots of things end up different from how they start out," she said.

At the time Perry assumed she was disappointed about some little development in her small world of womanly concerns—some dress that didn't fit right anymore or some recent tiff with her mother. He wondered now, as he recalled it all, if she had been thinking of something bigger, something involving himself maybe. But why hadn't she ever brought it up for discussion if that was the case? Surely a woman couldn't expect a man to figure out the maze of her mind with just a few cloudy intimations, a couple of overheard innuendoes. Of course, if he were going to be fair, he knew he would have to admit his resistance to discussing problems. Dinah *had* tried it several times, and—well, it never worked out. She had always ended up an emotional wreck.

Perry closed the little book. This would substitute for the birthday card he had given to Willard, he decided. He had already wrapped Dinah's birthday gift in brown paper and addressed it neatly. Now he cut off a shorter length of the brown paper and set about wrapping the book. What would Dinah think when she received it? What would go through her mind before she opened it, when she saw the return address? Would she laugh when she began reading it? Would she be cold and angry? Would she mail it back with sarcastic comments written in the margins—things like "Oh, sure—I'll believe this when the North Pole thaws" or "Too bad you didn't think of this years ago"?

He would mail them both today; that would allow plenty of time since her birthday was on Saturday. I *will so* mail it, he thought to himself as he ran a thick strip of packaging tape around the brown paper. He wouldn't go to all this trouble and then back out at the last minute; that would be something a teenager would do. But even as the thoughts ran through his mind, he envisioned the spiral notebook beside the bed where he slept each night. "Dear Dinah," each page began. He had been writing in it since August, off and on, usually at bedtime and always in pencil. It had started after a conversation with Dinah at the end of the summer, after he had talked with Troy one Sunday night.

"Mom wants to say something," Troy had said.

"Sure, okay—put her on," Perry had replied, trying to sound casual.

Dinah had taken the phone and said something to Troy then, her hand covering the mouthpiece, and had waited a brief interval before addressing Perry.

"There, he's gone upstairs," she said at last. "Perry, I'm worried about Troy."

"Worried? Why?" Perry felt his stomach tighten. Dinah never worried. That had always been Perry's function in their marriage.

"He's . . . well, he's having a real hard time right now. Maybe he's just dreading school and fourth grade and all, but it's got me concerned."

"Well, what is it? What's wrong?" Perry had asked. "He sounded pretty normal on the phone just now. He said he liked the Rollerblades I sent him for his birthday and told me about the party and all."

"I noticed that. I was listening to see how he'd be, talking to you. But you should have been watching him like I was. It's strange—he *sounded* all right, but it was like that electronically produced music. They say it sounds like the real thing, and I guess it does, but every time I hear it, I *know* it's not real instruments playing, but I don't know how I know. When I try to put it into words, I can't. Something just isn't right—either it's too subtle to catch, like I can *feel* it but can't hear it, or else it's too big, like it's the whole huge experience that isn't right and trying to explain it is too big a job. It's the same with all those pictures in magazines of tiny replicas of things—cars, furniture, and all. The first glance and you know it's a copy, yet when you examine it, you can't say why you knew it exactly. All the details are there in the right scale, down to the littlest things—but something's not right. You know it's not the real thing."

The "wash of words"—that's what Perry used to call Dinah's explanations when they were first married. He had been away from it for so long now that he had forgotten that sensation of being splashed and finally deluged with her words, the taking away of his breath with the suddenness of it all. It was different than Eldeen's monologues. Eldeen's were always specific, aimed at communicating particulars about people or places or events, whereas Dinah's might start out specific but always veered off into half-formed comparisons, irrelevancies, and always, always *feelings*. Actually, the music and replica analogies were pretty good, much more clearly expressed than most of what she came up with.

". . . and he hardly blinked his eyes the whole time," Dinah was saying now. "It's like he's on automatic pilot or cruise control—just sitting there opening his mouth like a ventriloquist's dummy or something. The words come out and they're the right ones, the expected ones, but it's his face and his posture and just his whole *appearance* that isn't right. And he's started bringing home the *weirdest* books from the library."

"Like what?" Perry wished Dinah would slow down.

"He knows right where they all are. He goes straight to the aisle—the five hundreds in the children's room—and drags them all off the shelf, sprawls out right there in the aisle and just *pores* over them. Books about hurricanes and volcanoes and tornadoes and earthquakes. Then when I ask him which *story* books he wants to check out to bring home, he sets his mouth that way—you know—and says he's checking *these* out. Then he brings them home and just loses himself in them for hours at a time it seems." So far nothing sounded all that critical to Perry; he used to lose himself in strange books when he was Troy's age.

"Then two days ago," Dinah continued, "I was so relieved to see him with his crayons and markers out, coloring and drawing, and I thought, 'Well, good—he's coming out of it,' but *do you know* what he was drawing? One picture was a tornado ripping the world upside down! There were little houses and people and animals just flying all over inside this gigantic tornado. And another one was a volcano erupting, with all kinds of black stuff gushing out the top, headed straight for a peaceful-looking little town. *And* I saw him out in the backyard yesterday, down on his hands and knees trying to look down inside a big crack in the ground and feeling around, kind of digging with his hands—we haven't had rain in weeks and weeks—and when I went out later, I walked over to where he'd been and there were three of his G.I. Joe men stuffed down inside that crack head first. He's a *disturbed* little boy, Perry."

"Well, I don't know. I went through a fascination with shipwrecks and floods and things like that when I was a boy."

"Fascination? Your mother said you used to have nightmares about being drowned."

When had his mother told Dinah that? Perry wondered. "Well, yes, I guess it was a combination of horror and fascination—like you were the time we watched *Psycho,*" he said. Dinah had sat on the couch with her eyes squeezed shut, clutching his arm till she almost cut off the circulation, but when he had suggested turning off the television, she had refused. "No, of course not!" she had said. "I want to see it all."

"You're getting off the subject, Perry," Dinah said. "What about Troy? I don't think it's normal for him to be so obsessed with all these violent acts of nature."

"Well, it's better than drawing pictures of people slashing other people's throats or shooting them with guns . . . I don't think we need to worry . . . it'll probably . . ."

Dinah interrupted with a cry of impatience, then a frustrated sigh. "Oh, I should have expected this. It's easy for *you* to say don't worry. You're hundreds of miles away! *Don't worry!*" She broke off with a mocking laugh. "That's what every therapist in the world says when you unload everything that's bothering you. 'Don't worry about it—try not to think about it so much—worry causes stress'—blah, blah, blah. I should've known that's what you'd say—not because you mean it, though; it's just your easy way out—the same old philosophy you've always been so good at—ignore it and it'll go away." Perry could picture Dinah cradling the receiver under her chin, throwing her arms about dramatically, pacing back and forth. What was this about therapists, though? What kind of therapist? Was she going to some shrink?

"Well, I don't know what else . . . have you tried talking to him?" Perry asked. "Tried to find out if he's got something on his mind?"

If only conversations didn't move so fast—if he weren't always expected to respond immediately. He needed time to prepare an answer, especially with Dinah. But he had learned a long time ago that she always interpreted pauses of silence as a lack of interest, so he always tried to come back with something quickly even though it usually fell far short of what needed to be said. He could think of brilliantly insightful, pungently pithy replies later—long after Dinah had exploded over what she once called his "thin, wispy" side of a conversation. "You leave me sitting high in the air on one end of the seesaw!" she had ranted. "You and your pitiful little thin, wispy comments—no wonder we can't have a decent conversation." He remembered getting lost in the metaphor—another one of her inept attempts at figurative language. If his end of the dialogue seesaw was so feeble, how could he hold *down* one end and leave her in the air on the other end? She hadn't thought it through obviously.

". . . so let me know when you have another one of your *inspired* ideas on how to help Troy," she was saying when he returned to the present, and after that all he heard was the enraged drone signaling the telephone's broken connection.

It had been that very night, back in August, that he had begun his nighttime letters to Dinah, recording things he thought of later that would have served as better answers. He had written about a variety of subjects eventually, but in the beginning it was all mostly about Troy.

But this little book was different, he told himself as he descended the porch steps toward his Toyota a few minutes later. He had intended all along to mail this—and he *would*. The spiral notebook beside his bed—well, that was therapeutic, that was all—a series of purgative mental exercises to prove to himself that he could think through a problem, discern likely causes, and draw up a workable course of action. The very fact that he used a pencil spoke for the fact that it wasn't anything permanent or really serious. But this—he had imagined it from the beginning as a conclusive, definite act. In spite of the niggling taunts of that inner voice, he had formed a clear image of himself at the post office window, letting the postal worker take it, weigh it, receive his money, stamp it, and carefully place it into a bin.

Perry passed Hardee's, the Texaco station, Thrifty-Mart, the bank, the G.O.O.D. Store. Farther on he drove past Wal-Mart, Darlene's Kreamy Kones, Arbuckles' Hardware, Bo-Nat's Barber and Beauty Shop. Finally, he saw in the distance the small brick building housing the post office, next to the flapping green and yellow pennants of Melvin's Used Cars. He depressed the accelerator a little more, driving now with devoted, single-minded fervor, eager to get the business done so he could put it out of his mind and get back to his chapter revisions.

Of course, it had been his chapter revisions that had led to this little digression in the first place. On Friday afternoon he had been going through the folder labeled "Prayer Meeting" and had come across a page of notes from one of Brother Hawthorne's Family Emphasis talks back in May. "A WIFE'S MOST BASIC NEEDS" was the title of the list. As he reread it on Friday afternoon, he had felt a mantle of guilt descend upon him. If this list were to be trusted—if Brother Hawthorne had indeed hit on the truth in his report of a wife's fundamental needs—then Perry had been a colossal failure as a husband.

It was after reading the list through for the fourth time, slowly, on Friday afternoon that Perry had stood up, forgetting the folder in his lap, and headed to the mall. *"She wants to know that you are thinking of her even in the midst of pressing outside obligations."* That was number five on the list. All right, he had thought, not even stopping to regather the scattered pages of notes on the floor, I can do that. I can let her know I'm thinking of her. Actually, he had been thinking of her upcoming birthday for several weeks now, wondering whether he should try to acknowledge it. Running across the list of a wife's needs had, of course, been coincidental—though he knew the churchfolks would argue about that—but it had served as a motivator, and once he had determined what to do, he felt something inside him settle peacefully, like the resolving of a chord. "Yes, this is the right thing to do," he said to himself.

The post office was almost deserted except for an elderly black woman wearing what looked like a shower cap over pink sponge curlers. She was buying stamps and was looking at several pages spread out before her. "I was wantin' somethin' purty," she said, raising a knobby finger in the air and waving it aimlessly. The uniformed counter attendant rolled his eyes at Perry, then pointed to a page of Joe Louis stamps.

"These are nice, don't you think?" he said.

"They's nice, but they's not purty," the woman said, shaking her head sorrowfully.

The attendant turned to another page. "Well, here's some of Hank Williams," he said. "They're bright and colorful."

"I ain't wantin' no *man* on my stamps." Another hater of men, Perry thought bleakly. Just as he was trying to imagine the source of this woman's grievances against man, she added, "And no *woman* either. I wants somethin' purty—like butterflies or flowers or stars or somethin' that jest *is* purty without tryin'." She emitted a guttural groan and turned to address Perry. "The longer I lives, the more I sees how *ugly* folks is." She looked him up and down as if confirming her opinion, then turned back to the postal worker.

She finally settled on the circus stamps, grumbling that they still weren't satisfactory, but since she had to have something, she'd take these. She bought only ten stamps, folding them methodically, accordion-style, and placed them deep inside the pocket of her long brown coat before moving away from the counter.

Perry set both the large box and the smaller package on the counter and pushed them toward the postal worker. "First class, please," he said. Had his voice really cracked or was he only imagining things? Thankfully, the attendant hadn't seemed to notice anything.

"Four thirty-five," the man said, pounding both packages several times with a large stamp.

"Will they get there by Saturday?" Perry asked. Why did his throat feel so constricted? He thought the postal worker was looking at him suspiciously. Maybe all postal employees underwent training to detect questionable patrons, ones likely to be mailing bombs or illegal substances. He forced himself to speak again. "Sure hope she gets it by her birthday." There, that sounded more natural except for the nervous laugh at the end. The worker was probably thinking, "Oh, sure, buddy, a *birthday* present. Tell me another one."

"It should be there by Thursday," the man said curtly. As Perry watched him drop the packages into a large, dirty canvas bag, he was suddenly filled with alarm and dread. What had he done? What kind of fool was he to write the things he had written and then actually mail them? He tried to find his voice, to ask for the little book back. He could pretend he had forgotten to include something or had picked up the wrong package by accident. Or he could try to distract the postal worker—tell him someone was stealing a postal Jeep right this minute and point urgently toward the back entrance—then dash around the counter and retrieve the parcel for himself.

Perry lifted his hand and pointed to the canvas bag. He cleared his throat and opened his mouth.

"I said I need another dime, sir," the postal worker said, looking at him curiously. Here was a way out. He could pretend he didn't have any more money; then the man would say he was sorry, they couldn't mail things on credit, and then he would have to return one of his packages— the smaller one. Perry reached inside his pocket as if searching for change.

Just then another postal worker came from the back, cinched up the big canvas bag with a quick jerk, and carted it off. Somewhere in the rear of the post office, Perry heard the sounds of a large door sliding open and the warning beeps of a truck backing up. He laid a dime on the counter. The sight of it was disgusting; it looked so despicably shiny and efficient.

"Were you fixing to say something?" the postal attendant asked.

"No . . . no, I was just thinking . . . how . . . *interesting* post offices are," Perry said, turning to leave.

Chapter 30

There now. You just set yourself down and do your work. I'll have these clothes done up in a jiffy." Eldeen pointed to the chairs over against the window of the Derby Wash-a-te-ria.

Perry stood for a moment, indecisive. He knew he should offer to help her, and it wasn't that he didn't want to—but it seemed such a personal thing to handle someone else's laundry.

"Go on now, scoot!" Eldeen said, waving her hand. "I've bothered you enough already today; you get on to your work. You can sit there by that little table and spread your things out like a desk."

"You sure you don't need me for anything?" Perry said.

"Well, I sure needed you earlier this morning I tell you—and you sure pitched in, like you always do—but I been doin' wash since I was six, so I don't reckon I'm liable to need any help with this. 'Course, I used to do it all by hand when I was a little girl, but I been doing it this way for a long time too. Go on now and get yourself set up at that little table before somebody else comes sashaying in and gets dibs on it." Eldeen lifted the towel off one of the plastic baskets Perry had carried in for her. He watched her grab an armful of white clothes and dump them unceremoniously into an empty washing machine, then pour laundry powder into her hand and sprinkle it over the clothes.

"I sure am glad nobody else is here right now," she called back to Perry, inserting her quarters into the coin slots. "Guess all the mamas are still recovering from the hubbub of getting their children off to school this morning." She stooped over the basket of dark clothes.

Perry walked to the corner and started to sit down in one of the vinyl-covered chairs by the low table but noticed sticky brown stains all over it. Someone must have spilled a can of pop. The chair on the other side of the table had no back; the chrome braces were still there, but somehow the padded support had been knocked off. He picked up another chair from in front of the window to move it over beside the table and felt something warm and oozy against his fingers. A candy bar—someone had smeared chunks of a candy bar all over the back of the chair. He saw now that the rest of it still lay in its wrapper under the chair. Some child no doubt. Probably a fussy toddler whose harried mother had bought him the Baby Ruth in hopes of quieting him. And it had probably worked. While she was busy folding laundry, the kid had used the back of the chair as an easel of sorts, probably licking his fingers as he painted. Perry inspected the mess on his hand.

"Now what's that truck you got all over you?" Eldeen exclaimed, shuffling over. "Well—if that don't beat all! Here, come over here and wipe it off." She waddled back to one of the washing machines and lifted the lid. Fishing out a washcloth, she wrung it out and extended it to Perry.

"I hate to get it all dirty," he said, taking it with his clean hand.

"Oh, pooh!" Eldeen said. "It's already dirty, else I wouldn't of just put it in the washing machine. Here, let me do it." And she grabbed the washcloth back and began scrubbing Perry's hand vigorously, fussing the whole time. "If they'd keep this place clean, it'd sure be nicer to come to! Spider webs everywhere you look and nasty cigarette butts all over the floor! And these filthy-dirty chairs! And that plate glass window—you can't hardly even see the pretty fall colors through it! Why, if it wasn't such a disgrace, it'd almost be *funny* to come to a place like this to get your clothes clean!" The thought came to Perry that someone entering the Wash-a-teria right this minute or walking past the window, seeing them standing here this way, might think he was a retarded adult being tidied up.

"There, that's fine," he said, pulling his hand away gently. Eldeen picked up the tattered magazines from the little table and ran the washcloth over the surface. "Look at that!" she cried. "I bet nobody's touched that table with a cleaning rag since we used to come here back before we got us a washing machine." She wiped it off thoroughly, then stacked the magazines on a chair and walked outside. She came back a few seconds later, shaking the wet washcloth. "There, I rinsed it off at a little spigot around the side." She set about wiping off the chair seats, then patted the one closest to the little table. "Now then, finally—your work space is all fixed up. Sit down!"

"Well . . . thank you," Perry said, but Eldeen waved her hand impatiently.

"I'm the one that's got *you* to thank, dragging you off from your morning's work the way I did. I sure hope Mr. Garland can come take a look at our washer tomorrow, but he said it might be Thursday before he makes it." She began laughing. "It sure threw me into a tizzy the way it just all of a sudden spewed water all over the kitchen—what a shock first thing in the morning!"

It had been a shock to Perry too. He had answered the telephone a few minutes past eight o'clock to hear Eldeen's hoarse shouts: "Oh, Perry, come quick! It's a flood, it's a flood, it's a flood!" He had raced over to find her down on her knees in the kitchen, with garments of all types—blue jeans, aprons, shirts, even socks—spread out on top of an enormous pool of water around the washing machine. At first he had thought the machine had somehow belched a load of clothes onto the floor, but then he realized she must be using all the dirty clothes to try to soak up the water.

Thinking back over it now, he was pleased at how quickly he had reacted—leaping forward to turn off the washer, then hurrying to the bathroom and gathering up an armload of towels. They had gotten the floor cleaned up without much trouble, although he had almost lost his balance and slipped trying to help Eldeen up afterward. Then he had moved a kitchen chair into the hallway and had her sit down while he went over the whole floor with a sponge mop.

"You are one nice neighbor," she had kept telling him. "Not everybody would come to the aid of a old woman the way you do—time and time again you get us out of scrapes. Yes sir, the Lord did a good thing when he brought you here to Derby and moved you to Blossom Circle right next door to us!" Perry couldn't help wondering if she was really thinking about what she was saying—did she really consider it a "good thing" that his wife had kicked him out of his house and that he had been forced to come live in Beth's house because he had nowhere else to go? Did she really think that part of God's big plan for the universe included moving Perry Warren next door to her so that he could help her clean up a washing machine overflow?

No sooner had these thoughts come to his mind than he wondered if she had somehow sensed them. "You've enriched our lives, Perry, that's a fact. No, now don't you go looking up at me that way, I know what I'm saying. And I hope in some tiny way we can give you something back someday. God's got his eye on you, Perry Warren, don't you think he doesn't. He knew what you was in for when he plunked you down here next door to us, and I know beyond the teensiest shadow of a doubt that he's going to work something good out of all this." She extended both arms to take in the whole kitchen, but Perry knew she meant it to include far more.

"Oh, I know you came here to write your book about us and all that," she continued, "but what folks don't realize is that *their* reason for doing a thing might not be the same as *God's* reason for letting them do it. We just see such a little bitty part of the whole story"—and here she stopped to put both hands up to her eyes as if she were looking through binoculars—"while God sees it all." She lifted her hands in the air and opened her eyes wide.

As Perry squeezed out the mop over the sink, she concluded emphatically, "Yes sir, Perry, the Lord's going to reward you for being so good to us. You wait and see." She paused, then spoke again matter-of-factly. "But first he's got to woo you and win you to hisself."

Perry avoided looking at her but took another few swipes with the mop around the base of the washing machine. Eldeen bent over and peeled off the furry yellow slipper-socks she was wearing. "These are sopping wet, and my red pair's in the washing machine right now. I'll just have to put on a pair of Joe Leonard's socks I guess, although I like these lots better because of the little rubbery grippers on the bottom." She stood up from her chair and walked down the hallway toward one of the bedrooms.

Perry lifted the lid of the washer and peered inside. The clothes were pressed damply against the sides of the tub. What was Eldeen going to do now? The sink was full of the other load of wet clothes—the dirty ones they had used to soak up the spill. He couldn't offer the use of Beth's washing machine, for it hadn't worked in almost a year; Beth had told him she wasn't going to have it fixed until she moved back home. For that reason Perry had become a regular customer of the Springtime-Fresh Drycleaners down near Hardee's. Once every two weeks he took in a big bag of dirty clothes and got them back clean and folded a few days later.

Eldeen came back into the kitchen wearing a pair of tube socks under her bathrobe and carrying a Planter's peanut can. "My, my, the floor's almost dry already," she said cheerfully. "Having the doors open sure helps air things out. Glad it's still mild outdoors." She sat down at the table and emptied the can. "Oh, looka there!" she said, beaming up at Perry. "There's plenty here in my change can to take all the clothes to the Wash-a-teria if I have to, but first I'm going to call Mr. Hal Garland. He fixes things like washing machines, and maybe he can come look at ours—it might be just a loose bolt or something, who can tell?"

Perry doubted that a loose bolt was the problem, but he didn't say anything. Soon Eldeen had Mr. Garland on the telephone, speaking slowly and loudly as if talking to a foreigner over a high wind.

"This here's Eldeen Rafferty, 16 Blossom Circle in Montroyal. You remember me, don't you, Mr. Garland? You came over once and fixed our stove that had quit heating up right, remember? That was two years ago this coming Christmas, right when my daughter Jewel was in the middle of baking a Christmas cake. You fixed our stove up like a charm, and it's been working fine ever since, although that cake sure was a flop. But now we've had us a calamity this morning with our washing machine, and I'd be obliged if you could come and see if you can fix it for us." She paused and her thick eyebrows drew together. "Oh, well, now that's too bad, but it's understandable with all the stoves and refrigerators and washing machines there's got to be here in Derby. But that'll be just fine, just whenever you can come by. I'll have to go to the Wash-a-teria today I reckon since my grandson needs his gym clothes done up for tomorrow." After she had hung up, she said to Perry, "It was sure a shame about that cake—it was in the shape of a Christmas tree, and Jewel had even tinted the batter green with food coloring. It called for six egg whites, too, I remember that!" When she stopped talking, Perry had of course offered to take her to the Wash-a-teria.

Perry slid several printed pages from a large yellow envelope and laid them out on the little table. It had been harder than he had expected to get going in the "Cast" section of his book. There was so much to say—first, all the general facts about median income of the church members, political affiliation, variety of occupations, size of families, and so forth, all of which he had collected from anonymous survey forms Brother Hawthorne had allowed him to make available after church one Sunday morning. He was also working on a chapter of character cameos to develop some of the people as individuals. For this chapter he had already interviewed two church members—Harvey Gill and Curtis Chewning—to find out more about their backgrounds, and he still had three more to go: Eldeen, Vonda Snyder, and Tricia Finch. He wanted a variety of ages and occupations represented, along with a mix of longtime Christians and newer converts. Perry read the opening sentence in the first "Cast" chapter: *The members of Gospel Lighthouse view themselves collectively as a city set on a hill and individually as the lights of that city.*

Eldeen went back outside to rinse the washcloth again, then returned it to the washing machine and sat down two chairs away from Perry with a small paperback book entitled *Invigorating Your Vocabu-*

lary in her hands. As he continued slowly through his draft, making corrections and jotting notes to himself in the margins, Perry could hear Eldeen chortling with satisfaction as she read her book. From time to time she'd sound out a word and say something like "Mel-*lif*-lu-ous. 'The actress spoke in a soft, *mellifluous* voice.' Now that's a good word—I'll have to remember that one!"

Perry was on his second page when a black woman and five preschoolers entered the Wash-a-teria. Eldeen looked up with interest. The children were so close to the same age that Perry couldn't see how they could all belong to the same family. Eldeen must have wondered the same thing, for she asked, "Are these fine-looking little youngsters *quintuplets?*"

The woman shook her head. "Naw, I babysit 'em." She pointed to the chairs against the window. "Sit down there," she said to the children, who, to Perry's surprise, obeyed, although two of the boys shoved each other trying to lay claim to the same chair. "Y'all stop that, Leroy," the woman said tersely, and they did. All five children finally got themselves arranged in their chairs and sat studying Perry gravely, their little legs dangling far from the floor. Perry felt like pointing to Eldeen and telling them, "Stare at *her*. She's a lot more interesting than I am."

The woman dug down into her laundry basket and removed five big picture books, which she distributed to the children. "Y'all read while I put the clothes in," she said, and all five children opened their books. Perry knew this activity was destined to be short-term. Images filled his mind of shrieking children chasing each other around the Wash-a-teria, crawling under the chairs, and smearing his pantlegs with chocolate.

"Aren't little Negro children the cutest things?" Eldeen said to Perry in a loud whisper. He glanced again at the silent row of children and nodded. One of them, he noticed, wore an oversized sweatshirt with Michael Jordan's picture on it. It looked brand-new; Perry wondered if the boy's mother had gotten it on sale now that Jordan had announced his retirement. One of the little girls had her hair meticulously groomed into neat cornrows with bright coral beads somehow woven in.

The woman was busy sorting through the laundry basket, tossing clothes into two washing machines and softly singing something mournful in a deep, rich contralto. At least it sounded mournful; Perry couldn't catch the words. Watching her, he couldn't help wondering what sorrows she had known. "Man is born unto trouble, as the sparks fly upward." He almost spoke the words aloud, for he had been rereading the book of Job recently and couldn't get this verse out of his mind. And wasn't it true? Everybody had his own share of trouble.

The woman was tall and athletically built, probably close to Perry's own age. It was funny how you could tell even from so simple a task as sorting laundry whether a person possessed natural grace of movement and physical coordination. Perry didn't think he would want to challenge this woman in any sport. He could imagine her annihilating him in a game of badminton.

Eldeen was still admiring the children, a look of restrained eagerness on her face. From time to time she looked back at the book she was holding, but never for long; her eyes always returned to the row of wide-eyed children staring at the pictures in their books and swinging their little legs.

Suddenly one little boy pointed to a picture and broke out into gales of laughter. "That crazy old dog's turnin' a flip!" he said. The other children clamored to see, two of them getting down out of their chairs.

The woman came over and took the book away without saying a word. At first Perry thought she was punishing the children for their enthusiasm, and he wished he were brave enough to speak up in their behalf. But when she pulled up a chair, sat down in front of them, and opened the book, he saw that she meant to read the story to them. Eldeen got up and moved over to sit beside the children.

Perry stopped trying to read over his manuscript and listened to the story of Barkley, a dog whose curiosity led him to snoop around inside an old tree trunk. After each page the woman read, she held the book up and showed the children the pictures. The turning of the flip had resulted from the dog's getting attacked by the bees inside the tree trunk. The children giggled uncontrollably when the last page showed Barkley with his snout and posterior bandaged.

Eldeen clapped her hands and laughed. "I reckon that's a different way of saying 'Curiosity killed the cat,'" she said, leaning forward to address the children. "Only this time it was a dog named Barkley, not a cat, and thank goodness he didn't get hisself killed, only hurt! Wasn't that a nice story?" The children looked at her, open-mouthed, and nodded.

"Read some more, Shekinah!" the little girl with cornrows said.

"Read this one, Shekinah!" begged the boy in the Michael Jordan shirt, handing his book to the woman.

"Is that your name—Shekinah?" Eldeen asked the woman, who simply nodded and opened the other book to the first page.

"How *fascinating!*" continued Eldeen. "Were you named after somebody in particular?"

"Naw," said the woman. "My mama heard it from a preacher."

"Well, now, I was wondering about that," said Eldeen. "I was sure you must know what your own name meant, but I was wondering how you came to get it."

"Read it, Shekinah," said the little boy named Leroy, pointing to the book in her lap.

"This preacher used to always talk about the Shekinah Glory," the woman said, "so that's what my mama named me—Shekinah Glory." The woman studied Eldeen's face closely as if ready to turn defensive if she needed to.

Eldeen gasped and grinned at the woman. "What a reminder you've got of the divine, holy presence of God!" she said. "A name like that—now *that* must be a blessing! And do you believe in Jesus, Shekinah?" Usually it took Eldeen longer than this to work up to her favorite subject, but Perry had to admit that the woman's name did provide the perfect bridge.

"Yes, I do," the woman answered briefly, her eyes locked with Eldeen's.

"Read, Shekinah!" demanded the boy in the sweatshirt.

"You mind your manners, Bufort!" she said. To Eldeen she added, "Some of these babies I keep needs lots of teachin'."

"Do you go to church anywhere regular?" Eldeen asked. "I'd sure be pleased to have you visit the Church of the Open Door if you don't—and all these sweet little children too." Perry was surprised. He had never once seen a black family at the Church of the Open Door. Had Eldeen checked this out with Brother Hawthorne? Did they need to vote on it at a business meeting?

"I go to the Temple of Philadelphia over on Summit Street," said Shekinah.

"And I know *right* where that is!" declared Eldeen. "We went right past there one time when they had part of Fredericks Road blocked off for repairs, and I said to Jewel—that's my daughter—'That sure looks like a thriving church!' There were cars just parked all over the place and folks just pouring in through the front door. I expected to see that little building start puffing out like it was going to explode!"

"We sure could use us some more space," Shekinah said.

"That's wonderful to hear!" said Eldeen. Then she threw her head back and started laughing. "I just thought of something! I just now thought of it!"

Shekinah and the children looked at her expectantly.

"Philadelphia—that's one of them churches John writes about in the book of Revelation, you know." Eldeen licked her lips excitedly. "Right after the part where it says 'He that openeth, and no man shutteth; and shutteth, and no man openeth,' the Spirit of God says to the church of Philadelphia, 'I know your works, how you haven't denied my name, and behold, I have set before you an *open door.*'" Shekinah looked at Eldeen, puzzled.

"See, *I* go to the Church of the Open Door," Eldeen continued, "and *you* go to the church named after the one God promised to open the door for! Why, I feel like you and me's got a real bond already, Shekinah, and we just now met each other. Isn't that the way it is with Christians, though? We're all brothers and sisters through the shed blood of Jesus!"

Shekinah cocked her head and studied Eldeen as if weighing her in the balance of everything she knew about white people. After a moment she smiled at her. "That's the truth," she said. "That sure is the truth." Then she looked down at the book in her lap and started reading aloud: "Tommy Toad and his friend Carlo Cricket were sipping a cup of apple tea under a big mushroom."

An hour later, as Perry carried Eldeen's laundry baskets into her kitchen, she was still exclaiming over Shekinah and her five small charges. "And that little Leviticus—he was Shekinah's own little boy, I found out, and wasn't he the cutest thing with those big old round eyes just a'starin' so . . ." She glanced at her vocabulary study book as she groped for a word. "So . . . *somber.* And little Jasmine with her . . . *vivacious* little elf-face. Oh, and *Ontario*—now isn't that a different kind of name for a little girl? She sure was something, though, the way she just hung on every word in them books. Bright? Don't you know it! I bet she'll be at the head of her class when she starts school!"

"Well, I guess that's everything," Perry said, setting the box of detergent on the table. The clock on the kitchen wall said ten-thirty, he noticed. He could get in a couple of hours of work before lunch.

"That sure does beat all how I could come up missing one red slipper-sock," Eldeen mused as she removed a stack of folded towels from the top of one basket. "I *know* I put it in the washing machine this morning before we had that big flood, but now it's come up short—it wasn't anywhere to be found when I went to fold everything back at the Wash-a-teria. That is just a *mystery* the way things get lost in the wash! You'd think it chews 'em up and swallows 'em."

"Maybe it's still inside here," Perry said, peering inside the washing machine. He ran his hand around the inside but felt nothing. He suddenly remembered something that had happened several years ago, when Troy was just a baby. Their washing machine had leaked all over the floor, and Dinah had called a repairman, who had pulled out one of Troy's little booties and said it had probably gotten swept over the top rim of the inside tub somehow and lodged in the discharge pipe.

Perry shoved the agitating basket to one side and tried to peer down the side but couldn't see anything. He examined the top of the washer. There was a top panel that probably lifted up if he could figure out how.

"Do you have a screwdriver?" he asked. "I want to check something." He doubted that anything the size of Eldeen's slipper-sock could get washed over and wedged between the agitating basket and the tub, but it was worth a try. "And a coat hanger too," he called after Eldeen as she headed for the hall closet.

When he pulled out the coat hanger ten minutes later with a large fuzzy red sock snagged on the end, Eldeen gaped in disbelief. For a moment Perry thought she had truly been rendered speechless, but then she launched into a display of ardent emotion in which she spun together into an amazing speech a number of the new words she had been studying, including "culprit," "recalcitrant," "laudatory," and "ingenious."

As he closed the screen door behind him, Perry heard Eldeen talking to Mr. Garland's answering machine: "This is Eldeen Rafferty again, and I just wanted to tell you to mark us off your list, for our smart neighbor has gone and *cured* the malfunction in our decrepit old washing machine."

Wouldn't Dinah laugh if she knew about this, thought Perry. He had actually lucked onto an idea and swiftly executed a solution; he had come across as a hero. He saw a picture of himself dressed in shining armor, riding a white steed, brandishing a gleaming rapier from the tip of which flapped a bright red, furry sock.

Chapter 31

P erry, there's been an accident." Something in the chill of Jewel's voice and the frozen blue of her eyes told Perry that this was more than a washing machine overflow. She was supporting herself with one outstretched hand against Perry's front door jamb; her breath was coming in shallow gasps.

Later Perry couldn't remember the act of moving toward her, but somehow he found his hands grasping her shoulders—partly, he thought, to steady her but also to prepare himself for what was coming. In the fleeting moment before she spoke again, he chastised himself for forgetting during these past few months how shaky the course of a day could be; he had allowed himself to be caught off guard, and he had vowed almost a year ago never to let that happen again. When Dinah had calmly announced her defection that morning, he had reminded himself thereafter to expect only the worst from a day. Thereafter he had begun waking each morning with a sense of dread, tiptoeing through the day's routine, wondering at what moment the next blow would fall, reminding himself that anything pleasant was only temporary, only a decoy to tease him into relaxing his vigil. And it had worked; he had never let life take him by surprise again—not until now.

He swallowed hard. How long they stood there looking into each other's fearful eyes he couldn't have said. He wondered later if Jewel had seen his fragility and purposely delayed telling him or if perhaps he had simply experienced the suspension of time common in moments of crisis. As she opened her mouth to speak, he tried to hope that it wasn't as bad as he feared. Maybe Hormel had gotten hurt; maybe someone at the church had taken ill; maybe a neighbor had fallen and broken a leg; maybe Jewel's car had been stolen. But no, he could see the station wagon in the driveway behind her; in fact, he could hear it idling.

"Can you drive us to the hospital?" Jewel asked, her voice trembling. "I don't trust myself to drive."

"Who's *us?*" Perry heard himself ask and immediately despised himself. Anyone else, he knew, would have asked what had happened, but he had asked who would be riding in the car with them. It was his old custom of postponing the inevitable—trying to avoid ingesting the whole horrible truth in one huge gulp, asking for it in small bites, hoping to piece it together by indirect clues. Maybe if he heard the names of those he'd be transporting, he could eliminate a few possibilities in the array of tragedies now playing themselves out in his mind.

"Mama and me," said Jewel. Just then Perry heard a door slam and saw Eldeen approaching the station wagon, her gray cape flaring behind her. She looked toward Perry's front door and motioned wildly.

"Come on, no time to waste!" she shouted. "Joe Leonard needs us like he's never needed us before!"

So it was Joe Leonard. Something had happened to Joe Leonard.

"Let's go," Perry told Jewel. "I'm ready right now." He gave only a passing thought to the fact that his computer was still turned on, that he was wearing jeans, an undershirt, and rubber thongs. He took Jewel's arm and led her to the car. As they backed out of the driveway, Perry saw the big orange pumpkin Eldeen had brought home from Thrifty-Mart a few days earlier. It was sitting on the front steps, its thick stem curled on top like a sprightly cap. He felt a terrible ache of sadness now, remembering how excited Eldeen had been about the pumpkin, what happy plans she had laid for the carving of a jack-o-lantern and the dispensing of Halloween treats in a few days to "all the little spooks and goblins" in the neighborhood. She had told him about Joe Leonard dressing up every year like a hobo to greet the children at the door and Jewel playing scary music on the piano. And now Joe Leonard was at the hospital, Jewel was sitting pale and motionless in the backseat, and Eldeen's face was a contortion of agony. How quickly things changed.

On the way to the hospital he learned some of the details about the accident. Jewel told them herself in short clusters of words, stopping often to catch her breath. She held her hand at her throat, Perry saw through the rearview mirror, and her eyes stared over his shoulder at the road ahead. It was cruel, Perry thought, how gentle the autumn breeze was, how crisp and clear the October air, how vivid the russet dogwood leaves even in the dimness of the lilac dusk. The maples along Iris Street, halfway into their autumn transformation, incandesced with citrus colors: lime green, lemon yellow, tangerine. To the west the sky was grapefruit pink, the clouds bruised purple. Everywhere he looked he saw the kinds of pictures they put on calendars. In stories, the weather was always blustery and foreboding during a disaster. Why couldn't the weather sympathize in real life?

It was cruel, too, how blithely the rest of the world was going about its business. In fact, it angered Perry. He saw a woman reach over and kiss her toddler in a car at a stoplight; at a corner two paperboys were laughing uproariously; a police car cruised Fredericks Road, the officer inside speaking into his radio. Perry had murderous thoughts toward a squirrel sitting beside the trunk of a pecan tree, busily prying with his little paws. Overhead a large flock of birds suddenly blackened the sky on some urgent migratory pilgrimage. Where are they going, Perry wondered. Why don't they stay here? He felt a swift hatred for birds. The first hint of trouble and off they flew.

Joe Leonard had stayed after school that day for basketball tryouts. Jewel didn't know the whole story yet, but around five o'clock Joe Leonard had evidently started walking home, then realized he must have left something he needed—maybe a book—back in the locker room at school. When he went back to get it, he had stumbled into a fight in progress in the locker room. Actually, Jewel said, it was pretty one-sided, with three boys ganging up on one. There were knives being flashed around, and the boy on the floor was bleeding pretty badly— though it was hard to tell if he'd been stabbed or just beaten and kicked. When Joe Leonard had crawled out of the locker room to find help a few minutes later, he was holding his own side with one bloodied hand. Rob Finch, the assistant coach, had been the one to call Jewel. But first he had stayed with Joe Leonard and the other boy while Coach Hampton ran to call the police and an ambulance. The three attackers had fled, but Joe Leonard had recognized them all and gave their names to the police.

"If he could tell their names," said Eldeen, "then maybe he's not hurt as bad as my heart tells me he is." But Perry remembered all the stories and newspaper accounts he'd read of dying people gasping out the names of their killers with their last breath.

As they neared the hospital, Eldeen began reciting Scripture verses. Perry recognized them as coming from the book of Job, but he wasn't sure she was quoting them in sequence. Still, it struck him as remarkable that she had such a storehouse of Bible verses at her disposal.

"Is not God in the height of heaven? and behold the height of the stars, how high are they! Acquaint now thyself with him, and be at peace: thereby good shall come unto thee." The whole time she recited, she swayed slowly back and forth, her eyes shut, her hands clamped together on top of her big black purse. "When men are cast down, then thou shalt say, There is lifting up; and he shall save the humble person. He shall deliver the island of the innocent: and it is delivered by the pureness of thine hands. . . . But he knoweth the way that I take: when he hath tried me, I shall come forth as gold. . . . He stretcheth out the north over the empty place, and hangeth the earth upon nothing. . . . For he looketh to the ends of the earth, and seeth under the whole heaven. . . . I know that thou canst do every thing, and that no thought can be withholden from thee. . . . In whose hand is the soul of every living thing, and the breath of all mankind. . . . Which doeth great things past finding out; yea, and wonders without number."

In Sunday school Harvey Gill had recently conducted a series of lessons on the book of Job, and Perry had found himself studying ahead each week for the next lesson. Eldeen could be quoting so many other verses from the book that would be more applicable, Perry thought now—the ones about the arrows of God being set against Job, poison invading his spirit, terrors besieging him, misery besetting his soul, traps lying hidden along the path; others about God hiding his face, striking down the righteous, casting his fury upon the weary, delivering the godly into the hands of the wicked. How was it, he wondered, that those were not the verses that came to Eldeen's mind in her own time of trouble?

When they entered the emergency room of the Dickson County Hospital, Perry walked briskly to the secretary standing behind the admitting desk, trying to scrunch his toes together to keep his thongs from snapping so loudly. Jewel and Eldeen followed him. A television blared in the waiting room: "Police have apprehended a suspect in the bombing of one of Columbia's oldest and largest churches," the resonant voice of an anchorman declared.

"We're looking for Joe Leonard Blanchard," Perry said to the woman behind the desk.

"Just a minute, sir," the woman said, looking up at him quickly and then leaning over to press a computer key. Perry tried to search her face for clues about the boy's condition, but all he could see was her brow, slightly furrowed, and her full, pouty red lips. They should have a more optimistic-looking person working here, Perry thought, someone who could understand what people must be going through when they came to this desk. The woman squinted at the screen and crimped in the corner of her mouth. Was she trying to think of a way to tell them Joe Leonard was gone, that the doctors had done all they could?

"He's in surgery now, sir," she finally said, looking up from the screen. "Are you his parents?"

"I'm his mother," Jewel said quietly, stepping forward.

"And I'm his grandmother," Eldeen said. "This here's our good friend," she added, pointing to Perry.

"Can you tell us anything about him?" Perry asked.

The woman shook her head and her face softened. Perry saw that he had misjudged her, for she reached over the counter to touch Jewel's arm sympathetically. "I need some information about your son if you're up to giving it," she said. Jewel nodded, and the woman turned to Perry and Eldeen. "Why don't you sit down over there in the waiting room? We won't take long. The doctor will be out as soon as he's done and talk with all of you. It's hard to know how long it'll be, though."

"Did you see him when they brought him in?" Jewel asked, her eyes fastened on the woman's face.

"No, not out here," she said kindly. "They took him straight to the operating room. He's in good hands, Mrs. Blanchard. Try not to worry." Perry wanted to scream out the same words Dinah had said to him on the telephone: "It's easy for you to say don't worry!"

Perry led Eldeen to a row of empty chairs along a wall, glad that she walked so slowly; maybe no one would notice his flip-flops. Around forty people sat scattered throughout the waiting room, all with exhausted faces, all watching the television screen with glazed, stupefied expressions. Could it be, thought Perry, that this many people in Derby and the outlying towns are going through the same emotional disruption in their lives that Jewel and Eldeen and I are going through? An elderly woman across the room had a blood-stained shirt clutched to her chest as she stared unblinking at the television. A baby cried fretfully and strained to get out of his father's arms; the man looked beaten and disheveled. A teenaged girl at a pay phone wept convulsively.

Suddenly Brother Hawthorne and Edna entered the waiting room, followed closely by Willard Scoggins and Harvey and Trudy Gill. The women embraced Jewel up by the desk, and Jewel laid her head briefly on Willard's shoulder. Brother Hawthorne then led the way toward Perry and Eldeen and pulled the chairs around them into a circle. "Let's pray," Brother Hawthorne said simply, and they all bowed their heads.

The thought dimly emerged from Perry's consciousness that he was actually *participating* in this event, not merely observing; though he wasn't praying aloud, his feelings were fully engaged. He wasn't trying to record the details in their proper sequence, to phrase them with words that would accurately describe the situation to a reader. The fact that he was writing a book about these people seemed far removed from the present. Perry realized also that he felt not the least twinge of embarrassment to be part of a prayer circle in the middle of a hospital waiting room. That he was wearing inappropriate footwear suddenly seemed entirely insignificant. Eldeen emitted a deep, agonized groan as Brother Hawthorne prayed for the Lord's "healing touch and miracle-working power in the body of our dear, faithful young brother."

Young brother—Perry remembered Joe Leonard's words only a few short days ago at the Each-One-Bring-One youth activity, his awkward words of gratitude about Perry: "he's like a big brother to me, and I always wanted one of those." For the first time since coming to Derby, Perry found himself not simply marveling over the fervency and faith with which these people prayed but also intensely hoping that they were right—that they did indeed have a God who could hear their prayers, who wanted to give them the desires of their hearts, and, most of all, who had the power to do so.

Jewel joined them in a few minutes, and over the drone of the six o'clock news on the television behind them, she spoke firmly in her soft Southern drawl the words of supplication Perry was never to forget: "Our gracious and merciful heavenly Father, you knew about all of this a long time before we got the phone call, before Joe Leonard even stepped into that locker room. You knew it was going to happen before he was *born*. We know you're wise and almighty and that our ways are not your ways, but we also know you're loving and good and that you won't let us suffer above that we are able. I don't know, gracious Father, how much I'm able to bear," and here her voice broke, though she continued praying through her tears, "but I trust you to sustain us through this trial. Please, dear God, spare my boy. Please don't take him from me. He's my . . . he's my only son, dear Lord." She emitted a sharp sob, but finished her prayer. "I know you know about the love of a parent for an only son. You gave yours for us. But please, God, please, if you see fit, let my boy live."

It was while Harvey Gill was praying that Perry realized someone must have turned down the volume on the television, and it was during Eldeen's prayer that he sensed the stillness in the waiting room.

Eldeen had just said, "And be with that other poor boy too that was hurt, dear God, and his sorrowing family—and those three mean fellers that hurt 'em, too, who need to know Jesus" when Perry heard the approach of footsteps. Eldeen paused and they all looked up.

"Are you Joe Leonard Blanchard's family?" a middle-aged man

asked. The woman beside him held a large wadded handkerchief to her mouth; her eyes, though heavily made up, were red from weeping.

They all nodded, and the man's shoulders sagged. "We're the Harrelsons," he said. "It was our boy Howie that Joe Leonard helped." The woman pressed the handkerchief to her eyes and shook with sobs.

Howie Harrelson. Perry hadn't forgotten the name. So it was Joe Leonard's cocky friend, Howie, who had been attacked in the locker room.

"Oh, you poor, poor things," Eldeen said. "Here, let's pull up some more chairs so you can join our prayer chain. God can save our boys, Mrs. Harrelson; he's got the power to do anything! Here, sit down by me." Eldeen put one arm around Mrs. Harrelson and leaned over to comfort her, murmuring softly and smoothing her hair as if she were a child.

Rob and Glenda Finch arrived a few minutes later along with Coach Hampton, who had just learned that the three attackers had been found and taken into police custody.

"What'd they do it for?" Eldeen asked. "Did any of them say what was behind it all? Why would three of 'em gang up that way against one?"

Coach Hampton shook his head. "Their story is that it all started over something Howie said to one of them before tryouts. One thing led to another, I guess, and that boy got two of his buddies to wait with him after everybody left, and they just . . ." The coach glanced at the Harrelsons apologetically. "They just meant to rough him up, they said, but he fought back pretty hard, and they pulled out their knives just to try to scare him, but that seemed to make him madder than ever. Then Joe Leonard showed up, and *they* got scared I guess, and . . . well, the way one of them put it was 'We just lost our heads.'" Coach Hampton sighed deeply. "They aren't what I'd call bad kids really—they just wanted to be tough. They're all pretty shaken up."

Rob Finch spoke up. "One of them—the one who admitted to actually stabbing Joe Leonard—told the police that they tried to get Joe Leonard to leave. Kept telling him over and over to get out. Said they never would've used the knife if he hadn't tried to get them off Howie."

"I don't know," said Coach Hampton. "They might say that, but kids usually go to all lengths when they're in a gang—do things they'd never do by themselves. If Joe Leonard hadn't interrupted them, there's no telling . . ."

A nurse came out from behind two heavy swinging doors. "Mr. and Mrs. Harrelson?" she called. The Harrelsons stood up quickly. "I can take you back to see your son now," the nurse said, smiling. Mrs. Harrelson gave a soft whimper and leaped forward. "He's got some pretty ugly wounds," the nurse said as she pushed open the doors, "but he's going to be all right." The Harrelsons disappeared through the doors, and the rest of them could hear the rapid, muffled clicking of Mrs. Harrelson's high heels echoing down the hallway.

They were all silent for several long moments. Then Coach Hampton looked around the circle and asked, "I take it that the rest of you are all Joe Leonard's family?"

"And friends," Brother Hawthorne said. He went around the group and introduced everyone.

Coach Hampton sat down where Mr. Harrelson had been sitting and looked straight across at Jewel. "Joe Leonard is a fine boy, ma'am," he said, his hands resting on his knees. Perry felt a small fountain of hope well up inside his heart. He said *is*, he kept telling himself. Joe Leonard *is* a fine boy.

"I don't know if you're aware of it—probably not—but a couple of the guys used to give him a pretty hard time," the coach continued. Perry tried to ignore the fact that he had shifted to past tense. "Called him Holy Joe Leo and a few other choice names." The coach ran one hand over his forehead and back through his wavy hair. "It was really something, though. Joe Leonard was always so good-natured about it—in a quiet way. Never acted like it was of much importance to him; never said a word back, just went on playing like he hadn't heard it. Sometimes I've watched a guy like Joe Leonard get chewed up and spit out when the hot shots think he's too timid to stand up for himself; it'll make 'em all the meaner. But with Joe Leonard I don't know what it was—he never answered back and pretty soon they got tired of acting mean without getting any response, and the next thing I know, I hear one of the ringleaders say something like 'Nice shot, Blanchard.'"

The coach looked around the circle at all of them. "You've got you a real nice boy—I only hope mine turns out half as nice. I'm sorry it's taken something like this for me to get to meet you and tell you so." He lowered his eyes and shook his head. "I can't tell you how bad I feel. I'm always there in the locker room till it clears out—but tonight I got a call in the office, and then a parent stopped me in the hall. I had asked Rob to check on some things in the equipment room, thinking I'd be right back, but . . ." He lifted his hands, then dropped them to his lap again. "I sure think a lot of Joe Leonard. I'll never forgive myself if . . ."

"He sets a store by you too," Eldeen spoke up. "He was sure wantin' to do a good job in the tryouts."

"He did," the coach replied, nodding his head firmly. "He sure did. He's got a lot of natural skill—and of course, I'm always looking for mature kids too. Sometimes that's a whole lot more important than experience." He tapped his forehead. "Joe Leonard doesn't think and act like the typical sophomore. He's not out to impress the whole world."

"Thank you for those kind words," Jewel said, looking straight into Coach Hampton's eyes. "We're trusting God to raise him up." She looked over at Brother Hawthorne.

"Shall we continue our prayer meeting?" Brother Hawthorne suggested. "Willard, why don't you lead us next?" Eldeen was studying the coach closely as he dropped his head reverently. Perry was certain she would arrange a private talk with him before the night was over.

It must have been fifteen minutes later when a doctor came out and looked around. "Blanchard?" he said. Jewel lifted her head and stood up immediately, her hands clasped under her chin. The doctor came toward them, his eyes traveling curiously and slowly around the circle as if wondering if this was some kind of game they were playing.

"I'm Dr. Whitaker," he said in a high voice. He was a small man, no taller than Brother Hawthorne and far less muscular. Everything about him was pale—his thin, washed-out hair, his skin, his eyes, his lips, even the light gray frames of his glasses. Perry could easily see him as the class brain in high school—first in scholastic standing, president of the National Honor Society, recipient of numerous scholarship offers, but the last one picked for teams in P.E. His voice, however, was surprisingly energetic as he said, "Well, you folks are lucky. I have good news for you." He continuously swayed forward on his toes and rocked back on his heels as he talked—a habit born from years of struggling with a height disadvantage, Perry suspected.

"Your boy's going to pull through fine," Dr. Whitaker continued. "The stab wound was pretty deep, but luckily it didn't puncture any vital organs. Missed the spleen by a hair's breadth—that could have been bad. We've got him all fixed up now, and I think he's going to be ready to see a face he recognizes in a few minutes. He's going to be sore for a while—won't be able to do any jumping jacks right away—but he's a lucky young man." Perry knew the doctor couldn't get away with referring to luck three times, and he was right.

"I beg your pardon, doctor, but luck's not got a thing to do with it!" Eldeen declared forcefully. "We been praying, and God's been working!"

The doctor stared at her, dazed. "Well, someone's sure on your side," he said, stretching his pale lips into a thin, taut smile.

"God is!" said Eldeen. "If God be for you, who can be against you?"

"Well, I like your spirit," said the doctor. He gave a weak cough and adjusted his glasses. "A nurse will be out a little later to take you up to his room." Frowning, he bit his lower lip and looked around the circle. "Maybe you'd better not all go up at once," he said. "The oxygen in the room might not hold out." He offered a half-smile, and everyone chuckled.

"Thank you, doctor," Jewel said, stepping forward with her hand extended. But instead of shaking the doctor's hand, she held it tightly as she looked deep into his pale green eyes. "There's no way to ever thank you for being here on duty when my boy needed you." As Dr. Whitaker waved off her thanks with his other hand, as if clearing the air of sentiment, she shook her head. "No, please, please let me say it. I know you must hear it over and over, and I sure can't say it like others can, like my neighbor here could," and she smiled at Perry, "—he's a writer—but I've got to say the words out loud or I just won't be able to stand it. Thank you for being God's instrument in bringing my son through. It's a wonderful thing you've done for him—and for me, and for all of us." Jewel's blue eyes were glistening with tears.

Perry had to look away. He knew he never could have expressed himself so sincerely and beautifully and openly if it were Troy instead of Joe Leonard who had just been rescued from death. He wasn't even sure he would have had his wits about him enough to think of making such a speech. He would probably have been too busy plotting the destruction of the three boys who caused the injury—thinking of various methods of physical torture he could inflict on them, of accusations aimed at their parents for raising such despicable hoodlums, of charges concerning the lax supervision after school that had allowed such an attack to take place.

At eight o'clock, after they had been allowed to visit Joe Leonard for a few minutes, Perry took Jewel and Eldeen down to the hospital cafeteria to eat. The other church people had left. Willard had been scheduled to close the library that night, and the rest had gone to prayer meeting.

"My grandson's gonna be all right!" Eldeen proudly announced to the girl working the cash register at the end of the line. "I got me a bowl of this here green Jell-O in honor of him—that's one of his favorites!" Her face crinkled into a maze of creases as she smiled radiantly.

The girl grinned politely as she totaled the purchases on Eldeen's tray.

"And," said Eldeen, "he's gonna have him a knife blade scar right here in his side for the rest of his life." She lifted her arm and pointed to the approximate place on herself, then spread her hands to show the length of the scar.

"Mama, people are lined up behind us," Jewel said.

Eldeen looked back at the couple behind Perry. "My grandson's on the mend, praise the Lord!" she called out, waving a friendly greeting. Then she picked up her tray and walked triumphantly toward the tables, smiling and nodding. "Good evening!" Perry heard her say to everyone she passed.

Chapter 32

I t was after ten o'clock by the time they had finished eating, visited Joe Leonard's room again, and talked again with the Harrelsons, who were allowed to take Howie home that night. Several church people had come by after prayer meeting to express their concern and to rejoice over the doctor's good prognosis. Willard had come back after the library closed at nine o'clock and had called the principal of Jewel's school to arrange for her to miss the next day's classes.

Pulling into Jewel's driveway at ten-thirty, Perry felt that weeks had passed since they had rushed off to the hospital, not knowing what they would find when they got there. The cool black of the October night felt vastly different from the mild twilight of four hours earlier. As he walked around the car to help Eldeen, Perry lifted his eyes to the stars shining overhead. In the darkness he smiled up at the sky and breathed in deeply.

"That poor Roberta Harrelson was sure a pathetic little thing," Eldeen said, grunting as she swung her legs out of the car and planted her feet on the pavement. "She made me think of a little sick, weak puppy the way she just shivered and whimpered. Which reminds me—Hormel's probably voracious with hunger about now. Joe Leonard usually feeds him before suppertime."

"He does look hungry, poor boy," Jewel said. "I'll feed him." And she started toward the side door. By the dim porchlight, Perry could see Hormel, his tail held at a rigid point, the brown cone of his snout protruding through the fence.

Eldeen shifted her weight forward and hoisted herself slowly out of the car. Perry grabbed her elbow to steady her. "Upsy-daisy, I'm all right," she said, chuckling. "You don't need to coddle me. Now that my mind's easy about Joe Leonard, I think I'll sleep like a little baby tonight! I feel like I been run through the washer, wringer and all.

Oooh—just look at them stars! If that's not a breathtaking sight, I don't know what is! Looks like somebody went and stuck a whole bushel basket full of straight pins into a big old pincushion."

"But straight pins don't come in bushel baskets," Perry wanted to say, "and pincushions aren't generally black"; the only ones he could think of were the small, plump red ones shaped like tomatoes that his mother had worn clamped onto her wrist.

"Bless her heart, at first she was just almost out of her mind with anxiety," Eldeen continued. "Then later she was all aflutter with relief!" Perry realized there was a time when he would have had to ponder over who the "she" was, and he wondered now how it was that he instantly understood Eldeen had simply returned to the subject of Mrs. Harrelson. Here was another dividing line to consider; when had he developed the ability to follow Eldeen's train of thought?

Jewel had come back outside with a large plastic scoop of dry dog food, which she emptied with a clatter into Hormel's plastic dish. Hormel sniffed it, then raised his head and looked through the fence at Perry. Perry imagined a little cartoon balloon floating above Hormel's head: *Hey, Oreo Man, where's the good stuff?* He was glad the dog couldn't talk. But Hormel didn't waste time wishing; he soon had his muzzle buried in his dish. Jewel picked up his water dish and filled it from the spigot.

Eldeen grasped the rail and headed up the side steps to the kitchen door. She looked back briefly at Perry. "You did it again, Perry. You stood by us in our time of need." She jerked her head in a quick nod. "I thank you. God is keeping accounts of all this." Perry felt like a child unaccustomed to receiving favors; he dug his fists into his jeans pockets and hung his head. "I'm going in," Eldeen announced abruptly, turning back to the steps. "I'm going to run me a hot tub of water and just soak my weary bones a little bit. Is that okay, Jewel? I won't stay in all night, I promise."

"That's fine, Mama," Jewel said, stepping back outside the gate. The metal latch fell with a gentle clang. "I need to catch my breath a little before I can even think about getting ready for bed. You go ahead and take you a nice, warm bath."

Eldeen disappeared inside, and Jewel stood facing Perry with her back to the gate, toying with the plastic scoop she was carrying. She looked as if she were struggling to speak, but Perry couldn't be sure. Maybe she was just thinking over the evening and trying to sort things out. He hated to leave her outdoors like this; he knew she must be exceedingly tired. What if she fainted right out here on the driveway?

"Well, good night," Perry said at last. But he didn't move.

"Wait, Perry," Jewel said.

Perry earnestly hoped she wasn't about to deliver a speech of gratitude as she had done to Dr. Whitaker. He felt his heart pounding as he watched her walk slowly, lightly toward him, then breathed more easily when she turned toward the steps and sat down on the top one. She set the scoop down and interlaced her fingers gracefully. How many times, he wondered, had he watched Jewel working with her hands in the kitchen, never hurrying, always performing even the simplest of tasks—the shaking of salt or the pouring of tea or the lifting of a pan—with languid, waltzlike movements. He had once mused over the differences between Southern and Northern women and decided that tempo was definitely one of them; Southern women took their time—at least the ones he had observed closely.

"Do you have a minute?" she asked him, waving toward the three steps below her.

"Sure," Perry said, a faint cloud of worry settling over him. Jewel wasn't generally one to talk much. How would the two of them manage by themselves? Of course, she had done a fair amount of talking tonight, he had to remind himself. Maybe it had loosened her up. He sat down on the second step, then wondered if this was what Jewel had had in mind. Maybe she meant for him to remain standing—or maybe sit on the driveway. Should he turn himself on the step partway or keep his back to her? He heard her sigh behind him and felt rebuked. Why did other people always seem to know what was expected of them while he went through life feeling like everything he did was clumsy and ill-timed? He turned slightly and placed his elbow on the step behind him.

At first he thought Jewel was inhaling the fresh autumn air, but after the third sniffle, he was appalled to realize she was crying. What had he gotten himself into? If there was one thing he avoided above all others, it was having to deal with a weeping woman. He had grown up fleeing the house whenever his mother cried, which was often. Beth had been remarkably self-controlled when she was younger, almost cold now that he thought about it, but one time when a boy she had liked stood her up, she had broken down at the supper table. Perry distinctly recalled leaving his plate untouched and walking out the front door. There had been a fresh outburst later when he came home, for Beth had assumed he'd left to find and punish the boy who had treated her so rudely. "What did he say?" she had asked him, her eyes still swollen from crying. "Who?" Perry had asked blankly.

He couldn't remember how many times after their marriage Dinah had cried before she had learned that his response would never vary. How many times, he wondered now, had he left the room while she wept alone, sometimes shutting himself away for hours until he ventured back to her, approaching cautiously, straining to hear? Exactly *when* had she stopped letting him see her cry? When had she recast her responses, relinquishing her tears and taking up anger and sarcasm?

Perry remembered a paper napkin he had stuffed into his pocket in the hospital cafeteria; he took it out now and handed it back to Jewel. She received it gratefully and put it to her eyes, then blew her nose.

"Oh, Perry, I'm so sorry," she said. "I don't know what's come over me. I guess it's just . . . everything. Joe Leonard and . . . well, Bailey and . . . Willard . . . and just *everything.*" She bent forward, laying her head in her lap, and Perry saw her shudder with sobs. At least she cried softly, not in great, heaving gasps, demanding attention, as his mother had. And at least she tried to explain her tears; Dinah had always indulged in crying exclusively, with no attempt to enlighten him as to the cause. Maybe she would have talked later, though, he thought now—if only he had endured the crying for a short while. He sat silently, uncomfortably, glancing back at Jewel from time to time. He could understand her venting her emotions this way over Joe Leonard, but what did she mean about Bailey and Willard? Why drag them into it?

It came to him again as she was crying that he could someday find himself in Jewel's place—suffering and waiting through a medical emergency involving Troy. How would he bear up? What if it had been Troy instead of Joe Leonard who was stabbed by a classmate? It could happen; public schools, even elementary schools, were dangerous these days. But the painful thought came to him now that if anything did happen to Troy, he wouldn't be there to help; he wouldn't be in the waiting room sharing the crisis with Dinah. Somehow, right now, that thought was even more oppressive than the idea of Troy's being injured. A wound could heal; a doctor's skill could set things right. But a wife agonizing alone was suddenly an unbearable thought. Poor Dinah. Poor Jewel. Maybe that's what she meant about Bailey; grieving alone had reminded her anew of his absence.

He looked up at the sky again; if Dinah were outside tonight, she could see the same stars he was seeing. He wondered if she ever thought of him. Did she ever wonder what he was doing—*how* he was doing? He realized that she would be receiving the packages he had mailed any day now. He pushed the thought far from his mind and turned back to Jewel.

"It's been a hard day for you," he said at last. He stared at his hand resting on Jewel's arm. How had it gotten there? He gently pulled it away.

Jewel's sobs subsided. She lifted her face and dabbed at it again with the crumpled paper napkin. Perry saw her raise her troubled eyes to the sky, almost wildly; he saw her shiver. "It all comes back so *plain,*" she said. "I sat right here on these steps the night . . . Bailey didn't come home." She stopped and pressed both hands against her temples. "I sat here and looked up at those stars," she said, pointing, "—those same ones—and I thought 'God, I know you're up there, and I know you love me, but how can I live out the rest of my life after *this?*'" She looked at Perry, her eyes wide with distress.

Perry couldn't think of what to say in the face of such deeply private revelations. Why couldn't she just dwell on the blessed outcome of tonight? Why did she have to dredge up dismal memories? Women were always doing that—reliving the past, slipping into some former melancholy like a favorite housecoat. Of course, what right did he have to condemn women? What had he been doing ever since he moved to Derby? Hadn't he been retracing every turn in the labyrinth of his relationship with Dinah? Hadn't he been wallowing in his failures as a husband and father? Trawling through his memory for clues to what went wrong? Wasn't he reminded on every hand of some previous carelessness of his own, some small act that had accrued harmful results, some besetting deficiency—and, yet, at the same time, the unfairness of the whole situation?

"But here was the thing I couldn't get over," Jewel was saying, calmly now as if her weeping had cleared her thoughts. Perry turned around farther so that he could look her full in the face, but she was still gazing up at the stars as she spoke. "I've never uttered a word of any of this to another living soul," she said, "but it's so heavy I don't think I can keep it inside any longer." Perry wondered with dismay if he had missed it; he almost hoped he had, for he wasn't sure he could bear such an ominous secret.

The kitchen door was ajar, and he could hear the sound of bath water filling the tub down the hall. Jewel dropped her eyes to meet his. She looked weak and vulnerable. "Don't say another word!" Perry wanted to command. "Don't strap me with your emotional baggage! I've got enough problems of my own!" But he kept his silence, and she continued, releasing each word slowly as if laying down a ponderous load.

"If it was just losing him—I could have gotten over that eventually," she said. "It would've been hard, but the Lord is merciful." She paused and lowered her eyes to study her hands; she turned them over several times, examining both palms and backs as if they belonged to someone else and held the clue to some mystery.

"We quarreled that day before he left to go fishing," she continued, more softly now. "I had been wanting to try to get a teaching job to help out with the finances, and I kept bringing it up every few days. Joe Leonard was fixing to go into junior high school that next fall, and I thought it would be a good time. Things were tight, and Bailey's job at the glass company was . . . well, it was steady but not very . . . rewarding." Perry heard Eldeen humming in the hallway; then a door closed firmly and the bath water stopped.

"Nobody was home that afternoon but Bailey and me," Jewel said. "It was a Saturday, and it had just rained that morning—a hard rain we really needed. Mama had gone with Marvella Gowdy to see somebody in the nursing home, and Joe Leonard was down at the church helping clean out the baptistry. He was trying to earn enough points that month for his 'Wings as Eagles' badge, I remember." Dinah used to do this when telling a story, Perry recalled. She would embellish the story line with all kinds of extraneous details, to the point that he was often tempted to shout, "Just get on with it! I don't care what they were all wearing or what kind of car they were driving!"

"And I started in on the subject of me working again," Jewel continued, "but he cut me off. I got . . . well, I got angry and started going over all my reasons again, but he just shook his head and said, 'I want you home.' It was always that: 'I want you home.' I'd tell him all my plans for keeping things the same at home—I'd use my Crock-Pot more and get up a little earlier and have Joe Leonard take over the vacuuming on Saturdays and on and on. But he wouldn't listen. He just said he didn't want to put me through that—rat race is what he kept calling it. He never would *listen,*" she repeated. "He'd just cut me off."

Perry felt a surge of impatience at the injustice Jewel had suffered. Bailey should have listened, he thought. At least given her the courtesy of hearing her out.

"Then he stood up," Jewel said, "and said he was going fishing, just like that, and he walked over to the kitchen door—this one right here." She glanced behind her, then pressed her lips together for a moment and held her breath. *"And then that's when I said it,"* she said heavily, looking straight at Perry. He could see her eyes filling up with tears again.

He couldn't help himself. "Said what?" he asked.

Jewel lifted her head, exposing her long, white neck. Her voice quivered as she spoke to the black sky above: *"Why don't you go jump in the lake?"* she whispered.

It took Perry a moment to understand. When he finally put it together, he realized he was staring at Jewel with his mouth gaping. Tears trickled slowly down her face. "But I didn't say it soft like that," she said. "I shouted it."

Perry couldn't stretch his imagination that far. He couldn't see Jewel shouting anything, much less something so childishly spiteful. But he knew it was true. She wouldn't make up something like this. In some different set of circumstances—a comedy routine or a funny movie perhaps—the scenario could be humorous. An old *I Love Lucy* plot maybe. Lucy and Ricky argue about money; Ricky says he's going fishing; Lucy tells him to jump in the lake; she receives word that his boat has capsized; she feels overwhelmed with guilt, thinking he has drowned; she delivers a penitent speech, vowing never to spend another cent unnecessarily; just then he walks in—having overheard her—sea-weed clinging to his hat, lake water dripping all over her carpet, and she embraces him remorsefully as Fred and Ethel join them in laughter.

But, of course, in Jewel's case, there had been no surprise entrance at the end, no embrace of reconciliation, and certainly no laughter. For over three long years she had lived with this unforgivably dreadful thought branded into her memory. How often she must have yearned to reenact that final moment, to change her response. Like she said, she could have somehow borne the grief of losing him, but to know that her last words to her husband had been so cruelly prophetic—Perry wondered how she had faced each day. How could a loving God do that to a woman like Jewel? How could he leave her haunted by such a horrible memory? Leave her to wonder if her thoughtless words had somehow predisposed the accident? How could she keep going to church, singing about the mercies of the Lord, hearing Romans 8:28 repeated endlessly, praying to a God who would dump such an onerous burden on someone he supposedly loved?

"Do you love Willard?" Perry asked, taken back at his own bluntness. Maybe the question sprang from an intense desire to get her mind off the subject of Bailey, or maybe, he thought later, he had guessed the present cause of her brooding.

He must have guessed right, for Jewel clinched her hands tightly and emitted a heart-wrenching cry. "That's what's got me in such a *state!*" she said. "How can I marry a good man like Willard, knowing what I know? Willard thinks I can do no wrong. I look at him, like I did tonight at the hospital, and see his love for me shining through his eyes, and I think, 'How can I let this go on, knowing what I did to Bailey?'"

Perry didn't stop to think about what he should say. It simply poured out. As he spoke, he watched Jewel's expression change from surprise to confusion to horror. "What *you* did to Bailey?" he said. "I don't get it. What about what *God* did to *you?* How come you're blaming yourself for this whole thing when, according to your theology, God is in control of everything? So you spouted off and said something you shouldn't have? So what? People do that all the time. Did that give God any right to penalize you by letting your husband drown? I don't see why you're so busy flogging yourself for something God could have prevented if he's really the kind of God you make him out to be."

Jewel shook her head in disbelief, her eyes wide, the paper napkin held tightly to her nose. "Oh, what have I done?" she said. "I shouldn't have told you . . . I can see how . . . but, oh, Perry, don't you *see?*"

"No," he said. "All I see is a woman who can't accept a man's love because God keeps beating her over the head with his club—the one called Guilt. Try asking yourself how God could do what *he* did instead of how you could do what you did."

Jewel covered her mouth with both hands and stared at Perry. When she finally spoke, she no longer sounded fragile and defenseless; her voice was full of vigor. "Perry, no one has any right to ask God that kind of question!" She leaned forward and put her hand on his shoulder. Her grip was amazingly strong. "If we were omniscient and omnipotent like he is, maybe then we could ask him why—but he's so far above us that even if he tried to explain his ways to us, we couldn't begin to comprehend." She shook her head energetically. "He took Bailey, and I don't question why. He had his reasons, and even if I never know what they were till I get to heaven, I still trust him. He loved me then, and he loves me now, and he'll always love me."

Neither one of them spoke for a long time. How simple this philosophy of life was, Perry thought. He remembered something Brother Hawthorne had said in a sermon: "Christianity defies the world's logic, for it is totally and utterly *simple.*" Suddenly he envied Jewel. He knew he should revile her, jeer at her lack of backbone, hurl insults attacking her faulty reasoning. But here he sat, envying her instead. To suffer as she had suffered and to be able to say with the deepest sincerity, "I accept this tragedy as part of my loving God's great, wise plan for my life" required a kind of strength he knew nothing about. Or *was* it strength? He felt curiously vitalized by Jewel's words, yet defeated too. He had studied these people for endless weeks now, yet he knew so little about them in any real sense.

"It's my own selfish, foolish words I can't forget," Jewel said finally. "That's where the blame lies. That's what I can't seem to get past. God didn't make me do that. And the devil didn't either. I did it all by myself. Every time Willard brings up getting married, I cringe inside. I see myself all worked up in my little tiff, and I hear those words ringing in my ears over and over. And I wonder, how long would it take before I said something ugly like that to Willard?"

So Willard was pushing for marriage. Perry had suspected it; he had originally hoped to observe both a wedding and a funeral to describe in his book, but he had been wondering lately if these last months would include a second wedding instead of a funeral.

"To answer your question earlier, yes, I do love him," Jewel said. She gave a low laugh. "Even if he is as crazy about fishing as Bailey was—maybe more—and even if he is younger than me and even if I did tell myself three years ago that I'd never ever marry again." She spread out the paper napkin, then smoothed it out on her knee. "Willard's a good man—so thoughtful and kind and . . . *upright*. I respect him in so many ways. But I just don't know if I could ever . . ."

"If you could ever *what?*" Suddenly Perry felt strangely assertive. Somebody needed to talk straight to Jewel, and there was no one here to do it but himself. "Jewel, if I understand your religion right, I think one of the cornerstones is the idea of forgiveness. Am I right? All those songs and verses about God washing you clean of your sins, forgiving your loathsome iniquities, and all that—are those just *words* you say without meaning them? If God could forgive somebody like Paul for killing Christians, don't you think he could forgive Jewel Blanchard for saying one mean thing? If God has a purpose for everything, who knows?—maybe he had a great big overall reason for letting you lose your temper that day. Your problem is that you can't forgive *yourself*. God is willing to—if he's the kind of God Brother Hawthorne keeps preaching about—but for some reason you think you've got to torture yourself and do penance for the rest of your life. If you don't watch it, you might miss out on Willard. What if God *wants* you and him to get married but you turn him down because of all this you've been telling me? Then you've gone and spoiled God's plan."

They stared hard at each other. Perry immediately regretted his words. Should he have spoken so rashly? Jewel must abhor him. A police siren droned in the distance, then grew louder, then faded. Hormel howled briefly in protest.

A slow smile gradually spread across Jewel's face. "Perry, you've put me to shame," she said. "You're absolutely right. My heart tells me that every word you said is true. Maybe God wanted to teach me to watch my tongue; he sure did that. I've never been the same since. Every time I open my mouth, I stop to think: Do I want this to be the last thing I say to this person? But the part about forgiveness—that's the sad part. Why should it take somebody like you, who doesn't even profess to know Jesus, to remind me that God stands ready to put my sins behind his back forever?" She bent her head and fit the tips of her fingers together thoughtfully. Perry heard Eldeen singing, low and muffled, behind a closed door.

"And as usual," Jewel continued, "the things you spend so much time wanting are never quite so wonderful after you get them." She rested an elbow on her knee and propped her chin in one hand. "I love the children I teach," she said, "but it's sure a harder schedule than I was expecting. Before, I was *begging* to work, and now I *have* to. Things sure change."

"Don't they, though?" Perry replied.

"Okay, turnabout's fair play," said Jewel. "You asked me, so I'm going to ask you. Do you still love your wife—it's Dinah, isn't it?"

Perry nodded, then sighed heavily. "Oh, yes," he said. "I still love her."

They sat in silence for a while. Perry heard Hormel noisily lapping water from his dish behind the fence.

"You won't put any of this in your book, will you?" Jewel asked, looking sharply at Perry.

He shook his head. "My lips are sealed," he said, smiling.

Eldeen must have opened the bathroom door, for the words she was singing suddenly became clear: "My life, my love, I give to Thee, Thou Lamb of God who died for me; O may I ever faithful be, My Savior and my God. I'll live for him who died for me, How happy then my life shall be! I'll live for him who died for me, My Savior and my God."

As he listened to Eldeen repeat the chorus, Perry remembered clearly the rest of what Brother Hawthorne had said: "But for all its simplicity, Christianity costs, in the words of T. S. Eliot, 'not less than everything.'" It was a simple swap these Christians and God had worked out between them: your life for mine.

Eldeen's deep, thick voice broke off halfway through the next stanza. Perry heard her heavy steps drawing nearer, and soon she was standing at the kitchen door in her long pink chenille bathrobe. The sash was twisted and cinched crookedly around her ample waist, one end dangling almost to her knees. She had a single wire curler speared by a white plastic pick on top of her head, and all Perry could think of was a small bone in the hair of some primitive native.

"What in the name of common sense are y'all doing still sitting out here in the chill night air?" Eldeen exclaimed. "You better come in and get to bed, Jewel! It's been a long, long day." She swung the screen door open, and Jewel obediently arose and stepped inside.

"What's that on the step?" Eldeen demanded, pointing sternly. Perry reached down and picked up the paper napkin that had fallen from Jewel's lap. It was damp and limp, shredded like a flag of surrender. Jewel winced apologetically and took it from him.

"Good night, Perry," Eldeen said.

"Thank you, Perry," added Jewel. As he headed across the driveway, he heard Eldeen say, "I wonder what they'll feed Joe Leonard for breakfast in the hospital."

Part 4
SUNLIGHT

Truly the light is sweet, and a pleasant thing it is for the eyes to behold the sun.

Ecclesiastes 11:7

Chapter 33

"All right now," said Willard, clapping his large hands lightly, "let's have prayer and get started. We'll do 'Manger Star' first and work out some of the kinks, then go straight through the whole program from the beginning. I know it's a sacrifice to give up your Saturday morning, and I thank all of you, but if we work hard, we can be done by noon."

As Archie Gowdy led in prayer, Perry could hear Eldeen's low, rumbling laughter in the Sunday school room behind the baptismal pool, where a group of ladies had assembled to finish making little white angels to serve as window decorations for tomorrow morning's special Christmas service. Then very plainly, right during the lengthy pause between Archie's "For these things we ask in the name of Jesus our Lord" and his booming "Amen!" the entire choir heard Eldeen's voice clearly: "And would you believe that that ostrich's whole digestive tract was just jam-packed with *feathers*, of all things!" Jewel quietly left her seat at the piano and slipped back to close a door.

"Well, on that solemn note, let us begin," said Willard, joining everyone else in laughter. Everyone was still chuckling as Jewel came back and slid onto the piano bench. Perry glanced down at Joe Leonard, who was grinning as he flipped through his choir folder.

"Manger Star" was a unique composition. Usually Willard arranged choir numbers based on familiar hymns, but for the Christmas program he had wanted something different, he said. He had written the piece especially for his choir, printing right on the music such notations as "Phil Spivey—solo," "Vonda and Louise join tenors," and "Birdie use chimes." The text was a narrative, beginning with Joseph singing of the long journey to Bethlehem; the entire choir sang the chorus each time, ending with "The manger star marked the Savior's rude throne, till the daylight broke and the Son-light shone." Perry wished there were some way for the audience to be aware of the altered spelling of Son-light; it made a difference in the effect of the line, he felt. Mary, whose part was sung by Edna Hawthorne, had the second solo stanza, and the shepherds sang the third. Then the whole choir, playing the role of the angel host, sang the fourth stanza.

It wasn't a bad piece of work, really. The words were far more polished than those in some of their other numbers; even the lyrics of some of the traditional carols Perry found to be sadly lacking in grace. Such as "The First Noel," in which so many of the accents fell in the wrong place—on the second syllable of *presence,* for example, and on words like *the, by, in,* and *that.* With all the redundancies and metrical stumbles, it sounded to Perry like some English schoolchild of long ago had written it.

"Manger Star" had a singable melody, yet not trite. Perry knew he wasn't the most qualified judge of musical merit, but he recognized a nice composition when he heard it, and he admired Willard for what he must have gone through to write this one. Putting notes together to form a song had to compare to making stories out of words, and Perry knew what labor that involved. But Willard hadn't stopped with the music; he had added lyrics. Perry wondered how he had gone about it. Did he start with the words or music? How did he ever come up with all the moving parts in the chorus that somehow meshed together so smoothly at the end?

Watching Willard now, conducting Phil Spivey through his stanza, Perry thought back over how much his estimation of the man had changed. After he had joined the choir back in the summer, he had grown to like Willard in an indirect, impersonal way, appreciating his politeness and good humor. But when he had begun to understand the man's intentions toward Jewel, Perry had opposed the idea for a good while, convinced that Willard wasn't a suitable match for her. He had finally admitted to himself that his resistance was based solely on physical appearance—he pictured Jewel with a handsome, slim businessman, someone tall and dignified like herself, not a round, jolly librarian four years her junior. The house next door seemed far too small to accommodate someone of Willard's girth; Eldeen took up enough space.

But Jewel loved the man; she had told Perry so that night as they sat outside on the steps. And the more Perry had watched Willard's chivalrous wooing of her, the more he had begun to hope for his success. There was something endearing about his undisguised esteem for Jewel. And about his unceasing *efforts*—Willard had even gone on a diet in August and had already dropped thirty pounds.

Perry realized he had missed the choir's entrance on the chorus, and he was glad Willard happened to be looking at the sopranos at the time, a pensive expression on his face. He held up his hand like a policeman stopping traffic. "Can you let that series of high notes *float?*" Willard asked the sopranos. "Right now it sounds like you're pushing." He pretended to hold up a necklace. "Think of those notes as pearls on a string; we want to admire the luster of each one, but only for a little while; just touch them, don't grab them and roll them around in your mouth and bite down on them to see how hard they are." Everyone chuckled, even the sopranos, and Willard raised his hands to begin again. "Let's start at the pickup to bar twenty-five," he said, smiling. This time he was pleased and nodded encouragingly as they continued through the chorus, stopping only once more near the end to point out the dotted rhythm of an eighth note.

As Edna began her solo stanza, Perry let his mind drift to the Sunday morning in November when Willard had announced his and Jewel's engagement to the church congregation. How brightly his face had glowed as he read his clever little poem, right after Brother Hawthorne's reminder about the annual upcoming post-Thanksgiving social that night. After Willard's surprising news, Bernie Paulson spoke up from the audience and asked him to read the poem again because he had turned his hearing aid down and didn't catch it all and he knew from everybody else's response that this was something he didn't want to miss out on. As Willard read it again, Jewel sat at the piano blushing happily, and the tips of Joe Leonard's ears turned bright red. Eldeen had said "Praise the Lord!" right out loud, and everyone had broken out into spontaneous applause.

After Willard's announcement, Brother Hawthorne had gotten up and repeated the announcement about the church social that night, saying he was afraid everyone would forget about it after the shock of Willard's news. The social after the evening service—a turkey soup supper—had turned into an engagement party, with everyone in high spirits over the prospect of two favorite church members getting married.

"Now you and Jewel can talk about the song selections on your way to church," Brother Hawthorne had teased, "and you won't have to pay her a special visit at the piano before services."

"Aw, shucks!" Willard had said, snapping his fingers, and everyone had laughed.

The churchfolks had pressed Willard to read his poem again at the social, and although he hadn't brought it along, he recited it from memory, his heart in his eyes as he addressed the lines directly to Jewel.

> The embers of my lonely life
> Will soon be kindled by a wife.
> On New Year's Day a new gold band
> I'll slip upon my sweet queen's hand.
> She'll be my crown, my diadem,
> My lovely bride, my Jewel—my gem.

Jewel had returned his affectionate gaze, her happy face upturned, her eyes like small blue flames ready to leap forth.

The rehearsal proceeded smoothly; Willard praised the men for their rousing rendition of "Go, Tell It on the Mountain," during which Glenda Finch, seated behind the dividing panel on the front row, tapped a repeated rhythmic figure on a tambourine. Perry couldn't help worrying a little that the audience would be so distracted trying to locate the source of the jingling that they might not fully appreciate the rich harmony of the men's ensemble.

As Jewel and Birdie played a piano-organ duet of "I Heard the Bells on Christmas Day," the ladies from the back room began creeping out into the auditorium to arrange their little clump of decorations in the center of each windowsill along both sides of the church. Each arrangement consisted of a small white angel standing amid several sprigs of holly and ivy. From a distance the effect was quite charming, although Perry knew the angels were only constructed of Styrofoam balls and cardboard covered with fabric from one of Jewel's old white tablecloths. The tiny halos, made of tinsel twined around copper wires and run up along the angels' spines, caught the sunlight now and glinted merrily.

After the organ's chimes had pealed their last note of the instrumental duet, Fern Tucker left the choir and went to the platform to deliver what she called a "Christmas reading"—actually just a story about a Sunday school pageant that went humorously askew but resulted in the salvation of a hardened old grandfather who had come to see his grandson play the part of a wise man.

As the other choir members listened to Fern's story, Perry watched Eldeen work on a windowsill near the front of the sanctuary. First she laid the greenery down, stepping back after every addition to study her handiwork. Then she set the angel gently in the middle, but he sat crookedly, one side of his cone-shaped body resting on top of a cluster of red berries. Eldeen pressed down on his head, but he sprang back up lopsided. She pressed down again, more firmly, and this time the little Styrofoam head popped off and rolled down between two pews. Perry let out an abrupt snort of laughter, then began coughing to disguise his slip. Several women looked back at him curiously, and Louise Farnsworth whispered, "Do you need a drink of water?" He shook his head and made an exaggerated show of clearing his throat. The next time he ventured a glance at Eldeen, she and Marvella were huddled together over the angel, whose head was in the process of being restored. Then Marvella spread apart the greenery and set the angel down in the center; this time he sat decorously level, and Eldeen moved on to the next window.

The children pantomiming the nativity scene arrived at eleven-thirty and practiced walking with majestic gait down the aisle and up onto the platform as the choir once again performed "Manger Star"—the finale. By the time they had finished, it was a few minutes before twelve o'clock. Willard smiled euphorically, thanked everyone for a "profitable rehearsal," and reminded them all to meet during the Sunday school hour the next morning for final preparations before the morning service. "Now, everyone has time to get to the mall," he said, looking at his watch, "to finish up your Christmas shopping."

"Oh, we got all next week for that!" shouted Sid Puckett. "I don't ever do mine till Christmas Eve." Dottie reached back and swung her choir folder at his head. "You *better* get my present before then!" she said, laughing.

As Perry lifted his eyes to the large clock above the center aisle, he felt the sudden resurrection of a memory; once again his mind played its old trick of calling up a past moment, triggered by the smallest detail, this time simply looking at the clock. As usual, it passed swiftly, in a heartbeat, but it was vividly realistic while it lasted. As he gazed at the clock, he heard words: *"Do you know for sure where your soul would live for eternity if your last second of time were to tick right now?"* He heard them clearly, in the elastic voice of a native Tennessean, Brother Hugh Laswell, who had preached a week of revival meetings here at the Church of the Open Door back in the fall. Perry had been sitting right here in this same seat in the choir and had instinctively glanced at the same clock to which his eyes were now fastened; he had even seen both hands of the clock pointed straight upward as they were now. The choir had been asked to remain seated behind the pulpit during the entire service that morning since there were so many visitors in attendance.

It had been the opening service of what they called "Revival Week," and Brother Laswell, the evangelist, had launched the week with a strong salvation appeal, citing story after story that Sunday morning of men and women he had known personally, who had stubbornly rejected the gospel, postponing salvation until they fulfilled certain goals—got older, got richer, got more education, etc., etc.—but then tragically lost their lives in a variety of accidents and all "slipped off into eternity, lost sinners on their way to hell, to that everlasting lake of fire." Brother Laswell had pronounced *hell* as "hay-yul" and *fire* as "fi-yer" and had drawn out all his *r*'s as if they were stuck between his puckered lips. Later in the service, near the end, he had leaned forward and spoken quietly into the microphone, his eyes running back and forth over the congregation: *"Do you know for sure where your soul would live for eternity if your last second of time were to tick right now?"* Perry would never forget dropping his eyes from the clock that day to note a mild disturbance in one of the back rows as a very old gentleman made his way from the middle of a pew to the center aisle and began hobbling toward the front, calling out in a weak, hoarse voice: "No, I don't, but I'm ready to make sure!"

Eldeen had been elated after church that morning, for it was Mr. Hammond, her acquaintance from the grocery store, who had finally responded to her invitation to come to church and had now accepted Christ. "You just never know—you just *never ever know,*" she had said joyously on their way home, "when that little seed you plant is going to start sprouting and bearing fruit!" Perry had written up the whole incident for the "Cast" portion of his book and intended to use it in the last chapter, the one he was working on now, in which he was highlighting Eldeen.

"Well, I guess we're done," Joe Leonard said. Perry looked away from the clock quickly and stood up, noting the puzzled look on Joe Leonard's face.

"Sure, sure," he said, and he was smitten suddenly with the thought that it was *sureness* that was the most incomprehensible, elusive quality about these people. They were so sure of everything. They would stake their lives on the truth of the Bible; they accepted every story without flinching, even the far-fetched ones about Jonah and the walls of Jericho and the parting of the Red Sea. They knew for a certainty that God created the world, that he had fashioned them for special purposes, that his hand could be seen in every part of their lives, that he would ultimately bring to pass all things wise and good to those he loved. They believed with all their hearts that God had sent Jesus to die for each of them individually, that their grandest prize awaited them in heaven, and that their final happiness was in no way related to anything material here on earth. But the paradox was that while it seemed to Perry the height of arrogance to be so *sure* you were right, yet these Christians were always stressing the importance of humility.

And they talked of death as a mere bridge—a short, stable bridge—to a wonderful land of promise beyond. How would it feel, Perry wondered, to look at a cemetery without the dark fear that had become so familiar to him recently? How would it feel to be absolutely sure about the future—not about every little particular circumstance, of course, but about the overall condition of well-being and protection? How would it feel to be able to meet suffering with the extraordinary reserves of character he had witnessed in these people over the past ten months, to live each day with spiritual aplomb, to anticipate with great joy what they sang about as "the meeting in the air"?

Jewel was helping Eldeen with her last window decoration, and Willard was stacking the choir folders inside a cardboard box on the front pew.

"I sure like that catchy introduction of 'We Three Kings'!" Eldeen called out to Joe Leonard, who was setting his tuba in its case. "It gives that sad-sounding song a little bit of life!" She turned to Perry. "You knew Joe Leonard wrote that extra part hisself, didn't you?"

Perry nodded. She had told him three times before. "I like it a lot," he said. Joe Leonard smiled, coloring slightly and avoiding Perry's eyes. As Perry watched the boy take a rag from his case and wipe a smudge off the bell of the tuba, he wondered how many other students were as careful about the instruments they were borrowing from their schools. He thought of the words of Mr. Beatty, Joe Leonard's band director, when he had come to the hospital back in October to visit Joe Leonard. As he had studied Joe Leonard in the hospital bed, Mr. Beatty had rubbed his hand along his jaw several times, his countenance shifting between despair and amusement. At last he had said, "Well, I thought I had heard every excuse in the book for not practicing, but in all my years of directing a band, I don't believe anybody's ever told me he couldn't play because the doctor said he'd rip out his stitches." Joe Leonard had smiled wanly, and Mr. Beatty had looked at Perry sitting beside the bed.

"I guess you're mighty proud of your son," he said. "I sure missed him today in band rehearsal; he's my key player in the low brass." Before Perry could correct the misconception, Mr. Beatty continued. "It's a rare thing these days to find a kid as serious about responsibility as this one." He nodded toward Joe Leonard, whose pale face seemed slightly rosier than a moment ago. "I sure wish you'd tell me how you did it," Mr. Beatty said to Perry.

"Did what?" asked Perry. "I didn't do . . ."

"Raised you such a fine young man," Mr. Beatty said. "He's the . . ."

"Wait," said Perry, shaking his head. "He's not my son. You need to tell all these nice things to his mother and grandmother. They're out in the hall talking to the doctor. You probably passed them on your way in."

Before he had left a few minutes later, Mr. Beatty handed Joe Leonard a twenty-dollar bill. "You told me last spring you were saving up for your own instrument," he said. "I know that'll take a while since tubas cost a little more than the average instrument, but here's a token of my confidence. I thought you'd like this more than a bouquet of flowers. Add this to your fund, okay?" Joe Leonard took the money, a look of wonder in his eyes. "Lots of kids tell me they're going to do this or that, and I just nod and say, 'Uh-huh,'" Mr. Beatty said to Perry. "But when Joe Leonard says he's going to do something, I know he'll follow through." He moved to the door then turned around and raised both arms as if preparing to conduct his band. "Oh, please hurry up and get well," he sang lustily to the tune of "Stars and Stripes Forever." After he left, Joe Leonard had turned the twenty-dollar bill over and over in his hands.

"Now just looka there!" exclaimed Eldeen, turning around slowly to take in the entire church auditorium. "If our little white angels don't just make the most *precious* decorations! That was a real original idea Marvella had this year. Lots better than them boxes and bottles last year that nobody knew what they was supposed to be. I don't know how many times I had to explain to folks that they was supposed to be the gold and frankincense and myrrh." She turned to address Perry. "Jewel and Willard's going to help me drape the choir divide with garland before we go," she said. "We can still count on you to come over tonight for some of Jewel's good chili, can't we?"

"You know me," said Perry. "Do I ever turn down an invitation like that?"

Jewel smiled as she lifted the dark green garland out of a brown paper bag. "Come at six. Willard wants to play Scrabble afterward if you'd like to stay."

"Sure," said Perry. "Oh, say, before I go,"—he turned to address Eldeen—"what was the story about the ostriches?"

"Ostriches? Oh, me!" Eldeen's face suddenly crinkled into its excruciating smile, and she bent over and slapped both hands against her thighs in unrestrained laughter. "Me and my big mouth! There I was just blabbing up one side and down the other, never dreaming in a million years that that door was open." She finally calmed down and wiped her eyes.

"Inez Cannon down at the G.O.O.D. Store was telling me about her son-in-law in Kentucky who's gone to raising ostriches," she said. "Gillam—that's his name—has these twenty or so ostriches in pens in his backyard, and Inez went to see him back in the fall and just couldn't get over them big old birds. She was telling us about how they'll get all worked up sometimes, the whole kit and caboodle of 'em, and they'll twirl around and around and pump their necks up and down and squawk and look just downright *deranged*. We was all just getting the biggest kick at the store yesterday out of her imitating them ostriches carrying on. You should of just seen her!"

"What about the one with the digestion problem?" Perry asked.

"Oh, *that!*" cried Eldeen. "Inez said Gillam has to keep the different ages separated 'cause they can get real mean to each other, and sometimes even the ones the same age will get into scraps. One day while she was there, Inez said one of the bigger ones got to pecking at one of his little sisters whenever she'd come near the food pan. He'd just peck at her, peck, peck, peck all day long,"—Eldeen stopped briefly, raised one arm to signify an ostrich's head, and made biting motions with her fingers—"and he just kept on and on blocking her from getting her rightful share. Gillam finally had to lock him up in the shed for a while so's that other little bird could get her something to eat." She finally dropped her arm and ceased her beak demonstration. "Well, later on—I don't know if it was the next day or what—but anyway, that mean ostrich started acting funny and jerking around inside the pen and just collapsing on the ground and all and not taking any interest whatsoever in the food pan anymore, and finally Gillam got so worried that he loaded him in his pickup and carried him to the veterinarian over in Paducah, and do you know what?"

"His whole digestive tract was full of feathers?" Perry asked.

"That's it! That's it! He'd done pecked so many of his little sister's feathers that he'd messed all his insides up, and that doctor had to do *surgery* on that ostrich and purge all them feathers out of its system! Now if that's not a lesson for us all!"

Perry stared at Eldeen, his mind quickly reviewing the anecdote. Another lesson—why did Christians always feel compelled to wrench a *lesson* out of everything? Or was it something that came naturally?

Maybe it was just a corollary to salvation. At any rate, the lesson wasn't immediately clear to Perry. What was the lesson here—don't eat feathers?

"Yes sir," she said stoutly, "jealousy and selfishness and meanness always catches up with you in the end. You can't get away with acting ugly forever. God's going to settle the accounts before it's all over!" Perry chided himself for not seeing the lesson at once—that one should have been easy. Once again he marveled at what these Christians could extricate from every small occurrence in life, even from an ill-tempered ostrich in Kentucky. They never took anything at face value; they always interpreted everything as an illustration of some scriptural truth. Saturated—that's what they were; their whole way of life was saturated with their own peculiar philosophy.

"Wait, Jewel, don't do the whole thing!" cried Eldeen. "I'm meaning to help! I just got a little hung up talking to Perry," and she hurried off toward the front of the church. "We'll see you tonight, Perry!" she called back.

Stepping outside the church, Perry squinted against the dazzling sunlight. Just looking up at the sky, without noticing the temperature of the air or the brown leaves blanketing the ground beneath the big oak trees or the large Christmas wreaths on the double doors outside the church, a person would think it was a summer sky. The clouds were frothy mounds of laundry suds, the sky behind them was the color of rinsed denim, and the sun blazed like a fiery copper rivet.

Chapter 34

Perry pulled out of the church parking lot and headed north toward Greenwood. He knew he was cutting it close to buy the gift today. Even if he could find one of those mailing services open this afternoon, with all the heavy demands at Christmas, he was running a risk of its being late. But it couldn't be helped; the idea had just come to him last night.

He had already ordered Dinah a practical gift—a "Classic Braided Rug" from the L. L. Bean catalog—and Troy an "Acadia Bike" with something called "grip shift," and those would be delivered sometime during the coming week he had been told. But what he was preparing to buy now would be something personal, something he hoped would carry an unspoken message to Dinah, though he wasn't sure he even knew what the message was supposed to be. The thought came to him now that maybe if he were forced to put it into words, it would have something to do with one of the "Wife's Most Basic Needs" Brother Hawthorne had talked so much about, the one that said *"She needs to know that you delight in her as a unique person and are vitally interested in her past, her present, and her future."* They had all sounded so corny and extreme to Perry at first, written down so succinctly in a neat little list, but after Brother Hawthorne had finished discussing each one, Perry had reconsidered.

He felt adventurous knowing what he was about to do. The birthday gift for Dinah back in October had been impulsive; he had never intended to look for Western wear—it had just been shoved at him more or less, and he had liked it and bought it without stopping to think. Of course, he had worried for days afterward that she would hate it, but she had dispelled his fears with her first words when he had timidly called later that week to wish her a happy birthday.

"Oh, Perry, I can't *believe* you!" she had said, but it wasn't at all the exasperated tone of voice with which she used to say the same thing after some disgraceful social gaffe she had observed him committing or after another of his domestic shortcomings. "I love it all," she said, "and I . . . well, really, I just can't believe you did this. I almost thought after I opened it that you may have remembered . . ." She stopped.

"Remembered what?" Perry had asked.

"Oh, never mind. You wouldn't. It did surprise me, though. You usually go for such . . . *safe* gifts. This was a real step out for you, wasn't it?"

"Remembered what?" he repeated.

"Nothing. It was so long ago I had almost forgotten it myself."

"What?"

"Oh, it's silly," Dinah said. "Really, it's dumb—just a kid thing."

"What? Tell me."

She had sighed after a long pause and then said, "A paper I wrote in school when I was a little girl. Maybe I never even showed it to you, though, who knows?"

But she had. Yes, she had, and Perry could hardly believe he hadn't thought of it the day he had selected the western outfit for her. How could he have forgotten? But maybe, he thought, maybe that was one reason he had so instantly liked the outfit when the saleslady showed it to him; maybe the memory of Dinah's school paper had prompted him without his realizing it. What he had considered an impulsive purchase may really have been soundly, though unconsciously, motivated. Memories carried great power even when dormant; he certainly knew that to be true.

Dinah used to carry the sheet of notebook paper folded up in her billfold until it started wearing thin along the folds. Then she had put it away somewhere, in a scrapbook maybe. Perry remembered how fond she had been of the little essay, one of those "What I Want to Be When I Grow Up" kinds, and she had shared it with him on one of their first dates, then brought it out occasionally during their courtship. She must have written it in third or fourth grade, for her cursive handwriting had obviously been in its formative stages. He remembered their laughing together over the spelling of several words, the creative punctuation, but most of all the actual content.

The essay had begun forthrightly: "*When I grow up I want to be a cowboy.*" Not a cowboy's wife or sweetheart, not even a cowgirl, but a cowboy. He remembered his amazement when Dinah's father had entertained him at their first meeting with stories of Dinah's tomboyish childhood. Perry had looked back and forth between Dinah and her father, wondering how she could be sitting there so clearly and completely feminine in every way yet having done the things her father was telling. Surely this beauty with the amber hair could never have shinnied up the flagpole of her elementary school on a dare—wearing a dress. Surely she hadn't grabbed Buddy Gower by the collar after school and given him a black eye for picking on her cousin. It couldn't be true that she had challenged every boy in her fifth grade class to an arm wrestling match—and won. But she confirmed every story her father told and offered a few more of her own.

Perry had already seen the school essay by the time he learned of all these bold exploits, but he had assumed until then that the cowboy ambition had been only a passing fancy or maybe even a joke Dinah had played because she thought the assignment was stupid. That would be like her. After hearing her father's stories, though, he remembered feeling vaguely threatened by the thought of dating a woman who had despised dolls and playhouses and whose birthday lists always included things like a gun holster, a ball glove, a Lone Ranger mask, and cowboy boots.

He realized now that he had very possibly suppressed the memory of her essay on purpose, filing it away under "The Way She Used to Be" and desperately hoping it would never get mixed up with "The Way She Is Now." It would have been interesting, though, now that he thought about it, to pursue the matter further had he not been so intimidated. He wondered what she would have said if he had asked at what point she had changed. What had marked the division between tomboy and lady? Surely a little girl didn't just wake up one day, pack away her baseball bat and rifle, and dress up for a tea party. What had initiated it all?

The essay hadn't been long, but if he remembered correctly, it had been packed with colorful details she had read about things a cowboy did—branding cattle, driving the herd to the railway, busting broncos, and fighting off Indians. Dinah had wanted to do it all. The essay had ended abruptly, he recalled: *"I want to ride the range in the hot sun and wear a red bandanna around my neck."*

During his phone call on her birthday, she never once mentioned the little book he had mailed. He had held his breath the whole time, hoping she'd say something about it, yet dreading it too. Would she laugh scornfully at the things he had written? Would she take issue with him about some minor point he had tucked away in a dependent clause somewhere? Would she complain about his writing it all instead of saying it? Or would she soften and thank him for the time and energy he had put into it? But she hadn't said a word about any of it, and he hadn't dared bring it up.

It hadn't been until several weeks later, when she had answered the phone one Sunday night at his regular calling time, that she had let it slip that she had received the book—and read it. But maybe it wasn't a slip after all; maybe it was carefully calculated. Whatever it was, before handing the phone to Troy that night, she had said, "By the way, that flirty guy in my philosophy class you wrote about—the one you said you always hated—was named Rick, not Rich."

When Troy had gotten on the phone a few seconds later, Perry had asked him, first, if Dinah had left the room. When Troy said she had, Perry asked him how she was feeling these days. Okay, Troy guessed. Did she seem happy? Most of the time, Troy said, except sometimes . . . Sometimes, what? Well, sometimes he thought he heard her crying at night after he was in bed. Did she ever go out with . . . uh, friends or other people? Yeah, she and Rebekah had gone to a movie once not long ago. Anyone else? Yeah, she and Joan drove to Chicago one Saturday and let him stay with Grandma. Did any . . . *men* ever come over? A man came and fixed something on the stove one day. Did she ever talk about *him*—Perry? "Yeah, oh, I guess so—I don't know," Troy had said crossly. "Why don't you ask her all these questions yourself?"

Dry Gulch Western Outfitters was located thirty miles away, in a string of outlet stores outside Greenwood. Perry pulled in and parked. Inside the double glass doors was a small vestibule, then swinging wooden saloon-type doors leading into the store. On his way through the swinging doors, Perry met a huge man with a finely groomed handlebar mustache. The man wore a leather jacket that jiggled with fringe, tight jeans, and a pair of brown lizard boots with pointed toes.

"Howdy," the man said brusquely, striding past Perry; his boots made a clopping sound against the wooden floor. Perry felt light-headed, almost giddy. What would the man do if he responded mockingly: "Howdy, *pardner*"?

Inside, Perry was taken back by an enormous splash of color. Everywhere he looked were vibrant reds and splatters of turquoise, orange, and purple. Beside the cash register stood a clear acrylic mannequin wearing a full-skirted yellow dress the color of Marvin Gardens. The points of the collar were tipped with shiny metallic silver, and small silver stars studded the belt. Down both sides of the bodice were stitched brilliant green cacti, outlined with silver thread. At first thought all the colors seemed incongruous to Perry with the life of a cowboy—all those cattle, the dusty trails, the bunkhouses and corrals, the rattlesnakes. But then, too, there were those magnificent Western sunsets. And perhaps the colors were more symbolic than literal—representative of a lifestyle of exciting hazards.

It took a moment after the visual assault to realize there was music playing over the intercom—cowboy songs, of course—the warm, mellow sound of men's voices with guitar, harmonica, and banjo accompaniment. It was "Good-bye Old Paint" right now, the story of a roving cowboy "off to Montan'" with "my foot in the stirrup, the rein in my hand."

Perry heard the sharp rat-a-tat of heels coming toward him, but he didn't see the woman until she was almost upon him; suddenly he was looking down at one of the smallest women he had ever seen. No wonder he hadn't seen her—she was no taller than the clothes racks. She couldn't be much taller than Troy for that matter, and he was sure her feet weren't as big as Troy's. Though her size was childlike, her face was that of a woman about Perry's own age. He tried to keep his eyes on her face and not stare at the rest of her—at the miniature red cowboy boots she wore, at her scrap of a Navajo-print miniskirt, at her short chartreuse blouse with the tails cinched tight across her tiny bare midriff. He couldn't help thinking how chilly such a costume must be at this time of year. But her face gave no sign that she felt the slightest bit underdressed; she wrinkled her button of a nose at him and shook her two shiny brown ponytails saucily. Two little brass horseshoes bobbed from her earlobes.

"How ya' doin', honey?" she asked, smiling up at him. "What can I help you with?" Her voice was squeaky and decidedly Deep South, but it might pass for a Texas drawl if customers weren't very discriminating.

Perry had already reviewed his strategy on his way to the store. That was before he knew the salesperson would turn out to be the size of a toy, of course, but he decided to go ahead with what he had planned. "I want to look at four things for my wife," he said, counting them off on his fingers. "A pair of boots, a belt, a hat, and a bandanna. If you'll show me where they are and let me look by myself, then I'll decide on something and let you know when I'm done."

The woman laughed, revealing two tiny rows of teeth the size of rice kernels. "Okey-dokey, honey, I can take a hint," she said. "So you don't like a leechy salesclerk, huh? I don't blame you the least little bit—I'm the same way—and I like a person who speaks his mind." She pivoted neatly and said, "Follow me, darlin'." She led him between round racks of clothes then down a few steps to the back half of the store. "This part down here is where we keep all our accessories," she said, spiraling an index finger above her head. "Hats along that wall," she continued, pointing, "belts on this rack over here, ladies' boots on those aisles in the very back, and scarves and bandannas over here on this table—anything you need help with, just holler." She gave him another pixieish smile, then turned and left.

Perry saw her approach two scruffy, gangling men in low-slung jeans over by the hats, who grinned at each other when she spoke to them; one of them leaned down, put his hands on his knees, and said, "Well, now, ain't you a cute little thing?" Perry was tempted to walk over and sock the man in the jaw. But the little woman must have been used to such comments; she took a step back, looked up at the man steadily, and replied, "If you need help with the merchandise, mister, just let me know. I might not be very big, but my brain works just fine." The two men stared as she marched away from them toward the front of the store, where several more customers had just entered. "Little fireball filly, ain't she?" one of them said, and they both laughed coarsely. Perry sincerely wished the roof would cave in right over where they were standing.

He walked back to the boots first and found the size eights. He wondered if Dinah would be surprised, thinking he had remembered her shoe size. Actually, he hadn't; he had cheated a little. When he had left home back in February, he had dumped all his desk supplies—the pens and pencils and paper clips and things—in an old shoebox, which had turned out to be one of Dinah's. Since he had no desk here in Derby, he had kept everything right in the same shoebox all these months, within easy reach on the right-hand side of the shelf board on which his computer sat. Every day he saw the shoebox, with its handprinted masking tape label on both ends: *Black patent slingbacks*. Dinah was big on keeping her shoes and jewelry organized, although most of her drawers were in constant disarray. So when the idea of buying her a pair of cowboy boots had entered his mind late last night, he had checked the end of the shoebox and had seen "8M" stamped on it.

He saw the pair of boots he wanted almost immediately: a dark rich brown the color of a well-polished saddle, with loops of decorative stitching around the toe. He pulled out a box of eights and headed toward the belts. He didn't know Dinah's exact waist measurement, but he knew it was small; he was relieved to see that most of the ladies' belts were sized in small, medium, or large. There was a case of belt buckles, most of them heavy and ornate, beside the belt rack. Perry bent closer to look at them.

An intercom speaker was mounted on the wall right above his head. A plaintive song was playing now—something about the "curtains of night." A cowboy was lying out on the prairie looking up at the moon and thinking about his sweetheart back home. Stop whining, Perry wanted to say. If you love her so much, hop on your horse and go get her. It was exactly at that moment that his eyes lighted on an oval sterling silver belt buckle with a brass inset of a cowboy riding a galloping horse. Another one of those odd coincidences that didn't necessarily mean anything—but it took Perry by surprise. *If you love her so much, hop on your horse and go get her.* Wasn't he in a fine position to be giving such advice? He bent down closer, his nose almost touching the glass case. The oval belt buckle looked lighter and more delicate than the others; maybe it would work for a woman's belt. He could buy one of the plain leather belts and add the buckle.

He slid the door of the case back and removed the buckle, holding it in his palm to test its weight. When he read the price tag of "$129.99," he almost put it back, but he took another look at the finely beaten silver and the plucky brass horseman and decided he couldn't. An old phrase of Dinah's sprang to his mind. Whenever she brought home something new that she thought cost too much, she would say, "I couldn't help it; the two of us *bonded* in the store."

Okay, soul mate, you're mine, Perry thought, setting the buckle gently on top of the boot box. He chose a soft brown belt then headed to the hat racks. The other two men had left by now, but Perry thought he could still smell something tainted in the air.

Size would have to be a guess here. He picked up a suede, buff-colored hat with a rawhide chin strap that he thought looked about right. It was too small for him but not much. Around the brim was a slender beaded band of turquoise, red, and yellow. He could see Dinah wearing it, her pretty features shaded from the sun by its wide brim.

As he set the hat on top of the boot box and turned to the display of scarves and bandannas, another song began playing over the intercom. The tune was familiar—"My Bonnie Lies Over the Ocean"—but the words were different. Perry tried to focus on the scarves laid out before him in neatly folded triangles, overlapping each other in a huge circle around the edge of the round table, but they all blurred together. Only the words of the song were clear. It was another cowboy dreaming under the night sky, but this one was thinking of eternity and mortality, wondering if he would go to heaven when he died. Now why did they have to go and put such a serious song right in the middle of the others about favorite horses and girlfriends?

Around and around the bandanna display Perry's eyes traveled as the song continued. Evidently one of Brother Hawthorne's predecessors had ridden a circuit out West, for in the second verse the cowboy singer developed an amazing religious allegory in which he spoke of another stockowner who always made room for the straying sinner, never forgot his own herd, even knew their every thought and action. Perry felt slightly dizzy after the last line of the stanza, which cautioned the listener to "get branded" so his name would be in the "big tally book." This was incredible. Here he was in Dry Gulch Western Outfitters thirty miles from the Church of the Open Door, and what was happening? He was getting preached at by means of a cowboy song over the intercom. He looked around, half-expecting to see the whole church congregated behind him, pointing their fingers at him. But all he saw was the diminutive saleswoman, standing on the top step of the upper level, her hands on her hips, like little wings on either side, her head tilted to the side like a curious sparrow's.

Perry looked back at the table of scarves, gently pulled out a large red bandanna, and set it down on top of the boot box beside the hat. Picking up his stack of purchases, he turned and walked toward the saleswoman, smiling. "I'm ready," he said, and her tiny red boots tapped smartly as she walked over to stand behind the cash register.

"You don't waste any time making up your mind, do you, darlin'?" the woman said. "That's great. My husband could never do this; he can't even decide what kind of milk to get when I send him to the grocery store." It hadn't occurred to Perry that she might be married. He wondered if her husband was a midget too. He wondered if she had ever borne children. "And, great day in the mornin'," she was saying now, "look at all the nice things you picked out! You're gonna have yourself one happy wife come Christmas, honey. If any of it doesn't fit, just keep your receipt and bring her back to try another size, okay?"

Perry noticed a small revolving display of earrings beside the cash register. He quickly removed one pair—two little pearl-handled revolvers, each one dangling from a large turquoise bead. "These too," he said, handing them to the saleswoman.

"Oh, I love these, I've got me a pair!" she said gaily. A happy song was playing now, one that kept repeating the phrase "Hooray for the cowboys!"

"I bet you can't wait to see her face when she opens all these," the woman continued, glancing up at Perry. But she fell silent, her fingers poised above the cash register. "What's the matter, honey?" she said. She reached over and tapped his hand. "You all right, darlin'?"

Perry forced a smile. "I'm fine," he said a little too cheerfully.

The saleswoman looked quickly toward the back of the store, where the other customers had drifted, then turned back to Perry. "Are you on the outs with your wife, hon'?" she said, her dark eyes clouding sympathetically.

How do women always seem to sniff these things out? Perry wondered. He would never forget how Dinah had foretold the doomed marriage of Prince Charles and Princess Di less than two years after their royal wedding. "She doesn't look happy," she had announced once, watching a brief news clip about the couple; Charles was holding his wife's elbow as they walked down a roped aisle among a throng of people. Dinah had pointed at the television screen. "See how he always looks away from her, over the tops of people's heads, like he's looking for someone else?" she had asked, and Perry had looked closer. All he saw, though, was the prince with a slightly worried expression, no doubt tired of all the public hoopla and ready to get away and play a little polo. "They won't last," Dinah had said shortly—and, although it had taken everyone else a lot longer to figure it out, she had been right as usual.

"Is she mad at you about something?" the saleswoman repeated, touching Perry's hand again.

Perry shrugged. "Oh, a little I guess," he said. He cleared his throat and straightened his shoulders. "But I'm working on it." He realized right then that he had never admitted to himself just what he was doing. He really *was* working on it—it was no longer just a hazy hope, but he actually had intentions.

The little woman's face brightened. "Well, all this should sure help," she said firmly, looking back to the cash register. "I could forgive lots and lots if my husband gave me presents like this!"

"That's what I'm hoping," Perry said.

A song of lament about a cowboy who fell in love with a girl on the Red River Shore began playing. When the girl's father objected to the marriage, the cowboy took off in a pique but returned later, only to find that his sweetheart had despaired and drowned herself.

The cowboy shouldn't have been so quick to leave, Perry thought, and he looked down at the silver belt buckle, which the saleswoman was just ringing up. He closed his eyes briefly but could still see the image of the daring, spirited rider straining forward in the saddle.

Chapter 35

As Perry listened to the rapid clicks of the rotary phone, he tried to think of all the things that were going on at the same moment all over the world. He often did this when he felt uneasy about something; he had done it since he was a child, when he had accidentally hit upon its calming effect. Somewhere in a rice paddie in Burma, he told himself now, a farmer's brown feet were plodding through soaked fields. But was it the right time of day for that? he wondered. And what about the season? For a moment he couldn't even think; everything he knew about geography was a muddle. He wondered what Queen Elizabeth was doing right now. What time would it be at Buckingham Palace when it was eleven o'clock at night in Derby, South Carolina? He used to know all that, but he couldn't remember the first thing right now. He knew the zero-degree longitudinal line ran through Greenwich, England, but . . . or was it *latitude* that went up and down? No, it was longitude; he remembered it because a giraffe's neck was long, and it went up and down.

Somewhere down in the South American jungle, he told himself, along the Amazon, monkeys were screeching and hungry crocodiles were floating along the banks. Beggars were crying in the streets of India, and Eskimos were eating the meat of seals in the Arctic. People right now were mountain climbing in the Himalayas, and others were lost in the Sahara. Somewhere on the planet a volcanic eruption was brewing, a river overflowing, an earthquake rumbling. Lightning was striking trees, maybe people. Women were having babies, old men were dying.

As he dialed the final number and heard the first ring, Perry spoke these words aloud: "In the vast mural of humanity, what difference does my little brush stroke make?" If Dinah hung up on him, the Burmese rice farmer would go right on wading through his fields, Queen Elizabeth would keep on wearing her dowdy little hats at royal functions, and the Eskimos would finish their meal and lie down to sleep.

"Hello." It was Dinah who answered, as Perry had expected. Troy would be in bed by now. She didn't sound sleepy or irritable, but her voice was flat as if she were preparing to listen to a telemarketing spiel.

"Dinah. It's Perry." He had tried to plan out his tone of voice and his opening words to provide the conversation with momentum, but again it all left him in an instant. He needed to learn to write it out on a notepad and have it sitting beside the telephone.

"This is Saturday night, not Sunday," Dinah said.

"Right," said Perry.

"Is something wrong?" Dinah asked.

"Well, in a sense, yes—but, strictly speaking, the way you mean, no."

"Then why . . . are you calling?" Quickly Perry tried to think of an adjective to describe her tone. Hopeful? No, that was too strong. Open? Friendly? Not exactly. Interested? Maybe, but not in an eager sense. Curious? Oh, surely there was a better word than that, one with more of a hint of optimism. But that was it, he knew it; if he were transcribing their conversation onto paper and adding adverbs to the dialogue tags, he would write, "'Then why . . . are you calling?' she asked curiously."

"Because I wanted to . . . talk to you," he said. The adverb for that one would have to be "stupidly," he thought. Why else did you call someone?

"Talk? *You* want to talk?" Incredulously, with a brittle edge of sarcasm, Perry thought. "Okay, let's talk," she said. Would that one be "archly" or "wryly"? He realized they weren't at all the same thing.

"What are you doing?" he asked. Then without even meaning to, he said aloud, "He asked nosily."

She laughed. "I'm addressing eleven Christmas cards. That's the least number I could get by with this year."

"Read me one," he said.

"What—a card?"

"Yes, what does it say? Read me one."

"Okay. 'Remembering you warmly during this very merry season.' That's it. There's a picture of a house on the front with a wreath on the door and a snowman in the yard and a Christmas tree in the front window, and all that."

"How are you signing them?"

"What?"

"How are you signing the cards inside?"

"Well, how do you think? With a pen."

"She said wittily," he replied, then immediately hoped she wouldn't take offense.

"Well, what do you mean, how am I signing them? You mean exactly what am I *writing?*"

"Yes."

"I'm writing, 'Sincerely, Dinah and Troy,' unless it's to somebody like Aunt Kay or Phyllis. Then I write, '*Love,* Dinah and Troy.' I mean, what else *would* I be writing?"

"You're late, aren't you?" Perry asked.

"What?"

"Don't you usually send Christmas cards the first week of December? It's the eighteenth."

"Yeah, well, I'm running behind this year. It's been . . . real busy."

"How's Troy?"

"He's okay. He's out of school now till the third of January."

"I bet he likes that." Perry was aware that this wasn't going anywhere. What was wrong? From somewhere inside him came a swift, grave command: *Quit asking her questions and start talking.*

"The church here is having a Christmas program tomorrow morning," he said, and without waiting for a reply rushed on. "I'm singing in the choir for it. My book is coming pretty well. I'm on the last chapter and hope to have it finished, revisions and all, by the end of January. Cal says it looks good so far. And speaking of Cal, he called last week with some pretty surprising news. I sent him a story and poem back in July, and he laughed. Well, no, not at first he didn't. They were . . . well, different from my usual stuff, and he thought I was getting sidetracked and all, and he didn't really even *like* them I don't think. But I told him to try to sell them, and I guess he did finally, and he called to tell me *Atlantic* had bought them both. *Atlantic,* of all places—not some hokey little magazine like he had expected. He said he decided when he pulled them back out and reread them to start at the top and work his way down. So he sent them to this friend of his at *Atlantic,* Fred somebody, and then forgot about them—until the friend called him one day and said they wanted them, both of them. And, let's see, what else? Oh, Beth called and said she's going to Canada for Christmas. Saskatchewan. She's met somebody there in Washington who's from someplace called Moose Jaw, and she and two other people are going to spend a week up there in a cabin with this woman's family. Can you believe it? Four mathematicians in a cabin in Saskatchewan—and one of them my sister, Beth? That's pretty amazing. And next week . . ."

"*Perry,* please." Dinah was pleading.

When he stopped, Perry found himself panting—only slightly, but nevertheless panting. "What?" he asked. "Please what?"

"Why are you doing all this?"

"All what?"

"Calling me like this and going on and on. You've never done anything like this before."

Perry couldn't think of an answer. Why *was* he doing this? He knew, of course, what his ultimate goal was, but he certainly couldn't state it bluntly to Dinah, not now. What *could* he say to explain his phone call? If he said the wrong thing, he knew well the contempt she was capable of expressing. He suddenly knew what Esther must have felt when she entered the king's court; her heart must have stood still as she awaited her fate: would she find favor in his sight or would he dismiss her with a curt directive?

At last Perry answered—slowly yet conclusively, as if he were just now gathering his thoughts and wanted to make no mistakes.

"I've changed, Dinah. I . . . guess I'm going on and on because I'm nervous. I just want you to know. . . well, I've changed."

"How?" It wasn't challenging or bitter, just—again—curious.

"Well, in a lot of ways I think, but it's hard to explain them all. I've done a lot of thinking, and . . ." He trailed off again.

"And what?"

"Well . . . men are . . . I mean, I never . . . well, if I could just . . . I think I could . . ." He broke off with a self-deprecating laugh. Dinah would have every right at this point, he thought, to fling back a caustic retort, something like "My, how aptly put" or "Oh, thank you, now I understand perfectly."

But she didn't say anything, and Perry finally took a deep breath and started in again, trying a lighter tone. "I told you I'm singing in the church choir now. Actually, I started back in June. That's one change. Did you ever know me to do anything like that before? And I've been trying out my hand in the kitchen more. At first it was nothing but spaghetti sauce from a jar or macaroni and cheese in a box, but I've been branching out lately. Jewel showed me how she makes biscuits— baking soda biscuits—and I've made muffins too. Last week I even tried lasagna one night, and it turned out pretty good. Willard took his spoon and scraped out the dish after we'd finished it. And I've learned to play tennis a little, and I've gone fishing four or five times. And I've read through the whole Bible and figured out a washing machine problem and . . . well, I've been thinking a lot lately, and . . ."

"Sounds like you're having yourself a real good time down there," Dinah said. It wasn't angry, really, but guarded—maybe even a little hurt. Perry realized how he must have come across; how would he feel if she proudly rattled off a list of new things she had learned to do over the past months during their separation? Again he had stumbled off down the wrong path. Could he grope his way back and try again?

"A good time?" he asked wonderingly. "Oh, Dinah, is that what you think I've been doing—having a good time? Look, I came down here pretty much out of necessity. Partly to write the book, of course, but also because I was . . . we were . . . well, I needed a place to live. It's not exactly like I've been living it up at some resort." He knew that if he had said it defensively, it could have sounded angry; it could very well have ended the conversation. But he had spoken calmly, kindly. Even as the words slipped from his mouth, he marveled that he was actually talking this way, that he was reasoning out the situation, seeking to fit the pieces together, not only to view their lives from Dinah's angle—as he had so seldom before attempted to do—but also, for her benefit, to try to put into words his own perspective.

There was a long pause, during which he heard Dinah sniff. His first response, when he realized she was crying, was to stiffen. He hadn't expected this; he certainly didn't *want* it. His mind was suddenly flooded again with memories of all the times he had simply vanished from Dinah's presence at the first hint of tears. Enter tears, exit Perry. The easy way out. He could do that now. He could so easily take the receiver from his ear and gently, selfishly set it down on top of the two black, springy buttons on the cradle of the telephone. The line would be broken. He began making up words to the tune playing through his mind: *Rock-a-by, Dinah, over the phone, when the tears start, then Perry will go. When the sobs break, then Perry won't hear, and Dinah can cry—a buzz in her ear.*

He waited a while, trying to come up with the appropriate words to say. He could say what he had said to Jewel that night on the steps: "It's been a hard day for you." But had it been? He had gotten the impression that Dinah was generally doing fine. He hadn't taken much stock in Troy's account of her crying at night; kids imagine strange things when they go to bed in a dark room.

"Dinah." When he spoke her name, she grew quiet. "Dinah, why are you crying?" He said it softly.

She inhaled raggedly, then answered in a broken voice, "I don't know."

They sat in silence for a time. He heard her blow her nose, an indelicate honking sound, and squelched the desire to make a joke out of it. "Dinah, won't you blow, Dinah, won't you blow, Dinah, won't you blow your horn?" he could have sung. But he didn't, of course.

"What's wrong? Are you okay?" Perry asked.

"In a sense, yes, but strictly speaking, no." It was her old habit of repeating his words but in a different context. He'd forgotten how often she used to do that, always playfully in their happy years together, but later on, with blatant sarcasm. Once, a year ago, Troy had asked Perry why some parents let their children believe in Santa Claus, and Perry had replied, "So if the children don't like their presents, they can say it's his fault." Later that day Perry had heard Troy ask Dinah why she always left the room when Dad entered, and she had sighed heavily, then replied, "If I don't like his presence, it's his fault."

"What's wrong?" Perry asked again.

Dinah took a long breath and let it out slowly. "I don't even know how to answer that," she said in a small voice.

"Is it something at work?"

"No, work's fine," she said.

"Is it something about Troy?"

"Well, no, not exactly, but . . ."

"But what? Is Troy having some kind of trouble?"

Her voice suddenly grew stronger, more aggressive. "Is Troy having some kind of *trouble*? Perry, Troy is a nine-year-old boy who lives with his mother and wonders every single day of his life why his . . ."

Perry didn't press her to complete the sentence.

"I think it's safe to say that Troy is having some kind of trouble, yes," she continued. "Did *you* ever have any trouble when you were a kid, growing up with only a mother around?"

The question hung in the air like an stultifying vapor. *Trouble, trouble, trouble*—the word echoed inside Perry's head. A picture of hideous witches stirring a noxious concoction leapt to his mind. "Double, double toil and trouble, fire burn and cauldron bubble." But what was a nasty gruel of newt's eye, adder's tongue, and goat's gall compared to what Perry had experienced growing up? He would have gladly drunk the witches' hell-broth, the whole cauldronful, in exchange for a normal childhood.

But Troy was far more resilient, more confident, more rugged than Perry himself had been as a child. There was no possible way Troy could be wandering in the same emotional wasteland Perry had gotten lost in. His nights couldn't possibly be as long and black as Perry's had been, his days as full of frightful insecurities.

He realized after a while that he didn't know whose turn it was to say something. Had Dinah asked a question? Or had he? He heard a slight rustle on the other end of the line and wondered if maybe Dinah was crying again.

"Dinah."

"Wait a minute, Troy's here. He says he's thirsty." He heard her lower the receiver. "Use the glass there in the sink," she said. So she was in the kitchen; all along he had been imagining her in the den. "It's Daddy," he heard her say. "No, not now, he'll call you tomorrow," she said. Then, "Okay, just tell him hi and then off to bed."

"Dad, is that you?" It struck Perry that at the moment Troy's voice sounded anything but resilient, confident, rugged. But the boy was tired and sleepy; what could he expect?

"Hey there, Troy. So someone's in the kitchen with Dinah, huh?" Troy didn't laugh. Maybe he didn't even catch the allusion to the song.

"Off you go," Dinah said from the background. She paused, then added, "Yes, I'll come see you in a minute."

After a few moments, Dinah spoke again. She sounded exhausted. "I feel so tired, Perry. I feel like I can't drag myself from this chair. Some days I feel like my feet weigh a ton, like it's a major accomplishment to pick them up. I wonder what quicksand feels like."

"A lot of points," Perry said.

"What did you say?"

"Nothing, nothing at all." He berated himself silently. How could he be so dumb? How could he tell her at a time like this that he had won the Scrabble game at Jewel's house less than an hour ago, barely beating out Willard in the end and that "quicksand" had been the word that had earned him eighty-four points? What would she say if he went into an enthusiastic explanation of how Eldeen had claimed the left center "Triple Word Score" with her word "sand," spelling it vertically, and had scored fifteen points, but then *he* had added the word "quick" to "sand," beginning in the top left corner, which was another "Triple Word Score" square and had accumulated eighty-four points, counting the "Double Letter Score" for the letter *c*? What would Dinah have to say to Eldeen's outcry, "Perry's just too smart for the rest of us, that's what!" He was glad Dinah hadn't been there to offer her own opinion of Perry's intelligence.

"What do you mean, a lot of points?" Dinah asked.

"There are a lot of points to consider," Perry said.

"Like what?"

"Like have you been to a doctor? Maybe you just need to take some vitamins or something. Have you been getting enough sleep? Are you eating right? Getting any exercise?"

"A doctor would just tell me what I've already heard a thousand times: 'You're reacting to stress. Get your mind off your worries.'"

"So who's told you that a thousand times?" An old suspicion stirred inside him; was Dinah going to some kind of therapy sessions?

"Oh, everybody," she said wearily. "I was so tired last night— you'll like this—that I sat on the sofa in the den and watched a whole basketball game on TV. I couldn't even get up the energy to change the channel."

"Who won?"

"Who cares? I didn't mean I really *watched* it."

"Not even the coaches?"

She laughed a short, humorless laugh. "Not even the coaches."

How many years ago was it, Perry wondered, that they used to watch sports together on television? Sometimes Perry would watch for a few minutes to see what the score was before flipping back to another channel, and during that time Dinah would study the coaches pacing along the sidelines. "They act like this is the *biggest* deal!" she would say. "Like somebody's really going to care who won this game a year from now." She had other similar comments for the sportscasters, whose frenzy made her laugh. "I'd be mortified to be a grown man acting that way," she'd say. Other times she'd watch for a few minutes, then say something like "I wonder how he treats his wife. Or if he even has one. He probably didn't act that excited when his first kid was born."

"Can I do anything to help?" Perry asked now, then immediately sensed how insincere he must sound. He might as well have said, "Can I give you a ride to Pluto on my magic carpet?"

"Can you do anything to help?" Dinah repeated. "Well, now, that's a tempting offer." Was she making fun of him? He couldn't tell. "What do *you* think, Perry?" she continued. "Do you think there's anything you can do to *help?*"

"Well, if I were . . . you know, closer, I . . . I could, well, I'd be glad to . . ." But what *could* he do? Did she have something in mind?

"Well, yes, now that's very true," she said. "If you were . . . you know, closer, you . . . well, you could . . ." This time there was no doubt that she was making fun of him. He suddenly thought of a tribe of

Australian aborigines roasting a kangaroo over an open pit. How carefree their lives must be. And the Indians living with their alpacas high in the Andes Mountains of South America—their main concern was to keep from slipping off those rocky precipices. What did they know of broken relationships and wounded feelings and the steady, throbbing knowledge of personal failure?

"Are you going anywhere for Christmas Day?" Perry asked after another hollow, silent interval.

"We'll eat dinner at Mother's," Dinah answered. "That will take all of an hour, the way she does it. Then we'll open her gifts to us, and she'll open ours, and that'll take another thirty minutes. Then she'll want us to stay all afternoon and on into the night, and we'll want to come home, and we'll probably both end up mad at each other."

"Well . . ." It seemed to Perry that she was determined to see only the bleak side of life tonight. "I guess I'll talk to you later," he said. "I just wanted to see how things were going. Troy doesn't exactly fill me in on all the details, you know." He made an effort to chuckle, but it caught in his throat. "I guess you can get back to addressing your eleven cards," he said.

"Right," Dinah said. "I guess that's what I can do all right."

After they hung up, Perry sat for several minutes, his hand still resting on the telephone receiver. The two little black buttons had been depressed; the line was cut. Somewhere, he thought—many, many places, in fact—there were people, all kinds of people like Spaniards, Danes, Irishmen, Thais, Laplanders, Turks, Tahitians, Egyptians, all going about their daily routines totally unaware of the icy weight in the pit of Perry Warren's stomach in Derby, South Carolina.

Chapter 36

Look at all them umbrellas!" said Eldeen, pointing to the wall as they stepped inside the vestibule on Sunday night. "That's one thing I like about rainy church days. Isn't that just the cheerfulest sight—all them different colors and sizes? Funny, them looking so perky when they're used on rainy days and all. They look like a row of little youngsters waiting in line to march into church."

"Somebody's going to need to mop up the floor out here after church," Jewel said. "It's a shame, too, because Nina and Jarvis just waxed it yesterday afternoon."

"Isn't that the way it goes?" Eldeen said, stamping her black boots on the mat. "Seems like from the time I was a little girl, it's never rained at the right time. It's always too early or too late or too much or too little or right before a ball game or right after a big washing when all the clothes are hanging out on the line to dry—or right after you got your floor all spic-and-span, and then everybody tracks through and messes it up again. My mama used to get so provoked over that! 'Course, that's looking at it from a human standpoint. God plans it all. Like it says in the Bible, 'He sendeth rain on the just and on the unjust,' and 'to every thing there is a season.'" Perry didn't understand the connection between the two verses.

"Well, it sure is a good thing the rain held off till tonight," Jewel said, adding her blue umbrella to the others along the wall.

Perry couldn't remember anyone even talking about what they would have done if it had been raining like this during the special program that morning, but maybe he hadn't been paying attention when the subject was brought up. He thought now about how inconvenient it would have been for the choir members to have had to walk around the side of the church in a downpour during Fern Tucker's story, when they all went back to the Sunday school rooms to put on their coats and scarves and then reenter from the rear of the sanctuary to stand in scattered clusters along the center and side aisles like carolers in a Dickens scene. Then by the time they had changed again from their caroling clothes into their long white robes and once more trekked around to walk sedately down the aisle for the finale, their shoes would have been soaked and the ladies' hairdos would have gone limp. And the children would have gotten their costumes all wet, maybe even muddy, tramping around the building before the pantomimed nativity scene. They would have dripped all over the new burgundy carpet, and the wise men's decorated paper headgear would have sagged.

"I was about to get worried about you," Willard said as they filed in to sit beside him in their regular pew.

Jewel smiled. "We just took our time," she said. "It was nice for a change not having to be here early. I even took a nap."

"Me too," Eldeen told him. "There's nothing better than a nap on a rainy afternoon! Why, I might still be sleeping if Howie hadn't of knocked so loud on the door when he came to pick up Joe Leonard. He does these real fancy knocks like he's playing the drums. Rap-a-diddle-rap-a-diddle-rap-rap. I don't see how in the world he does 'em. Here, Perry, let's sit that box here on the floor between us." Then, leaning over to Willard again, she poked his leg and pointed to the box. "You should just *see* the things we brought for the White Elephant party! 'Course, I don't think anything could beat them neon green stockings I took home last year!" She turned back to Perry. "They had these silver sequins all over 'em and was just the *tackiest* things you ever saw."

As Brother Hawthorne walked to the pulpit, Eldeen emitted a snort of laughter and whispered loudly to Perry, "And you should of just seen the sunglasses Brother Hawthorne got last year! Earl Vanderhoff was the one who brought 'em. They was gigantic purple things with pink rhinestones in the corners!" She began shaking so hard Perry could feel the pew vibrate.

Brother Hawthorne cleared his throat and smiled out at the congregation. "Welcome to our annual Youth Service. We've looked forward to this all year."

"He put 'em on after he opened 'em," Eldeen whispered, "and everybody like to of *busted!*"

"Our young people have put together a fine service for us tonight," Brother Hawthorne continued, "and I know it will be a blessing to all of us. Let me introduce the teenagers for you before turning the service over to them. Then I'll have a few words at the end before we dismiss and meet again back in Fellowship Hall for refreshments and our gift exchange."

"Earl said he found 'em at a yard sale, along with a necktie that Libby wrapped up for her gift," Eldeen whispered. "Woody Farnsworth ended up with the necktie. It was bright orange with a big old black ape on it and . . . oh, shhh! He's telling about the young people." Eldeen put her hand on Perry's arm as if to silence him and turned her full attention to Brother Hawthorne.

". . . at the piano. Marilee will be turning fifteen next month. She's in the ninth grade at Derby High School. She sings in the school chorus, plays flute in the Dickson County Youth Orchestra, and is in her ninth year of piano lessons—I believe that's right." Marilee nodded from the piano bench. "And Joe Leonard Blanchard will be leading the singing," Brother Hawthorne said, turning around to motion to Joe Leonard, who was sitting behind him on the platform. "He's fifteen and is a sophomore this year. He plays tuba in the school band and would have been on the basketball team if he hadn't had a little accident in the locker room one afternoon back in October after tryouts." Everybody laughed softly, and Joe Leonard stared at the tips of his loafers. "But we all know it wasn't really an accident," Brother Hawthorne said. "God uses everything for a purpose." Eldeen murmured, "He sure does!"

"He used Joe Leonard's so-called accident," Brother Hawthorne continued, "to lead Howie Harrelson to the Lord, and Howie's whole family was saved as a result and joined our church last month." Howie was sitting on the front pew, his right arm stretched out along the back of the pew behind Joshua Chewning. Perry saw him smile and nod at something Joshua said. "Howie will be singing in the youth ensemble later in the service," Brother Hawthorne said, "and will also help with the offertory I believe. Stand up, would you, Howie, so the visitors will know who you are. Howie is a sophomore at Derby High also."

As the introductions continued, Perry studied the young people. In appearance they were quite a disparate group: Mayme Snyder, home for Christmas break after her first semester at college, was tall and willowy with a face that had always reminded Perry of a war refugee— hollow cheekbones, dark haunted eyes, and an expression of long-suffering innocence. Yet when she spoke or sang, her eyes widened and brightened and her lips melted into an ethereally sweet smile. Tricia Finch, pretty and sprightly, barely came to Mayme's shoulder though she was only a year younger. Bonita Puckett, sixteen, was plump and friendly, with clear green eyes and a headful of extraordinarily bountiful black hair. Marilee Tucker was the youngest of the girls and the plainest—the kind of girl who could easily pass through life unnoticed and unpraised if her parents hadn't provided her with opportunities to develop some compensatory skill, which in her case happened to be musical achievement.

The boys on the whole were a younger group, Howie being the oldest at sixteen. Though only five feet six, Howie's physical agility had earned him a starting position on the Derby High basketball team. He had shown up for the first practice in October with two black eyes and a dark, stitched gash on his left jaw and had played each game of the season so far with a single-minded zeal that had taken Coach Hampton by surprise. The coach, who had chosen Howie for his speed and quick reflexes, had prepared himself to endure the same braggadocio Howie had exhibited the previous year. But Rob Finch had told Jewel that before their first practice Howie had asked to address the team; he had looked them all in the eye and said he was sorry for his big mouth in the past and said he hoped they'd see a different side of him from now on. He finished by saying he meant to play extra hard this year to help make up for the doctor telling his buddy Joe Leo he'd better sit out this season. And from what Perry had heard and seen, Howie had made good on his promise.

At thirteen, the Chewning twins, Joshua and Caleb, were both comically graceless, though Perry could see them someday growing into their bodies and transforming into lean, muscular men. They both had blond hair with cowlicks and smiles that spread over their faces like warm butter.

As he studied Joe Leonard, Perry found himself wishing he had taken a picture of the boy when he first saw him back in February. Was it just a matter of getting used to him, or had Joe Leonard really changed as much as Perry thought he had over the past ten months? He knew for a certainty, of course, that he had grown taller; to Perry it had been like watching the summer corn in the Illinois fields back home. Joe Leonard must be close to six feet tall now, and his frame had begun filling out a little. Although he still had the habit of shyly diverting his gaze from people's eyes, he nevertheless held his shoulders back and took long, purposeful strides.

The service began with Joe Leonard introducing the first song: "First Peter 2:9 says, 'Who hath called you out of darkness into his marvellous light.'" He darted a sideways glance at Marilee, then swept his eyes across the congregation before fixing on the clock above the main doors. "Please turn to number two-sixteen," he said, "and stand

as we sing the first, second, and fourth verses of 'Sunshine in My Soul.'"
Marilee gave a rousing introduction, then Joe Leonard lifted his arms
and his pure tenor voice led out boldly: "There is sunshine in my soul
today, More glorious and bright Than glows in any earthly sky; For
Jesus is my light." Perry wondered if Joe Leonard had selected the songs
much earlier, before he knew there was going to be a cold, dreary,
unremitting rain falling tonight.

The song service proceeded, a mixture of Christmas songs and
regular, year-round ones. Apparently Joe Leonard had chosen them
carefully, for each of his transitional comments provided a clear bridge
between thoughts; Perry saw that he had written the Bible verses in
order on an index card. After several songs, Sid Puckett stood and
explained the Scripture memory program he and Dottie had started
with the young people, and then all the teenagers stood on the platform
steps and recited the first two chapters of James. Perry noticed that even
Mayme knew the verses, and he wondered if they had mailed her an
assignment each week at college.

After the Scripture recitation, Joe Leonard stood and read a few
announcements from the morning bulletin and then led in prayer before
Joshua, Caleb, Bonita, and Tricia passed the offering plates.

"Aren't these young people just the biggest blessing?" Eldeen said
aloud as Howie and Marilee mounted the platform together. Several
people sitting in front of Eldeen nodded and smiled their assent.

The offertory was a flute-drum duet of "Little Drummer Boy." If
he weren't sitting here watching Howie and Marilee, Perry thought, it
would be hard to believe the sound being produced was from two
teenagers. Maybe the flute was an easy instrument to play, and maybe
anybody with a modicum of rhythmic sense could make a drum sound
good, but the fact was that the number was beautifully and sensitively
performed.

Later, when the ensemble sang an arrangement of "Silent Night"
that Willard had written for them, Perry closed his eyes. If there were
churches like this all over America—and he was told that there were—
then there must be at least some small hope for the next generation.
But would these young voices he was hearing now, searching so
earnestly for harmonies, be enough to counter the other voices—the
ones in huge, inner-city schools where education was a mockery, where
children addicted to drugs sought to kill their teachers and each other
over the slightest affront, where condoms were distributed like hall
passes?

"The greenhouse fallacy"—wasn't that the term Cal had often

used? "Those people think that by sheltering their kids from real life," Cal had said, "they can escape." Then he had laughed a bitter-tinged laugh. "My mom and dad tried that route, but they found out that their little greenhouse plants didn't turn out like they'd expected. For one thing, they *couldn't* resist all the outside pollution if they wanted to, and, for another, they didn't *want* to. So there you have it. Try to smother and hem them in when they're little, and they'll run wild all over the place when they finally find a little crack in the greenhouse to get out." It made sense to Perry; in fact, he could see both sides. These eight teenagers looked like pretty solid proof to him that the Christians' plan could work, but then Cal and his brothers seemed to argue the other side. There had to be *something,* some definable key that explained the difference.

Which side of the line will Troy end up on? he wondered. But no sooner had the question presented itself than a response came, swift and severe, as if declared by a sardonic arbiter: "Troy cannot possibly end up like the eight teenagers standing before you since, first, Troy's parents are not born-again Christians, second, they do not espouse any religious doctrine, third, they have not adhered to the greenhouse principle of child-rearing, and, fourth, they do not even live together." But there were other good kids who weren't from religious families; Troy could be one of those. For a moment Perry tried to form an image of Troy as a teenager, but nothing took shape except a picture of himself as an awkward, introverted teen. He felt a prick of fear along the back of his neck; surely Troy wouldn't turn out like him—he wouldn't wish that on anybody.

Joshua Chewning had been voted on by the youth group to deliver what was called "the challenge to the congregation." As he stood behind the pulpit wetting his lips, his cowlick silhouetted against the white wall of the baptistry, Joshua looked exactly like what he was—a nervous thirteen-year-old boy. He looked so out of place, in fact, that several younger children in the auditorium began snickering until Eldeen whipped her head around indignantly and released a low, long "Shhhhhhh!"

Everything grew still as Joshua opened his Bible and spread it out on the pulpit. "A Father's Love," he said. His voice was higher than usual, but his eyes were serious; there was no sign that this was the same boy who tied people's shoelaces together and made jokes out of everybody's name: "Knock knock. Who's there? Howie. Howie who? Howie gonna keep warm without a blanket?" Marilee was "Marilee we roll along," and Tricia Finch was "Fisha Trinch." He called Bonita

"Bonita Chicana," which he explained was a variation on "Chiquita Banana."

Perry knew he should be writing down the sequence of events but decided he would condense tonight's service into a few paragraphs to insert in the chapter about the youth group. And if he did it tonight before bed, he probably could get by without taking notes. He wished this would quit happening, though. He hadn't counted on new material this late in the project, but things kept cropping up that needed to be included. He had spent a good part of the afternoon today, for example, adding six paragraphs to one of the chapters in the "Theme" section of his book about this morning's Christmas program.

All of a sudden something else came to his mind that he ought to mention in Eldeen's profile, and he dug his Daytimer out of his pocket. He wrote the name "Flo Potter" to remind himself, then decided to go ahead and jot a few notes about tonight's service. The trouble with the section about Eldeen was that he could write a whole book just about *her*. How could he possibly sum her up in three or four pages? The more he listened to the audiotape of the interview he did with her, the more frustrated he became. His book was almost finished now except for these final details he had to keep adding and the very last chapter, the one containing the five individual profiles. He looked over at Eldeen sitting beside him, her dark eyes intense beneath the thick, bushy ridge of her eyebrows. What would she say, he wondered, if she knew how he was struggling over the section about her? The other four profiles— the ones of Harvey Gill, Curtis Chewning, Vonda Snyder, and Tricia Finch—had fallen into place easily, but every time he sat down to work on Eldeen's, he was more convinced than ever that mere words were totally inadequate for the task. Maybe he should ask Cal about marketing a videotape supplement along with the book.

Joshua Chewning held up two fingers and said, "Point two—God didn't let his love get in the way of doing what he knew was the right and best thing to do."

Way to go, Perry scolded himself, sitting up straighter and staring directly at Joshua. It was going to be a little hard to include a summary of tonight's "challenge to the congregation" if he sat there mulling over unrelated problems instead of paying attention.

"I asked my dad about this," Joshua said. "I asked him who God loved more—Jesus or the world. How could he give up his own son if he didn't love the world more? My dad said that God didn't let Jesus suffer because he didn't love him as much as us, but he did it because . . . well, it's hard to explain, but because when he looked at everything, it was the *right* thing to do. It hurts a father to see his child hurt, my dad said. He even said it would hurt him more to see *me* hurt than if he got hurt himself. So when God gave Jesus to die, he was hurting himself, but he did it because it was the best thing to do. It would've been selfish for God to say, 'I know everybody will die and go to hell if I don't give Jesus, but I just can't do it because I love him too much.' A perfect, holy God wouldn't do that. Just like I've heard my dad say at home he doesn't *want* to punish us, but he does it anyway because it's the right thing to do and he won't let his love get in the way of doing what's best for us."

Perry thought Joshua was getting sidetracked now, bringing in the punishment part. That belonged in another sermon. After all, God wasn't punishing Jesus when he allowed him to be crucified. But he instantly felt petty; who was he to criticize a thirteen-year-old for letting a thread of logic go slack? Anyway, maybe he felt a tug of conscience about the point. Hadn't Dinah reproved him often for what she used to call his "misguided love" for Troy? "You say you can't spank him because you love him," she would say, "but I say you *won't* spank him because you're afraid he'll quit loving you." Her final comment during these lectures was always the same: "If you *really* loved him, you'd quit thinking about yourself and do what *needs* to be done!" Then she would storm out of the room and Perry would seethe at the suggestion that his love for Troy was flawed and that *he* had ended up being the target of Dinah's wrath when it had been *Troy* who had thrown a tantrum or been blatantly disobedient.

Joshua's last point about God's love was simple: "God doesn't let his perfection get in the way of his love for us." He went on to repeat a principle Perry had heard many times since coming here: "God loves us even when we sin." Joshua developed the point further. "God doesn't love people based on their good works," he said, "and even the best Christians can never, ever *earn* God's love. God doesn't say, 'I won't love you unless you're perfect.'" Though Perry had marveled at the way these Christians and their songs focused so much on man's sinful nature, he had to admit, when he compared God's love to his own fatherly love for Troy, that this last point of Joshua's made sense.

Several especially ugly, embarrassing scenes came to mind during which—to use the lingo of these Christians—Troy had graphically revealed the "depravity of humankind." But had he withdrawn his love for Troy during those times? Not at all. He even remembered feeling a strange, hot ache of sympathy once when he watched Troy kick Dinah's antique cherry serving cart until it tipped over and her prized set of

Limoges demitasse cups was scattered in shards all around the dining room and kitchen. "He's just a little *child*," he had thought. "He can't be expected to understand why he can't simply have what he wants." Part of him envied the boy also—his childish prerogative of venting his feelings so unreservedly. What a luxury.

Joshua closed with a responsive reading of John 3:16–21. With the rest of the congregation, Perry read the last verse: "But he that doeth truth cometh to the light, that his deeds may be made manifest, that they are wrought in God." Perry thought he felt Eldeen's gaze on him, but when he glanced at her, her eyes were closed tightly and her lips were moving slowly. She looked so weak and burdened—so pathetic, really—that he wanted to touch her. He wanted to remind her that it was Christmastime, that at her feet was a box of silly gifts waiting to be opened and laughed over in Fellowship Hall, that her daughter was getting married in two weeks, that her friend Flo Potter had finally come to church that morning for the special program and had promised to come back again next week—oh, yes, and that God loved her. *That* would cheer her up.

For the closing song, Joshua asked everyone to turn to "The Old Rugged Cross" in the hymnbook and to read the words as Joe Leonard played the melody on his tuba. It was a song they had sung many times; even Perry knew the words by heart now.

He heard Eldeen sniff and looked over to see tears flowing freely down her wrinkled cheeks and splashing onto the page of the hymnal. "Oh, come now," he wanted to say to her, "you're all worked up over nothing—at least nothing new. Joshua is only thirteen," he wanted to remind her; "that certainly wasn't *his* sermon he just delivered—his dad probably wrote out the whole thing and told him exactly what to say; he as much as admitted it. And besides, it was nothing you haven't heard a hundred times before. You've got to understand that a service like this is bound to elicit a sentimental response," he wanted to say, "but, remember, break it down into its component parts and it was just a motley crew of eight kids, a flute and a drum, a few Bible verses, some songs, a short talk about a subject you've heard over and over, and now a tuba. 'The Old Rugged Cross' is just a song, that's all; it's nothing to get all choked up over, except that maybe your grandson is playing it. Look on the bright side: Even if there ever really *was* an old rugged cross, all that was ages ago—and, anyway, look at the last line. Someday you're going to get a *crown*—won't that be nice? Think about *that*," he wanted to tell her.

Jewel dug in her purse and handed Eldeen a tissue; she wiped off the hymnal first. Then as Brother Hawthorne stood to say a few concluding words and lead in a closing prayer, Perry saw a picture of startling clarity in his mind: Eldeen, dressed in a long, flowing robe of luminescent white, was carefully bending to lay an armful of shining trophies at the foot of an ancient, weather-battered cross. And instead of a little golden cup on each trophy base, the small golden figure of a person adorned each one. One he recognized as Mr. Hammond, another was Flo Potter, another was Glenda Finch, and another was Roberta Harrelson. But there were many others that he didn't have time to identify before Brother Hawthorne's prayer ended and the scene vanished.

Chapter 37

The Golden Oldies of Derby had sought, and received, financial backing from almost every business in town when they had set out twenty years earlier to build their store. The G.O.O.D. Country Store was located on Lambert Street a block off Fredericks Road next to the city park. It was a neat little log cabin with red gingham curtains at the windows and several big red rocking chairs on the porch.

When Perry pulled up in front of the store on Thursday morning, it was still raining—a cold, steady drizzle. It had kept up off and on all week, ever since Sunday evening. People were beginning to wonder if it would rain straight through Christmas Day, which was only two days away now.

The leaves of the holly bushes in front of the porch railing were bobbing erratically from the raindrops. As Perry walked up the short sidewalk to the shelter of the broad porch, he heard a man's deep, hearty laugh from inside. A bell clanged stridently as the door flew open and an elderly woman emerged, briskly snapping open a black umbrella the size of a small satellite dish.

"Come back and see us, Blanche," said the man at the door. Then, catching sight of Perry, he called, "Hello there! Come on in here where it's warm and dry—that is, if you can get around Miz Fisher and her umbrella." The woman quickly raised her umbrella and stared at Perry, her eyebrows arched neatly and her prim mouth forming a small, round "o." Perry saw then that besides her umbrella and long khaki raincoat, the woman had a plastic rain hat tied around her head and clear plastic boots over her sensible shoes.

She fixed Perry with a severe scowl and said, "You are not dressed for this weather, young man. You will get sick." Perry felt sure that at one time in her life this woman had been a schoolteacher. He could clearly hear a younger version of her stentorian voice saying, "You are not prepared for this examination, young man. You will fail." He ducked past her and entered the store. The bell gave another cheery clank as the man closed the door.

"Miz Fisher's not one for small talk," he said to Perry, his small, red-rimmed eyes shining jovially. "I just tried to tell her a funny story as she was leaving, and when I finished, she glared at me and said, 'Life is too short for such folderol, Mister Abrams.'" He threw his head back and brayed with laughter, then extended his hand. "Hollister Abrams here," he said. "I'm working here today, along with Charlotte Dalby over there." He waved toward the cash register, where a silver-haired woman sat crocheting. She never lifted her eyes. "Don't believe I've ever seen you in here before," he said, and Perry shook his head.

Hollister Abrams had a gold tooth in front; that was the first thing Perry had noticed, though there were many other things to notice. The man's other teeth were worn down to short yellowish stubs, and from his large, flared nostrils and sizable ears grew tufts of dark hair. His watery eyes looked like two small mahogany beads embedded in the broad expanse of his ruddy, polished face, and stiff clumps of salt-and-pepper hair shot out at odd angles from his head. Perry wondered if Hollister was his own barber. His eyebrows were mostly gray, but several long, dark hairs stood out like spikes. Tall and husky, Hollister Abrams carried himself like a much younger man. Perry couldn't help wondering what he had looked like at the age of, say, twenty. Was it possible that he had ever been considered remotely handsome? Had there ever been a young girl madly in love with him, who wore his picture in her locket and gazed at it longingly? Had a child's tiny fingers ever traced the odd configuration of this face?

Hollister was pointing out the different features of the store, starting with the woodcrafts in the nearest corner, labeled "G.O.O.D. Country Carvin'," and moving around the room to the "G.O.O.D. Country Stitchin'," "G.O.O.D. Country Decoratin'," and "G.O.O.D. Country Cookin'."

"Then over here in this part," he concluded, gesturing toward the area by the cash register, labeled "G.O.O.D. Country Livin'," "we got a few miscellaneous things, like that doorknocker there on the wall made out of old Pepsi bottlecaps and those milk jug games on the floor."

"Thanks," said Perry. "I'll just look around."

"The prices are right here on the tags," Hollister said, picking up a wooden mouse with a clothespin glued to the end of its nose.

"What is that?" Perry asked.

"It's a recipe holder," said Hollister. "See, you hang it on the knob of your cupboard by its tail," and he demonstrated by swinging it from his index finger. That was when Perry noticed that the man was missing two fingers on his left hand. "Then you put your recipe card in here," he said, pressing the clothespin open, "and you got it right there at eye level." Hollister pointed to the price tag. "It says what it is right here by the price in case you can't figure something out from looking at it." And sure enough, in small, spidery letters was printed "$4.50 Recipe Holder." Turning the price tag over, Hollister continued: "And here on the back it tells the name of the person who made it," and he pointed to the words "Dash Pearson."

"I see," said Perry, wondering if someone's name really was Dash or if he had misread it. Maybe it was a nickname. Then, fearful that Hollister would hover at his elbow, he said again, "Thank you. I'll just look around." This made no impression on Hollister, however, who set down the wooden mouse and held up a highly varnished wooden plaque with "Home Sweet Apartment" stenciled on it in gold letters and bright bouquets of flowers decoupaged in each corner.

"Isn't this something?" Hollister said, his gold tooth flashing. "Rudy Sears just brought this in the other day. You buying any Christmas presents for newlyweds? This might be just the thing—well, maybe. I don't know. Personally, it wouldn't be my style."

"No," said Perry absently. As his eyes traveled over the shelves of wooden items, he perceived an overlap problem. Why was the wall plaque in the "G.O.O.D. Country Carvin'" section instead of "G.O.O.D. Country Decoratin'"? It seemed as if it could easily go in either section. And hanging on the wall right in front of him was an elaborately cross-stitched proverb—"Tall oaks from little acorns grow"—inside a frame made out of what the price tag said were "crushed acorns." Didn't it belong as much in "G.O.O.D. Country Stitchin'" as in "G.O.O.D. Country Carvin'"? The needlework may have even taken longer to do than the frame.

"That's the same problem I've had with my book," he heard himself saying aloud.

"What's that?" asked Hollister, his small, friendly eyes twinkling with interest.

"Oh, nothing," Perry answered quickly. "I was thinking about something else. It's not always easy to know . . . where things fit."

"Well, now, that's the truth," Hollister said, setting the wooden plaque down. "Everything in this whole world is so . . . so linked together," and he made interlocking circles out of his thumbs and index fingers. He wore a wedding band on his right hand, Perry noticed, for it was his left hand that was missing the two middle fingers. Hollister Abrams turned and looked Perry directly in the eye. It lasted only a fraction of a second, but in that brief time Perry was convinced that he and this man could communicate on a level requiring very little verbalization. Just then the bell on the door clattered again, and two women and a little boy entered. Perry saw Hollister glance at them, then over at the woman crocheting behind the cash register. Her fingers never stopped, and her eyes never lifted.

"Go ahead," Perry urged. "I can look around by myself."

Hollister cupped one hand around his mouth and leaned closer. "Charlotte Dalby is a nice woman in her own way, but she's got it in her head that her only job is ringing up the sales." Perry smiled understandingly, and Hollister gripped his shoulder firmly. "I'll check back with you," he said. "Just save your questions." As he turned toward the other customers, Perry heard him say, "Feels good in here where it's warm and dry, doesn't it, ladies? Hi there, young man."

It was then that Perry saw the jelly cabinet Eldeen had talked so much about last night on the way to prayer meeting; it was sitting in the corner of "G.O.O.D. Country Carvin'" next to a little wooden wheeled contraption identified as a "doll stroller" on its price tag. It had to be the one since there didn't appear to be anything else like it. Checking the price tag, Perry was sure this was it. "$95 jelly cabinet," it read, and on the other side "Oliver Peake." Perry examined it closely. Not exactly Ethan Allen, but a highly commendable job, especially considering what he'd heard Eldeen say about Oliver Peake and his weak nerves. "Somedays he says he shakes so bad he can't even button his clothes," she had said last night.

"Oliver said his wife helped him with it some," she had said. "Fact is, Neville Greer says he wouldn't be surprised if Oliver's wife didn't do the *whole thing* by herself 'cause he heard Oliver's next-door neighbor—that woman named Pauletta who makes all them different little animals out of old spark plugs—say she sees LaVerne Peake trottin' back and forth all day long between the house and the wood shop they got in their garage but she hardly ever sees Oliver step outside of the house. But it sure doesn't make a lick of difference to *me* who made it—but I think it's real sweet of LaVerne if that's true to let Oliver take all the credit for it. I'll swanee if it's not the most . . ." She drew her thick eyebrows together as she cast about for the right word, as if visualizing the columns of words in her vocabulary book. ". . . the most *meritorious* cabinet I ever did see!" she finished, smiling triumphantly.

She had gone on then to describe it in great detail, and as they pulled into the church parking lot, she had said, "When Oliver and his son brought it in and set it down, I thought my eyes was playing tricks on me 'cause I looked at it and just all of a sudden saw as clear as day every one of Jewel's jars of blueberry jam and apple jelly and applesauce and peach preserves setting on them shelves in straight rows, with all the different colors just sparkling like glass. I rubbed my eyes, I'll tell you what, and wondered if that was what folks meant when they talked about having a vision. But then I looked again—and them shelves was plum' empty."

All four of them had gotten out of the car and walked across the parking lot of the church in silence. As they started up the front steps, Eldeen said, "Yes sir, if I had me a hundred dollars, I'd buy that jelly cabinet in a minute! What a pretty sight it would be settin' in our kitchen filled up with all Jewel's hard work." She beamed at the thought of it.

"You always help me, Mama," Jewel said, smiling. "It's not just *my* hard work."

Eldeen snorted and dismissed Jewel's remark. "Oh, piffle. What I do is just child's play next to what you do."

"Well, stop thinking about that cabinet," Jewel said. "There's lots more things we could use worse than that."

"Well, it sure would give me pleasure," Eldeen had said, sighing. "But then, I can think of other things that would make me gladder." They were at the front door by that time, and as Perry held it open, Eldeen passed through, casting him an inscrutable look. Her countenance had darkened, hiding her smile, like a cloud concealing the sun.

As Eldeen had left the auditorium later, on her way to the Peewee Powwow meeting, she had said aloud, "I have a unspoken prayer request I'd be obliged for all of you to remember during prayer time tonight."

And, Perry recalled now, every single person who had stood to lead in prayer that night had faithfully requested a favorable and timely answer to Eldeen's "unspoken."

As he ran his fingers over the smooth wood and tested the little door latch, Perry heard Hollister Abrams behind him. "Now that's a fine piece of workmanship there. You got you a real eye for quality."

"I'd like to buy it," Perry said, turning around.

Hollister's little eyes glistened. "Just like that? You already made up your mind?" Again he grasped Perry's shoulder. "Son, I like you!" He threw his head back and laughed. It was at that very moment, warmed by Hollister's sunny laugh, that Perry realized this man would be about the age of his own father had he lived. What would it have been like, he wondered, to grow up with a man like Hollister Abrams as his father? What kind of man would he himself be today if he had heard those words over and over as a child, a teenager, an adult—"Son, I like you"? What would it have been like to live in a house of laughter, a house where pats on the shoulder were an everyday occurrence, where people looked into each other's eyes?

"I can't take it now, though," Perry said. "Can you put a 'Sold' tag on it and trust me to come back tomorrow? I'll pay for it today, but I need to borrow a bigger car to get it home."

"No problem, no problem at all," said Hollister. His smile suddenly faded and he stroked his chin with the hand that was missing two fingers. "I just thought of somebody who's going to be mighty disappointed to see this cabinet sold, though." Perry said nothing, and Hollister clucked his tongue regretfully. "She's been telling everybody here at the store for weeks that she's praying for a miracle so she can buy it for her daughter."

"Well, I don't hold much stock in miracles," Perry said.

Hollister cocked his head and once again looked full into Perry's face. His eyes had lost their twinkle; they looked almost fierce. "Son, when you've lived as long as I have and found yourself staring eyeball to eyeball at a Japanese soldier whose main goal was to blow your remains off the face of the earth and you end up telling about it fifty years later—well, then you don't have any trouble at all believing in miracles. It would be as easy as wiggling your nose for the Lord to work it out so that this lady I know could get this cabinet instead of you—if he had a mind to."

Perry stared at Hollister in disbelief. He'd never seen this man at the Church of the Open Door. These Christians seemed to be climbing out of the woodwork lately. Just last week he had been approached in the parking lot of Thrifty-Mart by a young man he'd never seen, who asked Perry if he would read a tract and think about what it said. Did Hollister really hold to all that stuff Brother Hawthorne kept referring to as the "fundamentals of the faith"? Did he believe in all that metaphysical speculation about the Trinity and the Virgin Birth and the Resurrection? In the few minutes since he had entered the G.O.O.D. Country Store, Perry was convinced that Hollister Abrams was the kind of man who would latch onto something and not let go, but could it really be that he was a Christian—a "sold-out believer," as Eldeen liked to put it? Or was he maybe just on the fringes—somebody who liked to talk about the all-present spirit of divinity in humankind? Somebody who liked the security of considering himself "religious" and talked about "the Lord" as if he were a philanthropic old uncle but who really didn't carry it as far as the folks at the Church of the Open Door?

Hollister's eyes softened and he smiled. "Sorry, that's one of my pet subjects. They've told us not to preach to people on the job, though, so I'll shut my mouth."

"No, please, I'd like to ask you something," said Perry, glancing around the store. The two women were looking at a lamp made out of what looked like an old blowtorch, and the little boy was playing with a beanbag game. "Let's just say," said Perry, "that I wanted to buy this cabinet to give to this same woman you're talking about—let's say her name was something different, like . . . oh, how about *Eldeen?*" Hollister raised his scraggly eyebrows. "Let's say I'd heard her going on and on about it," Perry continued, "and I decided I'd like to buy it for her. So I come down here and spend my own money for it because I want to make her happy. I got the money in the normal way, by working for it. It didn't drop down out of the sky with a note attached that said 'From God, for purchase of jelly cabinet for Eldeen.' So I buy the cabinet and then take it to her house and surprise her with it for Christmas. Now here's my question. Is *that* a miracle?"

Without a second of hesitation, Hollister boldly answered, "Yes."

"How?" asked Perry.

Hollister pointed at Perry. "God is using *you* as his instrument. Let me ask you something, son. Is Eldeen a relative of yours?"

"No." Perry shook his head.

"Well, it wouldn't change a thing if she was, but anyway, is she an old friend of the family maybe?"

"No." What was the man getting at?

"That doesn't matter either, but it makes it better this way. Are you in her debt for some reason? Do you owe her some kind of favor for something she did for you?"

"Well, no, I wouldn't say that."

"So is this something you do a lot of—buying jelly cabinets for old ladies?" Hollister seemed to be standing closer than before, although Perry hadn't noticed him taking a step forward. Perry started to see where this was headed and knew there was no way to avert it. "No," he said. Somehow his interest in arguing the point had dissolved.

"So how do you explain what you're doing, son?" Hollister asked gently. "Don't you see? God has put it in your heart to do this nice thing, and that's as much a miracle in my book as if he reached down from heaven and picked it up and plunked it down in Eldeen's house."

Perry nodded. "I thought that's what you'd say."

"Well, it's the truth," Hollister said. "You think about it and your heart will tell you it's the absolute truth."

The rain had grown heavier and was drumming on the roof. Perry looked out the window. Cars crawled by on Lambert Street, their headlights glowing weakly.

"I'll go get a tag to let people know it's already sold," said Hollister. "I'll be right back."

Perry moved over to the "G.O.O.D. Country Stitchin'" section. He walked slowly, taking note of everything from quilts, wooden backgammon boards, pot holders, and dish towels to embroidered handkerchiefs, puppets, aprons, and little crocheted dolls that served as toilet tissue covers. On a small table next to a rack of little girls' smocked dresses were displayed sets of pillowcases. He picked up a set stitched with green lambs on a mustard gold hillside. There were two more sets like it, one with gray lambs and the other with navy blue. Compared to the stitching on the other sets of pillowcases, Eldeen's wasn't nearly as skilled; even Perry could tell that. But hers had an appeal he couldn't think of words to express. They reminded him of Dinah's description of a little girl they'd seen in a restaurant once. "She's so ugly she's cute," she had said, and it was true.

"I bet I know what you're thinking," Hollister said, coming up to stand beside him again.

"What?" said Perry.

"Well, it's like this," said Hollister, picking up another set neatly and beautifully embroidered with trellised roses. He held them out at arm's length, then looked back and forth from the lambs to the roses. "Somebody fancy and stuffy without much imagination would pick this one," he said, nodding toward the roses, "but anybody that likes little kids and balloons and crayons and Ritz crackers and buttermilk and comfortable old shoes would pick Eldeen's."

Perry smiled and looked up at Hollister briefly. "Do you have any children?" he asked.

"A boy and a girl," Hollister said, his gold tooth gleaming. "And five grandkids." Perry imagined him at one time leading his children to a park swing, holding their small hands in his. What would it matter to a son if his father's hand had only three fingers—if that hand belonged to a man like Hollister?

"I think I'll buy all three pairs," Perry said, reaching for the other two sets of Eldeen's pillowcases. Good grief, he needed to get out of this place before he turned maudlin. If he didn't watch it, he'd be brushing tears out of his eyes and calling Hollister Abrams "Dad."

"Eldeen's are all cotton, you know," said Hollister. "Most of the others are only part cotton."

"I know," said Perry. "I've got one set already but can always use more." Maybe he'd even send a set to Dinah someday. He turned toward the cash register, then lowering his voice, he addressed Hollister again. "I'd rather not . . . you know . . ."

"I understand perfectly," Hollister said. "I won't say a word to anybody. It wouldn't do for the surprise to get spoiled."

As Perry approached the cash register, Charlotte Dalby rose from her chair and set her crocheting down. "Eldeen sure will be sorry her chest got sold," she said sorrowfully to Hollister, who was removing the tags from the pillowcases. Perry reached into his back pocket and pulled out his wallet. "Why, look at this," said Charlotte. "Isn't that a funny thing? He's buying the chest Eldeen wanted so bad *and* three sets of her pillowslips too. She'll be glad for the one but sure not for the other."

Hollister winked at Perry. "Well, that's the way it goes," he said. "First come, first serve." Perry counted out seven twenty-dollar bills. Charlotte took the money and slowly recounted it, turning all the bills to face the same direction.

On the wall next to the cash register, Perry saw a large, gaudy framed picture of a parrot. As he looked closer, he saw that it was actually a collage made of various colors of styrofoam pieces.

Hollister chuckled. "That ranks right up there with bullfighters painted on black velvet, doesn't it?" An eerie feeling crept over Perry. Hadn't the exact thought been in the process of forming in his own mind? Or was it only that Hollister's comment had once again struck a responsive chord?

Charlotte looked at Hollister quizzically. "What are you talking about, bullfighters and black velvet?" she said. Perry held out his hand, and she began counting out his change.

"Oh, nothing," Hollister said cheerfully, picking up the sack of pillowcases. "Sometimes I say things that don't make the least bit of sense." He walked with Perry over to the door and opened it. The bell jangled noisily. Handing him the sack, Hollister said, "Here, son, let me walk you out to your car," and he reached for a large striped umbrella beside the door.

Down the sidewalk they walked together under the big striped umbrella, "dry as toast," as Eldeen would say. Perry felt Hollister's warm hand resting lightly on his back.

Chapter 38

I t was Eldeen's poem, which Perry ran across again on Friday morning, that was the catalyst for the most courageous act of his life. He knew it was the poem that started everything; he had no delusions afterward that he had thought up the idea on his own.

Actually, he had had the poem in his possession for several months, in a file folder labeled simply "Eldeen." The *Derby Daily* had sponsored a poetry contest for all the local readers back in the early spring, and Eldeen had entered without telling anyone, a fact that Perry still found remarkable. When the newspaper published the winning poems in late March, there was Eldeen's at the top of the page printed in the boldest type with a big exploding star design beside it and the words "First Place" stamped across the top.

Jewel had brought it over to him late that afternoon, and after she left Perry had gone out and bought a paper, clipped out the poem, and filed it away in a new folder. He had suspected even back in March that he would need a separate file folder for Eldeen. There had been a big to-do at church over Eldeen's poem, and, curiously, it was the surprise element of the whole thing that seemed to please Eldeen most. Over and over she had clapped her hands and chortled gleefully: "I sure pulled a big surprise on folks!" She accepted the church people's praise graciously, but always it came back to "Weren't they all surprised, though!"

But the amazing thing was that Perry had forgotten all about the poem until he ran across it on the Friday morning before Christmas. Well, perhaps it wasn't so amazing after all, considering the overwhelming barrage of new experiences he had been stumbling through since March. March—wasn't that a decade ago? Besides, he had added so many other pages of hastily scribbled notes to the folder that the poem stayed buried in the back, and when he had started working last week on the sketch of Eldeen for his book, he had found himself in a daze, shuffling among scraps of paper, pages torn from his Daytimer, the audiotape, and random thoughts that kept springing to mind as his fingers searched the keyboard for ways to contain Eldeen on paper. He never even made it all the way through the folder. One day he had typed for three hours straight, then reread what he had written, and deleted every word. By Thursday afternoon he had begun to despair, realizing that he had already spent more time on the few pages about Eldeen than he had spent writing entire chapters. He couldn't even decide what name to give her; he had tried using several—Dorothy, Leona, Lucille, Iva—but none of them seemed right.

What does it really matter *how* you say it? he kept asking himself. Remember, there's hardly ever only one way to say something. Just put it down the way it comes out and let it go. But he found he couldn't; it had to be right. For some reason the part about Eldeen had to be *exactly* right. Okay, he told himself, you've used the word "simple" for the past ten months in describing these people and their religion. So how come it's so hard to write about somebody who's so simple?

Frustrated, he had gotten up from the computer late Thursday afternoon, put on his jacket, and stepped outside for a walk. The rain had finally stopped around two o'clock, and the sky had cleared to a weak, pastel blue as if the color had been washed out. Brown oak leaves clung wetly to the pavement. If he had believed in signs and wonders, he may have been tempted to assign an interpretation to the cloud he saw directly over the DePalmas' rooftop as he stood in his front yard. The cloud was gigantic, and the irregular scallop of its contour was brilliantly outlined with a bold ribbon of phosphorescent silver. For a split second Perry stood awestruck before he realized that this was no atmospheric phenomenon, but simply the common result of the sun going behind a cloud. The brightness had to go somewhere, so it oozed its way out around the edges.

But although he had reduced it to an ordinary, explainable fact, the sight must have in some way unsettled his mental balance, for it was directly after this that he had actually spoken a silent prayer. It wasn't long, and it certainly wasn't premeditated, but he was keenly aware of the words echoing through his mind: *Please help me finish this chapter right.* He continued walking along the curb, slowly, but his thoughts were racing. Had he really uttered that prayer? Why? And to whom? Did he believe that there really was a God on full-time duty who truly cared about him? Or was it an accident, a type of involuntary mimicry of what he had observed among the church people all these months?

Maybe he had been thinking so much *about* Eldeen that he had thought *like* her for just a moment. Or maybe it was simply an act of desperation—nothing else had worked, so why not give prayer a shot? But, of course, God didn't attend to the prayers of unbelievers, did he? That is, unless they were asking for salvation, praying the "sinner's prayer," as Eldeen called it.

Was it just another coincidence, then, that by the time he had walked halfway down Lily Lane, the perfect first sentence for the section about Eldeen had formed in his mind? The name fell into his mind, too, as if it were a piece of ripe fruit: Raynelle. The thoughts came easily after that, and as he repeated them to himself, they unrolled as from a smooth, seamless bolt. He found a Bic pen in his jacket pocket but nothing to write key words on. That was why, during the next two hours, anyone looking out his window as the sun slipped beneath the silver-rimmed cloud and the afternoon shadows deepened into dusk might have seen a tall man slowly walking along the streets of Montroyal, pausing from time to time to look up at the sky, and then bending his head again to write on . . . what appeared to be the palm of his hand.

He walked for almost two hours, up and down streets all over Montroyal, even circling the same blocks several times, before finally turning back toward home. He realized that anyone watching would have reason to regard him with suspicion, and if a policeman had pulled up at the end of the two hours and asked him what he was doing, he would no doubt have reported Perry as extremely neurotic, bordering on psychotic. He could well imagine the officer's stony face and narrowed eyes as he listened to Perry's answer: "I'm writing the final pages of my last chapter! See, I've got the outline here on my hand!"

It was almost seven o'clock by the time he got home. When he saw Hormel's dark shape beside Jewel's fence and heard him crunching pellets of dry dog food, Perry realized that he was craving food himself, and a sudden strong desire for meat seized him. Not a hot dog or hamburger, but a real piece of meat. A whole plateful of food, in fact—meat and vegetables and salad and bread. The light in Jewel's kitchen was on, and he could see the shadow of someone standing by the sink. They would have finished supper by now; he felt a twisting sensation in his stomach as he thought of what Jewel might have cooked. As he stepped inside his own house and turned on the light, he spread open his left palm and stared at it. The ideas weren't going anywhere; he might as well take time to eat. He would need plenty of energy for the long night ahead.

The man who answered the telephone at the Purple Calliope seemed to think there was nothing unusual about someone calling for a steak dinner to go. Thirty minutes later Perry was standing beside the cash register inside the restaurant holding a large, warm Styrofoam platter with a lid, and thirty minutes after that he had already eaten most of the steak, all of the baked potato, and was starting on the steamed broccoli and carrots. He couldn't remember eating a meal like this in a long time. Jewel never fixed steak, and it wasn't on the menu at Hardee's.

By eight-thirty he was at the computer. He had finished with Eldeen by eleven-thirty and got up to make a pot of coffee while the last chapter was printing. At twelve o'clock he sat down at the kitchen table, the manuscript for his entire book stacked before him, and began reading from page one, placing each page face down in a new pile as he finished. Occasionally he penciled in a change, but for the most part he read straight through. He had read each section as a unit, of course, before sending the chapters to Cal, but this was the first reading of the whole manuscript from beginning to end. As he read now, he recalled how gratified he had always felt in his earlier projects—even the children's novels—to take that final journey through the completed pages, to read a favorite passage and marvel for just an instant that he had really written it, to feel the swift twinge of joy—like the satisfying click of a full change purse—when he came to the last paragraph.

The sun was just coming up when he laid the last page upside down on the stack and pushed his chair back. From where he sat, in the doorway, he could see the pale glow of sunrise through the window over the kitchen sink; then, turning to the living room windows, with their blinds still open, he could see the shade of night in the west. Here it was again—another dividing line: day on one side, night on the other.

A question and an answer from Blake's *Vision of the Last Judgment* came to him out of nowhere: "'When the sun rises, do you not see a round disk of fire somewhat like a Guinea?' O no, no, I see an Innumerable company of the Heavenly host crying, 'Holy, Holy, Holy is the Lord God Almighty.'" Perry remembered how infatuated he had been with William Blake for a few months in college, how drawn to the poet's mysticism, how consumed with the yearning to sit in the company of the esoteric coterie of Blakean scholars. Knowing so little about the Bible, however, he had understood few of the allusions and had soon wearied of Blake's artistic flamboyance. It occurred to him now that if he were to read the quotation today for the first time, he would make all the right associations, including the seraphic praise in Isaiah 6 and the declaration of God's glory through nature in Psalm 19.

Perry closed his eyes. He had been alert, running on nervous energy, until now; suddenly he wondered if he could even make it back to the bed. On his way past the spare room, he saw that the green light of the printer was still on, so he walked in to turn it off. As he turned around, he bumped against the edge of the file folder labeled "Eldeen," which lay open beside the computer, and all the scraps of paper floated to the floor.

That was when he saw the poem. It landed six inches from his feet and even whirled around at the last minute so that it was turned in the right direction for him to look down and begin reading. Across the top he saw the words he had written: *$50 prize—used for car tax and license renewal.* He remembered now how Eldeen had told everybody that God had sent the prize money at just the right time because Jewel thought she was going to have to make a withdrawal from their savings account; together, the tax and renewal fee came to $49.79—another one of those occurrences of happenstance these people were famous for, which they called "answers to prayers." But he had had his own brush with answered prayer, or at least a semblance of it, on his walk around the neighborhood yesterday—and now coming across this poem. Did it mean anything? Was there more to it than just an accident?

He stooped, picked up the poem, and read it.

Streams of Joy and Peace
by Eldeen Rafferty

There used to be an apple tree o'er yonder by my wall,
Its big round fruit dropped right down at my feet!
It bloomed so nice in spring and gave me apples in the fall,
But I was just so careless of my treats,
I never did say thank you—oh such a simple deed!
Until one day a bad disease crept in,
That bad disease it killed the flowers, then it hurt the seeds!
I loved that tree and missed it so much then!

I used to have a deep, deep well, my, my, how cool and pure!
I always filled my bucket every day,
And was that water sweet and did it taste good? That's for sure!
But oh, alas, my thanks I ne'er did say.
And so one day when I went out and lowered down that rope,
I cried out, "There's no water anymore!"
I tried again, but it was dry, bone dry, alas, no hope!
I should have told my gratitude before!

I used to have a special friend, I thought he'd live so long,
But I forgot that life was just a puff!
I didn't make amends for lots of things when I was wrong,
And didn't say "I love you" near enough!
We went about our busy ways and thought we had good health,
But one day Mr. Death he snatched my mate,
And oh, what good is fancy houses, cars, and lots of wealth?
For once a soul is lost, then it's too late!

So open up your mouth and say those things—now go on, start!
Like Thank You and I'm Sorry and the rest.
And don't you dare forget the one that softens any heart,
Please say I Love You—that's the very best!
Don't let your tongue be lazy, please just stand up now and speak!
And if you do, your love will grow and grow!
So all you have to do to find the Light of Love is seek,
And streams of Joy and Peace will flow and flow!

Perry remembered now that Eldeen had said the contest rules had prohibited religious poems, and it interested him to see that she had complied to an extent. He realized as he read it a second time that something about the poem touched him deeply, though he knew if he were to critique it as a work of art, it would fall miserably short. He smiled over its excitable tone—the schoolgirlish fondness for exclamation points, the archaic ohs and alases, the feverish didacticism. There was so much to criticize if he were to analyze it as *poetry*—the triteness, the redundancies, the ill-chosen words like "puff" and "o'er yonder" and "bad disease," the subject-verb agreement error, the shift of person, the relentless strumming of the meter. Truly, if this was the winning poem, Perry wondered what the other submissions had been like.

Even as he noted the flaws, however, he leapt to Eldeen's defense; anyone who could instinctively manipulate rhythm and rhyme so *regularly* could surely learn the artistry of variation and substitution. Remember, he told himself, this was written by a woman who was forced to quit school at the age of twelve.

He read the poem a third time; there was something around the edges of his consciousness trying to get through. It was more than just feeling sorry for a kind old woman whose opportunities for formal schooling as a child had been turned off like a faucet, whose affection for himself had both surprised and warmed him. It was more than just the memory of her delight over surprising everyone and winning the fifty dollars. It was something in the poem itself.

And then it came to him. First of all, Eldeen had created a persona, though she probably wouldn't have known what to call it. Perry knew the "I" in the first three stanzas wasn't Eldeen herself. If she had ever had an apple tree or well, he was certain she would have effervesced with thankfulness, and to any special friend she had failed to appreciate she would have offered prompt and profuse apologies. But the average person reading the newspaper wouldn't know that about her, and it moved Perry to think that Eldeen would put herself forward so unflatteringly, as a tight-lipped ingrate.

He thought about the interview of Eldeen that he had recorded on two cassette tapes; he had had to stop her after an hour and insert a second tape, which she had also filled up. The interview was a virtual paean to God's goodness to her since she had been a baby; every memory she brought forth was steeped with gratitude. Even quitting school—as she had put it, "It just made me feel so *chosen* to know that I could help out my family by working that way, because I sure knew—I mean I *sure knew* my mama and daddy was working their fingers to the bone to provide for me and Arko and Klim and baby Nori." They had felt bad, she said, about asking her to go live with her Uncle Marshall, whose wife had just died, and take care of a brood of young cousins, two of them little twin newborns, but Uncle Marshall had offered to pay her, and, in her words, "I saw it as a real compliment that they'd ask me to accept a responsibility like that." About growing up poor, she said, "Now I wouldn't of wanted it any other way. It teaches you so much about life! Why, my favorite toy as a little girl was a little cardboard box my mama gave me. I fixed up little scenes inside it with paper and sticks and leftover this-and-that and just had me the biggest time with that cardboard play-pretty!"

About her first husband's death of a horrible, lingering cancer, it was "Malcolm was out of his head before it was over, but I counted it a privilege to be able to nurse him at home and see the blessed peace on his poor face when he finally breathed his last breath and entered the gates of heaven." She had been thirty years old and childless. "My, how I did want me a baby!" she had said. "I wanted one the whole twelve years Malcolm and I were married, but something must of been wrong—I never could have one. Then after he died, I kept thinking about how a baby would of given me comfort. There my sister Nori was just married a little over a year by then, and she already had her a little baby, and she was the *sweetest* little thing—but a niece just doesn't match up with having one of your very own." But even about the baby, she had said, "But I knew God could hear my prayers, so I had to hang onto his promise to supply all my *needs,* and I had to realize that a baby must not of been something I really needed right then."

Her first husband had been gone for almost thirteen years when she had met Hiram Rafferty, a widower with a little girl. "Oh, I just thought I was in heaven!" she had declared. "Here was a man who wanted me to marry him—and he had the most precious little blue-eyed angel of a child you ever seen in your whole life!"

Perry remembered how emotional she had become telling about this part of her life; she hadn't even tried to stop and get her weeping under control but had kept right on talking, her face crinkled into its peculiar mask of anguished joy in spite of the tears, her throaty voice trembling. "So, see, God gave me my own child in his own time, and I've never stopped thanking him for a minute! If I had of already had a baby, then Jewel might not of been quite so special, and God knew all that. 'Course, I was in my forties by then, so I knew I probably wouldn't ever be having any babies—but Jewel couldn't of been anymore like my own flesh and blood than if I'd carried her around here inside of me!" She had patted her stomach, then laid both her large hands on her face and wiped away the tears. Perry could clearly recall what she did next; looking up at the ceiling, she had said aloud, "Thank you, dear loving Father, for sending me Hiram—and little Jewel!" Looking back at Perry, she had leaned forward and pointed upward. "And later on he gave me a grandson besides!"

Not once had she grumbled. About Hiram's sudden death from a heart attack at the age of sixty, she had said, "But praise the Lord he didn't have to suffer! He was gone in a flash, the doctor said. Just think, being here one minute and then being in heaven just like that," and she had snapped her fingers. About Bailey's mysterious drowning, she had thought a moment, her eyes sunken deep beneath the dark hood of her eyebrows, then said, "Now that was a real hard time. It's been a heartache to see Joe Leonard without a daddy and poor Jewel so tore up, but"—and then her face had brightened—"but, oh, just see what God's done in bringing Willard along! Joe Leonard's going to have him a new daddy, and Jewel's happy again like I've not seen her since Bailey died. It just proves it's true! 'Weeping may endure for a night, but joy cometh in the morning'!" The whole interview, both tapes front and back, was like that. "Oh, God's given me a *good, good* life," she had concluded at the end. "He has just poured down blessings on me above all that I could ever ask or think!"

Perry was still standing in the spare room, still holding the poem, staring past it. How long he had been there he couldn't have said. His eyes fell again on the poem; he looked at the organization of the stanzas. The first one dealt with food; hadn't he heard apples called "the perfect food"? The second stanza was about water, the consummate sustainer of life. The third was about another essential of life: love. By placing love last, before the final moralizing stanza, Eldeen had pointed it up as most important. Had she done all that intentionally? Did she know about climactic ordering in effective argumentation?

He walked slowly from the spare room into his bedroom, rereading the poem once more. Behind his eyes a dull, heavy ache pounded. He lay down on the bed fully clothed and held the poem above him; the lines blurred together, then curled themselves into black circles that spun tighter and tighter.

When Perry woke up, it was a few minutes after three o'clock. It took him a moment to figure out why the sun was streaming through the window at three o'clock; then he remembered. It was three o'clock in the afternoon—and it was Christmas Eve. As he sat up and placed his feet on the floor, he knew exactly what he must do. What were people going to say if he tried to explain it? "It came to me in a dream" sounded like something a weirdo from the lunatic fringe would say. But he couldn't stop now to think about what people were going to say.

The poem had fallen to the floor, and he picked it up again. It was all so simple. Eldeen had written this poem for a local contest, but it might as well have been addressed directly to Perry. He was beyond defending himself; he knew he hadn't shown a minute's worth of gratitude during his entire life. And whereas before he would have vehemently argued that he had scarcely had cause to express gratitude, now he knew better. And "I'm sorry" and "I love you"—how often had he said those words—*said,* not *thought?* The verse from the book of Daniel came to him: "Thou art weighed in the balances, and art found wanting." He had been touched by poetry before, but never like this, and never ever by such a clumsily crafted poem. It was almost embarrassing to think that he was finally being propelled into action by something like this—a hokey little ditty written by an old woman.

He wondered now, as he swung his suitcase onto the bed and unlatched it, whether he would be doing this had the poem been written by someone he'd never heard of and he'd run across it in, say, a magazine. He'd have to think about that later, after he was on the road.

As he hurried around the room yanking open drawers and tossing clothes into the suitcause he counted the hours. Fifteen—that's about what it would take to drive straight through from Derby to Rockford.

If he got away by four o'clock, that would be three o'clock in Rockford. So he should get there by six o'clock. Was that right? He ran through it again. Yes—he should be there by sunrise on Christmas Day.

He set his Bible on top of his clothes in the suitcase and went into the bathroom to pack his shaving kit. A picture flashed through his mind a few minutes later as he strode down the cramped hallway and set his suitcase beside the front door. He saw himself on a strong, nimble horse, bending into the wind as it galloped toward the sun.

Chapter 39

When Perry thought about it later, the trip was one of those paradoxes of time, both fleeting and interminable. He arrived in Rockford long before he had worked out a proper stage entrance, though early during the course of the eleven hundred miles he had considered and discarded dozens of ideas—poses to strike, witty dialogue to toss off, meaningful gestures to convey attitude—and had developed a variety of scenarios in his mind to prepare himself for the many ways Dinah might respond upon first sight of him. In another sense, however, the miles seemed to creep by; with every road sign, he was disappointed that he still had so far to go.

Somewhere past Asheville, after an extended period of imagining an especially bleak chain of events upon his arrival in Rockford, Perry made up his mind to stop worrying and think about something else. He hit upon the idea of looking at the past ten months retrospectively, reviewing his life in Derby from every angle, trying to recall details of every incident. Happily, as he drove through the Smoky Mountains, he realized he had a wealth of memories from Derby to draw on; he was well stocked for the whole trip.

For a time thereafter the trip took on a two-tiered aspect. On the one level he was a man in a Toyota on a simple mission—driving home for Christmas. It was on this level that he took note of the red needle on his fuel indicator, the exit ramps, mileage signs, billboards. It was on this level that he was aware of the lights of the cities, the deserted parking lots of malls at the edges of towns, the darkened windows of houses as the night wore on, the relief of finding a truck plaza open on Christmas Eve and the sense of wonder that it was, another "Open" sign at a Waffle House farther on. He saw the winking of Christmas lights around cities, a little girl asleep on a pile of blankets in the back of a station wagon, a highway patrol car pulled up behind a stranded minivan on the emergency lane.

Nor were his concerns on this level purely objective; certain sights activated his imagination from time to time. He wondered if the car with the Oregon license plate really was headed for Oregon and where it had been; he tried to imagine why the driver, a middle-aged woman wearing glasses, was so far from home. He mused briefly about a farmhouse he saw, with a single light burning downstairs. Were parents still working frantically inside, trying to put together a dollhouse or a train set? How did the attendant at the truck plaza get stuck with the Christmas Eve shift? Perry wondered if the man had a wife who was fuming over being at home alone.

While conscious of these details of his trip, on another level he was walking through a book—not the book he had written, but a colorfully illustrated picture book of his months in Derby. At first he tried to start back in February and progress sequentially, but he soon ran into difficulty, for every earlier incident seemed to create a synapse to a later one, the memories moving as fast as nerve impulses, refusing the confines of chronological order. Was that all memories were anyway—nerve impulses zipping around inside the brain? Perry stopped to consider this a moment. Was there a lobe of the brain where "Memory" originated? He tried to remember the diagrams of brains in his old schoolbooks, the ones where little arrows pointed to sections labeled "speech center" and "motor skills"; he could remember terms—cerebellum, medulla, cerebrum, right brain functions, left brain functions—but he couldn't recall any teacher ever discussing how memory worked. Why did some people, even highly intelligent people, forget things almost instantly, while others, like Perry, hung onto the most trivial details, often things they didn't even realize they had noticed the first time, much less stored away to retrieve and rehash years later? Did these people have some kind of abnormally enlarged pouch somewhere in their brains? Yet these same people so often seemed to overlook the big, important principles of life.

Perry tried once again to put the events of February in order, but almost immediately found his memory hurtling forward to July, to an incident from the closing program of Daily Vacation Bible School, during which the visiting organizer—an authentic Australian who called himself "Wally B."—led the children in a song about a little lost "jumbuck" who wandered from the herd. The jumbuck, of course, came to symbolize a wandering sinner as the song progressed. Between the verses of the song, Little Levi Hawthorne had crawled around the platform on all fours, dressed in a woolly lamb costume, bleating pitifully. Wally B. had adopted as the theme for DVBS something he called "Boomerang Behavior," which emphasized the principle of "getting back what you give out." Perry remembered the frightening sound of all those light, childish voices joined in perfect unison as they recited, almost shouted, together the Vacation Bible School Verse of the Week: "Be not deceived; God is not mocked: for whatsoever a man soweth, that shall he also reap!"

After another failure at arranging in order the events of his first month in Derby, Perry stopped trying and reminded himself of the different ways there were to enjoy a picture book—in fact, of the way he used to modify picture books as a child, once the novelty of the story had worn off. He remembered the time as a little boy when he had shown Beth his trick of opening the book anywhere and starting a brand-new story from the picture, then flipping to another page and extemporizing the next part of the story. Beth had been horrified. She had fixed him with an indignant glare and plugged her ears. "That's *not* the right story!" she had shouted, and he had protested, "No, it's a *new* one." And Beth had gone to tell their mother, who said she had a headache and they were making too much noise. Perry thought she may have even taken the book away and put it on a high shelf.

But anyway, somewhere during adulthood, he realized now, he had almost forgotten that you didn't have to proceed through the pages of a book in order; you could skip around. Or even do like Dinah used to do; she always looked through magazines from back to front. After this, he allowed his mind to wander around Derby, sauntering from memory to memory, disregarding chronology. He felt as if the time started going faster after this, though each time he checked his watch he couldn't believe such a few short minutes had passed; he even wondered at one point if maybe the battery of his watch was weakening, but the radio confirmed the time.

Occasionally, things he saw along the interstate began triggering memories about Derby so that gradually the two levels of his thinking merged into one. Near Knoxville when he passed a sleek Thunderbird, for example, with a tiny pair of baby shoes dangling from the rearview mirror, he thought at once of the pair of cheap fuzzy dice he had received at the White Elephant gift exchange the previous Sunday night. Everybody had roared with laughter, and Phil Spivey had shouted, "I used to have a pair of them in my red fifty-seven Chevy!"

Eldeen had gone into convulsions of laughter when she opened her White Elephant gift—a book entitled *Nickel Savvy*. The subtitle was *All You Want to Know about the 300,000 Uses of Nickel*. "Three hundred thousand!" she had said. "My stars, I didn't know there was but one!" After she had quit laughing, though, she spent a good while looking through the book, and on the way home from church she had talked at length about nickel's resistance to corrosion and its usefulness in electroplating, a process she tried to explain until Jewel said, "That doesn't make sense, Mama. I'm afraid you lost me."

Jewel's gift had been a coffee mug bearing a picture of a dark-skinned native with a huge disk in his lower lip and the caption "Keep a stiff upper lip." Eldeen had looked up from her *Nickel Savvy* book and laughed along with everyone else, but then sobered and said, "You know, there's really lots of folks in the world who *do* look like that, sad to say—I've seen pictures in magazines of the awfulest things stuck in their noses and ears, stretching them all out of shape ever' which-a-way, and their bodies all painted up wild and scars all over from their wicked, pagan knives." She closed her eyes and shook her head. "And you just *know* most of 'em's never heard the first word about Jesus. Not the first word."

Joe Leonard's White Elephant gift had been a tiny mirror with a little battery that played "Oh, You Beautiful Doll" whenever someone picked it up by its handle. Willard had gotten a sickly green glow-in-the-dark rubber ghost. "That's from me!" Bernie Paulson had bellowed. "I got it on sale after Halloween!" Sid Puckett had gotten a tube of yellow "mood lipstick" that was supposed to change colors and adjust itself to your disposition once you put it on, and Trudy Gill had gotten what looked like a canister of potato chips that ejected a dozen or so wiggly rubber snakes when opened.

When Perry had realized that Sunday afternoon that he didn't have anything for the White Elephant exchange, he had walked through the house looking for something he could give. He had seen several items of Beth's that would meet the qualifications for the gift perfectly; according to the announcement in the bulletin, it was supposed to be "anything useless, tacky, outdated, and/or ridiculous." The lava lamp on a shelf in Beth's hall closet would have been great, as well as an old record album of a group called "Arabella and the Ding Dongs" or the plastic daisy clock on the kitchen wall. The ugly plaid couch would have worked too, except the bulletin had also stipulated that the gifts be small and "easily transportable." Just as Perry had been ready to wrap up a box of Band-Aids decorated with Disney characters, which he had mistakenly picked up instead of plain ones at the drugstore, he had thought of something.

He had walked into the living room and looked at the musical snowglobe on the small table beside the front door. It had been sitting there since February, and every Saturday Joe Leonard had faithfully dusted it off when he came to clean Perry's house. Perry picked it up and turned it upside down. The broken figure of the little boy floated up and swirled around amid the snowflakes. It landed on the housetop and slid off onto the ground beside the snowman. A person could make a game out of it, Perry thought. He turned it upside down again to see if he could get the figure to settle in the branches of the bare tree on one side of the house. It took a few tries, but he did it. Landing it in the tree could be five points, balancing it on the chimney of the house could be ten, and so forth.

As he stood there studying the small boy lying sideways in the tree, Perry realized he hadn't held the snowglobe for many months, and he marveled at his lack of feeling for this memento he had been so careful to confiscate when he left Rockford. What had happened? During his first few days in Derby back in February, he had been unable to look at the snowglobe without feeling a choking sensation. The few times he had made the mistake of turning it upside down, he had felt physically ill, as if someone had just flipped *him* upside down and shaken all his feelings about. Hearing the tune had been like a painful rehearsing of his failures. But somehow he knew that the snowglobe belonged to another era now, and he wasn't sure why. It wasn't as if anything had changed really; he was still the estranged husband, the absent father, the exile from home. When, he wondered, had the snowglobe ceased to claim his attention? Why did it no longer evoke the same responses? Was it simply because it was broken that he now felt what could only be described as a mild repugnance for it?

So two of the adjectives for the White Elephant gift clearly fit the snowglobe—*useless* and *outdated*. And even *ridiculous,* with the little figurine stuck in the tree. In the hall closet Perry found a box, quickly put the snowglobe inside, and used the Sunday comics for wrapping paper.

Libby Vanderhoff had been the one to end up with it. He recalled the confused look on her face as she had pulled it out of the cardboard box it was wrapped in. She had held it up at eye level and stared in awe. "Look, it's got a knob underneath," she had said to her husband, Earl. She had turned the knob, a hopeful crease in her brow, and everyone grew quiet as "Winter Wonderland" began playing.

"Who brought this?" Libby had asked, looking around the circle of happy faces.

"Isn't that yours, Perry?" Eldeen said loudly, and everyone turned to look at him. Perry felt his face grow warm as he nodded.

"But . . . but it's too *nice*," Libby Vanderhoff had said. "It still works and everything."

"It's broken," Perry said shortly. "There's a loose piece inside."

"You call that broken?" Earl Vanderhoff said. He took the snow-globe from his wife and peered inside, then turned it upside down and examined the wooden base. "I believe I might could fix that," he said. "It's gonna take some doing, but I got me some epoxy that'll hold anything." He ran his finger around the bottom of the glass globe. "The hard part's going to be getting inside there," he said. He scowled with concentration, biting down on his lower lip.

"Well, if anybody can do it, Earl can!" cried Eldeen. "Now me, I'd end up spilling all the water out and there'd go all them little sparkly snowflakes." Turning to Perry, she said, "Earl's the best handyman you ever did see! Once he fixed a cuckoo clock of Marvella's and it's worked ever since."

"All it needed was some oil," Earl said.

"Well, anyway, *I* couldn't of done it to save my life," Eldeen stated. "Mark my words, Perry, Earl's going to have that little feller fastened down inside of there before tomorrow's done! And then it'll be like new. I sure wish I had of said something the first time I ever saw it. I should of told you then about Earl's handy way of fixing things."

Perry shrugged. "Oh, it's all right," he said to Eldeen. "It's not really anything I'm attached to. In fact, I was looking for an excuse to get rid of it really."

Louise Farnsworth was holding the snowglobe now, admiring it volubly in her breathy voice. Grady Ferguson was telling Harvey Gill about one his daughter had brought back from Germany, and Vonda Snyder asked Louise to wind it up again so they could all hear the song. Perry heard Fern Tucker say, "I can't *believe* anybody would give that away!" and Nina Tillman said, "I wonder if he knows how much those cost in the stores."

Perry wished he had thought this through more carefully before-hand. "It's not the crown jewels, for Pete's sake," he wanted to say. Of course, if he had been told how the gift exchange worked, that they would all be sitting in a huge circle watching everyone open gifts one by one, he would certainly have brought the Disney Band-Aids instead. He might have known these people would make a big deal out of something like a musical snowglobe, even a broken one—or, maybe, *especially* a broken one. It would go right along with their obsession with broken hearts, broken spirits, broken wills, broken loaves, broken pitchers, broken walls of partition. "Broken Vessels"—hadn't that been the title of one of Brother Hawthorne's sermons a couple of months ago?

He felt a sudden tingle of panic. Although Perry thought it highly unlikely that Earl really could remove the base without breaking it, manage to keep the water and snow from sloshing out, glue down the broken figurine, then put it all back together, *what if he did?* Would such an act place some tacit demand on Perry—to repair his life, for instance, to pick up the broken pieces of his marriage, to figure out what he really did believe about God? On the one hand, he longed desperately to do exactly that, to pry his life apart and anchor things down, to oil it and make it run smoothly, then put it all back together again. But on the other hand, he feared that he never could; it was too big a job, and certainly not one he could do alone. He shot a glance at Brother Hawthorne, seated farther down the circle next to Edna, waiting his turn to open the bright red-foil gift in his lap. What did the pensive look on his face mean? Was he thinking right now of a way to use the broken snowglobe as a sermon illustration?

Stop reading meanings into everything, Perry told himself; that's what women do. And stop wrenching symbols out of everything; that's what preachers do. He took a deep breath and looked on around the circle. No one else seemed to be drawing any connection between the imperfect snowglobe and Perry's personal life. He relaxed and watched Louise Farnsworth pass the snowglobe down to Barb Chewning, who passed it on to Marjorie Eckles and then to Eldeen. Eldeen held it in her large palm and stroked the glass dome gently as if it were the bald head of an especially charming baby.

"My, my, my," she said, her deep voice tender and husky. "I'd forgot just how pretty it was." Then she turned her sunken eyes on Perry and said earnestly, "I *know* it can be fixed up."

Somewhere between Knoxville and Lexington, Perry turned on the radio again. "Santa Claus Is Coming to Town" was being sung by either a mature child or an immature adult, he couldn't tell which. Although he had heard the song every Christmas for as far back as he could remember, the words had never struck him as they did now. According to that song, Santa Claus wasn't really the nice guy he was cracked up to be. Watch your conduct, the song was saying, because Santa is spying on you; you'd better be good even when you're sleeping or else he'll cross you off his list.

What did that remind him of? It was something he'd heard not long ago. In a sermon maybe? Yes, of course, that was it. Brother Hawthorne had been talking about false perceptions of God, how some people see

God as a big snoop, lurking around corners, peering between the cracks in blinds, gleefully rubbing his hands together when he caught them doing something wrong, sadistically levying heavy punishments. "The God of the Bible isn't like that," Brother Hawthorne had said. "The desire of his great heart of love is to bless and reward us. True, he often allows us to suffer, but the God that I know from this book"—he had held up his Bible reverently—"is a wise and kind Shepherd; when the sheep of his pasture walk through dark valleys, he goes before them with his staff of love."

A small Honda Civic whizzed past Perry, its backseat and rear window crammed with gifts. He wondered if he would get to Rockford before Dinah and Troy opened their gifts; or maybe they already had. What if Dinah . . . but he stopped himself.

He thought of the gifts he had taken over to Jewel's before he left Derby. He had planned, of course, to present them on Christmas Day, but when he decided so suddenly to drive to Rockford, he had called and asked Joe Leonard to help him carry the jelly cabinet from his kitchen to Jewel's. When he came back a few minutes later with the other gifts, he had found Eldeen hunched over the cabinet, her face in her hands. She had looked up at Perry, her lined face distorted with joy, and had lumbered toward him with both arms outstretched. As she embraced him, he suddenly remembered how long it had been since he had felt a woman's arms around him. Eldeen was surprisingly strong but soft too, so that pressed against her Perry felt protectively cushioned. He felt her stiff gray hair brushing his cheek, smelled the faint odor of eucalyptus and talcum. He timidly raised his right arm and laid it lightly on her broad back. For several moments the only sound was her guttural crooning—"Mmm, mmm, mmm." Then at last she relaxed her embrace and held him at arm's length, gripping him with her large, solid hands. "You are a dear, precious boy," she said, and once again her forehead puckered, her eyebrows drew together, and a pained smile spread over her face.

Joe Leonard had grinned and blushed when he opened his present from Perry and found a dark green sweater, and Jewel had been delighted with her new metronome. She promised to give Willard his gift to open when he came over that night.

The last gift was in a small box. Perry had found it at the Hallmark store in the mall and had bought it several weeks ago. He handed it to Eldeen to open, and she exclaimed, "Oh, but you've done given me something, a *great big* something! I can't take this too!" But she had, and when she removed the lid from the small box, she gasped. "Oh, looka here, Jewel, it's a *suncatcher* to go with all our others! I'll be if it's not a little yellow *lighthouse!* If that's not the funniest thing. Think of it—a *lighthouse* for a suncatcher." She was laughing and talking at the same time. "What a twist-around *that* is. Why, normally a lighthouse does its business in the dark and then gets to rest up during the daytime. But this little feller's gonna just shine and shine all day, then take hisself a nap at nighttime. Somebody sure had a sense of humor to think this up!" She lifted it out and held it high. "If that's not just the prettiest thing—look at it when I hold it up to the light!"

Perry had told them then that he couldn't stay, that he had decided to drive to Rockford and that he needed to get on the road. For a moment all three of them had stared in surprise. Then Eldeen had hugged the suncatcher to her breast and said, "Oh, Perry, you just don't know how hard I've been praying for this. Your wife and little boy are going to have the best Christmas present ever!" Jewel had smiled warmly and said simply, "We'll pray for all of you." Joe Leonard had offered to help him load his car. Before he left, they had filled a brown paper bag with sandwiches and cookies for the trip, and a few minutes later Jewel, Eldeen, and Joe Leonard stood in their driveway waving as Perry backed out. "I'll be back in time for the wedding," he had called to them. "And for our birthdays too," he had called to Eldeen, who yelled back, "You got you a deal! This one'll be *eighty* for me, remember!" As he was ready to turn onto Lily Lane, he glanced back and saw the three of them framed inside the rear window, the sun a great golden sphere suspended above the treetops. Jewel and Joe Leonard stood shoulder to shoulder, but Eldeen had moved forward a few steps and was still waving good-bye, fluttering both hands at once.

Another song was playing on the radio now. It was "Jingle Bells," but Perry hadn't heard this version of it for years. It was a group of dogs barking the melody in different pitches. He thought of Hormel, of his alert little eyes and inquisitive nose, his vigilant ears and his aversion for strangers. He thought of the dachshund's stubby legs and his long, streamlined body, a physique perfectly suited to slipping through the small hole he had recently dug under the fence. He remembered Eldeen laughing over the phone call they'd gotten from Glenda Finch, asking if Hormel was missing. Glenda had seen him furiously digging at their neighbor's back fence, inside which lived a little female boxer. "Now if that wouldn't of been some kind of odd-looking puppies if Hormel had of gotten his way!" Eldeen had said, whooping with laughter. Joe Leonard had filled up the holes under both fences and had returned home with the thwarted but unabashed Hormel.

From Lexington to Indianapolis the memories continued to weave themselves through Perry's mind, smoothly sliding in and out, turning back on themselves, changing colors. He saw a billboard with a picture of a stately brick building advertising "Bennett's Mortuary—We Care for You in Your Time of Need." It dawned on Perry that the sedate brick building was really the only related object that could tastefully be pictured on such a billboard; it would be morbid to have large drawings of caskets, mourning wreaths, headstones, or even the face of a concerned funeral director gazing down at the freeway sympathetically. Perry suddenly remembered a comment of Cal's during his most recent phone call. "So, no funerals, huh? Those people must be a pretty healthy lot."

"None yet," Perry had replied. "A couple of relatives have died, but nobody around here." He felt a little guilty when he realized how disappointed both he and Cal were at the gap this was going to leave in his book.

The radio kept him going. It was amazing that in every song some detail looped a thread back to Derby, South Carolina. On his way to Indianapolis he thought about everything from the nesting dove in the Hawthornes' carport to Eldeen's brother Arko, who had ridden the bus from Arkansas to visit for four days at Thanksgiving. Arko had turned out to be a large, loose-jowled man with a deep, hollow, barking laugh; everything about him had reminded Perry of a walrus.

He thought of Chinese Checkers, surprise muffins, and the movie he had driven to Greenwood to see one lonely Friday night in August, the day before Troy's ninth birthday. "The summer's best story" it had been hailed. It had received thumbs up from Siskel and Ebert, in fact generous praise from both critics and the public in general, and Perry had been in dire need of a good story that weekend. He couldn't remember much about the plot, however, an understandable lapse considering he had left before the movie was half over. His sudden rising from his seat, stumbling past four people and stepping directly onto the toe of one of them—one of the women he was almost sure—had both surprised and puzzled him.

He remembered how hot it had been that August night, yet how blessedly cool it felt once he was out of the air-conditioned theater walking toward his car. He wasn't sure he could have explained to anyone why he left; he couldn't even explain it to himself, except that he had been troubled by the hard faces of all the women on the screen.

In one graphically steamy scene, he had been filled with something akin to loathing—but for what, he couldn't say. *Why?* he had asked himself. Any red-blooded man who had been living like a monk in an over-churched backwoods town like Derby should have welcomed a scene like that. But he recalled now that when the camera had moved in for a close-up of the woman's face a few minutes later, her full lips had parted and she had laughingly uttered a vile obscenity. She had been a beautiful, lusty brunette with deep dimples; maybe it was because her face, especially the dimples, had reminded him of Jewel's that he had leaped from his seat and pushed his way to the aisle.

As he had driven home from the theater that night, he had imagined the faces of women—Jewel's fair features, Eldeen's kind brow puckered with someone else's burden, Birdie Freeman's sweet plainness, Glenda Finch's radiant smile, Edna Hawthorne's rosy plumpness, Nina Tillman's gypsy-dark eyes, Barb Chewning's fresh, athletic glow. He saw Dinah also—beautiful in that wide, versatile way that some women have of looking childishly innocent one moment and gloriously sophisticated the next, but always with a heart wholesome and trustworthy and guileless. Women—the salvation of the world. If women fell, where was man's hope? He thought of the sad faces of Jewel and Eldeen if they ever found out he had been to such a movie tonight.

Between Indianapolis and Chicago, Perry happened upon a radio station playing traditional Christmas carols one right after the other. For several miles he thought about the recent Christmas program at the Church of the Open Door. Then suddenly "Thou Didst Leave Thy Throne" ended, and without any transition whatsoever, a man's deep voice began reading from the book of Isaiah. *"He is despised and rejected of men; a man of sorrows, and acquainted with grief . . ."* It was a resonant, expressive voice, artistic in its shadings of words, yet the thought occurred to Perry that the passage was inappropriate to the Christmas season. Had someone at the radio station made a mistake and punched the wrong button? *"Surely he hath borne our griefs, and carried our sorrows: yet we did esteem him stricken, smitten of God, and afflicted."* Why not a chapter from one of the Gospels, something pertaining to the birth of Jesus? *"But he was wounded for our trans-gressions, he was bruised for our iniquities: the chastisement of our peace was upon him, and with his stripes we are healed."*

The language was lovely, richly textured and mournfully evocative, but it didn't exactly foster the Christmas spirit. Surely any minute now someone at the station would notice the mistake and correct it. But the voice continued its grave intonation. Maybe the person at the control board had fallen asleep. Perry knew there couldn't be many other people listening to the radio at three o'clock on Christmas morning. The whole business would probably go unreported. *"All we like sheep have gone astray; we have turned every one to his own way; and the* LORD *hath laid on him the iniquity of us all."*

In the future Perry was to refer, privately, to the experience that followed as an epiphany, but at the moment he didn't think to put a label to it. All he knew was that by the time the reader had reached the final words several verses later—*"And he was numbered with the transgressors; and he bore the sin of many, and made intercession for the transgressors"*—something had illuminated his thinking, as suddenly as day must have sprung forth when God said, "Let there be light." Of course, he thought, what more perfect subject for Christmas than the Crucifixion? It's the whole reason behind the birth in the manger; it's the grand culmination of God's love to sinful humanity. You can't talk about Christmas without talking about the cross.

And the Crucifixion wasn't complete by itself either; the Resurrection had to be faced and dealt with. You couldn't very well believe in one and not the other. It made no sense to Perry to place faith in certain parts of the Bible but to discount others as lacking credibility. Every story in the Bible, from Adam and Eve in the Garden of Eden to the wise men's journey from the East to John's revelation on the Isle of Patmos, hinged on what one believed concerning the very existence and nature of God. It was all part of the big picture. You either believed it all, or you threw it all out.

Perry thought of Hollister Abrams's ruddy face as he had said, "Everything in this whole world is so . . . so linked together." And he remembered the words to a song Edna Hawthorne had sung recently: "What will you do with Jesus?" The question branded itself on his mind now. It had all been so easy before. He hadn't had to answer such questions before because he had known so little of Jesus except as a shadowy, controversial historical figure. But now—now it was different. He had read the whole Bible, had heard it preached regularly for almost a year; he had to admit that it seemed to fit together.

He thought of an axiom he had heard somewhere, one of those pedantic moralisms he had always hated: "Knowledge carries with it responsibility." So now he had a little knowledge. What was he going to do about it? He could feel the pulsing of his heart, could *hear* it in his head. What if it stopped all of a sudden? What if he suddenly just stopped breathing—or had a wreck? What then? He turned off the radio and drove in dark silence for many miles, pondering.

It was a little before six o'clock when he finally pulled into a motel on the outskirts of Rockford. A man came out from a back room when Perry opened the door; he looked suspicious when asked about renting a room for an hour, but he gave Perry a key anyway and took his money.

He showered first—a long, hot shower—then shaved slowly, ritualistically. He put on clean clothes; the shirt was one Dinah had given him for a birthday several years ago. He thought suddenly of his birthday coming up in a couple of weeks; he remembered the day several months ago when Eldeen had discovered that their birthdays were exactly a week apart. "January the sixth and January the thirteenth! Now if that doesn't beat all! There's another coincidence for you!" Perry smiled over her loose definition of the word *coincidence,* over her capacity to get excited about even the most trivial of circumstances.

When he returned the motel key to the desk, the clerk took it without smiling. The thought struck Perry that maybe the man was sulking over having to work on Christmas Day. "It could be worse," he wanted to tell the man. "You could be on your way to a house you had run away from, where you will probably face a lukewarm, if not a hostile, reception. You could be right now frantically groping around for something to say by way of introduction, hoping intensely for a miracle you knew you didn't deserve. You could be overcome with the sickness of dread, wondering why you had undertaken such a foolhardy task."

Exactly twelve minutes later, at 7:09 A.M., he pulled up in front of the house and turned off the engine of his Toyota. The sun was rising feebly. His heart was thudding, and his hands felt cold and sticky. What was he going to say when she opened the door—if she did? He hadn't come up with the first workable idea.

He tried again to think of all the things going on in the world at this moment, things to put his own small trial into perspective. Somewhere a fire was blazing out of control, wreaking destruction; somewhere a car was rounding a curve to collide head-on with another; somewhere a child was starving to death. But it didn't work. Fires and accidents and starvation were all impersonal; this meeting with Dinah was personal and it was *now.* He looked up toward the house. All right, God, let's see how this prayer thing translates to everyday life, he thought. This time I'm going to do it on purpose—not like that other time walking around the neighborhood. As he sat there in his car, his eyes closed, he felt calm for the first time during the entire trip. His mind was clear, his lips set in a purposeful line. He felt that he wasn't the only one interested in the outcome of this thing he was about to do. Could it be that Eldeen was awake back in Derby, kneeling by her bed, praying for him? She did get up early to pray; he knew that. The thought was comforting, but he didn't have time now to muse about possibilities. As he opened the car door, stepped out onto the street, and turned his steps toward the front door of his house, seven words filled his mind: "Dear God, please fix this broken thing."

Chapter 40

The night Perry returned to Derby, a week later, the moon was a shallow bowl of cream tipped above the treetops. When he pulled into the driveway and got out, he saw that the lights were still on inside Jewel's house. The stark yellow porch light was beaming also. Eldeen had evidently been looking for him, for she flung open their front door and slowly descended the steps, talking the whole time.

"Oh, Perry, Perry! We been looking for you all day! We been praying for you and your family ever since you left, and we just *knew* our prayers was being answered when you stayed gone so long. Did you patch it all up with your wife?" She squinted toward the car. "I was hoping you might bring her and your little boy back here with you."

Perry met Eldeen on the sidewalk and put both arms around her as she hugged him. She wore a thick, scratchy red sweater over a dark, loose dress that hung nearly to her ankles. As she released him, Perry looked down at her feet. She was wearing her black rubber boots.

"I had to get these out again," Eldeen said, noting his glance. "It got down to the twenties last week. But let's don't be talking about me. Tell me about *you*—how did things turn out for you and your family?"

"We had a good week together," Perry said. "A really good week. Troy starts back to school on Monday, so we decided I'd better come back by myself. I'll finish up things here and then go back home for good in another week or so."

Eldeen clasped her hands under her chin. "*Home for good*—now that's just got to sound like music to your ears!" She bowed her head briefly, then looked back up. "Speaking of music, you'll never guess. Libby Vanderhoff called me and said Earl got that glass ball off and back on. Used a X-Acto knife and just kept going round and round the seal real gentle and heated it up a little too. He was scared the glass would break, but praise the Lord it didn't! Got the little feller anchored down nice and tight, too—I believe Libby said he *welded* it—but he's got it all propped up upside down on a high shelf to let the base set so the water can't seep out. Libby's so proud of it but said to tell you it's yours in a jiffy if you want it back."

Perry shook his head, but before he could speak, Eldeen continued. "*Home for good*—that just warms my whole insides up! 'Course, it's going to be a mixed blessing for *us*—losing you as our neighbor and not knowing if we'll ever see you again. I sure have been enjoying that jelly cabinet. We got all Jewel's jars lined up inside so pretty. And that new suncatcher's just a sight to behold! Wait till you see it in the daytime. Every morning when I pull open the drapes, I stand there and admire it all over again. It catches the light and shines like it's just drinking in the sun!" She pointed back toward their front window. "I still can't get over it—a little lighthouse slinging out its beams in the daytime!"

Joe Leonard came out to help Perry carry his things inside, and Eldeen stood at the front door of Perry's house, informing him loudly as he went back and forth of everything that had happened in his absence.

"And poor old Mayfield Spalding, his nephew found him laying on the bathroom floor in his pajamas," she said. "The doctor doesn't give him much hope. Says he probably won't live through the night. They said it probably happened early this morning sometime because one of his neighbors saw him letting his cat in late last night. It'd be a real shame if he died during the holiday season—now what *am* I saying? I take that back. It's *never* a shame when a Christian dies and goes to heaven! Christmastime would be a wonderful time to meet Jesus." She broke off to cluck her tongue sadly. "Maybe God will give him a peppier disposition in heaven, bless his heart. Mayfield's had a lot of hardships in his life, poor old thing, and I think folks has judged him unfair sometimes, although *they* sure didn't mean no harm—how could they know everything he's been through?" She shook her head. "No sir, we never know somebody else's heart, do we? Never, never, never.

"Oh, and you'll never *guess* who came to church last week! Remember Mr. Beatty, Joe Leonard's band teacher? He normally goes to a little Presbyterian church out on the highway toward Tryon, but he came to our church last week and brought his wife too, who I found out works at the Russell Stover candy shop in the mall. That reminds me, she was talking about the awfulest thing that happened over in Berea two days ago—it was in the paper. A woman shot her husband with a deer rifle because she found him eating her last piece of candy from a Russell Stover box that she had hid away in a special hiding place. Can you *imagine?* I told Mrs. Beatty, though, that there had to of been a *lot* more to that story. That woman wouldn't of just flew off like that over a piece of candy; it had to of been just the last straw in the haystack. Anyway, Mrs. Beatty knew that woman—said she used to come in the store all the time while she was working.

"Oh, and you know what? When Jewel took me out to the mall last week, just *guess* who we saw in Sears. Remember that man at the Purple Calliope who waited on us? Stanley? Well, there he was buying vacuum cleaner bags—still had on his waiter's suit, even the little purple jacket. I had a real nice talk with him, and we asked him if he'd come eat supper with us sometime when he wasn't working—and he said he would, and so we set up a date right then. Next Thursday's his day off, so he's coming then. I been praying and praying for that man, and I just feel like God's going to answer my prayers someday if I just keep on. You just never know—sometimes he answers 'em real quick, and sometimes he . . ." Eldeen stopped talking suddenly, and Perry could feel her looking at him. He avoided her eyes, pretending to rub a smudge off the handle of his suitcase.

Joe Leonard came in carrying a small box of books. "Did you want these brought in too?" he asked.

"Oh, sure," Perry said, coming forward to take them. "I plan to do a little reading this week." He wondered if Joe Leonard had noticed the Bible among the other books.

"Mama just told me to invite you over for our New Year's Eve dessert at midnight tonight," Joe Leonard said.

"Oh, *do!*" Eldeen begged. "We'll have us the nicest time! And you can tell all of us about your trip home and how your little boy and wife acted when you showed up."

"Well, I guess I can," Perry said. "I need to make a couple of phone calls first, but I can come after that."

"Good!" said Eldeen. "It's something we do every year. Jewel makes a special angel food cake, and we eat a piece at midnight to start off the brand-new year. She's whipping the cream for the frosting right now. Willard's coming too."

"He just got here," Joe Leonard said, peering out Perry's front door.

The sound of firecrackers spattered in the distance, followed by several loud pops nearby. Eldeen pointed to the clock on the bookcase. "Oh, my, looka there! They've done started up a whole hour early. Come on, Joe Leonard, let's get going and help your mother get things ready. Bless her heart, baking a cake on the night before her own wedding. Perry, you come on over directly, and you can tell us all about your Christmas while we eat our cake." She almost shoved Joe Leonard out the door. "We'll have to show you the locket Willard gave Jewel for Christmas," she told Perry as she started down the steps. "It's pure twenty-four carat solid gold!" She laughed loudly. "I told Jewel she better not wear it in a thunderstorm, though." Starting off down the sidewalk, she called back, "You remember that story back in the summer, don't you, about that lady in Walhalla who always wore a Saint Christopher medal around her neck, and one day she was running from her car to the house in a terrible storm and a great big bolt of lightning struck right on that Saint Christopher medal and nearly electrocuted her!"

Perry called Dinah first, then dialed Cal's number. Cal answered on the eighth ring, just as Perry was ready to hang up. He sounded sleepy.

"Hey, Cal," Perry said. "Did I interrupt your New Year's Eve party?"

"Perry? Where are you?"

"Back in Derby. I just got in an hour ago, and guess what? We might have our funeral."

"Oh . . . yeah," Perry heard Cal yawn, slowly inhaling a great whoosh of air, then expelling it loudly.

"Well, let's not get too excited about it," Perry said.

"Hey, ease up, it's going on eleven o'clock at night."

"So?"

"So I've been asleep for an hour and you wake me up, telling me somebody I don't even know died, and I'm supposed to be thrilled?"

"Cal, it's New Year's Eve. You've been asleep since before *ten o'clock* on New Year's Eve?"

"I told you I lead a dull life these days." Cal yawned again. "So whose funeral is it?"

"Just somebody at the church. A man named Mayfield Spalding. He hasn't died yet, but he had a stroke this morning, and they say he probably won't make it another day."

"Well, good . . . I mean, it's good for your book. Not so good for poor—what's his name? Mayfield?" Cal laughed hoarsely, then broke off.

"I wanted to tell you to hold the manuscript for a few days or so till we see about the funeral," Perry said.

"Yep, I will," Cal said. There was a silent pause, then he added, "It was good to see you last week. The chapters look good. Thanks for driving over while you were home. How did things . . . turn out at home anyway?"

Perry started to say, "Fine" but caught himself. One of the things he and Dinah had discussed was his reliance on pat generalities when asked a question. "Well, we still have some potholes to fill in," he said. "Maybe even a few new roads to build." He laughed awkwardly; *that* was certainly no improvement on the standard "Fine." He couldn't help wondering what would have gone through his own mind if someone else had answered a question of his with such metaphorical claptrap. "Things are looking hopeful, though," he said. "It's going to take some work, but we'll get there."

"Well, I'm glad for you," Cal said. He sighed and added, "Why didn't anybody tell us family life was going to be so *messy?*" There was a long pause before Cal continued. "Say, I might be coming down that way in a couple of days. My mother called . . . she's not feeling too good. Says she wants to see me."

"Why don't you stop by Derby and see me?" Perry said. "I could show you the church, and . . ."

"Yeah, and maybe I could even attend the funeral with you, huh?" But neither of them laughed. "Well, we'll see," Cal said wearily. "I don't know what Mom's up to. Hope this isn't just some trick to get me down there so she can preach to me. I wouldn't put it past her."

"Well, don't be too hard on her," Perry said. "You never know . . . you might . . . well, she's not going to be around forever, and . . ."

"Yeah, I know—maybe it's time to try to reconcile," Cal said, sighing. "Who knows? I sure don't."

Perry walked next door a few minutes later. Jewel met him at the door and welcomed him home.

"Well, I guess *home's* not going to be the right word for much longer, from what Mama told me," Jewel said, smiling. "She says you're going back to your family." Her blue eyes glowed steadily, like pilot lights. "I'm so happy for you, Perry," she said. Willard came in from the kitchen, his round face shining with goodwill, and shook Perry's hand vigorously.

As they sat around the kitchen table a few minutes later, Perry told them all about meeting Dinah at the front door on Christmas morning, about his last-minute impulse to carry his suitcase in one hand, like a tool kit, and a screwdriver from the trunk of the car in the other, then when she opened the door, to say, "Hello, ma'am, I got your call and came right away. Don't worry about the high rates on a holiday; my prices are reasonable. Now exactly what is it that needs fixing around here?"

They all laughed. "And what did she say?" Jewel asked.

"She just stared at me for a minute," Perry said. He didn't tell them that it was the longest minute of his whole life, that he had stood there during those endless seconds castigating himself for choosing such a stupid introduction, telling himself to turn around and get in the car and head back the way he had come but stubbornly refusing to do so until he got some signal from her that she still hated him. He didn't mention either that he was still praying silently.

"Then Troy called from inside and asked her who it was," Perry continued, "and she kept staring at me like I was some kind of ghost and said, 'It's the repairman I called.'" Then all of a sudden she had started crying, he said, and "she looked up at me smiling and crying at the same time and pointed to her eyes and said, 'Come on in. Do you fix leaky faucets?'"

Eldeen almost choked on a bite of angel food cake. "How did you two ever think up such a thing?" she said after she had gotten herself under control. "That's the funniest thing I ever heard!" Perry could imagine her telling and retelling the story to people all over town.

Outside, Hormel began howling—a thin, pitiable wail.

"Aw, listen there," Eldeen said. "I bet Hormel wants some attention. He knows we're all in here having us a good time, eating cake and laughing, and he's feeling sorry for hisself left outside in the cold."

"He's probably just nervous about all the firecrackers," Willard said.

"Well, I'm going to give him a little sliver of cake," Eldeen said, getting up. "Hormel's a funny dog—I don't know if you know it or not, Perry, but he just has the biggest fit over anything *sweet*." She cut a small slice of cake and put it on a paper napkin. "This'll let him know we haven't forgot him."

"Be careful on the steps, Mama," Jewel said.

"I will, I will," Eldeen said, taking her gray cape off the coat peg behind the door. "I never have fallen yet." Perry watched her leave. He felt the rush of cold air as she opened and closed the kitchen door, heard her slowly stumping down the steps, calling eagerly to Hormel, her voice pitched in the high register normally reserved for talking to babies: "I hear you, Hormel, you sweet little thing. Here comes old Eldeen with some dessert for her favorite little pooch."

Perry felt a sudden urge to go after her, to talk to her alone, to tell her about all the things he had learned from her, about the voice on the radio reading from Isaiah, about reading the same passage to Dinah last week, about the beautiful sunrise he and Dinah had watched together early this morning before he left Rockford, about the poem he had quoted to her: "I'll tell you how the sun rose/ A ribbon at a time/ The steeples swam in amethyst/ The news, like squirrels ran/ The hills untied their bonnets/ The bobolinks—begun/ Then I said softly to myself/ 'That must have been the sun!'" Eldeen would like that; she appreciated Emily Dickinson.

Willard was looking at him, smiling expectantly.

"Sorry, did you say something?" Perry said.

"I said you'll have to come back to Derby in the spring so we can go fishing again and try out all the tips in the book you gave me."

"Oh, right—the book," Perry said. "I had forgotten. I hope you didn't have it already."

"No, not at all." Willard shook his head. "You'd think since I like books and fish so much that I'd at least have seen it, but I hadn't. It's really interesting; I was reading the chapter on the striped bass just this afternoon." Perry couldn't imagine reading a book about fish on the day before your wedding, but then he didn't have the slightest recollection of how he had spent the day before his wedding. He had probably done something every bit as incomprehensible. What were appropriate prewedding activities anyway?

"Well, since we're talking about Christmas presents, Joe Leonard has something to show you," Jewel said as she refilled Perry's cup of coffee. "Mama didn't already tell you, did she?" she said to Perry.

"I don't think so," Perry said. Of course, Eldeen had told him so much as he was unloading the car that he couldn't be sure. Joe Leonard grinned and left the table. He came back into the kitchen a minute later carrying his tuba case. Upon closer look, however, Perry realized it was a different case; the green tape around the handle was missing, and the latches on this one were bright silver.

Joe Leonard laid the case on its side and slowly raised the lid. Inside, against a deep blue plush lining, lay a shiny new tuba. Joe Leonard lifted it out and brought it over to Perry, his eyes sparkling with pride.

Perry pushed his chair back and gingerly took the instrument. It felt cold and solid. He looked back up at Joe Leonard. "This is really yours?" he asked, and the boy nodded.

"Willard gave it to me for Christmas," he said.

"Well, not totally," Willard said. "Jewel got a special price on it from this place over in Greenville."

"Pecknel Music Company," Jewel said. "They give discounts to music teachers."

"And Joe Leonard already had over three hundred dollars saved toward it," Willard continued. "Sometime last year I had started putting back money for a piano for my apartment, but then when Jewel and I got engaged and we decided I'd move in over here, I knew we didn't need another piano, so I just switched my plans to a different musical instrument. So, you see, I didn't exactly buy it for him; we all pitched in together."

"Well, he bought most of it," Joe Leonard said. "And Mr. Beatty drove over to Greenville and helped Mama pick it out," he told Perry.

"And Mr. Beatty came to church last Sunday to hear Joe Leonard play a solo on it," Jewel said. She looked at Joe Leonard and smiled. "And I believe he played better than he's ever played before. It was so quiet when he finished that I almost wished we could have just sat there for a while thinking about the words to that song."

"Play us some of it, Joe Leonard," Willard said. Joe Leonard looked embarrassed, but he took the tuba from Perry and put it to his mouth. Perry recognized the tune at once; it was another favorite song at the Church of the Open Door. The words came swiftly to his mind as if he had known them all his life: "I hear the Savior say, 'Thy strength indeed is small, Child of weakness, watch and pray, Find in me thine all in all.'"

Joe Leonard had just begun the chorus—"Jesus paid it all, All to him I owe"—when it occurred to Perry that Eldeen should be back inside by now. He glanced toward the kitchen door, but there was no sign of her. "Sin had left a crimson stain, He washed it white as snow." It was a simple hymn, one Perry had liked the first time he had heard it almost a year ago. He still remembered the names printed under the title—Elvina M. Hall and John T. Grape. He remembered wondering which had come first, the words or the music. Had Elvina sent the poem to John to set to music, or had John written out the melody first and asked Elvina to write words for it? Had the two even known each other?

"I like it," Perry said. "I like it a lot. The tuba and the song both."

"I've always loved that song," Jewel said.

Perry looked over to the kitchen door again. There was no sound from outside except the occasional crackling of fireworks. What was taking Eldeen so long?

Joe Leonard stooped down to set his tuba back inside the case. Jewel stood to gather the empty cake saucers, and Willard got up to run a sink of hot water. Perry stood and stretched, then walked over to the door and pulled back the green-checked curtain. The porch light shone on the empty concrete steps, the slender black handrail, the station wagon in the driveway, the back fence gate.

It was the gate that sent a chill of alarm through Perry. It was open, flattened back against the fence, the dark backyard gaping ominously behind it. There was no sign of Eldeen or Hormel.

At the exact moment that Perry reached for the doorknob and turned it, a car horn blared, followed immediately by the sounds of screeching tires and crunching metal.

The other three turned to look out the kitchen door, which Perry had now opened. Jewel set the saucers down with a clatter and crossed her hands under her neck. "That was close by," she whispered.

Perry was the first one out the door. He ran out to the street and stopped. From the middle of the cul-de-sac, he could see it all. Even as he stood there, a piece of metal loosened from one of the cars and fell to the pavement with a dreadful, final clank. The accident had happened right where Blossom Circle turned off Lily Lane. The angle at which the two cars were melded together made it impossible to tell what had happened. The hoods of both cars were badly crumpled, and shards of glass glittered over the road like ice crystals under the glare of the streetlight. It wasn't the cars themselves that froze Perry to the spot; it wasn't the sight of the two car doors opening almost simultaneously, one of them buckled at an odd angle, nor the sight of two drivers, alive and apparently unharmed, stepping out and looking around in a daze.

It was Eldeen. She had fallen over face down, as if bowing to some god. The cars, crushed together in a mutilated "V," formed the backdrop; she was center stage, hunched in a great motionless mound on her knees under the spotlight.

Perry realized that Willard, Jewel, and Joe Leonard had run up behind him and were flanking him, panting as they took in the scene. He heard Jewel's injured cry, "Oh, dear God in heaven, no, *no!*" He saw them run forward; even Willard ran surprisingly fast. He had always thought action slowed at moments of crisis like this, but there they were, the three of them running like Olympic sprinters toward the horrible drama ahead of them. The two drivers, both of them men, were approaching Eldeen, one of them bending to touch her broad back, the other one kneeling in front of her. "Stay away from her!" Perry wanted to yell, but his throat felt closed.

How could this happen? He felt guilt-stricken when he remembered his phone call to Cal only an hour ago, his anticipation over the prospect of a funeral to add to his book. How could he be so callous about a human life? How could he have known that the funeral might end up being for . . . But he refused to put her name in the blank.

Perry heard a siren growing louder; someone must have called EMS. He saw the two men step back as Jewel arrived; he heard Jewel's sobs as she flung herself down beside Eldeen. But still he could not force himself to move forward. He felt a great tide of sorrow washing over him. Why hadn't he obeyed his urge to follow Eldeen outdoors earlier? He could have saved her from this; once again his hesitance had led to disaster. When would he ever learn?

He saw Willard kneel down on the other side of Eldeen and lay his hand on her broad shoulder. How could God allow Jewel and Willard to suffer so on their *wedding day* of all things? What kind of God . . . his mind whirled with a confusion of thoughts. Was this what he must prepare himself for as a Christian—interminable, unpredictable trage-dies, one after the other, as Jewel had suffered? Was it the foreordained lot of this lovely woman to reel through life from one calamity to another? Hadn't God taught her enough already? What more would he require from her?

And why hadn't God even given him a chance to tell Eldeen what had happened to him over Christmas, to give her another praise to mention in prayer meeting next week? To tell her how her poem had spurred him to action. Then he remembered with shame that it was his own weakness that had held him back from telling her; he *had* had a chance, but he simply hadn't taken it. And they had been planning to celebrate their birthdays together next week. It was a minor disappoint-ment, true, but on top of everything else it came as a profound loss. A police car pulled up, its blue light flashing obscenely.

Perry had read books with endings like this, and he hated them. The main character would reach a turning point; the gullible, hopeful reader was made to think that the hero was ready to step forward and make things right. Then some unforeseen catastrophe would knock the whole story off-kilter and all hopes would be dashed. The story would end despondently, with the unstated confirmation of humankind's purposeless existence tolling like a funeral bell.

Two policemen stepped out of the squad car and rushed to where Eldeen had fallen. Perry saw Jewel shake her head, heard Willard's sympathetic murmur: "No, sir." The officers turned immediately to the two wrecked cars. The drivers met them in the middle of the street, both of them extending their hands beseechingly as if eager to clear themselves. The blue light still spun crazily.

In spite of the speed of motion in the scene before him, the machinery of Perry's mind moved ponderously. The wheels of realization began to grind when he saw Willard tugging gently at Eldeen's shoulders, then reaching under her and pulling something out. Perry hadn't even thought of Hormel until he saw Joe Leonard bend down to take the small, limp body from Willard. So Hormel had been struck also. Perry felt himself flush with anger at the sight of the policemen now talking quietly to the two drivers. What did they think they were doing? Who cared about a collision of *machinery* when a woman's life was ebbing away—perhaps already gone? Then it came to him that that must be why they seemed so unconcerned; they must already know it was too late for Eldeen. One of the drivers had an excitable voice that carried all the way to Perry. He heard disconnected phrases: "darted out of nowhere," "heard a thump," "slammed on my brakes," "other lane," "old woman."

Perry heard the throaty keening for several moments before he isolated it as a separate sound. At first he must have assumed it was the siren winding down; when he finally heard it distinctly, he thought it might be Hormel—until he returned his gaze again to Joe Leonard, still holding the lifeless dog. No, the sound clearly wasn't coming from Hormel. Perry started walking toward the scene of the accident, slowly. Maybe the sound was a party horn or a stereo; that must be it. There were five or six cars around the DePalmas' house, and through the windows he could see what looked like dozens of teenagers crammed inside, gyrating in a huge mass to the beat of muffled bass thrums. Most likely they hadn't even heard the squealing of tires and the crashing of metal. Another sickening example of the pitilessness of life; there was a terrible isolation in sorrow. Ultimately you were just a lonely bystander watching a parade; nobody waving from the floats or marching in formation would flicker an eyelash if you dropped dead. And those standing around you would simply step over you so they could see better.

But the wailing was coming from somewhere outside, somewhere ahead of him. He continued walking forward, uncertainly. Could it be Jewel? Perry had heard her sobs earlier, but this was different. He wasn't sure Jewel could make such a sound if she wanted to. He remembered that Montroyal was once a mill community; perhaps the old whistle at the abandoned factory had somehow been set off by a group of mischievous kids out to have fun on New Year's Eve. Or maybe it was some new kind of fireworks with special audio effects.

As he drew near, Perry saw Jewel and Willard begin to rise from either side of Eldeen, each of them taking one of her arms and slowly hoisting her to her feet. *"What are you doing?"* he almost yelled. But he stopped abruptly and put both hands to his face, fully aware of the fact that he must look like an awestruck schoolgirl. He thought fleetingly of the resurrection of Lazarus in the Bible. What was . . . ?

Slowly they turned around, Eldeen between them, facing Perry. Jewel was talking to Eldeen as if she were a child: "It's all right, honey, you're all right, come on, I'm right here with you, Mama." Eldeen's face was a mask of misery; the wails had died, and from her mouth came deep, low moans. She stood looking at Joe Leonard holding Hormel, then shifted her eyes to Perry. Her cape had gotten twisted sideways, and her hair stuck up on top like the ragged plumage of a homely bird.

"He wouldn't listen," she groaned, tears coursing down her cheeks. "I tried and tried to call him back, but he just kept going. He didn't know any better. He just ran right out. Oh, I should of been more careful! He just slipped right out the gate lickety-split soon as I opened it and didn't even stop to see the treat I had brought him. He was probably going over to visit that little girl boxer dog again. I tried to catch him, but I was too late—oh, I was *too late*. That green car hit him and threw his little body over a ways, and then that other car swerved trying to miss it and ran smack into the green car. Poor little Hormel was already dead by the time I got there. His little heart was just as still as night." This brought on another labored moan.

"Shhh, let's go home, Mama," Jewel said softly. Then to Willard she said, "Maybe you better talk to the policemen to see if there's anything they need. Perry can help me get Mama home. Joe Leonard, you take Hormel and go on ahead. Just lay him in the backyard, and we'll talk about what to do after we all get home."

"Be sure to wash your hands good," Eldeen called sadly to Joe Leonard.

Perry walked forward quickly and took Willard's place beside Eldeen. He placed one arm firmly around her back and braced her elbow with the other. Together he and Jewel guided her gently home, the clasps on her black boots tinkling faintly with each step she took.

The night was pitch dark, except for the glowing crescent of moon and the occasional sparkle of fireworks. But the sun would come up in the east, Perry told himself as they walked toward Jewel's house. The sun would come up and shine through all the windows, and color would spill out over the new year.

About the Author

Jamie Turner has been a teacher for twenty-four years at both the elementary and college levels. For the past fourteen years, she has also written stories, articles, plays, and poems. Born in Mississippi, Jamie has lived in the South all her life, currently residing in Greenville, South Carolina. *The Suncatchers* is her first novel.